Blade's Edge

Virginia McClain

Other Works by Virginia McClain

Rain on a Summer's Afternoon:
A Collection of Short Stories

VIRGINIA McCLAIN

BLADE'S EDGE

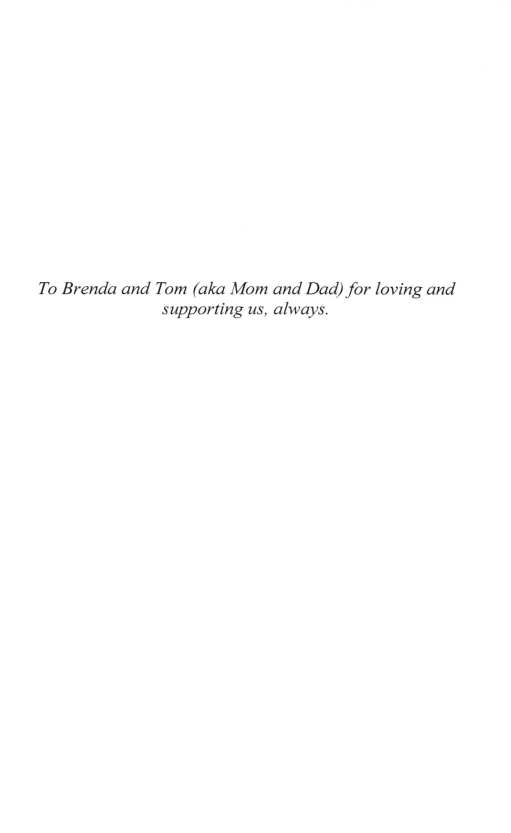

To Brenda and Tom (aka Mom and Dad) for loving and supporting us, always.

Foreword

So, first things first, if you're not the kind of person who really enjoys reading forewords... probably best if you go ahead and skip to the story. No really, there's nothing all that exciting here. The good bits are in the story!

Of course, now you're probably wondering why I'm writing this at all, if it's not part of the 'good bits.' A very fair question. The answer is, this book has a lot of stuff borrowed from feudal Japan and I'm here to clear up a few things about why that is, and how it is in NO WAY historical fiction, even though there are a couple nuggets of inspiration from feudal Japanese samurai culture. So, if hearing about that sounds like your cup of tea, by all means, stick around! If not, head to the story. That's why we're all here anyway. You can come back and read this later if you decide you're curious.

It's your call, but you've been warned. The good stuff lies ahead. This is just a lengthy disclaimer about how this book isn't actually about Japan.

Ahem.

Hi there! If you're still here then that must mean you like forewords a lot, or perhaps you've gotten to the end of the book and thought, *I can't decide if that was supposed to be historically accurate or not. Is this book really about Japan?*

The answers, quite simply, are No and No.

This is a fantasy book. The world in which it takes place is completely fictitious, in both space and time. Gensokai doesn't exist anywhere, and it never has. That said, if parts of the story make you think of Japan (or of the Japanese language) that's because I was living in Japan at the time that I wrote the first draft of the story, and the more I learned about Japanese history, culture, and geography the more bits of inspiration I found for this tale. The fictional culture of the book was inspired by feudal Japanese samurai culture. The physical landscape of the book was inspired by the Japanese landscape. And the thing that was most heavily inspired was the language. As a language nerd (I majored in Spanish linguistics in University, and have been obsessed with learning other languages since I was a kid) I thoroughly enjoyed picking words (or sometimes just pieces of words) out of Japanese and using them to make my own.

So, as you go through this story, you might find that parts of it seem taken from a Japan you recognize as either current or historic, and then you may find other pieces that don't fit that mold at all. I'm afraid the inspiration was loose, driven by a love and appreciation for all the things I was learning at the time, but not bound by the reality of any of them. I definitely made up words that do not exist in Japanese, and the place and history of Gensokai is entirely a product of my own imagination. The only reason I use Japanese at all, instead of a completely fictional language, was that I felt it helped establish the feel of the book, and also I lack Tolkien's patience when it comes to creating a new language from scratch.

Glossary of Terms

Some of the following terms are actual Japanese words, however, most of them are fabricated words made strictly for the purpose of this fictional work. Some are based in Japanese roots, while others are simply English terms made to apply to things in the book. While Gensokai is its own world and is not actually based on Japan, lots of the vocabulary for the book is taken from Japanese to help give it the feel of the feudal Japanese culture that the book was inspired by.

Eihei - The elite guard of the Rōjū (an actual Japanese term meaning elite guard)

Fuchi - The well of one's ki (taken from the actual Japanese word for abyss)

Gensokai - The name of the island realm in which our adventure takes place (taken from the Japanese words for element and world)

Ha - The actual Japanese word for the sharp edge of a blade

Hakama - The pants worn by Kisōshi (actual Japanese term for divided skirts that men wear on formal occasions or for certain martial arts)

Hebi-kyū - This is a made up term containing the actual Japanese word for snake (hebi) and the actual Japanese word for level or rank (kyū). In the context of the book, Hebi-kyū is the lowest rank for a Kisōshi (it is the first rank they achieve through testing) whereas the highest is Ryū-kyū.

Hishi - The elite assassins used by the Rōjū (taken from the Japanese word for secret history)

Josankō - The school where all josanpu are trained (taken from the Japanese words for midwifery and school)

Josanpu - A woman trained in the arts of birthing and care for women's health (the actual Japanese word for midwife)

Kami/kami - This word is taken from the actual Japanese for spirit or deity. For the purposes of this book the capitalized Kami means deity and the lowercase kami means spirit.

Katana - the long curved blade used by all Kisōshi (the actual Japanese word for a single edged sword)

Ki - A person's spirit or energy (actual Japanese word for spirit/essence)

Kimono - Traditional clothing worn by men and women throughout Gensokai (the Japanese word for clothing –especially traditional Japanese clothing)

Kisaki - The point of a blade (actual Japanese word for the point of a blade)

Kisō - Energy manipulation (taken from the Japanese words for energy and manipulation –note that the actual Japanese definition differs from this made up usage)

Kisōseki - A rare person who, due to an overlap in elemental powers, is able to track using kisō (word fabricated from a combination of energy manipulation and tracking)

Kisōshi - Elite warriors trained in fighting who possess an innate ability to manipulate one element (word taken from Japanese for "energy manipulation person")

Kisōarashi - A rare person who is able to monitor storms due to an overlap in elemental powers (word fabricated from a combination of energy manipulation and storm)

Mooncycle (moon) - Three tendays in Gensokai. Most common usage is "moon"

Mune - The blunt back edge of a blade (actual Japanese word)

Obi - The wide decorative belt worn with kimono (actual Japanese word)

Oni - Demons or bad spirits

Rōjū - The ruling council of elder Kisōshi in charge of making all decisions for Gensokai (using the actual Japanese word for the Shogun's council of Elders)

Ryokan - A traditional inn (actual Japanese word)

Ryū-kyū - See "hebi-kyū"

Saya - A scabbard (actual Japanese word)

Seiza - A folded seating position (actual Japanese word)

Senkisō - A Kisōshi with elemental ties to fire or air and thus to battle (taken from the Japanese words for energy manipulation and war/battle)

Seasoncycle (cycle) - The term for a year in Gensokai, most commonly referred to as a "cycle"

Shoji - sliding screen door or window (actual Japanese word)

Shinogi - The widest part of a katana, the part between the mune and the hasami (actual Japanese word)

Shuriken - A small sharpened disk used as a weapon by the hishi, often coated in poison (actual Japanese word for "throwing star")

Tatami - A mat made of dried woven grass and straw typically used as flooring, also a standard measure of length: approximately one meter by two meters in size (actual Japanese word)

Tenday - A period of ten days (taking the place of weeks in this world)

Tsuka - The hilt of a katana

Uwagi - The jacket worn by all Kisōshi (taken from the Japanese word for a traditional jacket)

Wa - Harmony (taken from the actual Japanese)

Yukisō - A Kisōshi with elemental ties to earth or water and thus to healing (taken from the Japanese words for energy manipulation and healing/medicine)

Yūwaku - The all female ruling power in Gensokai before the Rōjū took power

Anatomy of a Katana

tsuka - hilt
mune - back edge
shinogi - middle (widest point if looking at a crossection)
ha - front edge (cutting edge)
kisaki - point of blade
saya - scabbard

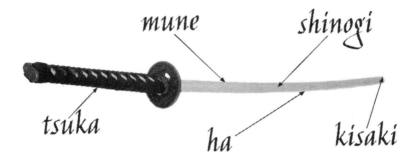

Tsuka

１１０９年

In winter we see
the reality of trees
exposed in cold truth

30日 12月、老中 1109年

⇒ Taka ⇐

THE SCREAM MADE Taka drop the snowball she had just been aiming at her best friend's head and turn towards the gate to see what was happening. In a single heartbeat Mishi was by her side and crawling onto her shoulders to get a better view.

"Mishi-chan!" she hissed. "I can't see when you do that!"

She brushed her younger friend's hands from her face, where they had strayed to cover her eyes. Mishi was a cycle younger than she, but barely smaller. Still, the girl insisted that her two fingers' width of height deficiency meant she could use Taka as a staircase whenever she pleased. Mostly Taka didn't mind, but someone had just screamed. This was serious.

Once she had cleared her vision of her friend's hands, she was able to see what was happening at the small gate that led into the snow covered garden.

"Mishi-chan... is that... is that Rika-san?"

She didn't give Mishi time to reply, for in a single breath they both recognized the older girl, and in one move Mishi had dismounted from Taka's shoulders and they had both begun running in Rika's direction. As they neared her, they saw that her face was streaked with dirt and tears, her clothes soaked with melting snow, and her body a mere shadow of what it had been when she had left them only two moons before.

"Rika-san?" they both called, as they ran towards her. Why had the older girl screamed? She was stumbling now, through the small wooden gate and towards the door to the orphanage's kitchen, which lay only a few tatami lengths away from her across the snow buried garden. Her breath faltered and her limbs shook, and Taka was sure that the girl would collapse at any moment.

Taka and Mishi were rushing to help the older girl when they heard a deep voice shout from the gateway.

"Stop her! Stop that girl!"

They had no sooner heard the voice than they were nearly thrown to the ground by three grown men rushing forward to grab Rika. Just as the men reached her, the girl let out another yowl of despair. The noise was so awful that Taka would have covered her ears if her hands hadn't been busy holding Mishi up from the packed snow that she and her friend had been flung down on.

Taka couldn't make sense of what she saw before her. The men appeared to be normal villagers, men she would have recognized from the town market if it had been a normal day. But these men were all grabbing Rika as though she were some sort of dangerous criminal and dragging her back towards the gate with them. They were forced to drag her, her legs flailing as she tried to free herself, her ragged clothing and jagged bones cutting an ugly scar in the snow as they pulled her towards the gate and the black clad man who had first shouted that she should be stopped.

Mishi regained her footing first and jumped forward as though to confront the men, but Taka grabbed her friend's shoulder in order to hold her in check.

"But Taka-chan, she doesn't want to go with them," Mishi said, and Taka knew it was true. She didn't need to read the girl's emotions with her kisō to know that Rika wished to be anywhere but in the hands of the men who held her, a fact made clear enough by the way she thrashed with what little strength was left in her frail body.

"I know Mishi-chan, but what are you going to do against three men and a Yukisō?" she asked, her grip firm on Mishi's shoulder. "They'll never let her go just because you punch someone in the knees."

Mishi's lips turned down at the reminder of how small she was, but Taka still held the younger girl's shoulder. Taka was having a difficult time restraining herself from helping Rika too, but she was convinced that there was nothing that either of them could do except...

Mishi-chan, run and get Haha-san! she said without speaking, projecting her thoughts and emotions at her best friend instead. Mishi nodded, turned on her heel, and began running towards the kitchen door, but when she was still a full tatami length away from the door it opened on its own and out came Haha-san.

"What's going on here?" the older woman demanded, as she hurried into the garden and wrapped herself more firmly in her winter shawl.

Hope began to bloom in Taka's chest. Haha-san wouldn't let these men take Rika when she was so clearly upset. Haha-san took good care of the children in her orphanage. She would protect Rika. Taka was sure of it.

The black clad man's lips narrowed and his gaze fixed coldly on Haha-san's face before he replied.

"This miscreant has run away from the Josankō and is to be punished," he said.

Haha-san hesitated before replying, and stepped back from where the man stood with the three villagers encircling the now quietly sobbing girl. Taka's hope began to waver.

"Has she done something wrong?" Haha-san asked, her voice now subservient and her gaze directed at the ground before her, rather than the man clad in black.

"Aside from being born a josanpu and disobeying her instructors, nothing at all." The tone of the man's voice suggested that either of those offenses were more than enough to condemn a woman.

Taka's hopes shattered then, as she watched Haha-san simply stand back and observe as the three villagers and the man clad in black walked away with a sobbing Rika carried between them.

Taka had been sure that Haha-san would do something to protect the older girl. Were they really going to stand there and let her be dragged back to whatever place had left her looking like a shade? She had seemed half starved. Haha-san might occasionally treat her wards harshly, or punish them for breaking rules, but she had always done what she could to make sure that the children at the orphanage were healthy and well cared for. Taka didn't think she was the kind of person to let a girl be so poorly treated, especially not one of *her* girls.

"You two should get back inside before the cold gets to you," Haha-san's voice rang out from the door to the kitchen. Taka had been so focused on watching Rika's procession away from the orphanage that she hadn't even noticed the woman's retreat. As she registered the older woman returning to the kitchen door, a small part of her world view shattered.

Taka turned to look at Mishi and saw that her friend was staring just as wide eyed at the procession of men and girl as she had been herself only moments ago.

"Taka-chan?" Mishi whispered. Even as Taka grabbed Mishi's shoulder to turn them both back to the orphanage and what small warmth the place had to offer, she began to wonder if it could truly protect them from anything worse than the cold.

"Yes, Mishi-chan?" she replied at length.

"You'll never let them take me away like that, will you?" Mishi's voice was as small as the spots on a sparrow's back.

"No, Mishi-chan," Taka replied, hoping the words were the truth.

Rika had been the only other girl in the orphanage that Mishi and Taka had shared their secret with. Taka had been only three cycles old when Rika had caught her healing a small scrape on Mishi's arm after the two cycle old toddler had fallen. She had warned her very sternly then that Taka should never allow *anyone* to see her using her powers, that she should hide her kisō as though her life depended on it.

Despite the initial warning and the occasional reminders, the older girl hadn't been very close to either Taka or Mishi. She was three cycles older than Taka, four cycles older than Mishi, and much too old to care about what they did with themselves. But Taka had learned enough in the intervening years to know that Rika's warning had saved her from a horrible fate, the same fate that had somehow found Rika now. Taka wondered how the girl had found herself exposed? Had she healed someone and been turned in because of it? Taka thought that the most likely answer. Was it impossible to hide who you really were forever? She already knew how difficult it was to know you could help someone, but have to sit by and watch instead because healing them would condemn you.

Taka swallowed then, her mouth suddenly much drier than it should have been, as she took in the silver grey gaze of her best friend.

Mishi was a hundred times more powerful than Rika would ever be. Was there really any way that Taka could protect her from the people who would notice her abilities? She didn't know what she could do to stop the people who would try to take Mishi away from her, but she was certain that she would do her best.

She nodded then, more to assure herself than anything else.

"I'll never let them take you away."

Mune

1 1 1 1 年

The spring tadpole
changes to a summer frog
the tail falls away

21日 6月，老中 1111年

≈ Mishi ≈

MISHI STRUGGLED AGAINST Haha-san's grip. She tried to sit down, tried to make herself as heavy as the sun; as heavy as the weight in her chest that told her that leaving Taka behind would never be alright, no matter what the adults told her.

It didn't do any good. The plain, white halls of the orphanage passed by in a tear blurred haze, despite her best efforts to burden Haha-san to the point where she would be unable to move forward. The only acknowledgment of her hollow sobs was their echo off the paper walls that enclosed them, and the tang of her sorrow on her lips.

Mishi's mind flipped through every scenario of a life without Taka and every thought left her feeling another slice of herself being torn away. No more Taka to share secrets with, no more Taka to heal her when she fell from the garden wall, no more Taka to tell her stories, no more Taka to show off her new fire tricks to. It was more than she could bear to think about. She didn't know what she had done to anger the Kami, but she would do anything she could to appease them. She would light a hundred sticks of incense and meditate for a cycle if that's what it took, but they couldn't take her away from Taka!

A hand struck the side of her face then, and she realized she must have cried part of that last thought aloud because Haha-san was shaking her and saying, "Stupid girl. You'll have a good life. You'll be a servant to Kisōshi in training. It's an honor most honest women would die for. I don't know what you've done to please the Kami so, but you should be thankful, not crying about your worthless friend."

Haha-san shook Mishi once more and then straightened her clothes and wiped the tears and snot from Mishi's face with a cloth she pulled from her obi.

"Don't embarrass yourself with such a display, little idiot. You should be proud. If Taka-chan is any kind of friend at all she'll be happy for you. Now stop blubbering and disturbing everyone's wa."

Mishi tried to take a deep breath, but she choked on a sob instead. Haha-san grabbed her and pulled her forward to push her out of the open doorway before she had a chance to drag in another shuddering breath.

"Here she is," Haha-san said to a woman who stood next to a small cart drawn by a single, giant horse. The woman, who still looked young but had a streak of silver that ran the length of her thick, black hair, smiled at Mishi and bent down to talk to her.

"You look upset, child," she said as she put a hand on Mishi's shoulder. "Why is that?"

Mishi tried to answer, but couldn't get words to form without bringing forth all the tears once more.

"She's just frightened of the horse," Haha-san said dismissively.

That made the woman squatting before her raise an eyebrow, but Mishi was unable to utter any other explanation. The woman with the silver streak in her hair raised her hand to Mishi's cheek and wiped away a tear. Somehow the gesture was much more tender than it had been when Haha-san had done it mere moments before, and something about the contact pulled some of the sadness from Mishi and lessened the emptiness that she thought might swallow her.

"Whatever is upsetting you, child, you should know that where you are going is not a bad place. You'll be well looked after and be among friends."

Mishi was about to explain how no number of 'friends' could make up for losing Taka, when a faint but familiar contact brushed against her mind.

An image of Mishi in her favorite hiding place in the vegetable garden filled her mind. A message with a clear meaning, one full of hope, that enabled Mishi to step forward and put her hand in the older woman's outstretched one.

"My name is Tenshi," the silver streaked woman said.

"My name is Mishiranu," Mishi answered through the next sob.

I will always find you, said the image that Taka had sent to Mishi's mind.

⟊ Taka ⟊

Taka tried not to scream. She wouldn't scream, because this couldn't be happening. Haha-san wouldn't do this to her, not really. Not in the same day she'd taken Mishi away. It was too cruel.

She denied the scroll that she'd seen Haha-san sign, the koku of rice—enough to feed her fellow orphans for the next mooncycle—that the man had unloaded from his cart. Her eyes had seen it all, but her mind refused to accept it.

The Kisōshi ran his hand from her kimono covered shoulder down to her exposed wrist and yanked her along by the arm. Taka bit her lip and tried to breathe through her nose. She wouldn't cry. She'd cried all morning for the loss of her best friend. Now she didn't need to cry, because this couldn't be real.

She had seen it happen before, of course. She and Mishi had watched from the kitchen door, too stunned to move or help, as this same Kisōshi had bought another girl five moons ago. The way the man had laughed as he'd carried the screaming girl from the orphanage had been enough to terrify them both. But nothing he could have done that day would have frightened Taka more than seeing the same girl three moons later when she had wandered into the vegetable garden looking like a starved and broken doll, much the same way Rika-san had two cycles before, but with less fight in her. The emptiness behind the other girl's eyes had given Taka nightmares for tendays afterwards. Haha-san had taken the empty-eyed girl across the village and Taka had never seen her again.

Her mind could not accept that this thing was happening to her, even as she was pulled from the hallway of the orphanage that had been her home since the time she was only a single cycle old and into the bright light of the afternoon sun.

Then the smell of dirt and horse manure somehow made the whole scene real to her and, just a few arm spans from the man's cart, Taka began to dig her heels into the earth beneath her.

"No," she said, trying to wrest her arm away from him, her voice finally emerging with the waking of her mind. "No!" she said more forcefully.

The Kisōshi didn't speak. He barely turned to look at her. Without releasing her wrist with his right hand, his open left palm came across her face, making heat spring to her cheek and tears jump to her eyes.

Taka knew that screaming wouldn't help, she knew that fighting back would only give him more reason to hurt her, and that since the man had bought her he could hurt, or even kill, her without anyone objecting. It didn't matter that Kisōshi were supposed to be the protectors of all of Gensokai. It didn't matter that he was supposed to represent justice and be a bringer of peace to the land they all lived in. He was Kisōshi and his word was law. He had bought her, and as far as anyone else was concerned, he had every right to kill her.

Taka knew all of this, had known it since she was old enough to know anything, but suddenly, she didn't care. She didn't care if he killed her here in the street, she didn't care if no one thought she had the right to protest, to defend herself. She wanted to live but, more importantly, she didn't want to end up with the empty gaze of the girl that Haha-san had sold to this man five moons before.

All of this coalesced in her mind in a single instant. She never made a conscious decision to scream, never made a conscious decision to claw at the man's face with her free hand. She barely felt the blows he rained down on her as she did it. Barely noticed her lip split beneath his fist, barely felt the skin separate over her eyebrow, never felt the skin swell her right eye shut.

Yet she felt the arm that wrapped around her waist and pulled her away from the man, and she felt the voice rattle through the chest of the man that held her.

"Iizuna-san, I see that you are having some trouble," said the voice. "Perhaps I can be of assistance?"

"Washi-san," the Kisōshi who had bought her said with a slight bow of deference. "I did not know anyone was patrolling through our fair village."

"Oh?" Washi-san asked. "It's on the regular patrol schedule. Though I admit I might be moving a day or two ahead of schedule. The roads have been unseasonably dry. Can I help you resolve some dispute?"

Taka didn't have to turn around and look at the man behind her to know that he was another Kisōshi. It was obvious in Iizuna's face, and in the fact that the man hadn't drawn his katana to 'protect' his property. Taka tried not to allow hope to surge through her. She reminded herself that another Kisōshi was the one who had just bloodied her face.

"No, no, Washi-san," Iizuna said, trying to sound casual. "I'm merely teaching some discipline to my new servant."

"Ah, a new servant, is it? I see. So you'll be paying her for her work then?" Washi-san's voice sounded pleasant enough to the ear, but Taka could sense the anger rolling off of him.

"Paying? Yes, of course. She'll have all the food and shelter she could want," Iizuna muttered.

Washi-san said nothing for a moment and Taka wondered what he thought of the other man's lie. Certainly, providing food, clothing and shelter to a servant was considered sufficient pay in many regions of Gensokai, but Taka was well aware that 'all she could want' was downright untruth, and she suspected that Washi-san knew it too. He was Kisōshi after all, and just as capable of detecting untruths as she was.

"Iizuna-san, this girl's face is bleeding rather badly. Do you mind if I inspect her wounds for a moment?"

Taka took a deep breath to steady herself. If Washi-san didn't take her away from Iizuna, she was fairly certain she would not survive the night, but she didn't know what Washi-san could do that would be within his rights. He gently led her to the other side of the dirt road that formed the center of their small town and knelt down to look at her. Taka was so bewildered by a Kisōshi meeting her eyes that she saw nothing else of the man's face, just earthy pools of light creased with gentle concern.

"Iya, child! That bastard has made a mess of your face," Washi-san said in a low rumble, as she stared thoughtlessly at his earth colored eyes. She didn't know what to say to that. She was already using her kisō to assess her wounds. She couldn't heal herself with anyone else around to see it, she knew better than that, but her kisō reached out and assessed the damage almost automatically.

"Eh?" the man turned his head to one side and looked at her through half lidded eyes. Then Taka felt a soft wave of contact, the same as whenever Mishi extended her own kisō to Taka to see how she was doing. Taka had never experienced that touch from someone else, and it startled her enough to stop her assessment of her wounds.

"Josanpu?" he asked, though Taka wasn't sure who he was asking. Taka simply stared at him. "Child, do you have a name?" he asked, and this time Taka was sure he expected an answer.

"Taka," she said.

"Taka-chan, do you have some healing power?" he asked again, his eyes suddenly serious. "You're very young for it, but... do you have some ability to close up cuts, or make pain go away?"

Taka nodded. Those were the least of her powers, but she didn't think she should say that. In fact, she shook herself, and was horrified at what she'd just admitted. Had she learned nothing from Rika-chan's capture from the garden all those cycles before? Baka! She'd never told anyone her secret before except Mishi. How had this man gotten it out of her? He must have tricked her, must have used his kisō to make her tell the truth. She started to shift out of his grasp.

"Taka-chan, hold still, please, just for a moment. Let me ask you another question. Do you want to go with Iizuna-san?"

She shook her head violently. That was an easy question to answer.

"I would rather die," she said, and as the words left her mouth, she knew that they were true.

Washi-san's eyes widened briefly and Taka wondered if he was surprised by the answer, or only by her willingness to say it out loud. Then he nodded.

"Well," he said, taking a deep breath, "I'm afraid I can't stop Iizuna-san from taking you."

He must have seen Taka's eyes widen in horror, because he continued quickly.

"But, I can give you over to people who can."

Taka's eyebrows met in confusion above her nose.

"I'm not sure how much safer you'll be with them," the man said, and there was something in his voice that Taka couldn't place. Was it sorrow? "But if you'd rather die than go with Iizuna-san, then they're probably a decent alternative."

Taka said nothing, but nodded once more. She didn't trust her voice not to betray her at that moment. Was it possible that this man could actually save her?

"Iizuna-san!" Washi-san called from where they stood. "I'm afraid this girl cannot go with you today."

"Eh!?" Iizuna bellowed from his cart as he stomped towards them. "I paid for her. She's mine. I can show you the contract."

"I understand, Iizuna-san," Washi-san said, with mock formality. "However, I have discovered that the girl is a josanpu. I will be taking her to the Josankō immediately."

Taka felt the blood drain from her face as the meaning of the words cascaded over her. She'd heard the man say josanpu earlier, but she hadn't understood why until just now. If this man thought she was a josanpu, then he was obligated by Gensokai law to take her to the Josankō. Taka took a deep breath and tried to steady herself against the knowledge. She had meant it when she'd said she would rather die than go with Iizuna-san, but the Josankō was the very place that Rika-san had been attempting to escape on the day that she'd been captured in the garden.

3日 7月, 老中 1111年

～ Mishi ～

MISHI HAD BEEN trying not to let her hope be crushed under the weight of the thirteen days that she had spent in this Kami-forsaken cart. Tenshi had tried to speak with her, but Mishi had limited herself to one word replies and let her attention slip back to watching the green beauty of the mountains slip past her without appreciating any of it. All the rice fields they passed, and the mountains and rivers that lined their passage, were clouded by the knowledge that each day made it that much less likely that Taka would ever find her. Finally, on the afternoon of the thirteenth day, she was jarred from her sullen thoughts by the cart coming to a halt.

Mishi looked up and blinked as though waking from a dream, her senses returning to her as if she had been asleep since the moment she left the orphanage and only now could see and smell all that surrounded her. The air was suddenly hot and thick with the smell of wet, green life; the dirt so recently kicked up by the horse still hazed the world around her. The gate they had stopped in front of was massive; taller than a man, wider than a horse was long, and made entirely of iron.

Mishi worked to keep her mouth from dropping open as Tenshi offered to help her climb down from the cart. She ignored the woman's proffered hand and simply dropped to the ground.

"This is Kuma-sensei's school for young Kisōshi," Tenshi said, as she pushed open the large iron gate and led them through. "During the day, young Kisōshi train here to learn how to fight, and how to control their kisō, and you will be their servant."

Mishi began to follow Tenshi, but paused briefly to wonder if it was safe to leave the horse in the street. Just as she hesitated, she saw a girl only a few cycles older than herself shuffle forward with a quick bow to Tenshi and go to meet the animal.

"One of your duties will also be to tend the horses," Tenshi said, as she returned the bow and kept walking through the large gravel courtyard. The news made Mishi stumble briefly and Tenshi reached out a hand to steady her.

"You aren't truly afraid of horses are you?" Tenshi asked, with sympathy in her eyes.

Mishi shook her head and was finally able to find words. "I don't know. They're very big. I'd never seen one so close until we rode behind the one that brought us here."

Tenshi smiled and put a hand on Mishi's shoulder. "Don't worry, your duties will be explained in detail tomorrow. For now, I'm just to give you a brief tour and explain the generalities."

Mishi nodded. She wasn't sure what 'generalities' meant, but the idea that someone would explain her duties tomorrow helped to steady her breathing.

"This is the main courtyard," Tenshi explained, as they walked straight across it towards one of the three buildings that enclosed the gravel square.

"On your right are the classrooms for history, geography, mathematics, reading, and writing... scroll studies. The library is also in that building."

Mishi followed the woman's hand with her gaze and tried not to be overwhelmed by the idea of books, scrolls, and learning that many subjects. Would she be expected to take lessons and learn to read and write? The idea excited her, but she shook her head to deny the thought; surely there was no reason to teach a servant such things.

"On your left are the classrooms for kisō and budō, weapons classes, emptyhanded training, meditation rooms... all of those studies take place in that building, and in the courtyard on the other side of the residence hall."

"Do the students live here?" she asked, before she could stop herself. She dropped her chin and hoped she wouldn't be reprimanded for speaking out of turn. Tenshi did nothing but answer her question.

"Kuma-sensei and I, and the other servant girls, live here," she said, gesturing to the building that they were directly in front of. "This will be your new home. The male Kisōshi who study here go home at night, or if they are from farther away they board at a nearby ryokan."

Mishi was too awed by her surroundings to notice anything odd about Tenshi choosing the words 'male Kisōshi.' Mishi tried to take in the details of the building even as she attempted to keep up with Tenshi's stride. The sheer size of everything, not to mention the covered walkways that surrounded all the buildings, almost made her stumble as she walked. The orphanage she'd lived in her whole life along with dozens of other children could have fit within the main courtyard alone.

"I'll show you to your room in just a moment, Mishiranu-san," Tenshi said, as they entered the long low building that was the residence hall. "But, first I'm to take you into Kuma-sensei's rooms. He likes to meet all new students as soon as they arrive."

Mishi nodded again, but her brain tripped over Tenshi's last statement. New students? The woman must be tired after the long trip.

Mishi didn't correct her, worried that it would only earn her a scolding. Haha-san would have smacked her for correcting an elder.

Tenshi said nothing else as she led Mishi down the entire length of the sparingly decorated residential hall, dotted with sliding doors to the left and right, to the door farthest from the main entrance. Tenshi slid the shoji open and gestured for Mishi to enter.

Inside Mishi found a nine tatami room that was sparsely decorated with scrolls containing landscapes that captured all the beauty Gensokai had to offer. The first breath she took within its walls smelled of the dried grass of the tatami mats and the steam of green tea.

In the center of the room, a large man sat in seiza before a low table which held a small pot and two cups. The uwagi and hakama the man wore, along with the katana and wakizashi sticking out of his obi, marked him as a Kisōshi. As that truth dawned on Mishi, she threw her knees to the floor and pressed her forehead down to meet them.

"Get up, child," said the gruff voice on the other side of the table, even as Mishi heard the shoji slide closed behind her.

Mishi froze for a moment with her head still pressed to the tatami. Of course she should have known that the instructor at a school for Kisōshi would be a Kisōshi himself, but somehow she hadn't made the connection between that obvious fact and the name of the man Tenshi had been bringing her to meet.

Now, here she sat, frozen in obeisance to a man who could kill her simply for making eye contact with him, and he was insisting that she get up; an act that would require raising her head above the level of his own. An act punishable by death.

Was it a trick?

"It's not a trick or trap, child," Kuma-sensei said from his place behind the table. "I wish to see your face, and wish for you to see mine."

Mishi cautiously raised her head, though she still knelt, and her eyes instantly began to scan the room, looking for anything to focus on other than the man who sat behind the low table.

"Come closer, child. You can't drink tea from back there."

The man's voice was deep and gravelly, like a pile of rocks being pushed down the side of a mountain, but it was calm and kind. She could find no trace of anger in it.

"You need not fear me, Mishiranu-san. I have been searching for you for many cycles, and I wish you no harm."

That statement was so startling that Mishi forgot her fear and confusion for a moment and looked directly into the man's eyes. His eyes were the green of a deep forest, and shone with a light that Mishi thought she recognized. Was it mischief? His face was broad and open, golden from having spent cycles in the sun, and he had a few small scars on his brow and chin. His black hair was pulled into a tight knot on the top of his head, the style typical of most Kisōshi.

"Aha! There you are!" he said, as their eyes met. "This is much better, Mishiranu-san. I will not allow my students to hide their eyes from me. Yours are such a lovely grey. Haha-san informed me that that's why they called you Mishiranu at the orphanage. Understandable, I suppose, but I think I prefer the name your mother gave you."

Mishi's vision blurred, though not from tears, and she found her eyes locked on Kuma-sensei's even though she kept meaning to look away. Two thoughts warred in her mind and she couldn't decide which required her more immediate attention. Kuma-sensei had called her his student, and he had mentioned her mother. She was still trying to decide which statement made less sense to her when Kuma-sensei continued.

"Mishiranu-san, you are my student, or you will be if you like, as you are a Kisōshi, just like your mother before you."

~~~

Mishi sat on the tatami of her room–*her* room, no one else's, just hers alone–and tried to force her mind to understand all that she had been told.

"It doesn't make sense," she murmured to her hands in her lap.

"I can answer your questions!" chimed a voice from the doorway, where her shoji stood open. Mishi looked up to see a girl quite a bit smaller than she was dressed in the same type of kimono that Mishi had found folded into her new dresser. The girl's face was hidden behind a wide smile, but she had bright open eyes of a tawny shade and a wide forehead that made her face look pleasantly welcoming.

"Who are you?" Mishi asked, before she could stop herself. Iyah! Haha-san would have smacked her for her rudeness.

"My name is Ami," the other girl said, apparently taking the question as an invitation to enter, and folding herself onto the floor in front of Mishi.

"I'm Mishi," she replied.

"Nice to meet you, Mishi-san! I'm your sister! Sachi-san is around here too somewhere, but she said she doesn't want to meet you."

Mishi didn't know what to make of a statement like that so she stuck to the things that made sense to her.

"Nice to meet you, Ami-san. What do you mean you're my sister? I'm an orphan, I don't have any family."

"Oh? What's that like?" Ami smiled as she asked the question and then shook herself as though in scolding. "I'm sorry. You asked about being your sister. Well, all Kisōshi are considered brothers, so we are sisters."

Mishi tried to make sense of that statement, but was struggling.

"The boys who train here are brothers, even if they come from different families," Ami continued, as though she could sense Mishi's confusion. "So we must be sisters! Ne?"

Mishi nodded, simply because she didn't see any other way out of that particular point of conversation. Ami smiled again, and nodded enthusiastically.

"See," she said, still beaming, "I told you I could answer your questions. What else don't you understand?"

Mishi didn't think she could even list all of the things that she didn't understand, even if she just limited herself to things she had learned today, but she tried to focus on something simple. Like how the school worked.

"How is it that we can train here and no one knows about us?" Kuma-sensei had focused mostly on how Mishi's mother had come to be his student, but Mishi still didn't understand how this school managed to exist in secret.

"Because to everyone else, this is a school for male Kisōshi. The normal kind. What everyone expects. No one thinks female Kisōshi exist, so they don't look for us. The boys practice here during the day, which explains why Kuma-sensei has a school full of training equipment, and he even sends them off to test for rank when they reach their 17th cycles! They test with the Rōjū and everything." The look on Ami's face as she said this made it look as though she were envious of this distinction, but Mishi couldn't imagine why.

"So everyone is convinced that this is just a normal school for Kisōshi?"

"Yes!" Ami beamed at her, her smile radiating approval that Mishi had picked up the idea so quickly.

"But we train here at night?" she asked.

"Yes! And on holidays, when the boys don't come to train at all, we train all day."

"But we act as servants normally?"

Ami shook her head, and that confused Mishi even more thoroughly until she said, "We don't *act* as servants, Mishi-san. We *are* servants. We spend all day cleaning and mending, tending the horses. You will learn many useful skills here."

The way Ami said that last sentence made it seem as though it was something she'd been taught to repeat, but held little enthusiasm for.

"And after we spend all day working, we train?" Mishi asked, beginning to wonder when she was supposed to sleep.

"Oh yes!" Ami said, and the way her eyes lit up at the mention of training made Mishi suddenly more eager for it than she had been. "We learn everything that the boys do! History, math, geography, poetry... everything!"

Mishi's heart felt like it was burrowing its way to her stomach. Her face must have fallen as well because Ami asked, "Mishi-san, what's wrong?"

"I can't read or write," she admitted, before she thought to stop herself. She felt the blood run to her cheeks as she realized how stupid the other girl would think her now.

"Oh? Have you tried it before?" Ami asked, her face suddenly serious.

"No. No one has ever taught me."

Ami's face cleared and her grin spread wide.

"Silly, Mishi-san, if you haven't tried it then you don't know that you can't!"

Mishi almost smiled then. Ami's laugh was so infectious, but she couldn't help but wonder how many times she would hear that same expression in the next few days, and how many times her ignorance would prove that she was in no way meant to be a Kisōshi.

5日 7月, 老中 1111年

≈ Taka ≈

"A WOMAN'S NATURAL tendency towards evil cannot be trusted with strong kisō," said the black robed man at the front of the class.

Taka could barely remember the sequence of events from the moment Washi-san had taken her from Iizuna-san and handed her over to the Yukisō who ran the Josankō. A handful of days traveling and a chain of strangers passing her along had lead to her arrival at a small collection of buildings whose high walls and stern visaged keepers had made her feel more like a criminal than a student.

This morning, after being herded into the room with a dozen other girls between the ages of nine and twelve cycles, Taka had barely had time to take in a breath of the dust and oil filled air before this man had introduced himself as an earth kisō and healer, though he hadn't bothered to include his name. Then he had begun lecturing them the moment he had stepped in front of the rows of rigid desks that lined the room.

"In addition," he continued, "her body and mind are too weak to control kisō properly. Both of these factors contribute to a woman's imminent corruption should she possess any greater kisō than that of a josanpu. Because of this danger, measures need to be taken to ensure that females with such abilities are never born. As you all know, no woman could be born a true Kisōshi, but a woman might be born with a lessened version of that kisō. This would inevitably corrupt her. Part of your training will be to learn to recognize any kisō present at birth and to act accordingly."

Taka's mouth went dry. The way the man had said 'act accordingly' had made her shiver. What could he mean?

"What do you mean, act accordingly?" came a hesitant voice from the other side of the room.

One of the girls had raised her hand to ask the question. Taka was startled, not by the question itself—after all, she had just been thinking the same thing—but by the reactions of the other girls in the room. They were all staring at the girl with white faces and widened eyes. Taka couldn't fathom why they would react that way to a simple question.

"I meant that you will learn to take care of such situations as part of your training," responded the black robed man, "NOT today."

Then he motioned his pointer at the door and a guard appeared in the doorway.

"Take her to the cages," said the instructor.

The girl who had asked the question jumped from her seat.

"What? Why? What did I do? It was just a question. What are you going to do to me?"

The girls around her did nothing, but paled even more than they had before. The guard came forward, grabbed her by the shoulders, and began taking her towards the door.

"What did I do? I don't understand! What did I do?!" the girl screamed, as she was dragged from the room.

She struggled, but the guard was over twice her size and solid muscle. Nothing the girl did seemed to affect him. Before Taka could think about the repercussions she jumped to her feet. It was as though something inside her had broken on the day they had taken Mishi away. When before she would have stood still with fear, she now felt compelled to act. She didn't know where the screaming girl was being taken, but judging by the looks on the other girls' faces it couldn't be a good place. She wanted to help, but she didn't know what to do. She took a step towards the girl still struggling in the guard's arms.

"What are you doing, girl?" the instructor had turned his chilling gaze on her and no one else in the room made a sound.

"Where are you taking her?" Taka asked before she could stop herself.

"You'd like to know, would you?" the man asked, a cruel smile spreading across his lips. "Well, why don't you join her then?"

Taka almost screamed when another guard came forward and grabbed her about the waist, but she managed to contain herself. They wouldn't kill her for asking a simple question, would they? She tried to assure herself that it couldn't be that bad, but she was too frightened to move, too frightened to fight back. All the bravery she had felt at seeing the other girl taken had fled from her and she was left frozen. She simply let the man carry her away; too stunned to do anything else, and all the while wondering about the answer the other girl had never gotten. What *did* they do to female babies born with more kisō than a josanpu?

~~~

Taka's terror no longer gripped her like a talon. She and the other girl had been made to wait outside of the instructors' offices for so long that her backside was sore from sitting.

"Do you think we could escape?" the other girl asked. Taka had to blink to be sure she'd actually seen the other girl's mouth move. They had been silent for so long that she thought it might be her imagination. She cleared her throat before answering.

"There was a girl from my village brought here who tried to run away," she said, when she'd found her voice. "They came for her as soon as she returned to us, and after that we never saw her again."

The other girl nodded as if that was what she had expected Taka to say.

"So why are you here?" the other girl asked, after a long pause.

Taka felt color rush to her cheeks, though she wasn't sure why she was embarrassed. "I stood up, when they dragged you out of the room," she said, at length. "And I asked them where they were taking you."

"Oh." The other girl seemed to think about that for a while, but eventually she spoke again. "Thank you," she said, "for caring what happened to me."

Taka shrugged. "I don't understand why they would punish either of us for asking a simple question... at least, not in a way that made all the other girls so frightened.... Do you have any idea what they'll do to us?"

The other girl shook her head.

"I've only been here a few moons, but one or two girls have been sent to the cages since I arrived. They're not allowed to talk about it once they return though, so none of us know what it is. We only know we can hear the screaming all night long."

"Screaming?" Taka asked, but the other girl only shrugged.

"What's your name?" Taka asked, after another long pause.

"Kiko. And you?"

"I'm Taka."

"Nice to meet you Taka-san," Kiko said.

"And you, Kiko-san," Taka replied.

They sat in silence for a few moments and then, finally, another man in black robes and two more guards came to escort them out of the building that housed their classrooms, the mess hall, and the dorms. Taka had only been at the Josankō for one night, but she had already seen most of what there was to see of the compound.

As they were walked down a path that led to the far side of the grounds, the sky began to darken the edges of the horizon, catching starlight as it encroached on what was left of the day.

Taka was surprised when she realized that she was being taken past the outer wall of the grounds themselves, and even more surprised when they continued deep into the woods that surrounded the complex. Hadn't Kiko said that she had been able to hear the screams of the girls who were taken to the cages? How was that possible if they were so far away?

Either they were being taken somewhere different than the other girls had been taken, or the instructors must use air kisō to amplify the sounds of the cries so that they still reached the dormitories even from this distance. Not long after they passed the outer wall, Kiko was taken down a path branching off to the left and Taka almost cried out at the separation. Somehow, knowing she was going into this punishment with company had made it less terrifying. Now her legs began to tremble despite her best efforts to reassure herself that she would be fine.

They had walked for a short candle burn when they finally reached a small clearing, which contained a small bamboo cage that Taka could just make out in the scarce light that the last rays of sun provided. It was a cube, only an arm-span wide on any side. Taka was unceremoniously shoved inside the cage and the door was latched and then locked with a steel clasp. The instructor said nothing as he turned with the guard and headed back the way they had come.

~~~

Taka sat. The cage was only big enough for her to sit cross legged or in seiza. She tried leaning against the back of the cage, but there was no comfort to be found there. The bamboo had raised ridges attached that made leaning against the bars almost painful. Was the instructors' plan to torture her with discomfort? There had been barely enough light to see by when the instructor and guard had left her here, but at least what she had seen of the forest that surrounded her looked normal enough. Now, in the enveloping darkness, her mind came alive with all of the horrors that might lie in wait for her once the light was truly gone.

Why hadn't she asked Kiko more questions about the screaming?

The harder she wished for the light to hold, the faster it faded from the sky, and soon the darkness was complete. With the failing of the light every noise that emanated from the woods became ominous. What had earlier been the innocuous sounds of nature now became the hidden evil of the woods signaling its approach. She tried to calm herself, tried to remind herself that nothing about the woods had changed besides the lack of light, but her brain kept telling her that lack of light had never made a girl scream in a way that made other girls too afraid to ask a simple question.

Her heart picked up and then skipped a beat as she heard a shuffling noise behind her. She tried to whip around in order to see behind her, but the cage was too small and she couldn't turn around fully without rearranging her legs. As soon as she had succeeded in facing the other direction, she heard another branch snapping behind her. She turned again, still unable to see anything, and now there came the sound of breathing from the right. She whipped her head to the right and this time let out a sharp cry of surprise.

There was something huge in the darkness just beyond her cage. She could hear its ragged breathing, and she thought she saw the white glint of moonlight on teeth. Her impulse was to scream, but she took a deep breath and stifled the noise. She didn't have to scream yet, nothing had happened to her yet.

She tried to take another deep breath, but her chest was tight and her throat was convulsing as sobs tried to come forth. Her rational thoughts told her not to panic, not to be frightened. Kiko had said that the other girls came back, which must mean that they didn't get eaten... but that didn't change the fact that she was terrified. Well and truly terrified, and the beast whose outline she could see was huge, and its stance was menacing, and she was sure that it was going to attack her, and she was trapped, TRAPPED, in a tiny bamboo box.

She worked to ignore the panic, focusing her energy and breath the way she would if she were about to heal a cut. She was always calm when she healed herself or her friends, always. It was part of the practice; without calm she was unable to make her kisō do as she bid. As soon as she focused her breath and her energy, she found that some of the fear left her.

The beast wasn't going to be discouraged from killing her if she screamed her voice away into the night. *Just breathe*, she told herself, *it can't get to you while you're in here, just try to stay calm.* Her breath began to even out and she regained some composure.

And then the thing in the night lunged at the cage and its giant maw snapped at her, barely restrained by the bamboo slats that surrounded her, and all her composure was lost.

She cried out despite herself, but managed to bite the sound off. *Squeaky noises frighten animals*, she told herself over and over, as the tears streamed down her face. She tried to calm herself, but the creature returned and snapped at her once more, this time from the other side of the cage. The animal was able to insert its snout into the cage almost a hand's length and Taka had to keep herself centered in the cube in order keep a safe distance on all sides. The animal came at her again and again from all sides, with only brief intervals between lunges.

Taka fought the instinct to cry out, to scream, every time the creature lunged at her. The best she could do was keep to a low steady sob. She was sure her restraint would break, that she would start screaming soon and never stop, and that doing so would drive the creature into a frenzy that would give it the strength to destroy her little bamboo box...

But then a cloud shifted and the creature stilled for a moment, its attention briefly elsewhere, and Taka caught a glimpse of it in the full moonlight. The moon had been slow to rise over the trees, and patches of moonlight had only just begun to illuminate the glade that held her cage. When a patch of silver light crossed the animal's path, Taka's breath was taken away.

It was a wolf, and it was stunning. A sleek silver coat flecked with black covered its body, with particularly dark patches of fur around its tail, saddle, and a triangle between its ears coming down to a point just above its snout.

Taka's breathing stilled momentarily, but not with fear this time. The creature was magnificent, and for some reason, that caused Taka's fear to dissipate. With her fear gone, she remembered that she could use her kisō to calm another creature. She'd never tried it on a wolf before, but it worked well enough on the stray dogs she'd tried to heal at the orphanage.

First, she focused inward and used her breath to find a quiet calm within. Then, she focused all her attention on the wolf and pushed her own ki towards the wolf's, the way that she and Mishi had always done to each other when they wanted to know how the other was doing. The wolf's mind was strange to her, very different from a human's, but the emotional currents she could sense were much the same: fear, anger, frustration, a sense of urgency Taka couldn't understand, and the fact that the wolf was a female.

The wolf had paused in her attacks the moment Taka had reached out to her with kisō. Perhaps it was confused by the contact. Deciding to take advantage of the wolf's distraction, she refocused on her own inner calm and tried to send that feeling out towards the wolf. She had managed to keep stray dogs from biting her while she set a broken leg using this very tactic, and she hoped it would work now.

The wolf paced back and forth, as if trying to decide if she should attack again. Taka kept up her calming thoughts and found that if she wasn't succeeding with the wolf, at least she was having some success on herself. She found that her breathing came much more easily and her mind was clearer than it had been since the sun had begun to set. Soon the effect seemed to spread to the beautiful animal that shared the clearing with her and she saw the wolf slow its frantic pace. Before too long, it stopped altogether and then sat in front of her a few arm spans away, studying her.

Taka likewise considered the sleek grey beauty before her. She wondered what could be making the animal so afraid. Certainly a human child trapped in a box was no threat to a full grown wolf? What was the cause of her fear then? Why was she determined to attack?

Taka had learned that cornered animals would attack due to fear, but this animal was far from cornered. The wolf had vast expanses of woods to explore and instead she attacked defenseless girls trapped in boxes. Was it simply preemptive? Did the animal assume that if she didn't attack first that she would be attacked herself? Did she have something she was trying to protect? Was it her young? Taka couldn't make sense of it.

While Taka quietly pondered the wolf's motivations, the animal appeared to calm even further. Eventually, the wolf lay down, her eyes and ears still pointing directly at Taka, quite clearly on watch, but she no longer seemed intent on attacking.

Taka allowed herself to relax then, and she shifted her legs to a position that would enable her to rest her head against them. She and the wolf watched each other intently for a long time. The moon cast a beautiful silver light across the creature's already elegant features and Taka found that she could not stop marveling at her

~~~

Taka awoke to the sound of a distant howl. The clearing was empty. The predawn light shone through a layer of mist onto a sparkling layer of dew that covered everything, including her.

The wolf was gone.

Taka wondered briefly if the whole thing had been a dream, but a quick glance at the deeply gouged bamboo slats that surrounded her proved that it was not. She wasn't certain what had passed between her and the wolf that night, and she wasn't certain what it meant for her future at the Josankō.

She thought of Kiko and wondered if the girl had enjoyed a less troubled evening than Taka herself, and she thought of the wolf and wondered how the animal would treat her if she were ever sent to the cages again.

But mostly, she wondered if, despite the horrible night's sleep she'd gotten, and the negative reputation she was sure to be gaining with the instructors, she hadn't just made two new friends.

1日 8月, 老中 1111年

≈ Mishi ≈

"STOP!"

MISHI HALTED mid-punch, her feet shifting awkwardly on the ta-tami beneath her, and tried not to shrink away from Kuma-sensei as he came towards her in the soft lantern light of the weapons room. When she looked up, the anger on Kuma-sensei's face made it clear that she had not succeeded.

"A Kisōshi does not shy away from anyone," he growled. "Not even her sensei."

Mishi nodded and tried to stand up straighter, even though all she wanted to do was run away. Her own nerves combined with the summer heat to send a trickle of sweat sliding down her back.

"Yes, sensei," she said.

Kuma-sensei sighed.

"Do you know why I stopped you?" he asked, the anger gone from his voice.

"Because my punches are horrible?" she guessed.

Kuma-sensei chuckled.

"Not horrible, Mishi-san, but the motion must flow through the hips. Your feet are your foundation, and the power of your strikes comes from the earth beneath your feet. The whole motion is generated from the earth and flows up. Your hips transfer that power to your torso and your torso to your arms, and all of that power releases through your fist as you exhale. You need a stronger base."

Kuma-sensei stepped back and addressed all three girls.

"You all do," he announced. "So you will practice punches on the right side until Mishi-san executes one perfect punch. Then you will switch to the left side."

Mishi could hear the other girls groan and she worked to hold back tears. They had already been practicing for most of the evening. Why was it so much harder for her than for the other two girls?

She could hear Sachi's voice whisper to Ami even as they began the punches.

"I don't see why we have to keep doing punches just because she's terrible at everything. We'll be here until winter if we have to wait for her to do it right."

Mishi clenched her jaw, wiped away the tears collected at the corners of her eyes, and focused as hard as she could on executing the perfect punch.

~~~

Mishi sat before the low table in her room, her legs folded tightly beneath her, and tried to focus on the warm scent of melting wax and the slow motions of the brush she held to the parchment before her, rather than the memories of her recent practice, or her aching muscles.

"Iya! You can't write either," said a voice over her shoulder. "You're as dumb as a cow!"

Mishi cursed herself for leaving her sliding door open, but the summer night air was so stifling that she had wanted to allow any breeze that could be found into the room. Instead, Sachi had found her way in and Mishi hadn't even heard her approach.

"Where did Sensei even find you? Were you hiding under a rock somewhere?"

Mishi bit back the words that she wanted to shout at the older girl, and focused on the parchment in front of her. If Sachi was too stupid to know that orphanages never bothered to teach their children to read and write, it wasn't her job to correct her.

"I asked you a question, Mishi-chan! Are you mute as well?"

Mishi took a deep breath, but before she could even gather enough air to speak, another voice chimed in from the hallway.

"Why don't you leave her alone, Sachi-san? She's only been here a moon. You've been here since you were a baby. We're lucky. We were taught to read and write cycles ago. She's only bad at everything because she just started. You've been doing it all for cycles, we both have."

Sachi turned on Ami then and stalked towards the much smaller girl. Sachi was at least two cycles older than Mishi and Ami was at least a cycle younger than Mishi herself. The disparity in their sizes would have been laughable if Sachi hadn't looked as though she were about to strike the much smaller girl.

"So, what's your excuse then?" she asked, as she stalked closer. "Since we've both been here since we were babies, why are you so terrible at everything?"

Ami didn't reply, but she'd already started backing towards the doorway behind her. Mishi understood why when she looked down at Sachi's clenched fists. So far though, Sachi was still just talking.

"You're just glad this stupid cow is here to make you look good, aren't you?" Sachi continued, without waiting for a reply. "We used to have to stop a hundred times a day to fix *your* mistakes, but now Sensei has switched to fixing hers and you can finally look like you're almost half decent at punches and front kicks."

Ami's cheeks reddened and her eyes filled with tears, and Mishi decided she'd had enough.

"Sachi-san," Mishi said, as she stood up from her calligraphy practice, "I think it made more sense when you were being awful to me. At least I'm almost the same size as you."

Mishi tried to summon a confidence she didn't feel. It was true; she was quite tall for her age, and despite Sachi's two cycle advantage she was practically the same height as the girl. But that didn't change the fact that Sachi had been learning to fight since she was old enough to walk and Mishi had only started her training a moon ago.

The muscles all along Mishi's spine tightened as Sachi turned around to glare at her, but before the older girl could do anything, Mishi held up her right hand.

"And I think you should know," she said, as she met the older girl's eyes, "I'm not bad at *everything*." As she said the words she focused her kisō and brought forth a small ball of flame to sit on her hand. It was a trick she had practiced long and hard with Taka around to help in case the flame escaped her. She couldn't do anything with it yet, aside from hold it, but Sachi didn't know that.

Sachi's eyes widened until her eyebrows met her hairline, and she took an inadvertent step backwards.

"You... you're not allowed to do that. No fire inside our rooms. Sensei said!"

1 1 1 4 年

Seeds we sow in spring
lay dormant for many moons
until pain births truth

17日 3月, 老中 1114年

≈ Mishi ≈

MISHI TOOK A deep breath of foggy morning air and repressed a shiver as she looked up at the peak pushing into the mist before her. She had known from her first day as Kuma-sensei's student that her training to become a Kisōshi would be difficult, but she had never imagined that she would have to climb a mountain like this one by herself. It became suddenly clear why Kuma-sensei hadn't told her any of the details of her test until he'd brought her here.

If she had known she was going to be required to scale the infamous Ryūjinjasan alone, would she have agreed to the test? And, even if she had agreed, would added days to contemplate all of the dark rumors that the villagers told about the mountain have discouraged her? Would she have let the stories of grown men disappearing from the trails, or strange, violent storms that didn't extend past the mountain's base, cloud her imagination until she was frozen with fear? As it was, she predicted a large part of the test would consist of not allowing her imagination to overcome her common sense.

As she stared at the forbidding peak disappearing in the mist above her and took in the long, serpentine trail that cut through the side of the mountain, she understood why Tenshi had stuffed food into the coat she had wrapped into a bundle and strapped between Mishi's shoulders. Mishi could see from here that she would need all day simply to get to the top of this peak, hidden oni or unnatural storms aside.

"Better start now then."

She refrained from looking wistfully behind her to where Kuma-sensei had dropped her off on horseback only a few moments before.

She doubted he would be there still and she knew better than to think he would let her do anything but climb anyway. Besides, she knew she wanted to continue her kisō training and she had been honored when Kuma-sensei had told her that she was ready for a higher level of instruction. But, of course, if she wanted to earn that honor she would have to work for it.

The path was narrow and steep from the beginning, although it plateaued occasionally as it crossed small creeks. It wound back and forth along the side of the mountain, barely visible amongst the verdant undergrowth of the forest, and for a time Mishi felt as though she were swimming in an ocean of every shade of green imaginable. The trees' leaves were dark and heavy with morning mist, the ferns that covered the forest floor were the bright and vibrant green of a grass snake, and the vines and moss that filled the space from trunk to forest floor covered every shade between.

She climbed as steadily as she could, one foot in front of the other, slowly watching the trail pass beneath her and ignoring the small rumbles that sounded like distant thunder emanating from what felt like the inside of the mountain. Allowing the rumbling to frighten her would only slow her down.

It wasn't until midday that Mishi reached a waterfall where the path simply seemed to vanish. Looking up at the cliff face before her, she decided that she might as well eat while she puzzled out how she was meant to proceed.

As she unwrapped the rice balls filled with tuna that Tenshi had placed inside her coat bundle, she took a close look at the waterfall before her and the way that the path ran directly into the cliffside over which it flowed. If the trail were to be believed, the next part of her journey somehow involved the cliff.

The slopes all around her appeared to be a deep tangle of underbrush over more sheer rock faces, and looked slippery as well as steep. The section of cliff that the trail pointed to was clean of plant life, seemed to be dry despite the waterfall cascading down it a few arm spans away, and she could make out small ledges and crevices which she could use as holds for her hands and feet. The same could not be said of the other slopes around her. Where the rock poked through the underbrush, it seemed sheer and slick with mud. Where no rock could be seen, the tangle of plants seemed tight and forbidding, and not at all secure in their own purchase on the rock. There seemed to be little choice but to climb the cliff. It wasn't very tall… maybe only three times as high as Kuma-sensei. Falling would be… unpleasant to say the least, but she didn't see what alternative she had.

Even as she made the decision to climb the cliff, the sky seemed to darken slightly around her, and she felt as if the mist that she had been climbing through all morning had decided to collect directly on top of her. The air grew more damp, and it seemed as though less sunlight filtered through it than had done so only moments before. Mishi shivered even as she finished her rice ball. She must be letting the rumors affect her imagination. A mountain couldn't will her not to climb it, could it?

She repacked her bundle with more caution than was probably necessary and settled it snugly between her shoulders once more, the sleeves of the jacket Tenshi had given her tied in a tidy knot over her chest.

She stepped closer to the cliff and looked up. It looked taller now that she was directly beneath it. Perhaps it was more like four times the height of Kuma-sensei. She reached for the first small ledge above her, and, finding no other foot holds below it, put her right toes on the same ledge as her hand and began to pull herself onto it. The ledge was only slightly wider than she was, and she had to be very careful to keep her balance as she got her weight centered over her right leg and stood up.

"This had better be worth the trouble," she muttered between gasping breaths as she prepared to rise towards the next ledge. She tried to ignore the deep rumble that the mountain seemed to emanate in response. Her mind must be playing tricks on her.

There were a few smaller holds between her and the next ledge, only the size of her hand or foot, and she wondered how any adults managed to make their way to the top of this mountain. Some of them must make it there, else where did the rumors come from? And besides, the shrine atop the mountain was said to be one of the most powerful in Gensokai, surely many people must come here seeking aid. So why did she feel as though she was utterly alone? As though if anything happened to her no one would ever find her or even her remains....

She shook that thought away, took a deep breath, and kept moving. Kuma-sensei would not have sent her to do an impossible task, and he probably wouldn't have sent her to do something that was likely to kill her... at least she didn't think he would. She knew from her training that the most important tasks in her life would be difficult, and sometimes even dangerous. She assumed that this was no exception.

Slowly, carefully, but never pausing for long, she made her way towards the top of the cliff. Some of the places she had to put her feet were only large enough for her toes. Some of the handholds only allowed for her fingertips to grip them.

As she came close to the top of the cliff, the rumbling of distant thunder returned, now shaking the cliff beneath her in a way that she thought thunder should not be capable of. Her hands began to sweat and her grip began to slide from the rock each time she reached for a new handhold. She took a deep breath and the rumbling subsided. Then, as she pulled her right leg higher and tried to get her toe on the next foothold, the rumbling resumed with more force than before and her right hand lost its grip, causing her to start swinging away from the rock. She cried out and dug in her right toe as well as her left hand, clenching all the muscles in her stomach and back in order to prevent herself from peeling away. From there, she wasn't even sure what her hands and feet were doing, but she somehow managed to reach for the final ledge an arm span above her. She pulled herself over the edge, her stomach flat to the ground and her right leg stepping up to slide her along the ground, until more than two thirds of her body was resting on the gloriously flat surface at the top of the cliff. The exertion had taken every bit of strength that she had. As she lay there and flipped herself over to contemplate a sky that was now surprisingly blue, when only moments ago she had been swathed in mist, she wondered if she would ever have the strength to stand again. Her arms and legs trembled with exhaustion.

After a time, her arms and legs felt more solid and she was able to sit up, but she decided she should eat another rice ball before she moved on. Tenshi was always telling her and her sisters to eat more, especially when they complained of being tired from training. The three girls may have grumbled at the advice, but they had also noticed that it helped.

The view from the top of the waterfall was entrancing. The mists swirled around the base of the mountain, forming a silky chain around the range of mountains stretching into the distance. Mishi watched as a hawk reeled through the ether, caught between clear sky and mist, and the verdant peaks between. As she finished her rice ball, she concluded that she must be at least halfway to the top of this peak. She still felt weak from scaling the cliff, but she also felt confident that she could walk.

She gathered herself up, replaced her small pack, and continued up the small, brown thread of trail that wove its way through the trees and underbrush, hoping she would make the summit before nightfall. The sky remained clear above her and she hadn't heard the mountain rumble since gaining the top of that ledge.

As it happened, the trail finally rose to a ridge line that wound for about half a league to the final summit of the mountain and deposited her in front of an unpainted, but ornately carved, wooden shrine no larger than her room at the school.

She stood before it, disappointed at first that it wasn't more grand in stature, but then slowly becoming awed by it as she took in its details. Within the standard wooden roof, with its curved and decorated corners, stood a statue of a dragon that took Mishi's breath away. She was not mesmerized by the fact that the dragon statue appeared to be made of solid gold and silver, though that fact struck her with awe as well. What mesmerized her was the incredible detail with which the statue had been carved. Every single scale, from the small, dagger shaped scales on the dragon's face, to the larger, leaf shaped scales of gold and silver that gently curved away from the dragon's body, locking together and overlapping with each other and a series of jade plates, was carved with the most exquisite detail. She couldn't imagine the level of patience the artist must have had to include so many details, especially over such a large statue. Everything about the shrine looked delicate, even though the dragon statue, folded over itself many times to fit its lengthy body within the confines of the roof, filled all the space inside, aside from a small jade bowl used to hold burning incense. For a moment it was all Mishi could do to inspect the sculpture and appreciate its artistry.

Mishi shook herself from her stupor and then opened up her bundle to retrieve a stick of incense. Those had been the only instructions that Kuma-sensei had deigned to give her for this adventure: climb to the top of the mountain, find the shrine, light a stick of incense, and begin to meditate. The rest, Sensei had told her, would 'be revealed to her.' That, she had learned over the past few cycles, meant that part of the test was to determine what the test was.

Ignoring the strange sense that there were eyes focused on her, she dutifully lit the incense, stabbing the stick into the coarse sand that filled the jade bowl so that it would remain upright until it burned down to nothing. Then she cast about for a flat surface on which to begin her meditations.

She finally settled on a nice patch of comfortable looking ferns a few arm spans away from the shrine, and sat down with her legs folded beneath her the way that Kuma-sensei had taught her. In the past few cycles her meditation had improved greatly. What had started off as a task that always left her bored and fidgety had become a practice that helped her access her kisō more quickly and to much greater effect than she had ever managed before. Kuma-sensei had started training her in kisō not long after her arrival at the school, despite telling her that most students did not start their kisō training until the age of ten. Recently though, Kuma-sensei had told her that her kisō was ready for the next level of training, one she would have to complete a very special test in order to begin. Since kisō practice depended largely on one's ability to focus one's ki in meditation, even in the distractions of battle, she assumed the test before her would be one of focus.

She closed her eyes, took a deep breath, and began to clear her thoughts.

Though her eyes were closed and she was focused inwards, she could still sense the sun as it settled low on the mountain and began to sink out of sight. She waited. As the last rays of sunlight touched the roof of the shrine, Mishi thought she sensed movement behind her. Could someone else be on the mountaintop?

Determined not to break her concentration, and resolved that the noise, whatever its source, most likely formed part of the test itself, she remained where she was. She was confident that she would sense it if she were in any danger of being attacked.

The light breeze that had been blowing as she settled into meditation became a true wind. As it began to blow more forcefully, she wondered if the weather were changing. Still, she tried to remain focused on her meditation. She continued her breathing and returned her mind to clarity. She assumed this was part of the test. An attempt to distract her perhaps? She would remain focused. She would prepare herself mentally for any eventuality.

Yet nothing could have prepared her for what happened once the sun was fully gone behind the mountains and twilight set in. When the last rays of light left the shrine and then disappeared behind the mountains to the west, the rumbling she had heard on and off all day began to emanate from the shrine itself. The hairs on Mishi's neck rose and she struggled to keep her eyes closed and maintain her focus. Soon the rumbling became a growl, such a deep and thundering sound that Mishi found it nearly impossible to resist the urge to open her eyes and break her meditation.

The sound of wood splintering brought her head up, her ears perked in the direction of the shrine, but she managed to resist the urge to look. Finally, a hot wind blew in her face, and a voice deeper than the most melancholy thunder rolled past her and enveloped her.

"Who are you, child?" The voice didn't sound angry, but it didn't sound pleased either.

"I am Mishiranu; a Kisōshi in training," she replied, with as much confidence as she could summon given the enormity of the voice that surrounded her.

It took every shred of self control she had to keep her eyes closed and cling to her meditative state. She was desperate to know what the owner of that voice looked like and whether or not it was likely to attack her. If it did attack her, how would she defend herself? The urge to open her eyes and see the potential threat before her was powerful and tempting.

"A female Kisōshi? It has been almost a thousand seasoncycles since I have met one. The last one was not worth the meeting. I was compelled to eat her."

The way the voice so casually mentioned eating a Kisōshi made Mishi shiver.

"Are you cold, child? I can warm you up," the voice said, with an earth shaking growl that Mishi could only hope was laughter. Mishi swallowed and tried to keep her apprehension at bay. What kind of test had Kuma-sensei submitted her to?

"Why don't you look at me, child? It's rather rude to sit there so obstinately with your eyes closed."

The voice sounded gruff, but she thought she also detected amusement in its reverberating tones. She continued to keep her eyes closed.

"I don't think you mean to be rude, which is why I haven't eaten you yet, but if you persist I will have to assume it is intentional and the consequences of being rude to a dragon can be dire indeed."

Curiosity and fear overcame her, and all traces of her meditative state vanished. Mishi opened her eyes. What she saw before her left her mouth agape and her eyebrows reaching for her hairline. The dragon statue was no more, and a pile of tinder lay where once the small though magnificent shrine had stood. What had replaced both the building and the statue was more magnificent by far. A living dragon hovered before her, in all of its gold, silver, and jade glory, over a hundred times as long as she was tall and with a head large enough that the mouth within it could easily have consumed five of her in a single bite.

The longer she stared at the creature, the less afraid she became, though it occurred to her that perhaps that was not a rational reaction to such a creature. The dragon was magnificent, and ought to have been terrifying, but out of habit and without thinking, she had pushed out her own kisō to assess the dragon's intentions as soon as she had opened her eyes. The moment she had done so she had perceived that the creature meant her no harm… at least, not without provocation.

21日 3月、老中 1114年

~ Taka ~

TAKA AND KIKO walked arm and arm, padding as silently as they could through the darkened, tatami lined hallway. As they walked, Taka's mind wandered to consider why the Josankō even had a library. In the three cycles that she'd been there, the instructors had never once assigned the girls reading from any book or scroll. All of their 'studies' consisted of listening to the lectures of the male instructors and working their practical classes with their female instructors. She supposed the presence of the library must have something to do with the tours of the 'school' that were given to the family members of girls who were newly handed over to the Josankō.

Yet, in the past three cycles, the library had become one of Taka's favorite sanctuaries. It hadn't taken long for Kiko to discover that Taka hadn't known how to read or write, and once Kiko had made a point of teaching her, she had excelled at the activity. Now she read as many scrolls or books as she could.

However, she'd never felt comfortable having scrolls or books out in front of the instructors, especially not the ones on advanced medicine that she preferred to read, and she and Kiko confined their forays into the school library to after dark, when they were less likely to run into any of the instructors.

They paused outside of the sliding paper door and listened for a moment before entering. Taka heard nothing, as was usually the case, so she gently slid the door open wide enough for Kiko to enter before her, and slid it shut behind her after they had both slipped through the doorway.

Once inside, Kiko insisted on lighting a small candle that she had brought with her. Taka always thought it was a needless risk to attract attention with a light, but Kiko insisted that they were more likely to attract attention with a loud noise if they bumped into something in the dark. Taka had to admit that it made finding scrolls much easier than dragging them to the nearest window and hoping to read them by moonlight.

With the candle lit, the two girls made their way to the stacks that contained the information on herbs and medicines that Kiko enjoyed reading. Taka patiently held the candle for Kiko as she looked through a few scrolls in search of one that caught her interest.

"Eee! Taka-chan," Kiko said, turning to her with wide eyes, "did you know that willow bark can be used to reduce fever as well as pain?" she asked.

Taka shook her head and raised a finger to her lips.

"Sshhh..." she hissed, her mouth turning up at the corners even as she did it. "You'll let the whole school know we're here," she chided.

"But this is so important! I can't believe they don't teach us any of this."

Taka shrugged. "If you paid closer attention in class, you might have noticed that willow bark was in the paste they had us make for moonpains last cycle."

"Tsk..." Kiko chided. "No one remembers what the instructors say in that class except for you. You're the only one who ever gets the medicines right on the first try."

"That's because I listen," Taka rebuked. "You should try it sometime. Along with being quiet. Honestly, you'll get us in trouble before I've even had a chance to find my scrolls."

Kiko stuck her tongue out at her friend and Taka decided to walk away with the candle just to demonstrate her disdain. It was only a moment before Kiko caught up and had wrapped her arm through Taka's once more.

"Hey!" she chided even as she reestablished their arm link, "I was trying to find a scroll that will tell me how to get rid of these awful spots on my face!"

Taka glanced at Kiko's face and tried not to laugh.

"You should leave them. They're the only thing that keep the other girls from hating you for being so pretty."

Kiko laughed aloud and then had to throw her arm in front of her face to stifle the noise. Taka smiled, but she wasn't actually joking. Kiko was by far and away the prettiest girl in their class, and the other girls really were jealous. If Kiko didn't have the small spots she was so eager to cure, the other girls might dislike her as much as they disliked Taka for always getting her medicines right in practical classes. Taka sighed. At least Kiko never minded that Taka was good at healing. Or rather, she never got mad at her for it.

Taka reached the stack of scrolls she was looking for and handed the candle to Kiko.

"What are you looking for tonight?" Kiko asked, even as Taka began to run a hand over the scrolls that were on the top of the stand.

"More on animal healing," she said. "I need something to hide my advanced anatomy scroll, and the instructors will start getting suspicious if I don't move on from 'animal husbandry' soon."

That made Kiko giggle, and just as Taka brought her hand up to shush the girl, she heard the sound of the shoji opening on the far side of the room. Kiko's eyes widened even as Taka leaned forward to blow out the candle. The two girls stood as still as they could, desperately hoping not to make any noise. In addition, Taka worked desperately to tamp down on her kisō so that it matched the level of a normal josanpu, something she never had to bother with when it was just Kiko and herself.

The two girls tried not to breathe or shift or fidget, and for a few moments there was no sound that they could discern in the darkened library. Then Taka almost jumped from her skin when she heard the shift of a boot against the wooden floor not five paces from where they stood.

"Well, well…" the cold voice of one of the male instructors said, as a small flame flicked to life at the end of a match. "What have we here?"

Taka and Kiko were too stunned to speak. Taka wasn't sure what the actual rules about visiting the library were, but she imagined there was probably something against going there in the dark. Still, how bad could it be to be sent to the cages again? It had been a long time since she had visited her wolf friend. Just as she had the thought, a strange glint flickered in the man's eye as he took a second look at Kiko.

"Taka-chan, you'll be headed to the cages, but you… Kiko-chan is it? Holding a candle in a room full of parchment? Are you trying to burn the whole school down?"

Taka wanted to point out the match held in the man's own fingers, but couldn't get the words to move from her throat to her mouth.

"I'm afraid your punishment will have to be more… severe." Even as he said the words, the man reached forward to grab Kiko with his free hand and began to drag her towards the exit.

Taka followed along dumbly, trying to decide if attacking the man would do any good, and weighing it against how much more 'severe' Kiko's punishment could be.

1日 4月、老中 1114年

≈ Taka ≈

TAKA AWOKE TO the stifled groans of someone trying to scream in her sleep. She turned to see Kiko flailing on the futon beside her as though attacking an invisible enemy. Taka cautiously placed a hand on her friend's shoulder.

"Shh… quiet Kiko, quiet. It's just a dream."

When that did nothing to calm Kiko's thrashing, Taka placed hands on both of the girl's shoulders as she said the words again, this time finding her focus and pushing her own kisō out to Kiko in order to calm her.

Kiko's eyes flew open and she stared unseeing at Taka. After a moment her eyes focused and she seemed to recognize her.

"Taka-chan? Taka…?"

"It's alright, Kiko-chan. I'm here. It was just a dream."

Kiko nodded, but she shuddered once more and tried to pull out of Taka's grasp.

Taka wondered what had been the cause of Kiko's nightmare. After what they had learned in class today, she thought she knew. Yet she didn't know what comforting words she could offer. She was at a loss as to how a human being could kill an innocent child like that, no matter what they thought the child might become.

"Did your dream have to do with today's lesson?" she asked, unsure of what else to say.

Kiko looked puzzled for a moment and started to shake her head, and then seemed to realize what Taka meant.

"Oh… yes, I suppose it was. Dreams make so little sense…. How can people do such awful things to one another?"

Her voice was quiet as she asked the question, and something in her tone made Taka wonder if all she was referring to was the lesson from that afternoon.

"Kiko, what did that instructor do to you?" It was perhaps the hundredth time she'd asked her since the two of them had been separated over a tenday ago, when Taka was dragged to the cages and Kiko to somewhere unknown.

Kiko shuddered.

"I told you, I'm not permitted to speak of it," she whispered.

Taka felt her spine cringe as she considered Kiko's words.

"How would they know you had spoken of it?"

Kiko shook slightly, but remained silent.

"Kiko-san, please tell me what happened," she pleaded.

Kiko rocked slowly for a moment before replying.

"I can't, and even if I could, I wouldn't. I'm fine, Taka." She took a deep breath and spread a false smile across her face.

Taka wasn't fooled.

"You can tell me anything, Kiko-san. You know that, ne?"

Kiko nodded and her eyes glistened briefly before she dragged her wrist across them.

"I know, Taka-chan. You are the best friend a girl could ask for."

Kiko wrapped Taka in her arms then, and Taka didn't have the heart to ask her again. Kiko would tell her in her own time, and Taka would try not to imagine what horrible thing the instructor could have done to put that quaver in Kiko's previously steady voice. In the meantime, she held her friend in her arms and patted her back.

"Will you be able to sleep again?" she asked at length.

Kiko shook her head. "I doubt it," she said.

"Then I'll stay here to keep you company," Taka replied, leaning up against the wall behind the futon.

Kiko managed a smile that actually seemed genuine then.

"Thank you, Taka-chan," she said, joining her with her back to the wall.

For a time they held hands as they whispered made up stories to each other. Eventually, Kiko lay down again and closed her eyes. Taka sat beside her, a hand on her shoulder to calm her if necessary.

Taka wondered if she or Kiko would ever be able to get a good night's sleep again. Taka still doubted that today's lesson was the only thing making Kiko scream in the night, but if Kiko truly had been dreaming of the horrors of today's lesson she wouldn't be surprised.

Today they had learned the horrible truth about what was done to female Kisōshi at birth. The cruelty of it was stunning, and it brought to light what Taka was now sure was the true purpose of the Josankō. The school brutalized young women who had any kisō at all into thinking that they were either weak, stupid, evil, or some combination of the three. Once that was accomplished, or at least once the instructors thought it was accomplished, they revealed to the students the true purpose of a josanpu: to drown female Kisōshi at birth.

It was clever really, the work that the instructors put into making the girls fearful, then timid... wouldn't that timidity eventually lead to self doubt? She supposed it was easy then, once a person was no longer sure of her own self worth, to convince her that these babies deserved to die. A host of women became complicit in the destruction of all the female Kisōshi who had ever been born, and all to save their own lives.

How could her classmates and the women who had gone through the school before her believe that a woman with more kisō than a josanpu would be a danger to society? She found it amazing that the instructors could be so effective in their methods, that so many of the girls already took the information as just one more necessary evil in this world where women were considered inherently corrupt.

She wondered then, why didn't she believe it herself? What was the difference between her and the other girls in her class? Although she wasn't completely alone, since Kiko didn't believe women were inherently corrupt either... what separated them from the others? What made them resist the idea that women with kisō must be evil? Was it because they themselves had more kisō than the rest of the josanpu? Taka didn't consider herself evil, and she was sure that Kiko was not.

Then she thought of Mishi. She didn't know anyone with more power than Mishi, and Mishi certainly hadn't been evil the last time that she had seen her. If Mishi wasn't evil, then why should any female Kisōshi be? Yet the instructors had convinced whole classrooms full of girls to doubt not only themselves, but every other woman they might meet. She could barely believe that it had worked at all, but the evidence was right in front of her: Kiko was the only one screaming herself awake tonight.

4日 4月, 老中 1114年

～ Taka ～

KIKO'S SLEEP DIDN'T improve over the following weeks. If anything, it seemed to deteriorate, and Taka began to truly worry for her. Not only was the girl having troubled dreams, but the instructors had held her back after class twice in the last tenday.

As the days went by, Kiko drew within herself more and more, no matter what Taka did to try to bring a smile to her lips. Taka continued to ask Kiko what was wrong, but stony silence was all that she got in return.

Finally, on the day when Taka had resolved to pull Kiko aside that afternoon and examine her for injury or illness whether the girl liked it or not, an instructor rendered the point irrelevant.

It happened during one of their practical classes, the class devoted to aiding women with moonpains and pregnancy. Without preamble, the female instructor grabbed Kiko by the shoulder and escorted her to the front of the class. Kiko's face paled to a ghostly hue and her eyes were wide with fear and anxiety. Taka had to resist the urge to rush forward and comfort her friend, but she had no idea what the instructor was doing, so she decided to wait.

The instructor turned Kiko to face the rest of the class, her hand still on the girl's shoulder, and Taka wondered if the woman was using some of her power to restrain Kiko, or to keep her from fainting, something the expression on Kiko's face suggested was likely.

"Kiko-san has a confession to make," the instructor said, as she pushed Kiko away from herself and towards the students, as though she were an ill behaved pet being made example of.

44

Kiko opened her mouth a few times, but no words escaped her lips. The rest of the class was silent. All ears were tuned to what might come out of Kiko's mouth.

"I..." she finally managed under the glare of the instructor and the pressure on her shoulder from the instructor's hand. "I met a boy a few tendays ago." Her whisper was barely audible, even in the silence that pervaded the room, and her eyes were cast solely on the floor, she would not look at her classmates.

"And..." prompted the instructor.

"And... he... I..."

"Go on," the instructor almost shouted.

"We were intimate."

Her voice broke as she said that last word, and Taka could see her shoulders begin to shake with silent sobs. Taka's fists clenched and un-clenched at the sight. What Kiko said made no sense at all.

"In other words," finished the instructor, "the little yariman is preg-nant."

Kiko's sobs were now quite audible and only the sounds of the other girls' shocked gasps kept them from overpowering the room.

"While we would normally dismiss a girl for such abhorrent behavior, Kiko's timing is impeccable. We are just about to begin our unit on prac-tical examinations for pregnant women, from inception to childbirth. So, rather than bringing in an innocent village woman and asking her to put up with your inexpert care, we will use Kiko here instead."

With that, the woman began the lesson. Kiko was required to stay at the front of the class as the procedures for an early pregnancy exam were explained and demonstrated in detail.

Taka's mind reeled and she didn't hear a single word that the instruc-tor said for the rest of the lesson. She kept trying to get Kiko's attention, to make eye contact and be sure that her friend was alright. But Kiko kept her gaze to the floor and never once looked in Taka's direction.

All Taka could think of was the absurd idea that Kiko had met a boy and had time to be intimate with him sometime in the past moon. Grant-ed, she didn't spend every second of every day with the girl, but she might as well. The only time they'd been apart in the past few moons had been when Taka was sent to the cages or when Kiko had been held behind after classes during the last two tendays. Could she possibly have met and been intimate with a boy in that time?

Taka didn't believe it, but she couldn't come up with an alternative ei-ther.

~~~

"I still don't understand how it happened," Taka said quietly, as she and Kiko sat beside each other with their legs stretched out on Kiko's futon later that night. Taka had refrained from asking her closest friend this question all day. She hadn't wanted Kiko to have to endure any more jeers from her classmates just for her own curiosity, but now their classmates were asleep and Taka could no longer avoid the question that had burned through her mind all day.

"How did you even meet a boy, let alone bed him?"

All the color left Kiko's face and the glint of humor that had been there only moments before was gone from her eyes in an instant. Taka instantly regretted the question and was about to tell Kiko to forget it, but suddenly Kiko's voice was answering and Taka's curiosity would not let her interrupt.

"I…" Kiko hesitated and shook her head. Her eyes locked on her lap instead of Taka and she started again.

"I was sent on an errand to pick up some goods that were needed for the school. There was a boy there, at the vendor's shop, and he was nice to me. We spoke a bit. The next tenday I was sent to the same vendor to pick up more supplies. The same boy was there. This time he asked me to join him in a back room so that he could show me something. I went with him. He kissed me. I… I opened for him. I never saw him again."

Taka felt sick. Not because of the story. If it had been told by any other girl, or if it had been told in any other way, it might have been plausible, and she certainly wouldn't have held it against any of her fellow students for wanting some sort of intimacy outside of these cold and brutal walls. But the way that Kiko told it, the way her lips moved as she stared at the floor and the monotone in which she recited it, made Taka's stomach reel. She had never heard a more distinctly memorized speech, and the implications of it made the heat drain from her skin and her spine feel like ants were using it as a ladder.

"Kiko-chan…" she said, after a long pause. "Please don't lie to me like that. I don't know what really happened, but… please, you can tell me the truth. I won't tell anyone."

Kiko said nothing for a long time, only shook her head and let tears stream down her face.

"That's all I can tell you Taka-chan. I swear. That's all I can tell you."

Taka let those words dig into her soul. All Kiko could tell her? The girl wasn't swearing that it was true, she was only swearing that it was all she could say. Why was that? Taka wanted to rip the truth out of her, to find out what had really happened and punish whoever was causing the pained look on her friend's face. Instead, she took a deep breath and wrapped her arms around her trembling friend.

She pulled Kiko close and kissed the top of her head.

"If you can ever tell me the truth…" Taka stopped herself. For some reason Kiko couldn't say anything more. She wouldn't do anything else to hurt her. Kiko had clearly had enough hurt for one day… for many days. "I want to do terrible things to whoever is hurting you, Kiko-san. You don't deserve this."

Those words only seemed to bring more sobs to Kiko's breath, so Taka stopped talking and simply held her.

What had truly happened to Kiko? What had happened to the boy? Who was the boy? Had there actually been a boy? She couldn't answer any of these questions, but neither would she ask Kiko about them. It was more than clear that the subject brought her pain. Still, Taka swore to herself that if she could find out the truth without hurting her friend any further she would do it, and then she would make someone pay.

5日 4月、老中 1114年

≈ Mishi ≈

"AMI-SAN, WHY are you crying?"

Mishi stood outside of Ami's room, the door only three quarters closed, as though Ami had entered in a hurry and hadn't bothered to check if the door had slid shut behind her. The soft sounds emanating from inside were definitely sobs, and Mishi wondered if it was today's lesson with Kuma-sensei that had upset her.

When Ami didn't reply, Mishi slid the door farther open and stepped through. The sight of the scroll in front of the younger girl, whose hunched shoulders shook with the force of her sobs, made Mishi suspect her initial concerns were correct.

"Ami-chan? Why are you crying?" she asked again.

The other girl said nothing, but nodded towards the scroll that lay on the table before her. Mishi walked to the table, knelt beside her friend, and pulled the document towards her.

Before the rule of the first Rōjū council was the era of the Yūwaku, a dark time in Gensokai history which shall not be discussed, its memories too painful for those who lived through any part of it. This historian does not wish to inspire any future evil doers by listing the atrocities of the Yūwaku and their evil reign. Henceforth, their name in history shall be a blank.

"Do you think it's true?" Ami finally asked, between sobs, as Mishi pushed away the scroll she was already familiar with from her own studies. "Do you think what Sensei told me today in class is really what they do?"

Mishi's mouth flattened out to a hard line. Did her own personal history make it so much easier for her to believe that the Rōjū were capable of such atrocities? Was it simply because she'd learned the truth almost as soon as she'd arrived at this school? Or was it because growing up in an orphanage didn't afford her all of the innocence of childhood that Ami had experienced?

"Yes, Ami-chan, I believe what Sensei told you today. I have believed it for cycles."

"But how?" Ami asked. "How could they do that to so many of us? Is that truly what would have happened to Sachi and me if we hadn't been rescued by Tenshi-san? They would have drowned us? Killed us before we'd drawn more than a hundred breaths?"

Mishi saw the tears streaming down Ami's face and wished she could still feel that much sorrow for the babies who were being killed every cycle simply for being born Kisōshi of the wrong gender. She nodded, the horror at least strong enough to keep her from speaking easily, even if it didn't affect her the way it was affecting Ami.

"How can the josanpu live with themselves?" Ami asked, when she could finally draw enough air to breathe.

Mishi shrugged. She didn't know the answer to that. Then she thought of the rumors she'd heard of the Josankō, of the girl she and Taka had seen dragged back there after her brief escape to the orphanage, and all the other little stories the villagers had told of the place. She wondered what the 'school's' true purpose was.

"Maybe there are more of them like Tenshi," Mishi suggested, heartbroken at the sight of Ami's sorrow. "After all, my friend Taka survived to make it to the orphanage, and I don't think her parents had Tenshi at her birth."

"I thought your friend Taka was a healer. Would the josanpu have tried to kill her too?" Ami asked.

Mishi nodded, "From what Tenshi told me, they are instructed to kill any female child born with detectable kisō at birth, regardless of what element they're tied to."

"How did Tenshi ever make it through such training?" Ami asked, her voice going cold.

"I don't know, but you should probably ask her that. I imagine she's not the only one who found it too horrible to bear. That's why they require two josanpu at every child's birth. They're not only required to report on the birth of the child, but also on each other. The penalty for allowing a female Kisōshi child to live is death. How many josanpu would risk letting the other josanpu report them to the Rōjū? That's why Tenshi has always had to 'rescue' girls by removing them from their families. If your family didn't think you were dead, Tenshi's life would be forfeit to the Rōjū. The same was true for Sachi-san's rescue."

Ami's face grew paler as she considered the words, and Mishi wondered what the girl had thought all these cycles when she was told that she had been rescued and that her family thought that she was dead. Ami had known those facts since she was old enough to understand all the words that explained them. What had she thought she had been rescued from?

"Is that why your parents were killed, Mishi-san?" Ami asked, after a moment.

Mishi nodded, the question shocking her out of speech for a moment. "Yes," she said at length. "They refused to give me up. They knew their child would be a Kisōshi and of course there was a good chance that I would be girl, or as good a chance as there ever is, but they refused to let me be taken away. They asked Tenshi for help, and she removed me on the night of my birth, telling the other josanpu that I was dead, but then she returned me to my parents the next day. And somehow, even though they went into hiding, someone revealed my existence to the Rōjū, who sent hishi after them..."

Ami nodded. She knew the rest of the story. That Mishi's parents had been killed while trying to escape the Rōjū's elite guild of assassins was not a secret to either of her 'sisters.' What was a mystery to all of them was how Mishi had survived and been sent to the orphanage to begin with. Mishi thought it likely that her parents had protected her, managing to hide her somewhere before they were killed, and some kind traveler had found her in the wreckage of their carriage and delivered her to the orphanage. Or maybe that was simply how she liked to think of it.

It was then that Ami's tears began to surge again.

"It's just so unfair..." she sobbed, even as Mishi put an arm around her to cradle her. "For all of us," she said. "And all because of some stupid woman who lived a thousand cycles ago."

"Fear can be a powerful destructive force," came a voice from the hallway. Mishi and Ami both looked up from Ami's table on the floor to see Kuma-sensei standing in the doorway.

"Imagine," he continued, as he stepped inside the room and sat down on the floor with his back to the wall, "what it must have been like to live in fear for a hundred cycles."

"A hundred cycles? I thought there was only ever one leader of the Yūwaku," Mishi said.

Kuma-sensei nodded. "Kisōshi used to live longer than most people," he replied. "They used to be much stronger in general. Cutting out half of the Kisōshi in the world for the past thousand cycles has made us weaker than we ever used to be. But Hasaki-san was born from two Kisōshi in a time when Kisōshi were stronger, and she lived for well over two hundred cycles. So imagine, if you can, living in fear of all female Kisōshi for over a hundred cycles. And then think, what would you do when you finally managed to rid yourself of the woman who had either forced, recruited, or killed EVERY female Kisōshi in all of Gensokai to serve her, such that for almost a hundred cycles every female Kisōshi had been a member of the Yūwaku and a party to all the atrocities they committed? Would you ever trust another female Kisōshi?"

Mishi tried to think of it that way, but there was no part of her that thought any of those facts would make her able to drown a baby.

She must have spoken some part of that aloud, for Kuma-sensei said, "Yes, but what if you weren't going to drown the babies yourself, only force someone else to do it for you?"

Mishi's stomach turned at the thought and Ami's sobs redoubled.

"I'm sorry, Ami-chan. I didn't come here to make you feel worse about the Rōjū's crimes. I merely heard you speaking and wanted to try to explain that, from the perspective of the first Rōjū council, they were merely protecting the people."

Mishi shivered at the thought. How many baby girls had died in order to protect the people? As Ami continued to cry into her shoulder, Mishi wondered how long it would take for the girl to adjust to the fact that the world was sometimes an awful place. Then there was a soft tap on the door and they all looked up to see Sachi in the hallway holding a tray.

"I brought tea," she said, her cheeks flushing as though she had been caught doing something naughty.

"And Ami's favorite mochi," she added, as she crossed the room and set the tray of hot tea and sweet rice cakes in the middle of the low table where Ami and Mishi still sat. She crossed back to the door almost as soon as she'd set the tray down, but she turned just before she crossed the threshold to the hallway.

"It's not all bad, Ami-san," she said, her voice sounding the most unsure that Mishi had ever heard it. "If not for the horrible Rōjū and their crimes I would never have gotten to have two such beautiful sisters." Red flushed not only her cheeks, but all the way down her neck, and she turned and left the room as quickly as she had come.

Mishi caught Kuma-sensei smiling at the doorway before he coughed to clear his throat.

"I will leave you two girls to enjoy Sachi-san's gift," he said, as he stood up and headed for the door. "Certainly we have much to be thankful for," he added, just before he exited the room and slid the shoji closed behind him.

Mishi turned to see Ami's eyes wide with wonder even as she reached for a rice cake, and Mishi marveled at how beautiful and cruel the world could be, all at once.

~~~

Mishi knocked gently on the sliding door before her and listened for an answer.

"Come in," came the soft reply within.

Mishi slid the door back, stepped through, and found Sachi sitting on the floor before her low table, a scroll of parchment and ink well in front of her and a thin calligraphy brush in her hand.

"What is it, Mishi-san?" the older girl asked, without looking up. Mishi simply watched her older 'sister' write for a while. Her black hair cascaded around her shoulders as her hands moved with systematic grace, and her eyes never strayed from the characters she created.

"It was kind, what you did for Ami-san today," Mishi said, after a long silence.

Sachi shrugged gently, careful not to remove her brush from the parchment. "I remember the sadness I felt when I learned the truth of what the Rōjū were capable of... I cried long into the night. Ami-chan was very little then, I doubt she remembers. But one of the older girls who was still here then did something similar for me."

"Still, it was kind of you."

Sachi finally put down her brush, and turned to look at Mishi.

"Is it really so surprising that I would do something kind for my sisters?"

Mishi looked into the almond colored eyes of her elder sister and raised an eyebrow.

"I think you've done your best to make us think so," she replied after a moment.

That caused Sachi's lip to curl at one end and she turned her body fully around to look at Mishi.

"I've known Ami-san since she was a baby. Even if she annoys me at times, I do love her."

Mishi nodded. She thought she understood the feeling, but she'd never had a true sister, only Taka. She supposed the feeling was similar. She still felt Taka's absence every day, even three cycles after they had been separated. Would Sachi miss Ami like that if the two were ever forced apart?

"Ami-san and I may not be as close as we could be, and I know I was horrible to you when you first arrived," Sachi continued. "But I love you both, and I want to help you when you're hurting."

That startled Mishi. She had understood Sachi's feelings towards Ami, but she'd never expected to hear herself included in that bond.

"Don't look so surprised, Mishi-chan," Sachi said, her eyes glinting with humor. "I know you think I'm a horrible cow, but I do care about you. You're my sister. We must care for one another. We have no one else."

Mishi thought about that for a moment. She understood the word 'sister' as an idea. She had even begun to understand the concept as applied to Sachi and Ami, two girls who were not actually related, but had grown up together as sisters and whose bond was that of sisterhood as Kisōshi. But Mishi had never truly considered herself one of them, not really.

"I suppose I'm not used to the idea of having family," Mishi said. "Orphans don't have family, even though we have each other…"

Sachi narrowed her eyes at Mishi and tilted her head to one side. She thought for a moment before she replied.

"Kuma-sensei once told me that the family we choose is even stronger than the family we're given."

Mishi thought about that. All that she knew of her true family she had learned from Kuma-sensei. The only family she had in this life was her chosen one. Eventually she nodded. Then something occurred to her and she was shocked that it had never occurred to her before.

"Sachi-san, are you ever allowed to see them? Your given family, I mean."

Sachi's eyes clouded briefly and she shook her head.

"No. No, they think that I'm dead. They were told that I died at birth, just as all parents of female Kisōshi are. It's the only way to keep them safe. If the Rōjū were ever to discover that I still lived, and if they ever suspected that my family knew… it would put all of our lives at risk."

Mishi nodded. She had known that her sisters had been rescued from birth, but she hadn't really understood the full implications of the manner of their rescue. Was it worse to be a true orphan, or to know that your family still lived, had wanted to keep you, but had never had the chance? Mishi sighed, and then did something that she had never done before.

She knelt beside Sachi and embraced her. Sachi hesitated for a moment, but then returned the embrace, and if warm liquid slid from their eyes and mingled on the cheeks pressed side to side, no one ever spoke of it.

1日 1 2月, 老中 1114年

≫ *Taka* ≪

TAKA SIGHED AND mopped the sweat from her brow with the sleeve
of her kimono. The candles they had lit at the beginning of Kiko's la-
bour were mere puddles, and one of the other girls had been sent to
bring more to replace them. Between the heat from the candles and the
bodies crammed into the small birthing room, the room suffered from an
overpowering odor of sweat, laced with a slight tang of fear. Taka's job
on this rotation was to keep track of Kiko's pulse and breathing. She
held her friend's hand for comfort, and touched her wrist lightly to keep
track of her pulse. Every now and again she tried to smile reassuringly
at Kiko, but the girl barely ever opened her eyes, her pain was so great.

Sweat drenched Kiko's body from head to toe, and every few minutes
her whole body contracted in what seemed to Taka to be the worst pain
a person could endure. She didn't seem to be doing well, but so far the
instructors didn't seem overly concerned.

Taka and her classmates had been rotating through the birthing room
for a fifth of a candlestick each. It was a practical exam for them, and
they had been split into five groups of three. Taka was just starting her
second rotation with another two girls from her class when the candle-
sticks were replaced. She was already exhausted, she couldn't imagine
how Kiko was feeling.

In the past few tendays the instructors had become more and more
convinced that Kiko carried twins. Taka had to admit that it seemed likely. She had been sorely tempted to check using kisō, but it seemed there
was never a time in which she could do so safely without anyone noticing. She had tried once, in the middle of the night, to see how many

55

minds responded from Kiko's futon (two, three?) but there was some form of protective barrier between her mind and the other girl's. She thought she might be able to get around it, but not without the risk of alerting whoever had put it there. If it had been Kiko that wasn't a great risk, but if it hadn't been... She decided her curiosity wasn't worth possibly alerting the instructors to the abilities that she wasn't supposed to possess.

As Kiko's belly had grown larger than anyone had expected, the rest of her seemed to be slowly disappearing. She was getting thinner and thinner, and while the instructors assured Taka and her classmates that this was not unusual for such a young girl who was pregnant, they also admitted that it wasn't healthy for the mother or the babes.

Taka had been worried for her friend for tendays now, and had actually been somewhat relieved when Kiko went into labor a full moon before her predicted birthing time. If she did carry twins, this was perfectly normal. If not, it seemed that the baby was large enough that an early birth would be unlikely to harm it. Either way, Taka was hopeful that with the babies out in the world Kiko would be able to regain her health.

It wasn't until Taka's third round of assisting in the birthing room that Kiko started screaming. Taka scrambled to Kiko's side to find out what was wrong. Kiko couldn't take breath to explain, so Taka moved to the foot of the bed and was horrified at the amount of blood that she saw there. Kiko screamed again, and the instructor who had been leading them pushed Taka out of the way.

"What is it?" she asked the girl. "Where is the pain?"

But the only response she got was another scream, followed by more blood.

Taka tried to fight her way back to Kiko. She wanted to hold her hand, and she wanted to use her kisō to sense for injuries. She could help, she was sure of it, but an instructor had grabbed her arms and was pulling her away from the raised futon on which Kiko lay. Taka didn't know where the extra instructors had suddenly come from. Originally there had only been one instructor there to monitor the girls as they performed their practical, but all at once there were five of them in the room, three of them engaged in holding back the three josanpu in training.

"Get out!" screamed the lead instructor.

"I can help!" Taka yelled in response. "Let me help!"

The instructor holding her pushed her towards the door.

"There's nothing you can do that a fully trained josanpu can't do. Now get out. We need to work."

She was shoved out of the door, along with the other two girls who had been testing with her.

Taka blustered at the door that had been slammed in her face, with two voices fighting in her mind for supremacy. Part of her wanted to rush back into the room and heal her friend. She knew that she could do it, that she was a better healer than any of the instructors at this school, but another part of her screamed that the action would be foolhardy. She would be exposing herself and risking everything. The Josankō would have her locked up, or worse, if she revealed what she was truly capable of. The first part of her insisted that it would be worth it if she could save the life of her friend, but the second part tried to convince her that the josanpu and healers would know enough to help Kiko.

Deep down, Taka knew better. Her friend was in danger, she had to help.

She pushed against the door. It was locked. She shoved it. It held. She threw herself against it. It didn't move. She backed up, charged the door at full speed and... she bounced off. She knocked loudly and began to yell.

Suddenly, the door before her opened. She didn't wait for anything to be said, she simply launched herself into the room.

"Are you trying to kill her?" shouted the instructor who grabbed her around the waist and began dragging her from the room.

"I can help!" Taka shouted in the woman's face as she struggled to make her way to Kiko's bedside. "Please, let me help."

"We do not need an untrained novice in this room, and you are frightening Kiko-san. If you continue to distract us, Kami-sama help her. Be silent!"

Without waiting for a response from Taka, the woman threw her from the room and slammed the door. Taka was left in a stunned silence on the other side. She pushed once more against the door, but it was locked again, barred from the inside.

Taka pushed her kisō out to Kiko to see how she fared, and screamed when she made contact and her friend's pain flooded her. She beat her fists against the door and shouted to be allowed in to help her friend. She no longer cared if she was caught and killed for revealing her kisō. All that mattered was helping Kiko and keeping her alive.

She screamed until she could hear nothing else, until her whole body was numb to everything but the feel of the wood beneath her hand. She never heard the instructor walk up behind her, never noticed the thick hand that clamped itself on the base of her neck, or the kisō that coursed through her and brought blackness to her world, until it was too late.

5日 12月, 老中 1114年

≈ Taka ≈

TAKA LET THE tears wash down her cheeks and tried to pretend that the smoke was making her eyes water. None of the other girls were crying.

The wind threw the acrid smell of smoke into her nostrils, and she thought it wouldn't be difficult for anyone to believe that that was the reason she cried. When she was overcome with the urge to sob she pretended it was a fit of coughing. One of the other girls asked her if she was alright. She wasn't alright. She wasn't sure she would ever be alright again.

She had failed her friend. She had let the instructors push her out of the birthing room, and Kiko had died. She could have stopped it. She knew it in a place beyond reason, with a physical surety that made her feel weak and hollowed. Her kisō was strong enough to have healed Kiko's bleeding. The instructors would have punished her for it, might have even killed her for it, but Kiko would be alive and mother to two tiny babies that Taka had never even gotten a chance to see before she had been rendered unconscious by one of the instructors.

Taka feigned coughing once more, as a sob wracked her body. She didn't know what would happen to those two children. She could only hope that they were still alive.

Taka stared at the fire. She watched as the wrapped figure within was consumed by flame, along with the wood beneath it. At some point the tears stopped. The pain and anger continued, as did the grief, but she held the fire in her gaze and didn't move. Part of her longed to throw herself on top of the flames and join Kiko in leaving this place. She had failed to save her friend. She hadn't fought hard enough, and now perhaps she deserved to join her. Her weight shifted forward slightly, without thinking about it, but before she could even step forward a voice surprised her into stillness.

"You are Taka-chan, ne?"

Taka blinked, through vision hazed by smoke, and saw that the fire had burned low and all the other students and instructors were gone. An old woman that Taka had never seen before stood close by, her gaze never wavering from the pyre before them.

Taka nodded, even though the old woman wasn't looking at her.

"Kiko-chan spoke kindly of you the last time I was permitted to visit her."

Visit her? She had never seen a visitor here in the three cycles since her arrival, aside from the families who dropped off their daughters when they were first placed here.

"They are quiet about it," the old woman said, seemingly answering the question that Taka hadn't asked aloud, "and I imagine most of the girls aren't allowed visitors at all, but my family will not be denied."

Taka took a closer look at the grey haired woman and realized that her kimono, while plain in color and design, was very high quality; nicer than anything Taka had seen before.

"Who are you?"

Taka's grief must have been making her incautious. Such a question was unthinkable from someone as low ranking as a josanpu in training.

The old woman's mouth turned up in a smile that wasn't reflected in her eyes at all.

"I am Kiko's grandmother."

Taka bowed low in an attempt to make up for the rudeness of her earlier question. She said quietly, "It is an honor to meet you."

The woman finally turned towards Taka, allowing Taka to see the embers of rage that burned in her eyes, even as the coals of fire before them shrank in their brightness.

"She left two letters, one for me and one for you, along with this package."

The older woman placed a small package wrapped in light parchment into Taka's hands.

"I'm not sure why. I've looked through it, and it seems a useless thing to me, but you take it, Taka-chan. It's obvious that you two were close, and she wanted you to have it."

Taka tried to form some kind of reply, but her throat seemed to constrict with grief and she couldn't get the words out.

The old woman turned to go, and Taka was left staring blankly through a veil of salt water at the small package in her hands. As the woman walked away Taka heard her voice, a mere whisper on the wind: "Someday I'll burn this place to the ground."

1 1 1 5 年

Challenges become
instructors of the most cruel
yet beautiful truth

5日 3月, 老中 1115年

⤜ Mishi ⤜

MISHI SAT BY the waterfall and considered what remained of her ascent to Tatsu's shrine. After over a cycle of training with Tatsu-sama, she was coming to enjoy the journey up the mountain, and not only because of the time she was able to spend with Tatsu once she reached her destination.

What had once been a physically desperate journey was now simply a somewhat challenging hike, and even the small cliff she was forced to scale every time she ascended the mountain had become a pleasant challenge rather than a life threatening grasp for the top. She enjoyed the slight exertion she felt in her calves and ate the onigiri she had prepared for herself; her favorite rice steamed to perfection, filled with a delicious salted salmon, and wrapped in her favorite seaweed.

She considered the mild strain she would feel in her upper body once she reached the top of the cliff, and stretched her arms in anticipation. She had gotten much stronger in the past cycle, a benefit that she noticed in her day to day training with Kuma-sensei, and even in her chores as a servant for the male Kisōshi. The pails of water she carried for cleaning, the barrows she pushed to clean out the stables, all felt lighter to her, and she felt as though she could train for longer than she had been able to previously. Of course, part of the reason for that was also how much she had grown over the past cycle as well.

She finished her onigiri and stretched her back and shoulders before repacking her small sack and positioning it between her shoulder blades in preparation for the short climb next to the waterfall.

She began the climb as she always did. There was a small ledge to the right of the waterfall that provided good purchase, even though it was slightly damp, and that was her preferred starting point. The climb was so routine to her now that she barely paid heed to where she placed her fingers and toes. Holds that had seemed desperate and tiny just a cycle ago now felt large and comfortable. There was even a corner in which the span of her legs alone would hold her, and she could rest her shoulders against the rock and let her arms relax. She made it to that point quickly and smoothly, and barely took advantage of the chance to rest, so confident was she now in her abilities.

She should have expected what happened next. If she had really thought about it, she would have seen it coming, but she hadn't. She had thought that here on her mountain with Tatsu-sama she would be safe from Kuma-sensei's propensity for surprising her with tests.

As she moved up and to the right from the pleasant corner where she could rest her arms, the first hold she placed the fingers of her right hand on was wet, and as her fingers slipped helplessly from a hold that normally presented her with little challenge, she realized that someone had covered it in fish oil. Luckily, between her left hand and her strongly placed feet, she was able to keep herself attached to the rock. But as her right hand explored farther, she found hold after hold covered in the greasy substance that allowed her no purchase.

Mishi tried to contain her panic. She was more than halfway to the top of the cliff, and to fall from her current position would be painful at best. At worst she would break something, possibly her neck. Her left hand still clutched a hold that was not slick, and she clung to it desperately as her right hand fumbled to find a hold that would not slip from her grasp. When she finally found a small incision in the rock that she could slide the front pads on three fingers into, she tried to gain control of her breathing. She only hoped that the oil on her hands wouldn't cause that small hold to prove treacherous as well.

She breathed deeply, trying to still her mind. She had two options: she could climb back down to the bottom and safety, reusing the holds that had been clean on her ascent thus far, or she could climb her way to the top using whatever holds Kuma-sensei had left grease free, and hope that she didn't slip from the rock entirely.

As usual, she didn't think Kuma-sensei would try to kill her, but the chance for injury was great and she couldn't guarantee that she wouldn't fall. Still, she didn't think Kuma-sensei's goal was to cause her to give up and return to the base of the cliff. She took another deep breath and tried to focus her ki.

Her feet were still in a balanced position, and with solid footholds she could gain height without relying so much on her hand holds. She looked for a place to raise her right foot to that wasn't covered in oil. Her bare toes sought small crevices in the rock, but she could already tell that anything that might be considered a ledge was well greased. Finally, she found a small pocket no bigger than her large toe, and placed her right foot there. It held, and she shifted her balance to that toe so that she could raise her left foot higher as well, and then use that position to stand up and search for a higher handhold. Eventually, she found another tiny foothold that was ungreased and she placed her left toe there.

She almost laughed as she thought about how she must look from below, like some strange frog plastered to the side of the rock with both of her feet resting near her waist and her backside in between. But the beginning of laughter made her balance shift, and panic quickly caused the laughter to die in her throat.

What she needed to do now was maintain her balance as she stood on those small toe holds and hope that once she was standing she would have access to some hand holds that weren't covered in oil. She breathed deeply to keep her ki focused and maintain her calm. Keeping her weight as close as she could to the wall, she extended her legs, pulled inward, and then levered upward with her arms, standing up. Her balance held as her legs locked out, and she tried to keep her breathing even as she brought her right arm up—quickly wiping grease and sweat onto her hakama on the way—past her head to find a hold that was free of oil.

Panic started to take her when the best that she could find was a small crevice only wide enough for two of her fingers side by side and only deep enough for a single finger pad. Her legs began to shake against her will as she brought her left arm up, attempting not to disturb the tenuous balance held by three points of her body; cautiously enough that she barely touched her hand to her uwagi in a whisper of an attempt to remove the oil that might ruin everything even if she found a hold that was clear of it.

In and out, in and out, she had to remember to breathe, or her muscles would fail and her balance would collapse. The muscles in her body that held her at tension were all working frantically, probably using more energy than necessary, but there was nothing she could do about that now. She was barely keeping panic at bay as she slowly made her left hand crawl on the surface of the rock. Like a blind spider, it searched cautiously around the space above her, seeking a place that would let it gain purchase, at least for long enough for her to find another foothold. She was so close to the top, so close....

This time, search though she might, there was no small crevice where she could place her fingertips, no tiny incut bit of rock to pull on. The surface was a blank wall, and the only thing that she found ungreased was a small bump: a mound of rock that jutted out from the rest, but provided no flat surface on which to cling. It was simply a rounded blob that had some texture to it.

Mishi's legs began to tremble in earnest. The exertion, combined with the near panic of balancing on nothing more than her toes and a few fingers, was taking its toll. If her leg shook much more, it would collapse, and then she would fall. Fall, even though her hands were a mere arm span from the top of the cliff. Fall, even though she was sure to break some part of her body from a height like this. Fall, even though she was sure that Kuma-sensei had not meant to cause her injury.

She had to move upward. Upward lay safety, and success, and a lesson with Tatsu-sama, who would be proud of her for succeeding against such odds. Downward lay injury, failure, and disappointing all of the people who cared about her. She took a deep breath and shifted her weight so that she could raise her right toe. Her hands could go no higher if she couldn't get her feet up, and she needed another single arm span of height to reach the top ledge. She found another small hole, this one slightly deeper than the last, but still not deep enough to hold more than half of her big toe. Now her left leg was shaking uncontrollably and she could feel her fingertips begin to sweat. Since when did her fingertips sweat?

She had to remind herself to breathe again, and she could feel the muscles in her arms locking up. Her forearms felt stiff with exertion and were beginning to shake. Her grip was getting looser, even as she tried to tighten it. She had to push onward, or she would let go of the wall entirely. She tried to lift her left leg.

Her left hand slipped from the small round hold that it had clung to with nothing but the friction of her skin, and she could feel the skin she left behind as she watched the cliff pull away from her in a sequence so slow that it seemed to be taken from one of her own nightmares. She didn't think to scream, there was no time, even in that long drawn out moment when she felt her left foot and and hand swing wildly away from the cliff, with her right hand and foot following despite their desperate clinging.

The world seemed timeless for a moment, as she realized that nothing held her to the cliff at all and she felt a brief moment of weightlessness before the forces of nature pulled her downward.

Her fall was so short that she shouldn't have had time to think of anything at all, but somehow, in the midst of all that panic, her brain managed to wonder if death would finally reunite her with Taka. Then she saw the earth surging up to meet her, and in one final moment of defiance she screamed inside her head.

Suddenly, there was a bed of fire between her and the earth.

Fire should not have stopped her from hitting the ground. Fire was not a substance that could cushion her, or protect her from the solid ground that waited to meet her. For some reason, this fire did not seem to care about those rules. It cradled her. She observed, in awe, that it held her and kept her safe. And then blackness welcomed her, and she felt her body shudder as it slammed into the earth below.

6日 3月、老中 1115年

≈ Mishi ≈

MISHI WOKE TO a giant golden orb suspended over her head. She almost jumped when the glowing orb blinked, and then she realized that it was Tatsu-sama's eye.

"She wakes!" Tatsu's thundering voice shook the world around her, and her skull felt as though it were trying to pull itself apart at the seams.

"Ow," was all she managed to say, as she sat up. The effort made her vision darken around the edges and she let her head drop back to the ground. "Everything hurts," she reported with her eyes closed, while she lay as still as possible.

"That is not surprising," Tatsu said, his voice as soft as he could make it, but no less skull-splitting because of it. "You did your very best to kill yourself yesterday."

"Yesterday?" Mishi's eyes flew open, but she didn't make the mistake of trying to sit up again. "How long have I been asleep?"

Tatsu snorted, but luckily he had turned his head aside before doing so, and the flame that shot from his nostrils did no more than singe a small bush, rather than charring Mishi.

"Sleeping is not what I would call it. You were unconscious, child. You used more of your kisō than you have ever attempted to use before, and the drain could have killed you. Have I not told you before that if you pull too deeply from your fuchi, use too much of the kisō within, you can take away your own life force? I know I've encouraged you to practice enough to push your limits, as that is how one deepens one's fuchi and gains access to more kisō, but I thought you would have more sense than to try to use so much. If I hadn't been here to heal you…"

Mishi thought about that for a moment.

"Well, I might have died anyway if I hadn't slowed myself down. What was Kuma-sensei thinking anyway? What kind of test was that?"

Tatsu looked away for a moment and Mishi used her kisō to register his emotions. Was that guilt?

"Tatsu-sama… what do you know?"

If a dragon could look abashed, she thought Tatsu managed it. "It was not Kuma-sensei's test. It was mine."

"Yours? Yours! Were you trying to kill me?"

Tatsu shook his giant head.

"Of course not, child. It was only a test."

"Only a test? What did you expect to have happen?"

"I wanted to see what you would do, given that kind of challenge."

"Challenge? All the holds were greased with fish oil! Climbing up was nearly impossible! I almost died!"

"Ah, but you could have stopped. You could have climbed back down. You could have used your skill with fire to burn away the oil on the holds and then climbed up normally…."

Mishi's face was suddenly red with heat and her voice shook as she spoke.

"You expected me to cheat? Or to give up?"

"They were possibilities. I did not expect anything. Instead you used almost enough of your kisō to kill you."

"But what were trying to get me to do? I didn't even mean to use kisō. I didn't even know I could use it that way. You've never taught me to do anything like that. I didn't think my fire could be used to shield. How does fire protect someone from a fall?"

Tatsu looked at her again with just one eye, as though inspecting her thoroughly.

"It doesn't. You must have hit your head. Fire cannot be used the same way that wind or water can to cushion a fall."

Mishi touched the back and sides of her head. She could have hit it. It certainly hurt enough for her to have hit it. She didn't feel any bruises or cuts, though.

Tatsu watched her perform this inspection and then she felt him perform an inspection of his own. His kisō politely sought permission to mingle with her own, and when it was granted he performed a brief scan of her body and mind.

The one eye of Tatsu's that she could see widened, and he backed his head away from her for a moment.

"What?" she asked, certain that something he had found had troubled him.

"You have not hit your head," he replied.

"That wouldn't have you backing away from me. What's wrong?" she asked again, this time worried that he had uncovered some awful truth about her.

"Nothing is wrong... which is the problem. Your memory is accurate and you have no injuries to your head."

"So what's the problem?" she asked, finally sitting up and just barely managing to stay there.

"The problem, child, is that if your memory is accurate, you really did use fire as a cushion to save you from that fall, and if that is true..."

Mishi swallowed. Tatsu looked startled and unsettled, and Mishi did not want to have anything to do with something that could unsettle a dragon a hundred times her size.

"If that is true," he said, "it means that you have a power that no Kisōshi has possessed for hundreds of cycles."

10日 3月、老中 1115年

⇒ Mishi ⇐

MISHI SCREAMED AS her body rushed towards the earth. She desperately tried to create a bed of fire as she had days before, but nothing worked. She slammed into the ground with a force sufficient to shatter bones and woke up.

She sat up breathing heavily, and was amazed to find that she was still atop Tatsu's mountain. She had been having that nightmare nightly over the past four days, so that was no surprise, but she hadn't expected to find herself resting at the base of a large elm tree not far from Tatsu's shrine. She must have dozed off as she waited for her dragon mentor to appear. The perplexing thing was that the moon was now high in the sky and Tatsu had yet to arrive.

Mishi stood up and stretched, deciding that she should at least practice some of her kata while she waited. About half way through her third kata, she felt a warm breeze at her back. She decided to finish out the kata and only after the final bow did she turn to Tatsu.

"That is a pretty dance, child."

"You're late," she said. Mishi almost felt guilty for the lack of respect, but she was still angry about everything Tatsu had put her through in the past four days.

The enormous dragon snorted and she was thankful, not for the first time, that fire was her element and consequently less likely to burn her. She patted down a smoldering spot on the leg of her training hakama and glared up at her mentor.

"I arrived exactly when I wished to, child. It is not my fault if you were here early."

Mishi contained her own snort, but realized that arguing with a dragon was not only unwise, but also a waste of time. It was already late, so she might as well be practical.

"Yes, sensei," she said, bowing to the giant, scaled creature before her.

Tatsu seemed on the verge of snorting again, but managed to restrain himself.

"Very good. Now then, tonight I will need you to climb that tree behind you."

Mishi turned to look skeptically at the tree. It wasn't that she didn't think she could climb it, she was sure that she could, it was just that she doubted the dragon's motives.

"Why?" she asked.

"You know, for a tiny human you have trouble demonstrating the proper respect."

Tatsu eyed her, and if she hadn't known him better, the face he made would have made her quite nervous indeed. Still, if he was planning what she thought he was, she had good reason to be suspicious.

"And for a giant dragon who could eat me in one bite, you are awfully hesitant to answer a simple question."

Tatsu sighed.

"You will not like the answer, child."

"I thought as much," she said, a shiver coursing down her spine. "I'm not going to try again, Tatsu. We both know it won't work. I haven't been able to make it work since the first time."

Tatsu bared his teeth in the expression that Mishi had come to recognize as a smile.

"Ah, but the past four days have not been days with a full moon. Tonight is the perfect time to try it."

Mishi simply stared at the dragon.

"I don't understand."

The scales above Tatsu's eyes crinkled, first with confusion and then with concern, and Taka could see the moment when he must have realized some important truth.

"Of course, of course," he began happily, "I forget that your Kuma-sensei is a male Kisōshi from an age without female counterparts. It's possible that he simply doesn't know."

He paused, as if expecting some reassurance from Mishi, but as she had no idea what he was talking about, she gave none. He continued unperturbed.

"It used to be common knowledge, but it wouldn't be anymore, would it? It has been centuries since it was relevant. Well, you should certainly know, and by all means share this with your sisters. Did you know that a Kisōshi's power waxes and wanes?"

Mishi nodded.

"Yes, everyone knows that a Kisōshi's power is greatest when the sun is closest to the earth."

Tatsu nodded.

"A male Kisōshi's power is tied to the sun, yes. But a female Kisōshi's power is tied to the moon."

Mishi thought about this for a moment.

"Why?" she asked.

"As well ask why the tides follow her; they simply do. But so does your power. When the moon is full, so is your power. I should have realized it sooner. We've been trying for days, but we can't very well replicate a threat to your life without risking your actual death, so the experiment is only partially effective. Tonight, however, you will have access to your kisō at its fullest strength, and my hope is that it will enable you to call it voluntarily."

"Tatsu, yesterday I almost landed back first on a sapling that would have skewered me through the chest. It was only your tail that saved me."

It was true. They both knew it. Despite their various attempts over the past four days, she hadn't once been able to make her fire work as a shield. First Tatsu had tried to get her to conjure the shield voluntarily, since that was the ultimate goal of this training, but nothing they had done had enabled her to call forth flame that worked as a shield. For the next three days, Tatsu had hurled various objects at her—boulders, saplings sharpened into spears, even her own bokken—but nothing had worked. Yesterday, in desperation, they had tried reenacting the fall, thinking that the danger had to be more complete to trigger the kisō shield. It hadn't worked. Nothing had.

"And I believe that is because it was not the full moon."

Mishi nodded, but made no move for the tree. She trusted the dragon with her life, but she thought he was overestimating her abilities.

"Mishi-san, this will be the last time. If it does not work, we will let it go."

She nodded again briefly and walked to the tree. The climb would be easy enough. She only hoped that Tatsu would catch her when she fell.

A few minutes later saw her dangling from one of the uppermost branches. The creaking of the branch made her nervous. She knew that the point of this exercise was for her to fall, but she'd rather the timing was her own and not that of a rickety branch. She held her breath and waited for Tatsu to signal that he was ready to catch her if need be.

"Alright Mishi-san, whenever you are ready."

Mishi began to nod, but apparently that much motion was all the branch needed to cause it to snap. She felt the brief, hollow flip of her stomach as her weight began to pull her towards the ground. Panic surged through her, her mind froze—she would fall right on the sapling beneath her, it would skewer her, and she would die. She tried to breathe, tried to scream, tried to do anything that would free her from the nightmare that had awoken her every night since her first fall.

The ground rushed to meet her, there was nothing she could do to stop it, and suddenly there was a comforting bed of fire below her, cocooning her just as it had five days before. She had a brief moment to feel relief and a tiny bit of triumph, then a sharp pain slashed through her skull and darkness engulfed her.

~~~

When she opened her eyes again, she was cradled between four giant talons on a bed of scales. It wasn't until Tatsu's nostril appeared before her and took in a sudden gust of air that she realized she must be in the dragon's grasp.

The comforting, warm wind that was Tatsu's breath coated her face and she shook herself to wakefulness.

Tatsu gently laid her on the ground and backed away from her so that she could see his face. She almost wished he hadn't. He looked upset.

"What's wrong?" she asked.

Tatsu shook his head as though confused.

"I'm sorry, Mishi, I should never have made you do that. I assumed that with the power of the full moon to draw on you would be safe, but…"

Mishi didn't understand.

"You were right, though. It worked. Apparently all I needed was the full moon."

Tatsu nodded but didn't look reassured.

"Yes, it worked, but…" he sighed, and Mishi wondered what had him so upset. "Mishi, it almost killed you. I had thought before… with the stress of the climb, and it being the first time that you used your kisō like that, it had simply drawn on too much kisō… but this was a longer fall and even with the full moon…. Mishi, if I had not been here to heal you and lend you my own kisō, you would have used up all that you had. You would have died."

Tatsu hung his head, and Mishi took a moment to decide how she felt about the whole thing. It must have made quite the difference to have Tatsu there immediately after her fall, because she didn't feel half as awful as she had the last time she had overdrawn her power and lost consciousness. She considered being angry with the dragon, but the regret in his voice made it difficult, and besides, she was fairly certain he wouldn't make her attempt to bring forth a fire shield anymore.

"So, you're telling me," she began slowly, causing Tatsu's head to rise to meet her gaze, "that I can use my fire as a shield, but probably only if I can draw on the power of the full moon, and even then it might kill me?"

"Will likely kill you, unless a Kami or great healer is there to save you."

Mishi sighed. "That's the most useless power I've ever heard of."

Tatsu's gaze locked with hers.

"Mishi-san, I'm sor—"

"Tatsu-sama," she said, too weary to let the dragon make one more unnecessary apology, "I'm tired. Will you watch over me while I sleep?"

It was a silly thing to ask, a child's question, but she hoped that Tatsu would understand the message of forgiveness in it.

"Yes, child. Go to sleep."

She laid her head down on her arms and sighed contentedly, as the giant dragon curled his great lengths around her in a protective circle and she slipped drowsily into a warm, dreamless sleep.

11日 3月，老中 1115年

≈ Taka ≈

TAKA SAT DOWN and let the rain pour over her. Every scrap of her tattered kimono was already soaked through, so she didn't see the harm in sitting still for a moment to try to find her bearings. She leaned her head against the trunk of the tree behind her and tried to remember anything from all the scrolls that she'd read at the Josankō that would help her find shelter in this damnable rain.

She was sure that the wolves had been trying to help her. The emotions and images that they had shared with her as they led her to this forest over the past tenday had all been positive. Hope, peace, gratitude, safety… over and over again they had sent her a feeling of safety attached to these woods. Then, after they'd escorted her to a creek so that she'd have a water source, they'd simply turned and trotted away.

At first Taka hadn't been worried. After all, they'd made it quite clear that wherever they had been leading her was quite safe. But after wandering the same forest for a day and a half and becoming more and more convinced that she was just turning in circles, she was beginning to be sure that, safe or not, she would starve in these woods.

Taka tilted her head back and let the water dripping from the tree branches pour over her face. She held out her hand and let the water collect there for a moment before bringing it to her lips to drink. At least she wouldn't go thirsty, she thought wanly, as she stared at the deep greens of the forest that continued to mystify her.

"Are you in need of assistance?" asked a voice that was nowhere and everywhere at once.

Taka sat up and looked around her in a panic; she hadn't heard any-one approach. Had one of the instructors managed to follow her this far? Her eyes were no help. There was no one around her.

"Hello?" she asked, sure she was losing her mind. Could simply not eating for a day really cause her to hallucinate?

"Hello!" said the same disembodied voice.

Taka stood up with a jolt and spun in a frantic circle, but her eyes still didn't see anything but the greens and browns of the forest.

"Who's there?" she asked.

"Mmm... difficult question to answer, I'm afraid. Most humans have very little success pronouncing my true name."

Taka spun around again, more slowly this time, but still didn't see an-yone.

"What am I talking to?" she asked.

"Aha! Good good, that's an easier question to answer. I'm a tree kami and the guardian of this forest."

"A tree kami?" Taka asked. Of course, any number of people prayed to the tree kami that protected their local forest. There had been a shrine to a tree kami in the town that she and Mishi had grown up in, but she'd never expected that a tree kami was someone she could simply meet in the woods.

"Well, where else would you meet one?" the voice asked, as though it had been listening to her thoughts. Had it?

"Well, you broadcast them readily enough, youngling. It is difficult not to listen when you make them loud enough for all the world to hear."

Taka had no idea what to say to any of this, nor was she entirely sure where she should be addressing her words. She still hadn't seen any-thing that resembled a creature that she could recognize as able to speak or hear.

"Hmm... yes, you wouldn't be used to me in my normal form. Hold on a moment."

Just then the largest tree before her, the one that she had been leaning against only moments ago, seemed to duplicate itself. For a moment there seemed to be two trees existing in the same place at the same time, and then the second tree shifted forward as though cut off just above the soil and its trunk and lower branches shifted and rearranged themselves to resemble the arms and legs of a human. Then, to Taka's horror, the tree's trunk shifted again, bark and knots rearranging themselves until a face appeared at twice the height of a human's and, as the creature stepped away from the still placid tree that had spawned it, its eyes opened to show glittering amber orbs that Taka found both beautiful and terrifying.

"There," the tree creature said, its voice now emanating from the mouth it had carved for itself. "That's better, isn't it?"

Taka stood dumb before the creature, unsure if she was even able to speak.

"Now tell me, child, what is your name?"

"T-Taka," she said after a long pause in which she tried multiple times to get her throat to work. "My name is Taka. I... my friends brought me here, two wolves..."

She wasn't sure why she was telling the tree kami that, but she couldn't think of anything else the creature might want to know about her, and after all, this was his forest. She supposed he might wish to know why she was there.

"Excellent! I do enjoy company! Come, let's find you a place out of the rain. You'll drown out here if you're not careful."

Taka shook her head. "Water doesn't bother me," she said, her eyes still wide as she took in the walking, talking willow tree before her.

"No," the tree kami said, as he inspected her with an incautious flick of his kisō that left Taka reeling from the amount of power contained within it. "You wouldn't be bothered by your own element."

He paused for a long moment, so long that Taka wondered if he had grown roots again and simply become another tree. Then, without warning, he began moving away from her.

"Come," he said, when she didn't begin to follow him instantly. "I haven't trained a true healer in ages! This will be fun!"

Taka's mind reeled. A true healer? Was that what she was? Fun? Training? What was happening? She was only seeking shelter.

"Ah, little sapling, I can provide so much more than shelter for you. You'll learn all I have to teach you, and we'll spend as much of your tiny life together as we can, and you'll do great things. Yes! How exciting. You can call me Yanagi. It's not my name, but it'll do. Come, come. There is much to show you!"

And with that the giant tree kami wandered into the woods and, after a brief pause to wonder at the strangeness of the world, Taka struggled to catch up.

Shinogi

1 1 1 9 年

Leaves turn and release
slow dance to the forest floor
change floats on the wind

3日 10月, 老中 1119年

≈ Mishi ≈

MISHI DREW IN a deep breath and focused her ki. She exhaled and centered herself. The delicate balance of her katana, resting in a relaxed but firm grip, became the focus of her world, and then that focus expanded outward to the scent of humidity in the grass tatami mats, the sound of a soft rain falling on the tiled roof, and the feeling of stillness in the air around her. She absorbed all those sounds and smells, making them part of her. As long as she held them, she would be able to sense the moment they changed.

Then she opened her eyes and dropped to the floor, her katana held close to her body as she rolled and an arrow flew above her head, embedding itself into the wall behind her. As she rolled to her right, she used the momentum to throw herself to her feet at the exact moment that a sai sliced through the air she had just vacated. Even as she stood, she dodged a set of three that left a trail in the wall behind her and then she ducked just in time to dodge the full force of a blow from Ami's jo. Still, the solid, wooden pole caught her across the back and almost knocked the wind out of her. She turned with the impact, swiping the blade of her sword across to meet with the jo and keep her attacker at bay, but she knew she had to keep moving or Sachi would hit her.

It had been six cycles since Mishi had first been gifted her own bokken, but it was only in the past cycle that Kuma-sensei had insisted that she and her sisters fight with real weapons and do their best to actually injure one another. He kept a close watch on their sparring, their blades were dulled sufficiently to make a mortal wound unlikely, and they had also started training in full armor. When Mishi had asked why they were bothering to train in full armor when it was unlikely that they would ever be permitted to wear it in battle, he told her that it was good training. If they could move quickly enough with full armor, he said, imagine how much faster they would be without it. Then he had thrown a lightly blunted shuriken at Mishi, which cut a deep groove in the plated wrist guard she had raised to block her face.

"And it will keep you alive in the meantime," Kuma-sensei added.

That had been the end of that argument. The fact that Tenshi was always nearby during their practices wasn't lost on Mishi either. The yukisō had tended a number of cuts, scrapes, and worse since they had begun training with real weapons.

But today Mishi couldn't allow herself to be distracted by her armor, or Tenshi's presence, or even by the jo that had struck her back and which her katana was now struggling to beat back. She had to maintain her center, hold on to all the threads that wove the room together. She must not lose track of Sachi, even though Ami was the closest threat. She had to be present. She had to be a part of this space as she had never been before, for to lose one thread was to allow the entire room to unravel. So she gasped breath back into her lungs, parried Ami's jo attacks with her katana, and waited for the next arrow to come.

Another sai came first, but that was alright because she heard it cut the air before her, felt its vibrations in the fabric of the room, and ducked, causing it to impact Ami's chest plate instead of her own helmet.

Mishi didn't take the time to appreciate the fall of one of her opponents; there was no time to take. There was only now. As Ami collapsed, Mishi stood and turned to face the arrow that had been aimed at her back. She brought her sword in front of her, and the arrow fell in two pieces. She dropped to the ground almost as quickly as the now-severed arrow, and a second arrow thunked into the wall behind her. She rolled to one side, just missing the shuriken that would have skimmed her face, and lunged to her feet. Without conscious thought, she charged Kuma-sensei, who dropped the shuriken he was preparing to throw and reached for his third sai. That was all the time that Mishi needed. Before Kuma-sensei's hand was even on the grip of his three pronged blade, Mishi had cut a deep groove across his chest plate.

Even as Kuma-sensei collapsed to the floor in mock death, Mishi was rolling away from where she had just been standing, as yet another arrow embedded itself in the wall. Mishi kept her breathing deep but even. It had taken her cycles to be able to do so while sparring at full speed, but Kuma-sensei had insisted and Mishi finally understood why.

Inhale, sense all the threads in the room; exhale, clear your mind of everything but the present.

She ran flat out and ducked into a forward roll on her third stride. As Mishi rolled, Sachi loosed another arrow, impaling the wall behind Mishi. Without hesitation, Mishi stood from her roll and continued her forward charge towards the far corner of the room, where Sachi was poised with her bow. Until that moment, it seemed she had been shooting only when she was likely to catch Mishi unaware. Now Sachi fired in rapid succession. Mishi assumed that Sachi's single goal was to take her down before she could close the distance between them.

Mishi's movements were calm and centered, but to an onlooker they would have seemed chaotic at best. She ran forward, then rolled to the side, stood up and rolled forward, ran sideways, jumped to touch the ceiling, and then rolled sideways again. She didn't make much forward headway except in fits and spurts, but Sachi's arrows kept missing. Finally she stood before Sachi with her katana at the other girl's neck and the arrow that Sachi had nocked dangled on the string.

"Well done, Mishi-san," came Kuma sensei's voice from his place on the floor. "You are ready."

"Ready?" Mishi asked. She hadn't thought this was a test, just a vigorous exercise.

"Ready for your first mission as a Kisōshi of rank," he replied.

4日 10月，老中 1119年

≈ *Mishi* ≈

MISHI KNELT IN front of the rack of weapons that covered the wall from ceiling to tatami and tried to ease the bruising on her ribs from yesterday's test by shifting her weight slightly. She winced, even as she smoothed a thin layer of choji oil over the length of the blade in her lap. Normally, she took comfort in the repetitive motions of applying the clove scented oil to the steel and carefully checking for any sign of rust. Today, her muscles objected to every wiping motion, her ribs protested her requests to remain upright, and her mind cried out for a chance to rest and focus on the mysterious mission that she would be asked to complete.

"Ah, Mishiranu-san!" said a voice from the other side of the room, making her fingers twitch in agitation. Luckily, her grip on the blade never faltered, and she did not sacrifice any digits to the oiling of the school's katana.

"I'm glad to find you in here," the voice continued, as it came closer. Mishi didn't need to look up to know who was addressing her, or to know that she'd rather remove one of her own fingers with the blade in her hand than continue the conversation.

"The weapons are always at their finest when you have treated them," Katagi said, finally stepping into view. Mishi could no longer ignore the boy without giving offense, so she looked up and bowed her head slightly in deference. The thing she hated most about her guise as a servant was the need to defer to all of the male Kisōshi in training that Kuma-sensei instructed during the day. Having just passed her first test of rank, Mishi was Hebi-kyū and consequently outranked Katagi, who would be leaving in a few days to test before the Rōjū for his first ranking even though he was a cycle her senior. Yet no one outside of Ami, Sachi, Kuma-sensei, and Tenshi was allowed to know that she was a Kisōshi at all, let alone a trained one, so she had to treat this boy with the same amount of deference that she would a Kisōshi who outranked her. It wouldn't bother her at all if she didn't find his incessant chatter so irritating.

"Where did you learn to treat blades so well?" he asked, looking at her eagerly even as she tried to continue cleaning the blade in peace. "Is your father a Kisōshi?" he prodded.

Mishi did her best to contain her emotions; allowing her kisō to slip in the presence of another Kisōshi would be a stupid give away, one she would be in no danger of if she weren't so exhausted from her increased training over the past few mooncycles.

Mishi briefly considered telling the boy the truth. *Yes, my father was a Kisōshi, and so was my* mother *for that matter, and I am one too, which is why I am so good at treating weapons. I value them as the tools that may someday save my life.* But that, of course, was not something she could tell him, and, in truth, she rather hoped the boy would just go away and leave her to her chores.

"I never knew my parents, Katagi-san. They died right after I was born." She hoped that would shut him up. She was too tired to deal with his usual nattering, the pain in her ribs, and the wall of weapons she had yet to clean, all at once.

"I'm so sorry, Mishiranu-san, I didn't know," Katagi said, as he folded himself to the floor beside her. His voice sounded sincere, which made Mishi flinch with a tiny bit of guilt. She hadn't meant to make the boy feel bad, only to make him stop bothering her. Unable to use kisō to scan him without his noticing, she simply looked at his face.

His golden eyes, set above high cheekbones and a narrow face, told the same story that his voice had. They were drawn together with concern, and his mouth was set in a soft line. For the first time, Mishi thought she saw why Sachi constantly tittered about Katagi being handsome, a fact that was generally repressed in her mind by his incessant need to let words dribble out of his mouth.

"It's alright," she said, refocusing on the blade before her. "How could you know? I never told you." She regretted the words as soon as she said them. She'd felt guilty for making the boy feel bad about her parents and then her resolve had been weakened by a moment of finding him handsome. Now that she'd said that, he was bound to try to keep talking to her. She glanced at him briefly out of the corner of her eye and was dismayed to find him dressed for weapons practice. A sure sign that he would remain here for a full candle's worth of practice at least.

"Do you know anything about them? Your parents, that is?" he asked, his face still emanating genuine interest.

Oh dear. This wasn't a safe topic at all. What Mishi knew about her parents was not information she could readily share with anyone. *Why yes, I know that they met here at this school, where they both trained to be Kisōshi even though female Kisōshi aren't supposed to exist, and then they had me and had to run for their lives when they refused to let the Rōjū kill me just for being born a girl with senkisō!* That was not the kind of information she could share with... well, anyone who didn't already know it. She hated lying, especially to another Kisōshi, but she wasn't sure what else to say. She decided on a lesser form of the truth.

"Not much, really. Kuma-sensei knew them both and was kind enough to take me in when he found me at an orphanage eight cycles after they died. He's told me what little I know."

"Iya! How horrible! Does he know how they died?"

Mishi blanched. Now there was a question she certainly couldn't answer honestly. Why was the boy so nosy? Did he have no sense of respect?

Katagi must have sensed her discomfort, or realized his blunder, for he very quickly began to reverse course. "I'm sorry, Mishiranu-san. What a terrible question for me to ask. It's none of my business and I doubt you'd want to talk about it even if—"

"They were killed," Mishi said quietly, for some reason wanting to tell him as close to the truth as she could manage, now that he had so earnestly retracted the question. "They were killed by bandits."

It was true, after a fashion. It was certainly what their deaths had been made to look like, according to what Kuma-sensei had told her, and anyone who would try to kill two new parents and their infant daughter simply because she was born a Kisōshi certainly met Mishi's definition of the term bandit.

"Iyada," Katagi said, as the blood left his face. "I should never have asked. It was completely thoughtless of me to—"

"Are you never quiet?" Mishi asked, as she sheathed the katana she'd finished cleaning and replaced it on the wall in front of her, grabbing the next one before returning to her place on the floor. She wasn't sure if she was upset with Katagi for his chatter, or herself for having revealed personal information to him. *Probably both*, she decided.

Katagi simply looked at her, his eyebrows high on his pale forehead, reaching towards the hair he kept pulled back in the standard Kisōshi knot. Mishi couldn't help it, she laughed.

"Is that all it takes to silence you? I wish I'd known that cycles ago." She unsheathed the katana she had retrieved from the wall and began her methodical application of the choji oil that would protect it from rust. After a few moments of blissful silence, Mishi looked up at the boy who was supposed to be a man, and sighed as she took in the fallen expression that lowered all of his features.

"I'm sorry, Katagi-san," she said quietly, as she continued her work. "I'm exhausted from…" she paused as she realized that she couldn't tell him why she was exhausted. "Well, I'm exhausted," she continued. "And I shouldn't take my frustration out on you. You were curious. That's fine. I have a strange past, it matches my strange eyes, and I should never be surprised that I'm a curiosity to the people around me."

She fell quiet as she continued her work on this new blade and she almost didn't hear Katagi when he next spoke.

"They're beautiful," he said, so softly that at first Mishi thought the sound was only in her mind.

"What?" she asked, before her mind processed what her ears had heard.

"Your eyes. They're not strange; they're beautiful." Katagi stood as he spoke, and then walked out of the room.

A heartbeat later Tenshi bowed her way into the room and stood before Mishi.

"Mishi-san," the older woman said, as Mishi tried to blink her way back to a reality in which handsome boys didn't tell her she had beautiful eyes and then walk away. "Kuma-sensei wishes to speak with you."

⚊ Taka ⚊

Taka ran a hand protectively over the pouch tucked into her obi, and brought forward the memory of Kiko telling her what province she had lived in before she had come to the Josankō. It was an affirmation more than anything; Taka had spent most of the past five seasoncycles trying to find a hall of records in Hokushin province that actually kept records for the entire area. The fact that there were ten towns that claimed to be the capital hadn't helped matters at all, and none of the seven she'd yet searched had possessed even local records of who was sent to the Josankō. The fact that she could only remain in any town for a handful of days before she raised curiosity to dangerous levels didn't help matters either. Unattached women who were not seeking employment drew attention that Taka neither wanted nor tolerated.

Taka had begun to doubt that anyone kept the kind of records she was looking for at all, until she'd overheard two clerks in a town a few days south of this one decrying how slow the provincial record keepers in Kengaishi were when it came to forwarding important documents. She hadn't had a chance to follow them, caught up as she had been in selling a brace of hares to a market shopper, but she'd made a mental note of the name of the town and beseeched the Kami that her eighth try would prove lucky.

So she was full of hope, as she used the tiny steel shim that she pulled from her obi to slide between the doors of the records hall and lift the latch on the other side.

~~~

It took her nearly a full candle's burn to find the records she was looking for. The Kengaishi hall of records was a maze of random stacks of scrolls and books woven through with the smell of musty parchment and drying ink. She found it easy to imagine that it took the people who worked here long enough to find anything, let alone copy and send it, that the clerks in Aokame complained. However, after a rather disorienting search in a darkened room with little interpretable organization, she finally came across something promising.

Josankō intake rosters Rōjū 1100 - 1115

Taka sighed. Fifteen cycles of names to search through, and she had to hope that Kiko had included her given name along with her family name. Still, hope sparked within her as she opened the scroll and pulled her small, shaded lantern closer. Was she truly this close to an answer?

~~~

Taka had already had to refill her lantern once from the small skein of oil she kept tucked within the sleeve of her kimono, but she was sure she was getting close to the entries that should contain Kiko's name. She'd brightened considerably when she saw that the majority of the entries contained the name of the town the girl was from. Yet, she was mystified by the sheer volume of names she encountered. She'd attended the Josankō, and she could attest that there weren't even half as many girls there as this document suggested. Where had the rest of them gone?

She didn't have long to consider the matter before she heard the quiet swish of a shoji screen moving down the hall. *Was someone here? Iya!* She had no excuse to be here that anyone would believe. She couldn't take the scroll with her, as that would ignite curiosity she couldn't afford. She scoured the page before her. She simply had to hope she could find the entry before—

There! She restrained herself from cheering aloud, as she heard the slow shuffle of cautious feet moving towards her.

Zōkame, Kiko-san Rōjū 1111 - 10 seasoncycles of age - Shikazenshi, Hokushin Province

Shikazenshi! Zōkame! Two answers in a single scroll, and all before whoever had shuffled down the hallway—

"What are you doing here?" asked a cold voice from the other side of the room.

Kami-curse it! How had he gotten here so quickly? His steps had sounded like the shuffle of an old man, and Taka had expected to have more time before he reached her.

Taka looked up, and was relieved to see that the man who confronted her was wearing the kimono of a clerk and not the uwagi and hakama of a Kisōshi. In addition, the fool had crossed the room and now stood on the other side of the desk from where she was. If she could find a way to distract him, the path to the doorway was clear.

"I'm looking for an old friend," she said, the truth making an oddly convenient lie.

"And you expected to find her hidden in the stacks of our scrolls?" the man sneered.

"She agreed to meet me here," Taka replied, leaving truth completely behind.

"Oh? And why would she do that in the middle of the night, I wonder?"

"She said she wanted to surprise her supervisor…" Taka hedged, hoping the hall of records had at least one female employee.

"She works here?" the man asked.

Taka nodded. "I'm worried though, she's supposed to have been here by now."

The man scowled at her. "I don't know what you and your friend are up to, girl, but I've no choice but to bring in the nearest Kisōshi. He'll handle this matter, and woe to you if you've been lying—"

Taka waved to the empty air behind the man. "Oh, there you are! What took you so long?" she said, with an excited smile plastered to her face.

The man turned around, just as she'd hoped, and she flipped the desk over in his general direction. She didn't think it would do much to stall him, but she hoped it would create a sufficient mess that they wouldn't be sure which scroll she'd been examining before her hurried exit. Even as the scrolls and inkwells from the desk were still hitting the floor, Taka was out the door and headed down the corridor to the main exit.

"Stop, THIEF!" the clerk shouted behind her.

Kami-curse him! She hadn't stolen a thing, only read some words and made a bit of mess, but she'd never have a chance to explain any of that if anyone heard the clerk's cries. Now she'd have to be extra cautious if she wanted to exit the town unseen. She slid back the wooden door that she'd first unlocked to break into the hall and flew down the steps before her, stopping only when she slammed into a wall that shouldn't have been there.

"What have we here?" asked the voice attached to the massive chest that she'd just bounced off of. Unfortunately, she hadn't ducked away before the hands attached to said chest had grabbed her arms.

"Did I hear someone call thief?" the voice asked. Taka kept her head down and stared at the two hilts sticking out of the man's obi. She cursed silently. If she got caught now, everything was over. She'd be killed for thievery, or killed for the presence of her name on a wanted poster that had circulated Gensokai for the last five cycles, but she would die, certainly, if she didn't get away from this Kisōshi.

"He went running that way!" she said, gesturing with her head in the opposite direction from where she intended to run. "I almost had him before he made it out of the office, but he tumbled a desk in front of me and got away." It was a gamble, using her own kisō to hide the lie to a Kisōshi. It might not work; if he discovered the untruth then she would only be killed more quickly for lying, and even if he didn't detect the lie he might not let her go. If the Kisōshi had been there long enough, he would know for certain it wasn't true, kisō or not. Taka held her breath and did her best to emanate the thoughts and emotions of a distressed female, using a small amount of her own kisō to push those outward. She had to hope that this Kisōshi was the heroic type.

"Wait here," he said, and he put enough of his own kisō behind the command that if Taka had been a normal citizen she would have had no choice but to obey.

With that he was off, running in the direction she had indicated, even as the clerk from the hall of records stumbled his way onto the steps exiting the building.

Taka wasted no time. She ran as fast as she could away from the hall of records and everything else in the town of Kengaishi, even as the clerk shouted for the Kisōshi to return.

It didn't matter, the man could call all he liked; she had the lead of a handful of heartbeats and that was all she needed. She hadn't seen a horse nearby, and the man had no hope of catching her without one. If there was one thing Taka had mastered in the past five cycles, it was the art of running.

~~~

Leagues later, with no horse hooves pounding the forest behind her and nothing but the moonlight and the trees for company, she finally allowed herself the chance to rest her back against a nearby cedar. As her breathing slowed and the cool night air filled her lungs, her hand sought out the small leather pouch tucked into her obi. She ran a finger briefly over the small journal contained within and then brought out the map she had carefully stolen so many cycles before. Unfolding it yielded a map showing just the northern region of Gensokai, centering specifically on Hokushin province.

"Shikazenshi… where are you?" she asked, scouring the map with her eyes.

"There you are!" she crowed in triumph, the last few cycles of desperation adding a deep feeling of relief to this one discovery. She marveled then at the oddities of life; the town was fairly large, and only about three days on foot from her home in Yanagi's forest. It would take her five days to reach it from here, but she needed to resupply first, so she would have to make the detour home.

"Zōkame-san, we shall meet again soon," she promised the night.

⤚ Mishi ⤙

"Come in, Ryūko-san," called Kuma-sensei's deep voice from inside his room. Mishi stepped inside and slid the door closed behind her. As she breathed in, she found comfort in the scent of fresh tatami and green tea that greeted her nose. The same beautiful landscapes hung from the same beautiful scrolls. Some things didn't change, even after eight cycles. But some things did.

"I wish you wouldn't call me that, Sensei," she said, crossing the room and folding herself down in front of the low table that separated her from the gentle bear of a man who had trained her for the last eight cycles. She looked him in the eye as she poured tea for both of them and waited for his reply.

"I know, Mishi-chan," the man said, switching to the name she had known her whole life. "But your mother would be upset with me if I didn't at least *try* to use the name she gave you at your birth."

A bitter smile touched Mishi's lips as she thought of Kuma-sensei knowing her mother well enough to know how she would react to things. She wished she shared that knowledge, but her only source of information about her parents was the man who sat across from her, and she was always hesitant to ask him for details, as the topic seemed to bring him so much sorrow.

"Would she truly be that upset with you, Sensei?" Mishi asked, wanting to prolong this rare insight into her mother's personality.

"Hmph," Kuma-sensei snorted, "she'd probably bash me on the head with her jo just for letting you get away with being called Mishiranu. Though I don't know how much it would really have bothered her—she would have simply loved an excuse to poke me with a stick."

That made Mishi laugh aloud. The visual was one she had considered more than once herself, but she would never dare to actually follow through with it.

"Sensei, surely she would never have hit you?"

"Never have hit me? Ha! Shows what you know, child, she'd jump at the chance."

"But you were her teacher!"

"Yes, I *was*. Was being the operative word. The moment she passed her first test of rank she threw respect for her elders right out the window. Used to sneak up on me after meals and drop frogs in my tea!"

Mishi put a hand to her mouth to cover her own laughter, but ultimately failed, and soon Kuma-sensei joined in and they were both wiping tears from their eyes. Finally, Mishi composed herself, and then she was left wondering what had brought on this new series of revelations.

"Kuma-sensei, why are you telling me this now?" she asked.

Kuma-sensei took a deep breath and locked his gaze with her own.

"Mishi-san, no matter what name you use, you should know that your mother would be very proud of you." Sorrow tinged his face once more, and Mishi noticed grey hairs now speckling his Kisōshi knot that hadn't been there eight cycles ago. Before she could ask what he meant by that, he continued. "You've passed your test for rank a cycle before most students do, and you're ready for your first mission. You have the finest fire kisō I've ever seen, and it's a distinct possibility that you can outfight even me."

Mishi felt the color rising to her cheeks at such high praise. Kuma-sensei did not say such things lightly; he never said a word of praise he didn't mean, and he rarely praised any of them at all. Yet Mishi had to wonder at such lavish compliments. She couldn't possibly be as good as Kuma-sensei claimed.

"I know you find that difficult to believe, Mishi-san. Kami know you find it difficult to believe the good in yourself, but I'm not telling you all of this to turn your head. I'm telling you this as a warning."

"A warning, Sensei?" Mishi asked, when he paused to take a sip of his tea.

Kuma-sensei took a deep breath, and Mishi wondered what it was that made him hesitant to continue.

"Your mission, Mishi-san, is incredibly important to our cause. It is also, I'm afraid, incredibly dangerous."

Something in Mishi's blood heated and she felt a thrill course through her body. She had wondered why Kuma-sensei would have called her to him if not to talk about her upcoming mission. The thought excited and terrified her.

"It is understandable that you are excited, Mishi-san," Kuma-sensei continued, his gaze never breaking from hers. "But I cannot emphasize the danger of this undertaking enough. There is a chance you could be captured. There is a chance you could be killed."

That last statement took all the heat from Mishi's blood.

"Killed?"

Kuma-sensei nodded.

Mishi had never considered that this mission might be the last thing she did. Of course, she'd considered it abstractly. Every day she studied the art of ending someone's life, and it was was only natural to consider the consequences of being on the losing end of that kind of conflict. But somehow, to have it stated so directly, to know that it was a strong enough possibility that Kuma-sensei needed to remind her of the risk that was ever present when one lived by the sword... it somehow made the threat real in a way that it had never been before, and, suddenly, Mishi wanted very badly to know why it was a necessary risk.

"Why?" she asked, her voice slightly more than a whisper.

Kuma-sensei raised an eyebrow, even as he raised his tea to his lips.

"Why should I be willing to die for this mission?" Mishi clarified. "What good will the loss of my life do?" She was surprised to realize it was a question that she'd never asked before, not even of herself.

Kuma-sensei swallowed slowly and then leaned forward, looking at Mishi with a gravity she rarely saw in him.

"Because it is time to fight, Mishiranu-san. It is time to fight for the world that we want. You should never have lost your parents. Sachi and Ami should never have needed to be rescued by Tenshi and taken from their families while their parents were told that they were born lifeless. We should not live in a world where any of that happens, and if we are to change things then there is only one recourse left to us. We must fight those who would continue to kill innocents."

"The Rōjū?" Mishi asked, her eyes going wide. "How can anyone hope to oppose them? They've ruled Gensokai for a thousand cycles! They have an entire army of Kisōshi at their disposal, not to mention all the hishi in the land. Are you telling me that we're going to stop them with three barely trained Kisōshi and their teacher? You're good, Kuma-sensei, but you're not that good."

Mishi hadn't meant to say such things to Kuma-sensei, but she found that she couldn't stop herself. The man must be crazy if he thought they could fight the Rōjū! She knew that they were at the root of the evil done to her and all the other female Kisōshi for the last thousand cycles, but she had assumed that Kuma-sensei's mission for her would entail accompanying Tenshi to save another female Kisōshi, helping to rescue a babe in arms the way that Sachi and Ami had been rescued.

"Mishi-san, I'm not asking you to single-handedly defeat all of the Rōjū's Kisōshi warriors in armed combat. Fighting them that way won't undo what needs to be undone anyway."

"Oh? Then what are you asking me to do?" she asked, with an edge of heat still in her voice.

"I'm asking you to infiltrate Rōjū City and steal a scroll that will enable us to release the Rōjū's grip on all of the Kisōshi."

~~~

Mishi sat with her legs dangling from the covered walkway and watched the rain start to fall throughout the empty training courtyard and the small garden beyond it. The soft patter of the rain soothed her, and the smell of wet earth and living plants filled her lungs.

"You'll need to sleep sometime," Tenshi said, as she lowered herself to the space beside her. Mishi said nothing, but continued to stare out at the falling rain as though mesmerized by the patterns the drops made in the rippling koi pond.

"Mishiranu-san," Tenshi began.

"If you're here to do Kuma-sensei's bidding, you might as well walk away. I won't be pandered to."

"Hmph," Tenshi bristled. "I thought Ami hit you in the ribs during your test yesterday, but if you think I'd do *any* man's bidding she must have hit you in the head."

Mishi tried to force the corners of her mouth down, but lost the battle.

"There, that's better!" Tenshi said, flashing her own generous smile in return. "Kuma-sensei told me you were upset, but he didn't explain why. Care to tell me?"

Mishi returned her gaze to the rain filled courtyard, and her mouth returned to the straight line it had been prior to Tenshi's arrival.

"Oh, nothing at all, only that he's asked me to die for his cause," she said, unable to keep the sarcasm from her voice.

Tenshi looked at her and raised an eyebrow.

"*His* cause?" she asked. "And when did all of this become *his* cause? Are you not a Kisōshi? Were your parents not killed by the Rōjū? Are your sisters not victims of the same system?"

Mishi resisted the temptation to grind her teeth together.

"Kuma-sensei has already reminded me of all those facts," she said, struggling to keep her voice even. "Kisōshi I may be, and I'm grateful for all that you and Kuma-sensei have done for me, and for Sachi and Ami, but… dying? Tenshi-san, I didn't ask for any of this! I didn't ask to be Kisōshi, I didn't ask to be 'the strongest fire kisō Kuma-sensei has ever seen.' I'm barely 16 cycles old, Tenshi-san, shouldn't I get a chance at living before I have to throw it all away?"

Tenshi was silent for a time, and the two women simply stared into the falling rain together.

"You should," she said finally, her voice just audible above the patter of raindrops on the tiled roof. "Certainly, you should have a chance at life. You deserve it, and so does every other girl in Gensokai. So tell me, Mishi-chan, what life will you have?"

"What?"

"If you don't help us overcome the Rōjū, what life will you have? Will you go out? Will you travel Gensokai? You can't take your katana with you, and you'll have to pretend to have no kisō. What will you do? Will you teach young girls how to fight? You would be killed for it. Will you bring peace to the land? If anyone thought you were a Kisōshi, or even remotely close to one, you would be hounded to the ends of the land and killed the moment you were captured, as your mother was. Will you give up using your kisō and start a farm? Settle down with a husband and raise babies? And what will happen to those babies if they are girls? What will happen when they are born Kisōshi, like their mother?"

Mishi tried to picture any of it—farming, raising a family—none of it appealed to her. She had no interest in those things, but even if she did, Tenshi was right. She would never be allowed to have it. Any of it.

"Gensokai has not been the land it was meant to be for well over a thousand cycles," Tenshi continued. "The Yūwaku were a scourge when they reigned and they committed many atrocities in the time that they ruled, but they were replaced by an evil just as insidious, and worse for being veiled as a good. You know the history books, you know why the Rōjū were established, but you also know the evil that 'corrective step' has caused. You've lived it. Would your mother have been killed if the Rōjū hadn't been put in place to keep 'another evil female reign' from rising up after Yūwaku? Would your father? Imagine what your life would be like, if your parents hadn't broken Gensokai law by trying to keep you alive at your birth. Imagine what your sisters' lives would have been, if they could have grown up with their families, training openly at a school as our boys do. Imagine what it will be like if someday you decide to have children, and you can keep the girls as well as the boys, no matter what power they're born with."

Mishi closed her eyes for a moment, not to picture that kind of world, but simply to contain the emotion that picturing a life with her parents alive in it brought her. It wasn't something she'd ever imagined before she'd come to Kuma-sensei's school and learned who they were. For the first eight cycles of her life, she'd never known if her parents were dead or if she'd merely been abandoned, like so many children in Haha-san's care. Even since Kuma-sensei had told her the truth about her parents, it was something she only rarely allowed herself to fantasize about. Why torment herself with a past that was impossible and a future that could never be?

Even before she spoke, Mishi knew she was done arguing. Tenshi was right that there was no other life for her with the Rōjū in power. Her choices were to succeed, and live in a world where she was free to be the person she had become, or to fail and die knowing she had fought for a world that was worth living in. But there were still answers she wanted…

"Why is he so obsessed with this, Tenshi-san? Why does he care so deeply? He's a Kisōshi. He could have land, be the peacekeeper for a whole town, have a life of his own. Why has Kuma-sensei dedicated so much of his time to saving the lives of female Kisōshi and training us to fight? Why should he care at all?"

Tenshi turned to look at her then, and her eyes had lost their usual glint of good humor.

"It's not my story to tell, Mishi-san, but... Kuma-sensei had a wife and child once. His wife was Kisōshi, though of course very few people knew it, and..."

"And?" Mishi asked, unable to restrain her curiosity.

"And so was his daughter." Tenshi stood up then, and grabbed Mishi's shoulder before turning to walk away. "He used to go by a different name," she said. "But that man died along with his wife and child, and Kuma-sensei is all that's left."

9日 10月, 老中 1119年

≈ Taka ≈

TAKA SAT ON a fallen log by the gently flowing creek and enjoyed the warming rays of sunshine on her face. She was much warmer for having replaced the thin silk kimono she wore in populated areas with her more usual leather leggings and tunic, but winter was fast approaching and she soaked up the last warmth of the cycle gladly. The smell of pine needles and wet rocks filled her lungs, as she watched Yanagi weave vines and loose branches together in a pattern so randomized it almost looked natural.

"You know, there's a good chance I won't even be here through the winter," she said, as the giant tree continued crafting the large, flat piece of weaving.

"So you believe you've found them?" he asked, without pausing in his work.

"Yes, I think I've found them. I have the town name and the family name, so it's just a matter of patience and listening to the right bit of gossip."

"You shouldn't stay there long," Yanagi cautioned.

"When do I stay anywhere long?" Taka asked.

"You know what I mean," the giant willow tree clarified, his voice emphasized by the rustling of his leaves and branches. "There are more Kisōshi there than usual, according to my sources, and you should be extra cautious not to draw attention to yourself. Especially if that Kisōshi from Kengaishi is spreading word about a young woman who matches the description of a certain five cycle old wanted poster."

Taka had to admit that Yanagi's sources were impeccable. The benefit of being the tree spirit of the entire Souryu Forest was having a constant stream of information from the wildlife, as well as some of the older trees. Taka wasn't entirely clear on how Yanagi's relay system worked. Whether the tree spirit simply couldn't explain it very clearly, or simply wanted to maintain some of the mystery of being Kami, Taka had never been sure. But she'd accepted his explanation of having 'a strong connection with the land to which I am beholden' without too many questions, even as a twelve cycle old girl.

So if the tree spirit said there was an increase in Kisōshi activity in Shikazenshi, Taka would take his word for it, but that wasn't going to stop her from following the first real lead she'd had in cycles.

"I'll be careful," she said.

"Will you?" the walking tree asked. "Will you make sure you don't throw away all you've become in this quest for vengeance?"

Taka sighed. It was a discussion they'd had before now, but Yanagi liked to bring it up any time Taka's quest seemed likely to put her in danger. He was awfully protective for a thousands of cycles old tree.

"It's not just about revenge, Yanagi-san. It's about ending an evil. You know as well as I do that the Josankō shouldn't be allowed to go on existing."

"That may be true, but I still don't understand why *you* have to be the one to bring it to justice."

"If this next bit of my mission goes as planned, I won't be doing it alone."

"Hmph... Some comfort that will bring me, if it winds up getting you killed."

"This from the eternal tree who keeps reminding me how fleeting my own existence is?"

"It's fleeting enough as it is, without you throwing it away for vengeance. I'll be very upset if the fleeting moment I'm allowed to spend with you gets cut even shorter through your own recklessness."

"Yanagi-san! When am I ever reckless? And when did you become my mother? I've never had one before, I don't need one now!"

"Child, I have been your mother, or father, or whatever parental figure you like, since you arrived in my forest half-frozen and wasting away for lack of food. You are as much my daughter as you were daughter to the woman who birthed you, and as a Kami, when *I* threaten to find you in the afterlife and torment you if you die before your time, you should heed the threat!"

Yanagi-san's anger was genuine, but that last statement made Taka laugh before she could control it.

"I will do my best to keep you from having to torment me in the after-life, Yanagi-san," she said, still chuckling.

"See that you do," the willow tree said, his voice emanating from no-where and everywhere. "The spirit world is not a forgiving pla—"

Yanagi was interrupted by a piercing cry from above them, and he and Taka both raised their heads to see the black speck of a hawk high overhead. Taka called back to the hawk with an answering cry and pulled the thick bracer she kept attached to her belt onto her forearm, where she fastened it in place.

By the time she was done, the hawk had circled low enough that his red and brown feathering could be made out against the blue of the sky. Moments later, the buffeting of wings by her head announced Riyōshi's arrival, as she raised her arm and the hawk's talons scored the thick leather that protected her wrist.

"I wasn't expecting to see you today, friend," she said aloud, out of habit. At the same time, she used her kisō to project the sense of mild surprise she felt and an image of a clear sky, devoid of hawks.

In return, Riyōshi nipped her ear 'affectionately,' a habit which al-ways drew a small amount of blood, and returned images of himself cir-cling the woods without finding any prey and checking repeatedly on his mate only to be squawked away from his roost.

"I see, so you thought you'd come and see if I was up to anything in-teresting?" she asked, turning a skeptical eye to her wooden mentor. "And Yanagi had nothing to do with your appearance?"

Riyōshi ruffled his feathers and smoothed them again, while looking between his two legged companions.

"I thought you could use some company on this adventure," Yanagi said, attempting to sound disinterested.

"You mean you thought I could use a chaperone?"

"Riyōshi-san is a useful companion to have," the talking tree spirit in-sisted.

"I'm aware of that, but I don't like taking him into populated areas. There are too many idiots who might try to put an arrow through him."

"Well, he volunteered. I'm sure you can keep him safe. You already promised you were going to be extra cautious."

"I did, did I?"

"Didn't you?"

"Whether I did or not, you know I'll be more cautious than usual if I have to look out for Riyōshi-san as well."

"Look out for him? Riyōshi-san can take care of himself."

"You know what I mean." Taka took a deep breath and let it out slow-ly. The only creature in all Gensokai who was more protective of her than Yanagi was Riyōshi. His ability to scout leagues of terrain ahead of her in the time it took her to walk a league on foot could be invaluable, but that didn't make his harping on and on about her safety any less tiresome.

"Well, I suppose you've both gotten your way," Taka said, after glaring at both of them long enough to make them each turn away and inspect the sky.

"Excellent!" Yanagi said, with a suspicious amount of enthusiasm. "Now let's see about getting this door in place." And with that, he flourished the woven mat he'd been constructing, a door that would withstand ten times the foul weather that anything that she could construct would, and Taka had little choice but laugh at how fortunate she was in her friends.

14日 10月, 老中 1119年

≈ Taka ≈

TAKA DIDN'T MIND the smell of the warm rice wine on the tray she carried, but when it combined with the stale sweat and cooking meat scents that permeated the izakaya, her nose twitched in distaste. She worked her way through the maze of private rooms and tried to single out the details of the various conversations within as she passed. She was grateful that most of the patrons she served had consumed enough sake that they were beyond caring if she took longer than necessary to bring them their next round.

This was her third day in Shikazenshi, and she had learned nothing of use in her inspection of the town. It was a time when she rued the wanted poster that still hung in all the Kisōshi meeting halls throughout Gensokai, which described "a young josanpu who might be seeking shelter or attempting to locate her associates: wanted for crimes against the Rōjū." The first time she had found the poster she had laughed at it for all its lack of useful description, since it didn't even detail her appearance—not that she had many outstanding features anyway—but the first time that offering her healing talents in exchange for room and board had raised enough suspicion that the town had sent the local Kisōshi after her, she no longer found it funny. She would give anything simply to be able to ask around for the Zōkame family, but she couldn't do it without raising people's curiosity, and she couldn't afford any undue interest in her presence.

Taka could suppress her kisō enough that no one would think her more powerful than a normal josanpu, but she struggled to make her kisō undetectable for any length of time and, consequently, any Kisōshi who bothered to scan her would find that she met the description of a young josanpu seeking shelter all too well. All of that meant that she had to find her information by eavesdropping on conversations, or, as was the case tonight, downright spying. She had become quite an experienced server of food and drinks as a consequence, so it was no longer difficult for her to seek employment at ryokan and izakaya as she found them. She found that the places where people slept, ate, and drank were always the best places to find useful news or gossip. The difficulty always lay in stumbling on the right conversation. The past two days hadn't brought her any luck so far.

Tonight was her last chance to learn something by eavesdropping, or else she would have to risk breaking into the local town hall, something that she was reluctant to do after her last effort. Getting caught breaking into records halls was even more suspicious than asking direct questions about the family she was looking for.

Taka reached the room that had ordered the tray of atsukan she carried, and knocked quietly before sliding back the shoji that separated it from the darkened hallway.

As soon as the door was open, she almost dropped the tray that she carried when she took in the room before her. Why had she agreed to deliver this tray for the girl downstairs? Kami-curse it, she was walking into a room full of Kisōshi, all of them dressed in hakama and uwagi, and all carrying katana and wakizashi. She cursed Yanagi-san for being right, then took a breath, composed her features, made sure that she was tamping her kisō down tightly, and entered the room.

"Pardon the intrusion," she said softly, though she knew no one would listen to her. As she hoped, the six men surrounding the low table within continued their conversation as though no one else were there. All she had to do was circulate their drinks without drawing attention to herself, and she could be on her way.

"You can't tell me everyone in town thought it was a good idea," one man said, from the far side of the table.

"That's right," agreed another, as Taka collected the empty clay jugs used for pouring warmed sake and replaced them with the three full ones she carried on her tray. "I heard two of the town council opposed it."

"Oh?" countered a third man. "Who was that, then?"

"Zōkame-san was against it from the start," a fourth man added, from closer to the door.

Taka took a deep breath and made sure her hand was steady as she moved to replace the third and final jug. *Had she really just heard the name Zōkame?*

"Eh? That old man? Well, that's not surprising."

"Bah, he lives on the north side of town with all the old money, what would he know about farming anyway!"

"Heard his wife came from a farmer's family, seems he might know more than most..."

Taka looked around the room for any excuse to stay and hear more, but she couldn't find anything that needed cleaning or attending. Besides, even with her kisō clamped down tight, she would still register as josanpu if any of these men bothered to scan her. She needed to get out of here before anyone noticed her. She stood as calmly as she was able and headed towards the door.

"Well even if he does know something about it, why should the rest of the council listen to him?"

Taka slid the shoji open once more, reluctant to leave, but triumphant at having already learned more than she had dared to hope, and exultant that she had escaped a room full of Kisōshi without being detected.

"Girl!" a man on the far side of the room called, just as she stepped through the door. Taka's heart skipped briefly. Had she done something to give herself away? Her hand began to tremble, but she stilled it as she remembered that she had neglected to ask if they needed anything else.

"Yes, okyaku-sama?" she asked, using the honorific reserved for customers in all establishments.

"Bring us some sashimi!"

"Certainly, okyaku-sama," she said, bowing slightly as she slid the door closed.

Taka almost skipped down the hallway as she returned towards the kitchens. She would make sure that someone brought the men their order of sashimi. *She* would be on the north side of Shikazenshi by the time it was ready to eat.

It wasn't until she stepped through the door that led from the izakaya's kitchens and into the back alley that she realized her mistake. The Kisōshi who had been closest to the door in that private room stood at the bottom of the steps to the izakaya and looked at her as though he'd been expecting her. The man didn't stand out in any way—average height, average coloring—she wouldn't have noticed or remembered him at all, had his uwagi not been a bright golden color.

She stopped on the second step, somehow sure that the man was waiting for her and unwilling to put herself any closer to him.

"I have wondered for cycles now about the mystery girl those posters describe. I never understood what the Rōjū could want with a stray josanpu anyway. But that's not what you are, is it?" the man asked, from a few arm spans away.

Taka said nothing. What could she say that wouldn't damn her? She would either have to attempt to lie to a Kisōshi (and this one seemed much less easily fooled than the last), or damn herself with the truth. Neither option appealed to her.

"You almost got away, little one," the man continued. "I never would have noticed if you hadn't seemed so elated as you left the room."

Taka frowned. She had kept her facial expressions carefully schooled during her exchange with the Kisōshi. How had he—

"Your face didn't give you away, girl. Your mind did, and your kisō. I'm much more... vigilant than most of my brothers," the man explained, without Taka even asking aloud.

She still said nothing, but wondered why the man bothered to explain himself rather than simply grabbing her and taking her to the nearest Kisōshi hall, or wherever it was that Kisōshi took prisoners for the Rōjū. Not one to waste an opportunity, Taka began scanning the alley for avenues of escape. The man didn't appear to have a horse nearby, so if she could make it past him without getting tackled, she might yet have a chance of escape. Certainly, she shouldn't wait here while his five friends gathered and made their way to help him.

"Running will make this much more difficult," the man said, once more responding when she'd said nothing.

Taka took one last look at the man and opened her mouth as if to speak, but instead she leapt to the bottom of the steps that exited the izakaya and sprinted into the alley. She made it a handful of strides before the man somehow managed to tackle her. Kami curse these blasted kimono! She hated not being able to sprint as fast as her leather leggings allowed. She rolled underneath the man, even as they went down, and drew the man's own wakizashi from his obi. But the man had either anticipated that, or he had the reactions of a snake. Even as she hit the dirt beneath them, he was pinning her arms to her side.

"I don't want to hurt you, girl," the man said. "But if you cut me, I'll have to let the rest of my brethren kill you."

Taka spat in the man's face and flicked the wakizashi away with her wrist. She didn't want to be killed for cutting a Kisōshi, but at least he wouldn't have the damned blade either.

"If you don't wish to hurt me, let me go!" she growled, as she struggled against the man's weight. He was at least one hand's span taller than she was, and substantially more muscled. She had planned to use her knees on his more sensitive spots, but he had managed to use his legs to pin her own, so she was left with no recourse but to spit and curse and try to lift his weight.

"I'll consider it," the man said. "If you'll tell me why the Rōjū are so keen on capturing you."

Taka shook her head.

"That just gives you more reason to capture me. I've broken their laws. What more do you need to know?"

He canted his head to one side and raised an eyebrow, even as he still held her pinned beneath him.

"I'm curious as to what you are. Your kisō is far stronger than any josanpu I've ever met. Even when you were trying to control it inside, it registered as high for a josanpu, and now that you're not focusing on keeping it contained..." The man whistled softly to emphasize his point.

Taka was incredulous. Pinned in an alley, in the middle of the night, under a Kisōshi who just wanted to know what she was? "Since when do Kisōshi care about minor details like WHY the Rōjū council wants people dead? Shouldn't it be enough for you that they think I deserve to be killed?"

"Not generally, no. The Rōjū ha—"

Just then a cry rent the air, and Taka called back before the man even had time to look up. In a moment, wings, talons, and a vicious beak were between her and the Kisōshi, leaving the man had no choice but to release her or allow his face to be ravaged by an angry hawk. Taka took full advantage of the man's distraction and pushed him off of her as his attempts to defend against Riyōshi left him unbalanced. As soon as she was free of his weight, she rose to her feet, pointed herself south (she didn't need this overly perceptive Kisōshi following her), and ran, the reassuring sound of flapping wings soon following close behind her. She truly hated it when Yanagi-sensei was right.

15日 10月、老中 1119年

～ Mishi ～

MISHI HELD THE horse's reins and tried to stop her hands from shaking. She took a deep breath and tried to focus her ki. Her mind traveled back to the small dinner she had enjoyed with Kuma-sensei, Tenshi-san, Ami, and Sachi last night.

It had been a quiet affair, but Tenshi-san had made her favorite sushi, and Sachi had told her the story of her first mission, while Ami told stories of a girl who had left a cycle before Mishi had even arrived at the school. Mishi was already familiar with all the details of Ami's story about the rescue of an infant Kisōshi with Tenshi-san, but she had listened happily anyway as her friend had regaled them with the story enthusiastically. Sachi's story had been part commiseration and part briefing for Mishi's mission, as her first mission had essentially been a scouting mission for Mishi's, completed two cycles ago. Mishi had heard some of the details before, but they had taken on a new meaning with her own fate now so closely tied to them. At the end of dinner, her sisters and Tenshi-san had given her warm hugs and wished her well, then left her alone with Kuma-sensei.

Kuma-sensei's face had looked dark even in the warm candlelight, and Mishi had begun to wonder what she had done or said that could have upset him.

"This is for you," he had said, as he handed her a long thin object wrapped in silk.

As soon as Mishi had held it, she had known what it must be. Nonetheless, she had opened the package carefully and uncovered a katana the likes of which she had only seen before in Kuma-sensei's personal sword collection. Tears had begun to fog her vision before she could even formulate a response.

"Don't thank me for it yet," Kuma-sensei had said. "You cannot have it until you return from your mision."

Mishi had looked up, her eyes asking the question that her mouth hadn't formed yet.

"Mishi," Kuma-sensei had said, "I cannot emphasize enough how dangerous this mission will be. It is paramount that you keep your cover for as long as possible. It is quite possible that your belongings will be searched when you enter the Rōjū compound. You cannot have a sword with you then, or all will be lost before it's even begun."

Mishi had wanted to nod, but picturing her life for the next few tendays without a sword was... difficult.

"Sensei... what if I need to defend myself?" she had asked.

Sensei's eyes had caught hers and locked with them.

"I have taught you to fight with and without a sword. Tatsu-sama has taught you many tricks as well, I'm sure. If you need a sword, take one. Take it off of your attacker, if you must. I know that you know how. But know that once you pick up a sword, your disguise as a servant is completely ruined, so only do it if your very life is threatened."

At that Mishi had nodded. She must have been too distracted to mask her feelings well, for Kuma-sensei answered a question she had only asked in her own mind.

"Mishiranu-san, I know this seems like an awful burden to put on one as young as you. Sixteen cycles is young indeed for a Kisōshi's first mission. This is no arbitrary right of passage. A Kisōshi must complete a mission that is potentially life threatening, yes... but this is much more than that, Mishi. Your mission is pivotal to what I've been working towards for so many cycles. If you succeed, we will have the tools to remove the power that the Rōjū has abused for a thousand cycles. I would do it myself if I could, but I would be recognized and killed as soon as I entered the compound."

That had given Mishi pause for a moment. She had thought of what Tenshi had told her so many nights before, when she was still trying to decide if this cause was worth her life...

"Sensei, Tenshi-san mentioned to me... well, she said it wasn't her story to tell, but she told me that you once had a wife and child. A daughter..."

She had wondered if Kuma-sensei would be upset that Tenshi had shared his secret, but the emotion that clouded the man's face wasn't anger.

*"I did once, yes. And, yes, before you ask, that is why I would be rec-
ognized and killed on sight at the Rōjū compound if I were to go myself.
The Rōjū happen to think me dead at the moment, but... I'm afraid I
didn't make a very good impression the last time that any of them saw
me, and while you and your sisters might consider me ancient, I'm not
yet old enough that they wouldn't recognize me..."*

The curve at the corners of Kuma-sensei's mouth hadn't given Mishi
the sense that he regretted whatever had given the Rōjū such a bad impression of him, but the cold anger behind his eyes had kept her from
asking any more about it. Instead, she had focused on a question that
was still bothering her.

*"Sensei, I still am not sure I understand. If this mission is so im-
portant and so dangerous... why me?"*

Kuma-sensei had taken a deep breath before answering.

*"Mishi-san, I sometimes forget how little you think of your own abili-
ties. Let me say something to you very clearly. This mission is very dangerous. That scroll is very well guarded, though not directly. As we've
discussed more than once, it will be far easier to get to the scroll than to
escape with it. Either of your sisters, or perhaps some of my former students, could get into that compound, they could even get into that library, but you are the only one who I am sure can get out again."*

Mishi had swallowed, realizing that her mouth had gone dry.

"You expect me to have to fight."

Kuma-sensei had nodded.

*"I would prefer that you didn't, and it is my sincere hope that you
won't have to. It's possible that if the plan works perfectly, you won't
have to. It's a good plan, but even the best plans have faults. If it comes
to fighting, I know that you can do whatever you have to to stay alive
and return to us."*

"But Sachi has been training so much longer and her skills with—"

*"Mishiranu-san! Now is not the time to question my judgment. You
are the best fighter I have trained in many cycles, perhaps ever, and
your abilities with kisō outshine even my own. You are the only one who
can do this. Now go. And may the Kami protect you."*

With that, Kuma-sensei had given her a hug, something he had never
done before, and sent her on her way, promising to look after her sword
until she returned.

A soft neighing and the fresh scent of horse manure brought her back
to herself and what she was supposed to be doing. She looked down at
the graveled courtyard in front of her and saw a fresh green lump steam-
ing back at her.

"You couldn't have waited five minutes?" she asked the horse standing placidly before her.

"Shall you get the shovel or shall I?" asked a voice directly behind her.

She cursed herself for allowing her thoughts to distract her so thoroughly that Katagi could sneak up on her without her noticing.

"I'm so sorry, Katagi-san. I will get a shovel right away," she said, as she bowed and hurried off to the stables.

Once the horse dung was dealt with, and the saddles were properly adjusted and loaded, Mishi and Katagi quickly mounted and were on their way. Katagi had been silent through the remainder of their preparations, yet they were barely outside of the courtyard when he began talking again, and Mishi remembered her first objection to the mission, one that had been summarily dismissed the moment she had uttered it. It was not important to the mission, apparently, that she disliked Katagi-san's company. Hours later, sometime after Mishi had placidly imagined herself fighting him unarmed a number of times, each time resulting in a more devastating loss on the part of Katagi, she noticed that he had finally fallen silent. She restrained a sigh of relief, worried that any sound she made might incite him to start speaking again.

"You're awfully quiet, Mishiranu-san," he said.

She silently cursed herself for having even thought about sighing. Apparently it had been enough to attract his attention.

"I wasn't aware that you required any response from me, Katagi-san," she said.

Katagi frowned.

"Not required... I mean... you don't have to... but I thought... don't you like to talk?"

Mishi held back her first reply and tried something only slightly less scathing.

"I do not particularly enjoy talking for talking's sake alone," she said, perhaps not succeeding in keeping all the disdain out of her voice.

As soon as she had said the words, she rebuked herself. She had to play the part of a servant, and a servant would not say such things to her master. Just as she was about to try to form an apology, Katagi laughed.

"You never cease to amaze me, Mishiranu-san," he said, as he brought his mirth under control. "You never reply the way I expect you to."

He smiled and looked as though he had just completed some kind of trick and was awaiting praise. When Mishi said nothing, he continued.

"This is a tenday long journey, so we have ample time to get to know one another," he said, with a broad smile that made Mishi want to punch his shiny teeth out. "What should we discuss first?"

Mishi tried to remind herself that she was doing this for a better future. Without Katagi-san, she had no reason to arrive at the Rōjū compound, no reason to be escorted into the guest's quarters willingly, no reason to wander the grounds and search the libraries while Katagi-san was testing… She sighed. She really couldn't beat him up and leave him on the road-side. It would absolutely ruin her cover.

≈ Taka ≈

Taka waited outside the tall, wooden gate and crossed her arms across her chest to keep her hands from fidgeting. Her fear mixed with excitement, creating a strange rushing sensation in all of her limbs that made them feel as though they were about to fly away from her. She took some deep breaths and tried to center her ki. What would Yanagi-sensei have said?

Let your mind flow down to your roots and up to the tips of your leaves, filling every branch and twig with the calm of the forest floor.

She no longer bothered to point out that she didn't have roots and leaves, since his meaning was clear enough. Taka focused her energy on the stillness of the earth beneath her and worked to spread calm from her toes to her hair.

By the time the guard who had answered the gate returned she was no longer shaking, at least not visibly.

"My mistress will see you now," he said, as he closed the small flap that had allowed him to speak to her and pulled back on the human sized door that would allow her entrance.

It was clear from the moment she stepped through the gate that the man who was ushering her in thought she had no right to be here. She was inclined to agree with him. She certainly wasn't the kind of person who would generally be granted an audience with his mistress, but this was where she needed to be. She had searched for so long, and it was finally time.

She continued to focus on her breathing and tried not to think about the various ways in which this could go wrong. She had to hope that the whispered words she had heard five cycles ago had been the truth. She needed an ally now more than ever.

The farther into the compound she was led, the more out of place she felt. She had understood the guard's initial disdain for her appearance. She was aware of what she must look like to him, but the more that she saw of the compound, the more obvious the disparity between her own station and that of her host's became. Not only was the compound huge, but it was also elaborate. The colors of the buildings were sedate and mostly natural tones, but the carvings in the woodwork were exceedingly detailed, and the quality of the wood itself was excellent. In fact, Taka didn't even recognize it, which was astounding, considering how familiar she now was with all of the surrounding forests.

She was led through a well manicured courtyard, around two wide, low buildings wrapped in covered walkways that most likely contained living quarters, and down a small pathway that snaked between one of the larger buildings and what smelled like a bathhouse, into a small but exquisitely maintained garden. A tiny pond was the central focus, but there were a number of small, lovingly tended trees and bushes, as well as a large willow that overhung almost the entire garden. In one corner sat a very small tea house. It was there that she was led and asked to wait.

She removed her shoes and folded herself onto her knees to wait for her host. As she waited it began to rain softly and she was taken by how peaceful the small garden was. She considered reaching out to the plants here to see how they fared, but she was risking enough as it was, simply by being here. A shiver took her as she sensed the familiar tingle of someone else's kisō making contact with her own. She stifled the urge to look around to see who had made contact with her, for such an act might betray her. Whoever had just scanned her should not have been able to sense her kisō unless they were incredibly adept at recognizing dampened power, as the Kisōshi from last night had been. A few moments later, a woman with the papery skin and silver hair of great age entered the tea house, silently removing her shoes as she did so, and gracefully folded herself and her simple but elegant kimono to the floor in order to mirror Taka's position on the far side of the small cherry table between them.

Taka instantly put her head and hands to the tatami before her, even as her chest constricted in recognition of the woman who had just sat down.

"Please forgive my uninvited visit," she said, her forehead still touching the grass mat in front of her, as she worked to control her voice.

"Your uninvited visit is most welcome," came the reply across the table. "Please, child, sit up and allow me to serve you some tea."

It was only as she sat up that Taka noticed the serving woman stand-ing at the entrance holding a tray with all of the amenities for tea.

The grey haired woman made a small gesture, and the serving woman placed the tray on the cherry table and then walked away, leaving them alone in the garden.

Taka sat quietly, watching as the older woman began the careful movements of the tea ceremony. Taka was awed, not just by the grace and focus of every small movement, but by the mere fact that the cere-mony was being performed at all, and in her honor, no less. It was some-thing that someone of her station had no right to expect, and, indeed, it was a ritual she had never seen before.

Taka searched her memory for the things that she was supposed to say and do in such a situation, but she had no experience to draw on, not even from the stories of others. So, she simply waited in silence while the tea was made, hoping that basic gratitude and humility would be sufficient to keep her from offending her host.

She worked to keep her eyes on the intricate ritual in front of her in-stead of on the face of the woman she had only seen once before, but part of her was so desperate to be sure that she had finally found her that it was difficult. Five cycles of planning, of searching.... Luckily, the woman was focused on the task in front of her and didn't notice Taka's furtive glances at her face and hands.

Taka's brain reeled with the importance of the moment before her, of the possible consequences that the next few minutes would bring. She pushed those thoughts aside and focused on the present. She listened to the soft rain on the teahouse roof, and the sound of the willow leaves dripping into the koi pond. She watched the graceful turns of the simple tea bowls before her and the careful whisking of the green tea within them.

Finally, she was presented with a tea bowl, and, not knowing what else to do, she accepted it with a bow, careful to show the proper defer-ence to her host.

"I humbly thank you for the tea, Zōkame-sama," she said, as she brought the small bowl to her lips.

The older woman raised an eyebrow at her, then. For a moment, she said nothing, simply sitting gently on her folded legs and sipping her tea.

"There are sweet cakes, child," the woman said after a moment, ges-turing to the small platter of rice cakes filled with sweet bean paste on the table.

Taka nodded and put her tea down before reaching for the small deli-cacies.

"I'm so sorry," the older woman said after Taka had taken a small bite of her dessert, "you seem to know my name, and by the way, please call me Tsuku instead of my family name, but I do not know who you are. You told my guard that you were a friend of my granddaughter's?"

Taka bowed her head low.

"Forgive my rudeness, Tsuku-san. It has been a long time since we last met. You have not changed at all since then, but I forget how much I must have changed in that time."

She looked up then, and tried to hide all of the worry she felt behind a small smile.

"I am Taka..." She hesitated before adding, "we last met at your granddaughter's funeral."

The smile faded from Taka's lips at the words, and a darkness seemed to pass briefly over Tsuku-san's face at the same time. For a moment, Taka was worried that all of her worst fears from the past five cycles would come to pass in a heartbeat; that Kiko's grandmother would throw her out, be unwilling to hear her, or worse yet, try to send her back to the Josankō. She held her breath, and for a moment was completely unable to read what passed on the older woman's face.

Then, eyes rimmed with moisture, the woman reached across the small cherry table and took Taka's hand.

"You made it out of that horrid place?"

Taka nodded. "I escaped a few month's after Kiko-san's death," she said.

That made Kiko's grandmother tilt her head in curiosity.

Taka smiled at the gentle worry in the older woman's eyes, and hoped it was a sign that she would not attempt to send her back to the Josankō. Unsure where to start, but sure that she should try to explain while she still had the woman's attention and good will, she began to speak.

"As soon as I learned the truth of what happened to Kiko-san, I could no longer stay at that... place. I arranged to be 'caught' borrowing books from the library and was sent to the cages. From there, I managed to escape."

Kiko's grandmother looked confused for a moment.

"I'm sorry, Taka-chan. What do you mean, once you learned the truth of what happened to Kiko-chan? What did you discover?"

Taka took a deep breath and tried to reign in the rage that even now burned through her when she thought of what had been done to her friend. It was important that she give this information clearly and concisely, so that Tsuku-san would believe her, understand her, and, most importantly, agree to help her with her mission.

"Did you ever find Kiko-san's story of how she met that boy a bit... strange?"

Tsuku-san scoffed, and Taka's hopes rose slightly as the formality the woman had maintained throughout their earlier exchange melted away.

"Strange? The whole story was complete nonsense. That girl could never lie. I don't know what really happened, but I know it didn't happen as she claimed."

Taka nodded, her confidence bolstered by Tsuku-san's easy acceptance of this all-important fact.

"Do you also remember the package and letter that you gave me? You said that you had looked through them."

Tsuku-san nodded, her mouth a hard line.

"I could never make sense of why she wanted to give you such a boring account of her pregnancy, and the letter sounded as though it had been written by a member of the Rōjū, it was so stuffy and proper. Mine was the same." The older woman's voice took on the hard edge of anger as she added, "Kiko-chan was never that formal with me."

Taka took another deep breath. The next part of her story was the most difficult part to believe, but everything would hinge on it.

"It took me some mooncycles to recognize that the letter and journal contained a hidden message," Taka said carefully.

Tsuku-san looked at her speculatively, but said nothing, so she continued.

"Did you happen to notice the many extra brush strokes all along the sides of the parchment, as though Kiko-san had lacked the scrap paper one would normally use to take excess ink from a brush?"

Tsuku-san thought for a moment before nodding.

"Yes, I had assumed the 'teachers' at that place had refused her any extra parchment."

Taka nodded.

"A reasonable assumption," she said. "But after a moon of staring at those marks and wondering why they covered the sides of every inch of that journal, I began to wonder if they were something more. It took me another moon before I was able to decipher the pattern, and one more after that to actually decode the whole journal, but it turns out that Kiko had written an alternate journal, entirely in code, in the margins."

Tsuku-san stared at her for a moment.

"Taka-chan, I would like to believe you, but my Kiko-chan had no reason to know anything about codes and ciphers. How could she possibly have written an entire journal in code?"

Taka smiled at that. She had thought the same thing herself, even as she was decoding the whole thing, but she said the same thing to Tsuku-san now that she had told herself while she had continued her work.

"It's not a particularly complicated cipher, Tsuku-san. Kiko-san could have thought of it herself without even knowing much about how these things usually work. Certainly, I was able to decipher it without the help of any prior knowledge of such things. It was only the mystery of why she had left so many single stroke marks on the sides of her parchment, when I knew she certainly could have found a spare piece, that made me wonder if the marks held any secret meaning."

Seeing the incredulity in Tsuku-san's eyes, and knowing that everything depended on Tsuku-san believing her, she reached into her obi and slid out the folded parchment and small bound journal that she carried there.

"May I show you?" she asked, even as Tsuku-san's eyes widened in recognition of the journal and letter she held.

Tsuku-san nodded, but said nothing. Taka unfolded the single piece of parchment first and placed it in the middle of the cherry table. She rose onto her knees, so that she could push the piece of paper closer to Tsuku-san and indicate the parts to which she referred.

"See the stray marks here, at the sides and bottom?" she asked.

Tsuku-san nodded, her eyes glued to the heavily worn piece of parchment that Taka had spread before her.

"Do you see the single dots that separate the marks every so often?"

Tsuku-san nodded once more.

"They are the key to the code," Taka continued. "They separate each character from the next."

Tsuku-san examined the parchment more closely and shook her head.

"No," she said. "If you combine the first four strokes before the first dot, you get 'dog.' From there you combine the next seven and get 'red,' and after that you get 'spirit' with the next six strokes. It's gibberish."

Taka-san smiled, glad that Tsuku-san had understood the most basic part of the code so easily.

"I thought the same thing," she said, as she opened up the journal to its first page and put it in front of the older woman. "But eventually, on a whim, I tried taking the top right stroke from each page until that place was marked with a dot." She flipped through the corresponding pages as she spoke. "I wrote them down as I went... and the first character I found?"

Tsuku-san met her eyes above the journal and locked with them. The emotion behind them pinned her in place and demanded the truth. She realized then with certainty that the kisō that she had felt contact hers earlier had been Tsuku-san's, as the woman used it now to insure that she couldn't be lied to.

"The first character," she continued, "was my own name: Taka. What followed…" She swallowed here, and decided that this woman deserved the full truth, no matter how difficult it was to say. "What followed was a detailed account of the repeated rape of your granddaughter at the hands of the male 'instructors' at the Josankō, and her subsequent pregnancy. In the final pages Kiko-san asked me to look after her babies— she was sure even then that she carried twins—because she feared that the instructors would wish to silence her after the children were born."

Tsuku-san's gaze held hers for a few moments more, and the cold rage that burned in those eyes, gracefully framed in long silver hair, kindled the rage that Taka had worked so carefully to repress until now. Taka's voice dropped to a harsh whisper, not out of any wish for secrecy, but only because she could not trust that her words would not break on the blade of her anger if she spoke any louder.

"I escaped less than a moon after I finished uncovering the truth of Kiko's death. Before I left, I attempted to find some record of where your family was located, but I found nothing. It seemed that all of the records relating to Kiko had either been destroyed, or had never existed. All I had was a reference that Kiko had made once to living in a province to the North. I did not even know Kiko's family name then, but I have been searching for you ever since."

"Only to tell me the truth?" Tsuku-san asked, after a moment.

Taka nodded. "And to ask for your help," she added.

Tsuku-san's eyes hardened for a moment, but she gave a slight nod that suggested that Taka had permission to ask. "What is it you would like my assistance with, Taka-san?"

Taka couldn't help but be pleased that the older woman had dropped the diminutive in her name. She was seventeen now, after all, and between the more respectful use of -san attached to her name, and the words she was about to utter, a small smile curved the corners of her mouth even while anger still glittered in her eyes.

"Burning the school of midwives to the ground," she said.

16日 10月、老中 1119年

⤞ Taka ⤝

TAKA ROSE FROM the futon having barely slept. After cycles of sleeping on a straw pallet on the floor of her small cave, the luxury of a down futon on a thick tatami and four walls around her was disorienting enough to prevent her from sleeping well. Now, as she rose to fold the feather pad away and the smell of the aging straw of the tatami filled her nostrils, she looked with dumb curiosity at the small basin on the far wall of the room that was reflecting the quiet dawn light back at her.

Ah yes. She was supposed to wash her face and hands. The hot bath she had enjoyed last night had been the first she'd experienced since escaping the Josankō that didn't require a lengthy hike into the mountain range containing Yanagi's forest. She had grown used to washing herself in the cold stream that flowed close to her small cave and considered hot water a rare treat, a reward for the full day of climbing into the mountains that it took to reach the nearest hot spring.

She scanned the room to find where her clothes might have been left. The maid who had escorted her to her bath the night before had taken them and told her that they would be washed. Yet the kimono, under kimono, obi, and accessories that she found lying an arm's span from the basin were not her own. A small sheet of parchment lay atop them.

Taka-san, please accept this small gift as a token of my esteem.
Sincerely,

Zōkame Tsuku

Taka picked up the kimono and held it to the light. The simple, black design was sparsely decorated with light pink and white sakura blossoms, printed on a medium weight silk that would be perfect for spring and fall. It was by far and away the most beautiful fabric Taka had ever held. While she could not refuse such a gift, she felt awkward dressing herself in a level of finery she was utterly unaccustomed to. She felt a familiar pang of longing for her leather leggings and tunic.

Finally, after painstakingly dressing herself and arranging her hair with the small decorative combs that had been laid out along with the clothes, she left the small guest room and headed for the main receiving room. The maid had shown her to it the night before on the way back from the baths, and informed her that she was to meet Zōkame-sama there the following day.

Taka had been stunned, at first, when Tsuku-san had invited her to stay the night. But the more she thought about it, the more she thought it made sense. After her uninvited arrival the day before Tsuku-san hadn't had much time to speak with her, yet both agreed that they still had much to discuss. So Tsuku-san had suggested—the kind of suggestion that one accepted as an order—that Taka stay the night, and that they meet again the following day, when Taka could be formally presented and they would have more time to speak. In addition, the appearance that she was a welcome guest would provoke less curiosity amongst the servants.

As she reached the double sliding doors that marked the entrance to the receiving room, Taka noted the intricate landscape that decorated them, another reminder of how far above her station Tsuku-san and her family were, and took a deep breath. She hoped this formal reception wouldn't last long. She had little education in formal etiquette and would be hard pressed to keep up appearances for any length of time.

As she slid the door to the side, the low murmur of voices that she had heard before entering dropped to absolute silence. Before she'd taken a full step into the room, an armed guard stood before her with his sword half drawn and she froze in place.

"Ah, my apologies, Zōkame-san. Allow me to present Otonashi-san, a recently arrived guest of our house. The maid must have gotten lost on her way to fetch her. Consequently, she has arrived without introduction, but I did ask her to join us this morning."

Taka's heart briefly stalled as she realized the horrible breach of etiquette she must have perpetrated by showing up without a maid to introduce her. She was so flustered that she barely noticed the surname that Tsuku-san had fabricated for her. When she realized that she was not being formally introduced to Tsuku-san, but rather to Tsuku-san's husband, her heart jolted back into action at twice the speed. Had Tsuku-san betrayed her? Taka had told Tsuku-san yesterday of the Rōjū mandate demanding her arrest. Had Tsuku-san decided to let her husband turn her over to them? There was little she could do to protect herself if it were so, since she was unarmed in a heavily guarded room. Her fate was in the hands of her hosts.

The guard stood to one side and sheathed his sword. Taka moved into the room as quickly as her restrictive new kimono would allow and folded herself to the floor, with her head and hands to the mat before her.

"Otonashi Taka-san, I present you to my esteemed husband, Zōkame Yasuhiko-san, Fifth Member of the Rōjū council."

The flesh all along Taka's spine prickled as she heard the title attached to Tsuku-san's husband's name. Fifth Member of the Rōjū Council? Tsuku-san's husband was a voting member of the Rōjū? She had been flung to the jaws of the enemy, and there was nothing she could do now. She did not dare to lift her head from the floor.

"Welcome to our home, Otonashi-san." The voice that addressed her now was a low baritone, and she had to assume it was Zōkame-san's.

"Please forgive my intrusion in your home." Taka had to cough to get her voice to work above a whisper.

"We would love for you to join us for our morning meal," said the baritone voice from the front of the room.

Taka sat up, fairly certain that etiquette required her to accept the invitation face to face with her host, but kept her eyes averted from Zōkame-san's gaze as she said, "I would be most honored to accept your invitation, Zōkame-sama."

In her peripheral vision she saw Zōkame-san nod, and immediately the servants and guards in attendance vacated the room.

"Otonashi-san, please, join us here," Tsuku-san called from the front of the room.

Taka wasn't convinced that her legs would hold her, but she managed to stand and shuffle her way to the front of the room, where servants were just returning with a low table and a series of trays laden with a morning meal, the extravagance of which Taka had never seen.

Taka took her time folding herself onto the small zabuton in front of the low table, cautious to keep her feet pointed away from her hosts and desperately trying to remember any other rules of etiquette she had ever learned. As soon as the servants had all exited once more, Tsuku-san spoke up.

"Taka-san, I hope you'll forgive me for hiding my husband's identity from you yesterday. I thought perhaps you would be unwilling to meet him if you knew it in advance. But—"

"What you should know," said Zōkame-san, "is that I loved my granddaughter very much, and no matter what the Rōjū may say about the matter, I will always be in your debt for the friendship you offered her."

Taka bowed once more, unsure what to do in light of this information. Could she truly trust that a member of the Rōjū would not turn her over to them simply because he loved his granddaughter? Would he have a choice? What would the consequences be to him if anyone discovered that he knew of her existence, had a chance to capture her, and did nothing?

Some of these doubts must have shown on her face, because Zōkame-san let out a small laugh that held no humor and then continued.

"I understand that it must be difficult to trust me in this, Taka-san, but you should know that Tsuku-chan told me of your identity last night, and if I were planning on turning you over to the other Rōjū I would have already done so."

Then he sighed, and Taka felt compelled to look at his face for the first time.

"You do know how to read my intentions, do you not?"

Taka hesitated, but then remembered that Tsuku-san had scanned her the day before. If Tsuku-san's husband already knew about her kisō and that hadn't already resulted in her death, perhaps she really was safe. Reluctantly, she nodded.

"Good. Then, please, scan me. I would have you trust me."

Taka took a deep breath, but then locked eyes with the man before her. It was the first time she had truly looked at him, and doing so made her breath catch for a moment before she pushed her own kisō out towards his. His hair was a silver to match his wife's, and his face held many folds of time and laughter, but his eyes were sharp and lit with a spark that Taka thought she recognized.

Yet, what had caught her off guard was the large scar that ran diagonally across the old man's face, from his left brow to the bottom of his right cheek, just barely missing his eye. Still, she ignored this physical distraction and pushed a small amount of her kisō out to touch his, just enough to check surface thoughts and feelings, enough to detect a lie.

She could tell that his feelings ran true to what he said, but that he was also hiding much from her. That was all she could ascertain without prying, so she drew her kisō back into herself and waited quietly.

"Do you believe me?"

Taka nodded.

"I do, Zōkame-sama, but I can also sense that you are hiding much."

Zōkame-san raised his eyebrow at that.

"First of all, please call me Yasuhiko," he said, with a smile that seemed to beckon the past. "Kiko-chan always did, and now no one but Tsuku-chan does, and I find that I miss it."

Then his face grew more grave and he added, "I was not aware how much kisō you hold. You are very good at repressing it. You should not have been able to sense that I am hiding anything. No josanpu should be able to."

Taka knew no safe reply to that comment, so she remained silent. A clinching feeling in her gut and a chill down her spine tempted her to fling her power outward to protect herself when Yasuhiko-san used his power to inspect her own a moment later, but she restrained herself.

"I see," was all that he said when he was done. The look on his face, which she had dreaded would be one of anger or fear, was instead one of speculation.

Tsuku-san took that opportunity to speak once more.

"You see, Yasuhiko-kun? She is well adapted to my plan, is she not?"

"More so than I believed at first, yes. But I still have many questions."

"Yes, yes, and she will answer them, but first let me explain things to her."

Tsuku-san then turned to Taka and reached across the table to hold her hand.

"Taka-san, we wish to help you. You know how I feel about the Josankō. You have known from the day that Kiko-chan's body was released to the Kami. But you may not know that we are fortuitously placed to help you in your mission, in a way that no one else can. To work together, though, we need to know more about you and you about us. We need to trust each other. Do you think you could trust us enough to tell us more of your story?"

Taka considered that for a moment. It was a serious question. She had come here for help, and had thought that Kiko's grandmother was a good place to look for it, based solely on a whispered promise she had heard five cycles ago. She had spent those five cycles looking for this woman, with the sole purpose of enlisting her help. Yet she had never known about the position held by Kiko's grandmother's husband. The Rōjū council was directly responsible for the very evil she was working to eradicate. How could she possibly trust someone who formed a part of that?

As if reading her thoughts (had she been that unguarded?) Yasuhiko spoke. "Taka-san, I know that it must be difficult to believe that I could want the same thing that you want, but please… scan me now and tell me what you sense."

As he spoke, the man opened up his kisō to her, not as an attack or even as a defense, but as an offer of submission. Taka sensed that, in that moment, she could overrun his kisō and do as she wished with it. She carefully made contact with her own kisō and used it to inspect his thoughts. It did not take long before she broke off contact out of a sense of respect and deep sympathy. Apparently, Kiko wasn't the only person Yasuhiko-san had lost to the evils of the Elder Council.

"I will trust you," was all that she said.

"Thank you," Yasuhiko-san said. "I realize that it is not an easy thing for you to do."

He paused then, and gestured at the feast laid out before them.

"Please," he added, "eat something while you tell us the story of how you escaped."

Taka smiled and used the hashi in front of her to pick up some food, putting it on the small plate before her.

"I'm afraid it's not the gripping tale you might expect," she said, putting a bite of fresh squid dipped in shoyu into her mouth.

She had to work to keep from exclaiming at the quality of the food, but she had never eaten so well in her life. It was difficult to make herself pause and speak rather than continue eating.

"After I learned what had been done to Kiko-san, I knew I could no longer stay at that wretched place. I arranged to be caught borrowing restricted books from the library, in order to be sent to the cages. Once there, unguarded except by a wolf I had already befriended, escape was simple. The only reason no one thinks of it when they're in the cages is that they're terrified of the wolf, but that wasn't a problem for me. Once free, I returned the favor for the wolf and made my way into the woods."

"I'm sorry, Taka-san, but what do you mean, you returned the favor for the wolf?" Tsuku-san asked.

"She aided me in my escape, so I aided her in return. Her mate was being held captive, and had been for cycles and cycles. The instructors were holding him captive in order to coerce his mate into attacking the girls who were sent to the cages. He'd been trapped in a cage barely larger than he was. His legs were withered from lack of movement, and his back scarred from years of abuse. I freed him and healed him so they could escape also."

If Tsuku-san or Yasuhiko-san thought this exchange was odd, they gave no indication, so Taka continued her story.

"So, then I was free. My plan was to seek you out and ask for your assistance. I thought perhaps you were the only person in the world who might not turn me over to the Rōjū for the bounty that was placed on my head soon after my escape, and who would be interested in vengeance, as I am."

Yasuhiko-san nodded, but spoke again. "But you haven't been roaming the wilderness searching for us for the past five cycles, have you? You are too well trained, and I know you didn't receive that training from the Josankō."

"True," Taka replied, but here she hesitated, as the truth of her training strained credulity.

"So what have you been doing? Who has trained you?" Yasuhiko-san prompted.

"His name is Yanagi-sensei. He is… an unconventional healer. He has been training me in the healing of plants and animals."

"The healing of plants?" Tsuku-san asked. "I wasn't aware that there were any mortals who knew of such things."

"Well, aside from me, there may not be," Taka admitted. "Yanagi-sensei is a tree kami."

"A tree kami? A spirit of the woods is your mentor?" Tsuku-san asked. "How on earth did you find him?"

"Actually, the wolves led me to him. After I healed the female wolf's mate, they seemed keen to lead me somewhere. I had no other direction to go, no information about where you resided aside from knowing that it was somewhere in Hokushin, and as the wolves wanted to lead me north anyway, I followed them."

"And they took you to a tree spirit?"

Taka nodded, then smiled, even as she reached for another bite of squid sashimi. "Well, they took me to his forest. I sort of ran into him by accident after that."

Yasuhiko-san shook his head. "Not a gripping story, ne? Wait a moment. I will ask the servants for more tea. I can see that we are going to be here for some time."

~~~

Long after the three unlikely companions had eaten their fill and sat sipping hot tea around the low cherry table covered in intricate carvings, Yashuihiko-san finally cleared his throat and leaned forward.

"Taka-san, you have been very gracious to share your story with us. I believe it is now our turn to show you the same courtesy. To tell you the entirety of both our stories would keep us here for days, but for now, let me say that we both have reasons to despise the Rōjū."

"But you *are* a Rōjū," Taka said before she could censor herself. "A voting member, no less."

"A position I have worked very hard to attain, Taka-san. It has taken me cycles and cycles to get to where I am today. Now I am perfectly poised to execute a plan that we have spent cycles preparing for."

"We have an ally, an old friend really, who has been running a very special school in the south. It is a school for Kisōshi, but while it trains male Kisōshi during the day, at night he holds classes for a very small group of female Kisōshi."

Taka's eyebrows raised to her hairline. A school for female Kisōshi? How could he do such a thing?

"Surely those girls are supposed to be dead... how can he run a school in such a way without getting reported to the Rōjū?"

"The girls are the school's servants, so no one thinks it strange for them to be there, or receive room and board there. The school is secluded, at the edges of a small town without many people...he manages. And as to the girls, yes, according to the Rōjū they should be dead, but according to the Rōjū, they are. He has a josanpu in his employ who has helped him rescue all of the girls that he trains."

Taka was astounded to hear the news, but it gave her new hope for her plan. If there were other josanpu who recognized the evil of the Josankō and the people who had orchestrated its existence, then perhaps she might have even more potential allies than she had originally thought.

"I see that the information has given you some measure of hope, and well it should, but we haven't reached the best part yet. These female Kisōshi are poised to complete one of the most important missions for our cause, and we believe that you could be a serious asset to that mission."

"And what, precisely, is your cause, Yasuhiko-san?" Taka asked, still finding it difficult to believe that these two nobles could possibly want the same things that she wanted.

Yasuhiko smiled then, as he picked up his cup of tea and drew it to his lips, "Why Taka-san, to overthrow the Rōjū council. What else?"

20日 10月、老中 1119年

≈ Taka ≈

TAKA STARED OUT of the small rocky opening and watched the rain drip from the vast green expanse above her. The sound of frogs croaking in the nearby forest and the smell of damp earth and clouds filled her lungs. She took a deep breath.

"It's good to be home, Yanagi-sensei," she said.

The ancient willow tree with glittering amber eyes who stood before her smiled, his knotted features bending in ways which trees generally didn't, but which Taka had gotten used to over the past five cycles.

"It is good to have you back, Taka-chan," the tree said, yet again breaking the standards of trees across the land.

Taka smiled at her mentor and leaned against the mouth of her small cavern home. She was tired from the three day journey from Tsuku-san's home to her own small valley, and she shivered in the slight chill that had rolled in with this late summer rain. As usual, Yanagi seemed unaffected by the weather.

"How long must you wait for this guide?" Yanagi asked.

"Tsuku-san said five days or fewer," she replied. "And I left her home three days ago."

"And where exactly will you be going?"

"I'm not sure—hence the guide. It's a school in the south, but apparently it's a bit remote. Tsuku-san and Yasuhiko-san said that the best ally I could have was a man named Kuma-sensei. I can find him across the mountain range and to the south, but as both this Kuma-sensei and I are on the list of people the Rōjū would like to see dead or locked up, I can't afford to take the roads that are patrolled by Kisōshi."

"What do you gain by finding this Kuma-sensei?"

"Tsuku-san said that he would do almost anything to see the Rōjū destroyed, that he has been working to that end for cycles. There's a plan they've been concocting for ages that I can help with."

"He sounds fanatical. Can you trust him?"

"Tsuku-san described him as dedicated rather than fanatical. She wouldn't give me details, but she implied that he used to have a family."

"Used to?"

"Mm. But doesn't anymore…"

"She said nothing more?"

Taka shook her head. "When I asked for more information, she said it was his story to tell."

Yanagi thought about that for a moment.

"Hmm… I wonder…" he said, bark furrowing in thought above his eyes.

"You wonder?" Taka prompted, after a long stretch of silence from the tree. Yanagi drifted that way sometimes, and Taka had to prod him to remember that she was not a tree herself, so her time wasn't infinite.

"Mmmm? Oh, nothing. The story of this Kuma-sensei may be one that I know, but I cannot place it. The name is not right…"

His echoing bass of a voice trailed off again and Taka decided not to disturb him for a moment. She was genuinely curious about the story of this possible future ally, but she had already resolved to hear it from his own mouth, so she didn't mind going without Yanagi's guesses. The tree spirit was old; older than her forest home, possibly older than the mountains that cocooned it. She wasn't sure, and based on the few times that she'd asked, neither was Yanagi himself.

She let her mind trail after such thoughts for a moment, attempting to contemplate the vast age of such a being, as she tried to avoid thinking about the topic at hand. She was leaving. She was leaving, and for the first time since Yanagi had taken her in five cycles before, she didn't know when she'd be back. Considering the possible dangers of this journey, she didn't know if she would be back at all.

"What thoughts have you looking so withered, young sapling?" Yanagi asked.

She smiled at the strange term of endearment Yanagi occasionally bestowed upon her.

"Well, ancient roots and leaves," she replied, in her best attempt at an arboreal honorific, "I'm thinking about this journey, and how long I may be gone."

That turned Yanagi-san thoughtful as well.

"Mm… and how long do you think you will be gone?"

"I don't know. Certainly a few tendays, possibly a few moons or more.... The journey there, alone, will take a tenday. After that... it depends on what this Kuma-sensei needs help with. Tsuku-san told me that he never shared exact details with them, due to their close relationship with the Rōjū and the possible interception of messages between them."

Yanagi shook his long dangling branches forward and back, in what Taka had come to recognize as a nod.

"I cannot fault him there. In fact, I wonder if you should trust Tsuku-san and her husband? How can her husband remain a member of the Rōjū voting council if he knows of its horrors?"

"I asked the same question," Taka replied. "Yasuhiko-san's response was simple enough. The best position possible from which to dismantle anything is the inside. They claim to have been feeding information to Kuma-sensei and others like him for a long time. They have held a grudge against the council since long before Yasuhiko became a member. Kiko's death was yet another grievance against them."

"And what of the Josankō? Had you not always planned to go after them first?"

Taka nodded. This had been a brief point of contention between herself and Tsuku-san.

"Tsuku-san made an excellent point when I tried to insist on that particular detail. I can fight to close the Josankō, but it is merely one small branch of evil on a corrupt and festering tree. Cutting it off does little good, when the entire tree must be toppled."

Yanagi shuddered at the metaphor, and Taka briefly regretted her wording, but her point stood.

"She makes an excellent point," he said, once he had repressed his initial reaction. He shimmied his long flowing branches, as if shaking the thought away. "Well, you should prepare whatever you need for this trip. I will, of course, keep your... erm... home ready for you."

Taka laughed at the thought of Yanagi trying to politely label her cave. It was small, dry, easily hidden from view, and it had served her well for the past five cycles.

Then a thought stole the laughter from her eyes and lips, and she gave voice to something that had troubled her since she had started the return journey from Tsuku-san's residence.

"Yanagi-san... what if I don't return?"

Yanagi's eyes locked with hers, and the sparkle seemed to dull from them momentarily.

"Do you not wish to come back?"

"Of course I do! This is my home now."

Yanagi's eyes lit once more, and his mouth spread into a wide smile.

"Then you will." He said it so simply, and with such confidence, that for a moment Taka found no room to doubt him. Then her concerns returned to her, stacking slowly like a wood pile laid across her shoulders.

"The Rōjū are no small obstacle. They already wish me dead, and I haven't even challenged them directly yet... Yanagi-san, you have to admit there's a chance that I won't return."

Yanagi swayed his many supple branches from side to side.

"Nonsense, youngling. You are a renowned healer, and an expert at living off the land. How could they ever harm you?"

"Renowned healer?" she asked, unable to focus past his initial point. "I don't see how that's possible, when I've worked so hard to hide my identity for my whole life."

"Amongst humans, of course, but the birds, wolves, and trees know better. So do all the other animals."

"Ha! And what good will that do me?" she asked. "Will the birds and the trees come to my aid, when the Rōjū is hunting me down to kill me?"

"Only if you ask nicely," Yanagi replied.

Taka was dumbfounded. Was Yanagi joking? Would the woodland creatures really move to help her if she needed it? Certainly she had spent the past five cycles healing and helping wherever she could, but—

A sharp cry rent the air, and Taka looked up to the greying light that filtered between the trees. She imitated the keening sound and waited.

Yanagi shuffled to the side of the cave, so as to clear more space overhead, even as Taka stepped forward with her arm raised. A small dark spot above her was growing rapidly larger, even as another keening cry rent the air. A moment later, the sky above her was blotted out entirely, as the smell of warm, damp feathers was pushed into her face in a few frantic bursts of wind and the feel of long talons sank into the leather that wrapped her arm.

"Hello, Riyōshi," she said, as the hawk rubbed his beak against her cheek and nipped her ear.

She didn't bother to express pain. The hawk knew that even that small bite hurt her, but he insisted on the greeting, and, in the cycle that she had enjoyed his company after healing one of his young, she had learned to bear it. The bird conveyed a series of images and feelings to her: strange human, approaching, warning.

"I think my guide may be here," she said to Yanagi.

The tree 'nodded' his branches. "Hmph... rude to arrive early, if you ask me," he grumbled.

Taka nodded, but didn't say anything. She had hoped to have more time with her mentor. More time with Yanagi before she left, more time with Riyōshi, more time in her home.... She sighed.

"I had better prepare my things," she said.

She used the same method of sending images and feelings to ask after Riyōshi's health and that of his family, and when he confirmed that all was well, she bid him farewell. The hawk did not release her arm.

He sent another series of images and emotions.

You seem sad.

She nodded and sent back, *I must go on a journey. Unsure when I'll return.*

Riyōshi looked at her momentarily and then flew off without bidding her farewell. Taka tried to blink back tears. Would all the animals she knew feel so betrayed? Certainly Riyōshi was the animal she felt closest to, the one animal who seemed to visit her solely for her company, or to exchange news, but how many others would be so hurt that they didn't even wish her a safe journey?

Yanagi moved slowly away from the cave, in the strange way that he had. Even after five cycles, it never ceased to amaze Taka to see a tree walk.

"I will let you pack your things," he said. "I will return in time to say farewell."

Taka turned towards her cave, telling herself that it was the rain that now soaked her clothing that made her tremble, not the way that Riyōshi had left. She had barely started assembling the few items she would bring with her when she heard a soft slapping against the wet rock behind her. She stood and spun round, the long bone knife she had been in the process of packing clutched tightly in her right hand.

"You'd better put that away before you hurt yourself," said a voice she didn't recognize.

A tall man wearing leathers much like her own stood in the opening to her cavern. As he was blocking most of the light from the entrance, and her fire was burning low, she couldn't make out the details of his features from where she stood.

"And who are you?" she asked, making no move to put away her knife.

"The guide that's been sent to escort some wayward girl across the mountains."

Wayward girl? She shifted her stance slightly in case she decided to use the knife she held.

That caused the man to raise one eyebrow at her, and Taka's shift in position changed the balance in light so that she could see more of his face. The man had eyes that were the greenish blue of a juniper tree. The rest of his face looked weathered and displeased, and it had clearly been a few tendays since he had bothered shaving. She was surprised to see that, despite the facial hair, he looked little older than she was, a few cycles older at most. Tsuku-san had assured her that the guide she was sending was experienced and reliable, someone she had been trusting to convey messages between herself and Kuma-sensei for cycles…

"I see our visitor has arrived," came Yanagi's voice from behind the young man, "and is polite as ever."

"How am I being impolite?" the young man asked.

"Taka is not prone to drawing knives on her guests, so I can only assume that you've said something to offend her, Mitsu-san."

The young man turned to Yanagi and opened his mouth to respond, but Taka interrupted him.

"Mitsu-san? Yanagi-sensei, do you know this man?"

Yanagi's branches swayed forward and back in assent.

"Yes, Taka-san, I'm afraid so. Though I'm surprised that this is the guide you were sent," he said.

"Why are you surprised?" she asked, ignoring the fact that Mitsu had opened his mouth to speak.

"Because I was unaware that he was acquainted with your new allies."

Taka nodded. "And how is it that you know him, precisely?" she asked.

"Hmm…" Yanagi eyed Mitsu speculatively and waved his branches noncommittally. "I'm afraid to say I raised him."

Mitsu made a noise of protest, as though he found this whole conversation objectionable, but Taka ignored him.

"Raised him? How is that possible? I thought you hadn't trained anyone for a hundred cycles?"

"Hmph… I haven't. I didn't train him. I raised him." Yanagi shifted his gaze between Mitsu and Taka. "But it's his story to tell, and you've days of travel ahead of you, so I won't bore you with it now. Are you ready to leave, Taka-chan?"

Mitsu seemed to have resigned himself to glaring at both of them, and Taka cleared her throat.

"I'll be ready soon. Perhaps you two would like to catch up…" she suggested as she turned back to her belongings.

Mitsu stepped away from the mouth of the cave with Yanagi, but spoke over his shoulder as he did so.

"Remember not to pack too much, princess. I'll not be carrying your bags for you."

Taka didn't bother to respond, but she might have sheathed her knife a little too forcefully as she returned it to its belt and strapped it on. She tried to focus on her breathing, the way she would if she were about to heal a patient, but her worries were multiplying. Not only was she off to pin all of her hopes for revenge on a Kisōshi she'd never met, she was now forced to travel with a coarse imbecile who called her princess. She tried to think calming thoughts as she organized the few belongings she planned to take with her. Inevitably, her mind returned to a thought that wasn't exactly peaceful, but somehow always calmed her: she thought of Mishi, and wondered where she was now.

21日 10月，老中 1119年

≋ Taka ≋

WOULD SHE REALLY have to put up with this for a full tenday? Their pace was grueling, and the trail they followed grew ever steeper and rockier, but none of that bothered Taka, even as they climbed over rugged, rocky outcrops and through dense forest. She was well used to the terrain and even the pace. She had needed to cover many hundreds of leagues in her five cycle search for Tsuku-san, and she had always held herself to a relentless speed. Nor was she bothered by the sting of the autumn air that filled her lungs as they pushed further into the mountains. The smell of pine needles that tinged the cooling air and permeated her every breath was soothing, rather than troublesome. What bothered her was the tactless oaf a few paces ahead of her who was constantly turning around to make sure she wasn't lagging behind, insisting on calling her princess, and sarcastically offering her a foot rub every time they took a break, even though she hadn't spoken a single word of complaint.

If she'd known how to get to her destination without the help of this 'guide,' she would have long since thrown him off one of the ever more frequent cliff ledges they traversed and continued on without him. Or, at the very least, she would have pulled ahead of him and shown him that his pace was not even pushing her to the full extent of her stamina. Yet there was no point in pulling ahead of him when she wasn't sure of their destination. Tsuku-san had shown her a map while she was still a guest at the woman's house, but all Taka knew was that the school was over a hundred leagues southeast of her cavern home. She would have had no difficulty finding her way there over roads, and she even could have made it there over mountains by herself, given enough time, but it would have taken her over a moon without the help of her guide; or so Tsuku-san had insisted when she had promised to send the man to her.

Now, as she walked behind the man and resisted the urge to step directly behind him and walk on his heels, she wondered if his presence was really worth the shorter trip. Tsuku-san had insisted that Mitsu was a valuable ally, not just as a guide but also as protection. Taka had found no argument against that. Yanagi-sensei had taught her many things; she could hunt, she could use a knife to clean game, and with the forest to aid her she could defend herself to some degree, but she had never been trained to fight. She had focused on healing instead. And wasn't that the whole reason she was being sent to this mysterious Kuma-sensei? To bring fighters to her cause? Not only had Kuma-sensei been planning to overthrow the Rōjū for some time, but according to Tsuku-san he was a highly ranked Kisōshi with a band of loyal Kisōshi at his disposal.

Taka sighed, as her thoughts strayed to all that lay ahead of her and how much was still uncertain, and then instantly regretted it. Mitsu heard the noise and took the opportunity to chide her.

"Are we tired, princess? Shall we rest?"

Taka wondered for the hundredth time since beginning their journey the day before if this man was deliberately trying to provoke her, or simply had no idea who or what she was. *Probably both,* she decided.

"I regret that your memory is insufficient to the task of recalling that I am not a princess, and I must insist, no matter how exhausted your little twig legs might be, that we continue."

She saw the smirk falter on Mitsu's stubbled face and thought that perhaps the twig legs remark had struck home.

"Is this the best pace we can make?" she asked, when Mitsu said nothing.

Mitsu raised an eyebrow at her and turned back toward the trail. The gap between them briefly grew, as he sped forward, and Taka smiled inwardly. She could go faster, and if the man had no breath to insult her, perhaps they might make it through their travels after all.

~~~

Later that day, they came to a small clearing by a creek and Mitsu spoke for the first time since that morning.

"Rest here a bit, princess. I'll be back soon," he said.

Taka was determined to ignore the fact that he continued to call her princess.

"Where are you going?" she asked, as he turned away from her and began walking into the nearby woods.

"Hunting," he said, without looking over his shoulder.

Taka rose to follow him.

"I said, stay here." Mitsu turned on her suddenly as he spoke.

"I can hunt," Taka said, clenching and unclenching her fists. "I can help."

The corner of Mitsu's mouth curved into a humorless smirk.

"You can help by staying here and out of my way," he said.

Taka's hand slid to the hilt of the knife in her belt and her fingers flexed, but she resisted the temptation. She was a healer, not a cutthroat. She was startled that she'd had to remind herself of that. Mitsu stalked off to the woods, and Taka returned to the creekside to refill her water skin and enjoy the sensation of the sun on her face contrasting with the chill breeze of the mountains.

She had already had to shift once, chasing the sun to the next boulder that was big enough to lie on, when she heard a distant scream. She was on her feet at once. The sound had come from the direction Mitsu had traveled, but farther to the north. She grabbed her pack and water skein and moved into the woods.

Taka would never have found him if she hadn't stumbled across a raven who had moved on after deciding that the creature scrabbling about on the forest floor didn't look likely to die anytime that same day. Luckily, since the raven wasn't concerned about preserving a meal, it was willing to communicate where she would find him. Taka was both relieved by the news that the crow thought him likely to live, and annoyed that Mitsu had managed to get himself injured when they were barely beginning their journey. She hoped it was something that she could heal quickly.

When she finally came to the small cliff ledge and looked down, she grimaced at the state of him. The raven had been right. He wasn't bound to die in the next day, probably not even the next week, but left untended those wounds could kill him. Mitsu lay at the base of a cliff that was only twice the height of a tall man, and his ankle jutted awkwardly away from his body, his leg clearly broken. Taka grimaced as she noted the large piece of rock to the left of where he lay, newly broken from the cliff. She began the careful work of descending a cliff she now knew to be crumbling apart.

"Don't!" she heard a soft wail behind her and shook her head. "The rock's loose," Mitsu continued.

"I can see that," Taka replied, without pausing in her descent. She hadn't spent five cycles living in her mountain valley and traveling without roads in search of Tsuku-san without learning a few things about getting over and around cliff faces. This one was just small enough for her to consider climbing (or in this case descending) it rather than finding a way around it. Anything taller and she wouldn't have done it. Still, even from this height, one could suffer an injury if something unexpected happened, as Mitsu had proven quite spectacularly. Testing every hold for her hands and feet before transferring her weight to them, she made her way to the bottom of the cliff band.

"We shouldn't both get stuck here," Mitsu muttered, through clenched teeth.

Taka only managed to keep herself from laughing by taking a good look at the man's leg. The leg was no laughing matter.

"I won't get stuck here, Mitsu-san," she said, as she began pulling some of her healer's kit out of her pack. "And, luckily for you, I've no intention of letting you be stuck here either."

She examined the contents of her pack and decided they would do. Or she hoped they would. It depended on how much additional damage there was beyond what had been done to the bone. She took out her knife and reached for Mitsu's pant leg.

"What are you doing?" he asked and started to flinch away, a move that clearly caused him a great deal of pain.

"I am going to heal you, if you'll hold still and avoid injuring yourself further," she said, as mildly as she could, reaching once more for his pant leg.

Again he shifted away from her, and again his face contorted in a way that suggested he was likely to vomit from pain.

"I'm not pregnant," he grunted between attempts to bite his own lip. "Nor am I suffering moonpains."

Taka had to remind herself that she needed the man to get across the mountains quickly, but it took effort not to just stand up and walk away from him.

"Can you heal it?" she asked.

"What?" Mitsu's face was a cross between pain and confusion.

"Can you heal it yourself?" she persisted. "You know, mend the bone, stop the bleeding... walk away?"

Mitsu shook his head.

"Of course not," he said. "No one can do that. Not even the Rōjū council's personal healers."

Taka took a deep breath and began the work of centering herself needed in order to heal Mitsu before dark.

"I don't know what the Rōjū Council's healers are capable of," she said, working to keep her breathing even. "But I can heal you enough that you can walk away. Carefully, mind you, it won't be completely healed for a matter of days, but if you don't do anything stupid it will be good as new in a few days' time."

Mitsu's eyes widened and she thought it unlikely that he would believe her. In this case she doubted it was just personal prejudice. It had been made clear to her on more than one occasion during her time at the Josankō that what she could do surpassed even what the instructors could do, healer or josanpu. She shrugged as she focused her power inwards, then reached for his leg once more.

"No, don't!" he said.

"Oh go to sleep!" she replied, touching his leg anyway and using her kisō to render him unconscious.

Taka sighed. It wasn't uncommon for her to have to sedate her patients, especially when she worked with animals, but it wasted valuable kisō if the subject was rational enough to remain calm. Clearly that wasn't going to be an option here. She used her knife to cut away the pant leg on Mitsu's left leg and, as she was able to see more of the wound, was suddenly glad that she had rendered the man unconscious. This was going to be difficult.

She had thought, initially, that the break might have been largely the result of falling at an unexpected angle, but she saw now that his shin had been at least partially crushed by the rock.

Once more she focused her kisō, and this time, through the contact of her hand on his leg, she willed it outward, into Mitsu, water drawn to water, searching out his blood and following it through his system, in order to look beneath the surface of his skin and sense what needed to be done. It wasn't as bad as it could have been. The bone had been partially crushed by the rock, but the bone shards were fairly large, and there weren't as many of them as there could have been. The majority of the bone was still whole. Also, he'd been lucky, and no major blood vessels had been torn. She had her work cut out for her, and they would need to spend the night here, but she could have him walking by tomorrow.

She focused her breathing, pulled on the depths of her fuchi, brought up a flow of kisō, and began to work.

~~~

It was fortunate that Mitsu had at least succeeded in catching a largish hare before falling from the cliff face. She supposed that he had been on his way back to where he had left her when he had suffered the misfortune of using a loose chunk of rock for a hand or foot hold. She had found the hare within a few feet of the man after she'd finished the healing, and she'd been grateful. It had been dark by the time she was done, and she would have been too exhausted to go hunt for their evening meal anyway. They still had plenty of dried rations to choose from, of course, but after that much healing she was in desperate need of a real meal. She'd left Mitsu sleeping to go collect firewood and then had come back to roast the hare.

When Mitsu woke, Taka was already enjoying a large hare leg and warming herself by the fire. The man blinked and rubbed his eyes a few times before speaking.

"What did you... I dreamt I'd fallen from a cliff," he said.

Taka took another bite of rabbit and decided to give him a moment to orient himself before speaking. He stared at his leg for a moment. The bloody shreds of his leather leggings contrasted with the soft white of the silken bandages that Taka had used to wrap his ankle and lower leg.

"I can't move my ankle," he said after a moment.

"That's because I've wrapped it tightly enough to stop you from moving it. It needs to set overnight before you'll be able to walk on it."

Mitsu looked from her to his leg once more. She could see the moment when he realized that the amount of blood on his pant leg confirmed that he hadn't dreamt any of it.

"It would be cruel to pretend that this will heal completely," he said after a long pause.

Taka nodded, "I agree. To pretend that it would heal would indeed be cruel, but as I told you before, as long as you don't do anything stupid to it, it will be back to normal in a few days."

"How did you find me?" he asked, taking Taka by surprise. Of all the things she expected him to ask, that wasn't at the top of the list.

"I heard you scream when you fell," she said. "That gave me the general direction. Then I was lucky enough to run into a disappointed raven."

"What?"

"A raven who was willing to tell me where he'd seen a meal he wasn't willing to wait around for."

Mitsu leaned up against the tree that Taka had propped him under while he was still asleep, and shook his head.

"None of this makes any sense," he muttered.

Taka shrugged, but didn't bother explaining.

"Would you like some hare?" she asked, instead.

Mitsu nodded, and Taka took that as a good sign. She must have done a good job managing the pain if he had an appetite already. That boded well for his recovery. With any luck, they'd be able to continue their journey the following day.

She cut the man a chunk of hare and passed him a water skein as well. She let the corners of her mouth curve upwards in a moment of smug satisfaction, though she said nothing.

Let him try to call me princess now, she thought, as she stared into the depths of the fire.

25日 10月, 老中 1119年

≈ Mishi ≈

ON THE SECOND to last day of their journey, Mishi's thoughts had begun to loop around the plan that she would soon have to enact and the many problems that might arise as she did so. For the previous tenday she had managed not to let her mind fall into that trap.

Mishi had hoped, after the awkwardness of conversation on the first day of the trip, that Katagi would leave her in peace for most of the journey. She had hoped in vain. He had barely paused for breath over the past tenday, as they rode slowly towards Rōjū City. Mishi had learned more than she cared to know about the boy—she couldn't bring herself to consider him a man, 17th birthday or no—than she had ever cared to. Yet over the past few days, despite her best efforts to focus on the slowly changing scenery, despite the kata she practiced in her head as a distraction, she was all too aware of what Katagi thought of her sisters, Kuma-sensei, Tenshi-san, and even each of the horses in the school stable. She knew how many siblings he had, and how much his parents were hanging on the outcome of this first test of rank, and what he would do in various testing scenarios once he was in front of the Rōjū council. Despite her best efforts to ignore him, the boy had waited for her replies, so she had been forced to listen and speak or risk appearing insufferably rude (something a servant would never do). She had kept herself entertained through the onslaught by imagining some of the more violent ways that she might get Katagi to stop speaking.

Today, though, her thoughts had turned to the possible failings of her and Kuma-sensei's plan. Katagi had been blissfully silent through most of the day's journey, but when they were only a league or so away from

140

the ryokan where they would be staying their final night on the road, he interrupted her reverie once more.

"Are you alright, Mishi-san? You seem troubled."

She reflected for a moment before speaking. She was troubled. She knew that her cover was a fairly easy one to keep, as long as she could remain close to Katagi and act the servant, but once she made her move for the documents...what then? If she were caught near her ultimate goal, would her cover be believed? It was one thing to be caught as a disobedient and overly curious servant, but it was quite another to be unveiled as a female Kisōshi in the depths of the lions' den. If she were caught by a Kisōshi, he might be able to sense her kisō and know what she was. She was able to mask her kisō most of the time, but if she had to use it in order to find the scrolls.... One of the benefits of her cover as Katagi's servant was not only getting into the compound, but masking her own kisō from others should she need to use it; in his presence, anyone who could sense kisō would assume that the power was his. If she had to use her kisō outside of his company... the risk of ruining her cover would be great.

She sighed, as she pulled herself away from those thoughts and sought some explanation for her apparent concern.

"I was merely thinking, Katagi-san."

"Well you seemed quite... distracted. Do you mind if I ask what you were thinking about?"

Of course she did, but she couldn't very well tell him that.

"I was just thinking of how nervous I would be if I were about to be tested before the Rōjū," she lied. "Aren't you worried?"

Katagi smiled briefly, then frowned.

"A bit, actually. More than I would care to admit. I have been going over kata in my head night after night, and I keep thinking that I'm missing moves...even on the most basic kata that I've known for cycles."

Mishi nodded. She knew that sensation well, though of course she couldn't say so. Testing for Kuma-sensei made her nervous enough to forget kata that she'd practiced since childhood.

"That sounds frustrating," was the only safe thing she could think to say.

"Indeed it is. I can't help but think that no matter what I do, I'll fail and be told that I am a disgrace to Kisōshi, and my family, and that my parents will disown me, and I will have nothing left to do but commit seppuku and be done with it."

Mishi grimaced. She hardly thought that ritual suicide was a reasonable response to failing a test, but she hoped that Katagi was exaggerating.

"Just the other night," he continued in a harried voice, "I had a dream that I was performing my kata before the Rōjū council and everything was going quite well, when suddenly, I was no longer wearing hakama! I had to run from the testing floor and pull my uwagi down over my buttocks as I ran!"

Mishi couldn't help but laugh. She didn't want to make Katagi feel any worse, and indeed his facial expression was one of true horror, but the image in her head was just too comical to ignore.

Thankfully, Katagi began to laugh as well.

"I suppose it is rather humorous," he admitted between chuckles. "But it was terrifying the other night."

Mishi had to gasp for the breath necessary for speech, and her ribs were beginning to ache from laughing so hard.

"I can imagine," she said, when she had finally collected enough air. "It would be truly horrifying if it happened in real life. But you have to admit that as a dream, it's quite funny for anyone who didn't have to experience it themselves. Besides, let's be honest, if all you have to worry about for this test is your pants vanishing mysteriously, then you're probably quite well prepared."

Katagi chuckled again, and some of the worry seemed to lift from his frame.

"You make a good point. I suppose my mind may be trying to tell me that I am sufficiently prepared and should stop worrying."

He paused for a moment as though considering something serious.

"But what would I do if my pants really did disappear in the middle of a kata? Suppose that's part of the test?"

Mishi's laughter roared forth once more at the sincere look of concern on Katagi's face.

"If that's part of the test," she said when she could speak once more, "then you should simply stand tall at the end of your kata and state that you felt you needed two swords instead of one."

The laughter that followed had both of them almost falling from their horses, even as they pulled up to the ryokan where they would stay their final night on the road, and the two companions were blind to the stares they drew from a group of young Kisōshi who had arrived only moments before them, while they led their horses to stable still chuckling.

~~~

Mishi's hands trembled as she groomed the horses in the predawn light, and she worked to keep her mind from repeating the same litany of thoughts about what could go wrong with the plan that had kept her from sleeping through most of the night.

It was only when she started to groom the horses a second time, simply to keep her hands busy, that she noticed that Katagi had not yet arrived at the stable. She had taken longer than usual with the horses, because she knew they would soon be under the scrutiny of the Eihei, the Rōjū City's private guards, and consequently she had taken extreme care with their grooming this morning. Katagi should have been here by now.

Rōjū City closed its gates at sundown, and if Katagi wasn't ready soon they would have to ride very hard indeed to arrive in time. And if they had to ride the horses hard all day, they were bound to undo all of the careful grooming she had just done. She went back into the ryokan in search of Katagi.

She found him inside his room with his head underneath his futon, his knees on the tatami, and his backside in the air. He resembled a large flightless bird that Mishi had once seen in a scroll of exotic animals in Tenshi-san's library.

"Katagi-san, what in the name of all the Kami are you doing?" she asked.

"I camt goh," came the muffled reply from beneath the futon.

Mishi stood at the door torn between laughter and rage. She chose laughter, because killing him would ruin her cover.

"And why is that, Katagi-san?" she asked, over her own amusement.

He finally removed himself from underneath the futon.

"Because I am going to fail. I am certain of it. I will not pass. I'll be sent home in disgrace and my parents will be forced to disown me. I'll have to commit seppuku."

Mishi watched him deflate as he spoke each word, and she was beginning to worry that she would have to drag him all the way to Rōjū City. She wasn't worried about carrying him, she was sure she could manage it, but he would no doubt struggle and cause a scene, and she could neither afford the time nor the energy that it would take to force him onto his horse. She briefly considered leaving him behind.

"That's not true, Katagi-san," she said, before she could give into temptation and walk away from him to find her own way into the city. "I'm sure Kuma-sensei would never have sent you to the Rōjū council for testing if he didn't think you were prepared. Do you really believe that he wishes to be the laughing stock of all the other Kisōshi because he sent an incompetent to test?"

Katagi eyed her and looked hopeful for a moment, but then collapsed once more.

"When he sent me on my way I knew what I was doing, but now I've forgotten everything. EVERYTHING. I don't know any kata. I got up early this morning to train and I started doing my first bokken kata, the very first and... I couldn't remember it. Not even the first move. My mind is blank. I've lost everything."

Mishi knew that laughing would shatter Katagi's already fragile ego, but it was still a struggle to keep herself in check. She thought about slapping him, but decided to try more words first. She knelt so that she was closer to eye level with him.

"We are nearly there, Katagi-san. We have one day of travel before us, and then it will be time for you to test. It is daunting, to be sure, but it is what you have been training for your whole life. Is there a chance that you will fail? Certainly. But if you don't go, you will have already failed. Imagine that, Katagi-san. Imagine the shame of returning to your family to tell them that you never even arrived at Rōjū City. What would they say to you then? There is no shame in doing your very best and awaiting the outcome, Katagi-san, but think of the shame in being too afraid to try."

With that, she turned on her heel and returned to the horses in the stable. She had to get away from the boy before she lost her temper. Was he a Kisōshi or wasn't he? He was testing for his rank; the worst that could happen would be to have to test again the following cycle. She was risking her life! Did he find her hiding under her futon this morning? *Baka!* she thought. *Show some courage.*

She took the horses into the courtyard and fought the urge to leave without him. Already her brain worked to devise some plan that would gain her entrance to the compound without Katagi. She wouldn't let his cowardice keep her from her own mission. She would—

Katagi walked out of the ryokan and came to take his horse's reins from her hand.

"Thank you, Mishi-san," he said.

She didn't know if he meant for the horses, or the talking to, but she wasn't about to ask questions. If they rode steadily and didn't take many breaks, they would reach the gates of Rōjū City just before sundown.

~~~

They were only a few leagues outside of Rōjū City when they overtook a group of six young Kisōshi on the road, centered around a single figure in a bright red and black kimono. Mishi was just wondering why the group looked familiar, when one of the Kisōshi called out to them.

"Ah, if it isn't the laughing Kisōshi and his faithful servant," the young Kisōshi called out.

One or two of the other Kisōshi chuckled briefly at the comment, but most of them didn't bother looking away from the figure in the black and red kimono, who was animatedly telling a story.

"You remember, Kusuko-san," said that first Kisōshi, "the ones who stayed at the ryokan with us last night?"

Now Mishi remembered why the group looked familiar. They had walked past them entering the stables the night before. They must have left while Mishi had been collecting Katagi from his room, and stayed ahead of them all day.

Mishi wondered why the Kisōshi would make such a fuss over laughter. Did they never laugh with their friends?

"Ah yes, his *servant* the giantess..." said another young Kisōshi.

Mishi's fists clenched on the reins of her horse at the way the man said the word servant. What was he implying? Then she realized that he'd called her a giantess, and blood rushed to her face. Her sisters constantly teased her for her height, but she mostly forgot about it when they weren't busy poking fun at her. It wasn't something most other people commented on, though she occasionally heard it whispered behind a hand or fan when she passed through a market square. She was taller than any other woman she'd met, taller, even, than most men.

Mishi kept her eyes on her horse and rode in silence, desperately trying to keep any more heat from rushing to her cheeks and neck, causing her further embarrassment. Just as she expected all eyes to be on her and someone to comment on how she was turning as red as a mountain beet, Katagi's voice rang out over the group.

"Are you so easily intimidated by the stature of a woman?" he asked the Kisōshi who had made the giantess comment. "How *small* a man are you, that such a thing frightens you?"

Mishi continued to stare at her horse, but she smiled inwardly. She thought those were big words coming from a man who had been hiding his head under his futon only this morning, but she still appreciated Katagi's attempt to come to her defense.

The Kisōshi who had made the giantess comment turned in his saddle and moved his arm to his katana, but the Kisōshi who had originally called out to them maneuvered his horse between the two of them before the first one could draw his blade.

"I'm sorry, my friend has a bad sense of humor," he said. "We're traveling to the Rōjū City for our second test of rank, and some of us are nervous."

Mishi could tell that the man was simply trying to placate them, which she thought was interesting since Katagi was an as of yet untested Kisōshi, while all of them had already past their first test of rank. Did he think Katagi somehow posed a threat, despite the fact that he traveled alone with only a single servant?

"Iwama-san here has forgotten how to be courteous to servants, since we sent all of ours ahead to prepare our quarters for us. All except for Kusuko-san here, who we have kept to entertain us with her stories," he continued jovially.

"I'm Saito," he said, after a pause in which neither Katagi nor Mishi said anything. "Please, join our group. We should make the gates with time to spare before sunset."

Mishi hoped that Katagi would refuse, but knew that there was no polite way of doing so, now that they knew they shared a destination.

"Pleased to meet you Saito-san," Katagi replied. "I'm Kazeki, and this is..." Katagi hesitated for a moment, and Mishi realized that they'd come to another awkward moment caused by her presence. Saito had introduced himself with his family name, so Katagi had done the same, but now he was left in awkward silence. As an orphan, Mishi didn't have a family name. In truth, she now knew her family name, but it would be suicidal to tell it to anyone.

"Koji," she said quietly, hoping no one would notice. It was more subtle than explaining that she was an orphan, but barely.

"Koji-san," Katagi repeated lamely, as his cheeks reddened slightly at his own blunder.

"It's a pleasure to meet you both," Saito said. "We're all traveling from Ushiomachi."

Mishi tuned out the conversation of the two young men, now that it was clearly focused on trivialities and no longer likely to break out in violence, allowing her mind to wander as she took in the passing scenery. Every now and again, the porcelain skinned woman wearing the red and black kimono, Kusuko-san, Saito had said, let out a high pitched giggle that distracted Mishi from her enjoyment of the mountains that lined the valley and drew closer together as they neared Rōjū City.

The peaks in the distance reminded her of Tatsu's mountain, and made her miss her mentor. She had gone to visit him briefly before leaving for this trip, but this was the first time since she had started her training with him five cycles ago that she hadn't visited him at least once in a tenday. She felt the absence keenly. Suddenly, she was very aware that if

146

things went poorly on this mission, she would never see Tatsu again. Somehow, that possibility made the prospect of death seem more real to her than anything else had. She had begun to contemplate why that might be, when she was suddenly drawn from her reverie by the view that appeared before them as they came around a curve in the road.

The mountains had narrowed over the past few leagues and funneled them into a steep valley, so that the rolling green slopes topped in rocky peaks had now become walls on either side of them, rather than just grey obstacles in the distance. But as they came around this last turn, the tight valley opened slightly, revealing a chain of multistory buildings with intricately decorated swooping roofs, connected by delicate looking bridges over a series of small gorges, canals, and rivers, all shrouded in a fine mist.

Mishi snapped her mouth closed as Kusuko pulled her horse forward into a light trot, towards the gate that nestled in the large stone wall that circled the city.

"Welcome to Rōjū City," she called over her shoulder, as she rode ahead.

26日 10月, 老中 1119年

≈ Mishi ≈

MISHI KNELT BEHIND Katagi and tried not to fidget, blush, sweat, or otherwise give away her current emotional state. She took a deep breath, in an attempt to calm herself, and found that it only made things worse. The tang of sweat and anxiety coming from Katagi and herself mixed with the scents of the tatami touching her forehead, the scent of the hundred strangers that filled the enormous room, and a bite in the air like a summer storm, which threatened to overwhelm her.

She had managed to hold herself together admirably as they had ridden through the gate to Rōjū City the day before; back straight, head inclined in the proper deference of a servant, leading both her horse and Katagi's, with him still astride, as she presented their papers to the Eihei that manned the gate.... But that had been a single Kisōshi inspecting them, and they'd had the benefit of a crowd of Kisōshi riding with them, all of whom were well known to the Rōjū City guard. Only one person to fool into believing that she was simply a servant and needed no additional inspection, an easy feat when surrounded by a group of Kisōshi that were already fooled. The man had paid more attention to the pedigree of the horses and the make of Katagi's sword than he had to her, and she hadn't even felt a moment of discomfort as they were assigned to their guest quarters and told they would be presented the following morning.

Now, as she knelt with her head bowed to the floor, under the gaze of hundreds of eyes, with a physical hum of kisō vibrating in the room due to the presence of so many Kisōshi gathered in a single place—and with no more than her own dampening and Katagi's kisō register to protect her—she nearly retched with the sense of vulnerability that enfolded her. She swallowed, and hoped that having her face to the floor would keep most people from noticing how nervous she was.

"Kazeki Katagi-san, and his servant," said the voice of the guard who had escorted them in.

Mishi's breathing hitched briefly at the mention of her position, but her name wasn't even given. She worked to even out her breathing. After shoring up her effort to dampen her kisō, she listened to the litany of Katagi's ancestry that he was required to recite for the Rōjū in attendance. His voice was strong and steady as he listed the long line of Kisōshi that had eventually led to his conception, and she thought that he seemed much less terrified today than yesterday. As she relaxed, her mind ran over the details of the hall they had entered. Like the rest of the city, the Rōjū audience chamber was larger than necessary and excessively ornate. The solid oak doors that they had passed through had been several times the height of a man, and thicker than Mishi was wide, not to mention carved with intricate reliefs of animals and landscapes. The chamber within had a ceiling even taller than the doors, and was large enough to host hundreds of onlookers, while still leaving ample space in the center for petitioners, or Kisōshi being examined, or those introducing themselves and reciting their lineage. Mishi hadn't had much time to take in the details of the room before she had knelt to the tatami behind Katagi-san, and she was thankful that she was required to remain with her head to the floor for the remainder of his introduction. As far as she was concerned, there was no safe place to let her gaze linger in this room, between the dais at the front of the room playing host to all the members of the Rōjū council, and the legions of visiting Kisōshi seated in the raised benches that lined both walls of the giant chamber...

A small flicker of kisō brushed past her then, and she clamped down on all of her musings. A shiver crawled over her, and the temptation to look into the crowd and find the pair of eyes that had been scanning her along with that tendril of kisō was almost overwhelming. Fear of discovery made her stomach clench and her chest constrict. She stared steadfastly at the tatami in front of her and made a point of counting individual strands of straw.

She felt no more flickers of power, beyond the hum that permeated the room, for the remainder of Katagi's introduction. When it was at last over, she shakily got to her feet behind her 'master' and followed him out of the great hall with her head bent and her shoulders bowed. She was almost to the door when she felt one last flicker of another's kisō pass over her. Before she even realized what she was doing, she looked over her shoulder to try to catch the eyes of whoever had scanned her. She saw a hint of motion in the crowd, someone turning their head away, although from this distance she couldn't even tell if it was a man or a woman. Silently cursing herself for looking and possibly drawing attention to herself, she instantly crouched to the floor as though searching for something.

Katagi appeared at her shoulder.

"Are you alright, Mishi-san?" he asked. His voice sounded constricted and Mishi wondered if the kisō that permeated the room made him feel as nervous and lightheaded as it did her.

"I dropped my fan," she replied, using a small sleight of hand to appear as though she'd picked it up from the floor beneath her kimono. "I'm sorry, Katagi-san," she said, bowing to cover her anxiety. "We should go."

Katagi nodded and preceded her out the door. Mishi kept her eyes ahead this time, and hoped that whoever had sent that tendril of kisō out to her hadn't noticed her reaction.

~~~

A single night of rest in their guest quarters had not accustomed Mishi to their size. Katagi's room was as large as a training room at Kuma-sensei's school, and the servants' quarters attached to it were still twice as large as her sleeping chamber at the school. The added space made her feel strangely vulnerable.

She had just finished laying out Katagi's uwagi and hakama for the following day, complete with obi, katana, and wakizashi, which she had spent a good portion of her morning cleaning. She was gratified to see that he had cleaned the blades himself over the course of their trip. If he was worth anything as a Kisōshi, he'd be sure to clean them again tonight, just to make sure she had done it properly. His test wasn't for another few days, since Kisōshi who had traveled for multiple days were granted some time to rest from their travels and prepare, but she expected him to keep them in the best possible condition in the days leading up to his exam.

She returned to her own quarters and slid closed the door that led to the hallway. A moment later she heard a soft call from the same door.

"Yes? Come in," she called.

She had expected to see Katagi open the door, perhaps wanting to clarify some detail of the plans for tomorrow, or to ask her if she knew where some article of his clothing or equipment was. The high-pitched giggle that emitted from the doorway therefore surprised her.

"Good evening, Mishi-san, is it?" the high-pitched voice said.

The face that accompanied the giggle belonged to a young woman not much older than herself, dressed in a bright pink kimono, and hiding half of a round and high-cheekboned face behind a gilded butterfly fan, dazzling emerald eyes peeking out above it.

"Yes," Mishi replied, frowning. The girl looked familiar, but with only half her face visible behind the fan, she wasn't sure from where.

She couldn't pinpoint what bothered her about the girl—perhaps the pervasiveness of the pink in her kimono? Another high pitched giggle came from the doorway, and Mishi thought she might be narrowing in on the problem.

"I'm Kusuko. I'm serving on this floor too. We traveled together briefly yesterday. I thought I should come and introduce myself, now that you're settled in."

If the other girl hadn't followed that statement with yet another giggle, Mishi might have appreciated the gesture more.

Now that the girl had mentioned it, she recognized her as the young woman in the red and black kimono who had been traveling with the group of Kisōshi they'd met on the road the day before. Mishi tried to smile at the girl, but worried that it had come off as more of a grimace.

"How kind of you," she said, so as not to have to hurt her face with false affability. "Are you here with another Kisōshi testing for rank?"

Kusuko giggled again.

"Of course," she said.

Mishi nodded, as she tried to fathom what the girl found so constantly amusing. She had been forced to dine alone in the servants' kitchens the night before, but she wasn't sure she was lonely enough to appreciate this girl's company. She tried to think of a way to excuse herself.

"I... I was just going to set out my master's robe for his bath," she said, gathering Katagi's robe and stepping toward the doorway. When Kusuko didn't move, she added, "You'll have to excuse me. I must place this in his room."

Instead of moving, the girl let out another series of high pitched giggles, even more enthusiastic than the first.

"Why go this way?" she asked. "It takes too long, and it is so indiscreet. You should use your connecting door."

"My what?" Mishi asked.

Kusuko stepped into Mishi's room and crossed to the adjacent wall, where she lifted up a light silk tapestry depicting swans on a still pond.

"Here," she said, sliding open what had been, until a moment ago, a perfectly concealed door.

"For convenience," she added, raising her eyebrows up and down and bursting into another fit of giggles.

Mishi stared at the other girl as her meaning slowly eked into the edges of her understanding. Was she suggesting... could she possibly mean that... that she and Katagi were... that her purpose in being here was... IYAAADA! She almost screamed the word aloud and threw Katagi's robe against the wall in disgust, but she managed to restrain herself. Her mission depended on not attracting attention. If this girl thought that she was a courtesan instead of a servant, so be it. She coughed to regain her voice.

"Thank you," she said with attempted equanimity. "This will be very useful in case I need to reach my master in an emergency."

She tried to move back towards the door to the hallway again, hoping that it would encourage the other girl to leave.

"I'm sure there will be plenty of 'emergencies' between now and when you leave, ne?" Kusuko asked, giggling once more.

Mishi inhaled deeply and only imagined collapsing the other girl's windpipe, instead of actually doing it.

"If you'll excuse me, I still have work to do."

"Me too!" Kusuko replied, smiling and winking at Mishi before she left the room in a fit of giggles.

Mishi left her room at the same time and went to lay out Katagi's robe for his bath. As she made a point of returning to her room through the hallway, she shuddered at the thought that anyone, or possibly everyone, in this city expected her to have sex with Katagi.

~~~

Mishi woke the next morning feeling more relaxed than she had in days. If all went well, she would not appear before the Rōjū again for the duration of their stay. In three days, Katagi would complete his test, an event that thankfully did not require Mishi's presence. At that time, with the majority of the Kisōshi residing at the compound engaged in testing, either as participants or spectators, she would attempt to acquire the Rōjū Scroll. In the intervening days, today included, her job was simply to acquaint herself with as much of the city as she could, in order to facilitate both the acquisition of the scroll and her escape afterwards.

After checking Katagi's rooms and finding that he had already departed for his morning meal with the other visiting Kisōshi, she made her way to the servants' commons, in search of her own morning meal.

Unfortunately, not long after she sat down, she heard a soft giggling to her right and turned to see Kusuko sit beside her.

"My, but I am tired from last night," she sighed, before erupting in another fit of giggles. When Mishi said nothing in response, the other girl continued.

"Aren't you tired, Mishi-san? I saw your man last night as he exited the baths... I bet he could keep a girl up for hours and hours, ne!" Kusuko seemed unable to resist her own humor and suffered yet another fit of laughter. Some of the other men and women nearby began to chuckle along with her.

Mishi kept her eyes locked onto her miso soup and began counting the ways in which a giggling courtesan might accidentally die between here and her quarters. She said nothing.

"Ah..." Kusuko continued. "So it takes more than that to tire you out, does it? Understandable. I sometimes find that one man in a night is hardly enough, ne! But still, last night was rather... athletic. I find that my whole body is tired this morning."

Mishi's jaw clenched so tightly that she was worried she would grind her own teeth to powder.

"I wasn't aware that you were required to train with your master," she said, forcing herself to relax at least enough to speak. "It's very kind of you to volunteer to be his sparring partner."

This caused Kusuko to vomit up another round of screeching laughter.

"Mishi-san! You are too funny! Sparring partner... that's good. I'll have to remember that one."

Mishi attempted to focus on her rice.

"Well, even if you aren't tired this morning, I hope you made good use of the little trick I showed you yesterday?"

"Trick?" Mishi asked, her brain attempting to ignore the girl's blather.

"About the door." Kusuko had dropped her voice to an exaggerated whisper.

"Ah, yes.... That is, no. I haven't used it yet."

Kusuko let out a small gasp and for the first time since Mishi had met her, she looked entirely serious.

"Oh, Mishi-san, you must be careful. That door exists for a reason. If you are caught being indiscreet, you will be punished."

Mishi reminded herself that no matter what this girl thought of her relationship with Katagi, her goal was to remain undetected. If Kusuko had information that would help her stay out of trouble, she needed to know it.

"Oh?" she asked, not sure what to say, but wanting to hear what else Kusuko might be able to tell her about the guest residence's security.

"Yes," insisted Kusuko. "I know this is your first time to the palace, so I'll warn you. I'm surprised that your mama-san didn't tell you before you left. Your presence here is tolerated and even understood. The necessities of a man, especially a Kisōshi, are accepted by the Rōjū, but you must be discreet. If anyone catches you in the corridors at night..." Kusuko's face paled as she continued in a true whisper, "I knew a girl who was caught last cycle and... well, when I saw her again I barely recognized her through all the bruises."

Mishi swallowed and almost choked. That single explanation had been very educational, yet it raised a hundred other questions that Mishi knew she would not be able to ask without giving herself away.

"Thank you, Kusuko-san," she said, after a moment. "I appreciate the warning. I will endeavor to be as discreet as possible."

The other girl smiled and finally began to eat her meal. Mishi savored the silence for a moment and thought about all that Kusuko had revealed in their conversation. What the other girl knew only reminded Mishi of her own ignorance. It could be dangerous for her to be caught out wandering the city by herself. She cringed as she realized what the best course of action would be, but decided to ask anyway. The other girl seemed truly eager to share what she knew about how things worked here, and it would be much easier to explain away the presence of a pair of girls touring the compound together than for her to explain her presence alone. Besides, Kusuko seemed to be known here, so perhaps no one would question her presence in a place like the Rōjū Library.

"Kusuko-san," she said, "you know so much about this place, and I have most of today free. I was wondering...would you mind showing me the city today?"

Kusuko beamed and let out a high pitched squeal.

"Eeee! That would be so much fun!" she shrieked. "Yes, yes! Let's go explore!"

Mishi smiled briefly and returned to eating her rice. The high pitched noises emanating from her new 'friend' made the skin along her spine move in two directions at once. She sighed, and hoped she wouldn't ruin everything by leaving an unconscious courtesan lying in the middle of a garden somewhere.

28日 10月, 老中 1119年

≈ Mishi ≈

KUSUKO HAD OFFERED little resistance to the idea of exploring the Rōjū City together on a day when neither of them had many duties—unless you counted giggling as resistance, in which case she had provided quite a bit.

Careful not to draw much attention to herself or her own interests, Mishi didn't specify any particular destination for their tour. She didn't want her curiosity to seem too pointed, and she would have one more day to explore if she didn't get a chance to visit the places she needed to see today.

Kusuko held her arm, giggling incessantly whilst describing the various men she had accompanied here in the past. For a girl who seemed not much older than Mishi, she had certainly had quite a few clients. Mishi supposed that was the way of a woman of the World of Winds. After all, wasn't that the point?

As a girl who had never even been kissed she found herself... not jealous exactly, since she wasn't sure how she felt about that kind of relationship with a man, but... curious? Certainly she had been listening more closely to what Kusuko had to say as they walked the gardens that bordered the residential buildings arm in arm, even though she was still putting half of her attention towards counting guards and possible escape routes.

Fortunately, Kusuko spoke freely and Mishi found she didn't have to respond much, or ask any questions. The girl still erupted in giggles every few minutes, and Mishi still found her effusive personality annoying, but she was certainly... informative.

As the two walked together, Mishi listened and watched, finding it difficult to picture Rōjū City as the center of all the the evil deeds committed in Gensokai for the past thousand cycles. The city itself was beautiful, a place of art and culture that contained buildings, bridges, and gardens of a finer design and layout than Mishi had ever seen or even imagined. Multistory buildings with swooping rooftops were connected by delicate bridges and stonework pathways. Even the bridges in the garden in which she and Kusuko wandered were intricately carved with delicate designs.

At one point, as they neared a small pond filled with koi in the lower gardens, Kusuko tugged on her arm and said, "Mishi, your master... how is he?"

"Katagi-san?" she asked, puzzled by the seeming non-sequitor.

Kusuko nodded, and brought her fan to her face to stifle another giggle.

Without the giggle, Mishi wouldn't have known what Kusuko was referring to, but the pink in the other girl's cheeks, even as she hid behind her fan, made her meaning all too clear. Mishi felt the blood rush to her cheeks and neck as she understood the implication.

"I don't know," she said, trying to force her blood to behave. "We have never..." Mishi couldn't even finish the sentence.

Kusuko looked slightly shocked.

"But he's so handsome!" she said. "Haven't you at least thought about it? You must have."

Mishi had never had time to think about boys, or men, or anything but her work as a servant and training as a Kisōshi. Until a tenday before this trip, she'd never actually said more than five words to Katagi-san. Since the start of the mission, she'd been worried about staying hidden and alive once she reached the scroll, not to mention all the time she'd spent wishing that Katagi would simply be quiet. Handsome? She supposed he was; Sachi always said so. He was as tall as she was, with much broader shoulders, he had pleasantly high cheekbones, and—

"And you wouldn't be disappointed with him, Mishi-san. I wasn't lying about seeing him come out of the baths!" Kusuko dissolved into another fit of giggles, but managed to continue speaking. "All those hard muscles from Kisōshi training... Mmmm!"

Mishi shook her head and willed herself not to look down at her own body, not that she could see it beneath her servant's kimono.... She wondered if she compared herself to Katagi, who would have more muscle. Then she shook her head to rid herself of the image that conjured. The last thing she needed was thoughts of her and Katagi standing naked beside each other (even if only to compare muscles) to distract her from her mission.

She was beginning to regret having asked Kusuko to accompany her on her 'tour,' when the girl suddenly redeemed herself.

"Mishi-san," she said, excitement dancing in her eyes. "Would you like to go look at the libraries?"

Mishi tried to mask her excitement at the mention of heading to the one place she was most interested in visiting.

"There's more than one?" she asked. Of course, she already knew that there were several. It had been part of her briefing before she left, but the more ignorant she appeared, the less likely she was to raise anyone's curiosity.

Kusuko nodded. "Oh yes, there are several. Shall we see them all?"

Mishi nodded emphatically. "That would be wonderful."

They walked arm in arm through more of the gardens, and then into a large building made entirely of stone. Mishi did her best to keep her grip from tightening on Kusuko's arm, as the two girls walked through the stone hallways. The building was like nothing she had seen before. Even the Rōjū audience chambers were in a wood and thatch roofed building. No one built buildings entirely from stone.

Even Kusuko had stopped her giggling and slowed her walk. After a moment, she spoke almost in a whisper.

"Almost no one enters here," she said. Then she smiled suddenly. "Which makes it a perfect place to share secrets!"

Mishi tried to return the smile, but the building was making her nervous and she was fairly certain there was no secret she wished to share with her giggly, gregarious companion.

"So," Kusuko continued, her voice solemn once more. "You can tell me now…"

Mishi cringed as she thought of what lewd questions Kusuko might ask next.

"Do you enjoy your profession?" the other girl asked, the smile gone from her face.

"My profession?" Mishi asked, unsure how Kusuko could have gone so quickly from smiling and giggling to the pale and stricken expression she wore now.

"As a servant?" Kusuko prompted. "I know you're not actually a consort," she admitted quietly. "I know you don't… do what I do. I just… well, it was nice to pretend that you did, first because it made you so nervous and then… then because you were still willing to talk to me. "

She shrugged, as though this were the kind of thing that happened all the time, and if Mishi hadn't been so uncertain in her surroundings she might have laughed. Before she could say anything, though, Kusuko spoke again.

"Being a servant... is it nice?"

"Nice?" Mishi asked.

"I mean... does it make you happy?"

"No, Kusuko-san," Mishi replied. "Being a servant does not make me happy."

Kusuko then tilted her head to one side, as though inspecting her.

"But you are happy, aren't you? You seem at peace with your life. You must be happy."

Mishi thought for a moment, then nodded. She couldn't tell this girl the whole truth, but perhaps she could convey some part of it.

"I take pride in my work as a servant, but it doesn't make me happy. I find that there are other things that I can do that make me happy, and I seek those out when I can." She pictured her home at Kuma-sensei's school, then continued. "I find happiness in reading, in walking in the sunshine, and walking in the rain. I find happiness in the falling of the snow."

Kusuko smiled then, but there was such emptiness in her eyes when she did it that Mishi found herself wanting to wrap the girl in a hug until that look went away.

"All of those things only make me sad," Kusuko whispered. "Falling snow makes me wonder about the peace of taking my final rest..."

Mishi stopped walking and turned to face Kusuko.

"How did you come to be a woman of the World of Winds?" she asked, though she wasn't sure she wanted to hear the answer.

"I was raised in an orphanage," Kusuko said, her voice faltering as she spoke. "I was sold to a man who... I was only 12. I didn't know what was happening to me, and even if I had, there was nothing I could have done to stop him.... He turned me out when he was done with me. No money, no food. I could have easily... but one of the Mama-sans in the village took pity on me. She brought me into her house and trained me. Offered me a chance to earn my food and shelter."

Mishi nodded, and they started their slow walk once more. How many times had she and Taka seen the same thing happen with girls in their town, in their own orphanage? She hadn't understood it very well when she was still living under Haha-san's roof, but over the cycles since then she had come to understand the cruel fate that produced the girls with the empty eyes. She had often thanked her karma that she hadn't been one of them, that Kuma-sensei had found her in time... and she worried and wondered about Taka.

She suddenly felt a kinship with Kusuko that she would never have thought possible, even that morning. The girl was an orphan, like her. But, unlike her, karma had dealt Kusuko a cruel hand. Kusuko dealt with it by creating a persona of giggling hysterics and mindless gossip, but Mishi could hardly blame her for hiding in whatever way she could. She wondered if there was anything she could do to help the girl…

"Kusuko-san," she said, after a moment of contemplation. "Would you leave, if you could?"

"Leave where?" the girl asked, perhaps distracted by her own thoughts.

"Leave your mama-san," Mishi said. "Change professions?"

Kusuko smiled for a moment, but then shook her head.

"How could I? I would have to buy my own contract from my mama-san. I could never afford it."

"What if I could?"

"You?" Kusuko seemed stunned. "How could you afford it?"

Mishi smiled for a moment before saying, "With some help from a friend."

Kusuko looked stunned, and for a moment seemed unable to speak, then she said, "I have trouble believing that you could do it. Even a contract like mine would cost at least five koku. Where in Gensokai would you get that much?"

Mishi shrugged.

"Never mind where I'd get it," she said. "If I could do it, would you want to come with me?"

Kusuko smiled, and for the first time, Mishi thought she saw the young woman behind the facade of the giggling consort.

"Yes," Kusuko said. "Yes, I believe I would."

~~~

It hadn't been Mishi's reason for offering to take the girl away from her current plight, but Kusuko had been very helpful after their small exchange in the secluded library halls.

Over the past two days, Kusuko had helped her cover acres and acres of Rōjū City. They had wandered through and between five tiered pagodas; buildings with spectacularly curved and tiled roofs; gardens with manicured trees, calming waterfalls, and rocks arranged in soothing landscapes; over bridges, and the gorges and rivers they spanned; and they'd made more than one trip through the libraries. By the time Mishi woke on the morning of Katagi's test, she felt confident in her knowledge of the layout of buildings, gardens, and guards. After she woke, but before she rose from her futon, she rid herself of nerves by focusing her ki and mentally going over the plan, step by step.

It was clear when she entered Katagi's rooms to make sure he was prepared that he had not done the same. He hadn't resorted to hiding under his futon yet, but he was pacing back and forth across his room and seemed unable to tie any part of his gi.

Mishi grabbed him by the shoulders to make him stop pacing.

"Hold still," she said, as she began to tie his obi for him. "You'll have no luck finishing your kata if you trip on your own clothes. Now I understand why you had nightmares about losing your pants in the middle of testing—if you don't tie them on, they don't stay on."

Katagi seemed relieved that he no longer had to fidget with his clothing, but he seemed no less worried than before. He looked at her with a face drained of all color.

"What if it happens?" he asked. "What if my pants fall off?"

Mishi stifled a laugh.

"Your pants will not fall off. I've tied them twice just to make sure. And remember, even if they do fall down, you have a plan: complete the kata as usual and at the end profess the need for two swords."

Mishi looked into Katagi's face to search for some sign of laughter, but he seemed to have missed the joke entirely.

"I can't do this," he said. "I can't. I'll fail horribly, I can tell. I—"

"Do you want me to slap you?" Mishi asked.

"What?" Katagi's brows rose to his hairline, and he seemed to be focusing on Mishi for the first time.

"Do you want me to slap you?" Mishi repeated, trying to keep her voice from rising. "You're panicking. And for no reason. Your life is not on the line. You are in no danger. You are simply going into a room full of old men to complete some kata that you know as well as your own name. You could pass this test with no pants on and your eyes blindfolded. The only reason that you're nervous is that you're worried that the old men are going to judge you. Stop. You know that you are qualified. You know that you will pass. You're simply letting your imagination run away with you. When people are nonsensical and need to be brought back to reality they are slapped. So, I'll say it again: would you like me to slap you?"

Katagi stared at her. She could see every word that she'd said hit him like a pebble on a pond.

"No," he finally replied. "No, somehow I don't think I would enjoy that." He looked her up and down. "I've never noticed it before, but something tells me you could slap with quite a bit of authority. I don't think I want to take this test seeing double."

Mishi smiled, only slightly regretful that he hadn't taken her up on her offer.

"A wise choice," she said. "Now, is there anything else I can help you with before you depart to meet your Kami-ordained fate, brave sir?"

She hoped the jibe would sting, but not demoralize. She only wanted to remind the man that he wasn't going to meet his death.

Katagi smiled.

"A kiss from a fair maiden always brings the hero good luck," he said.

Mishi laughed.

"I shall go forthwith to find a fair maiden, that she may kiss you! But, be warned, I may not be back in time for your test."

Katagi stepped closer to her then, and smiled again, but this time the smile was different and there was something about how close he was that made her... uncomfortable.

"I meant you," he said.

Mishi could feel the heat rush through her body. She thought she must have turned the color of a spring cherry, and she suddenly had no greater wish than to run from the room, but somehow she found that she couldn't move. Her body was betraying her.

"Me? But... I thought you wanted a fair maiden.... Surely—"

"Do you have any idea how beautiful you are?" Katagi asked, stepping closer. Mishi wanted to pull away, she wanted to step back, but her body refused to listen.

Her mind was spinning wildly. Katagi thought she was beautiful? That didn't make any sense. It must be his nerves talking. He couldn't possibly...

"But... you... and I... and—" she stammered, worried that he would come even closer to her, and unsure of what she would do if he did. "You ask me rude questions and... always make extra work for me... and you talk of nothing but yourself... you only occasionally ask me anything..."

She hadn't meant to say any of it. She regretted being so honest as soon as the words escaped her lips, but it was too late to take them back, so she stood there, waiting for him to be crushed, or angry, or maybe to hit her.

Instead he laughed.

"I was afraid to talk to you," he said, his eyes alight with humor and... something Mishi didn't really want to think about. "You're so beautiful, so silent, and you make me nervous. I find that every second that I'm in front of you, I want to try to impress you, or make you laugh, anything to get your attention and... and nothing works. No stories of my family, or my training.... You are as unaffected by anything I say as... as a tree! So, I'm always searching for something that will draw your attention. I know I sound like a complete fool, but... I can't help myself."

Just as Mishi was worried that Katagi would step closer, he resumed his pacing, and she let out a breath she hadn't realized that she'd been holding.

"It's so frustrating," he said. "You're gorgeous, and hard working, competent, confident... but you aren't interested in anything I say. You understand it all, you understand me... you give me good advice, but... I can't make heads or tails of you, and... you're a mystery to me. You're a puzzle that I'm dying to solve."

He stopped pacing and stood in front of her once more. "I can't stop thinking about you," he whispered, as he stepped closer to her.

Mishi felt another surge of warmth course through her, and she trembled. What was wrong with her? Why did half of her want him to come closer, while the other half cried out for her to run away? And why couldn't she make herself move?

"I think I love you," he said, almost closing the distance between them.

Mishi couldn't think, she could barely breathe. Why was this happening now? Today, of all days? She had so much at stake.... She couldn't afford this kind of distraction, and—

Katagi closed the final distance between them and leaned his head towards hers. Part of her wanted to scream, but another part of her was very curious about what would happen next. She waited, her breath held and her body alight with conflicting reactions.

Then he kissed her.

For a moment, she enjoyed the fire that coursed through her veins and thrummed through her head, and she leaned into the soft feel of Katagi's lips against her own. Then she felt like she couldn't breathe. Her mind froze and her body leapt into action. Her right arm shot across, grabbing Katagi's left. With a swift turn of her body, he was over her shoulder and lying on the floor staring up at her. Without even a second's pause, she ran from the room, down the hall, and into the gardens. She had to get away, she had to think, she needed to breathe. Why couldn't she think? Why couldn't she breathe?

Why had she let him kiss her?

1 1 1 9 年

As winter steals life
so it hides seeds under snow
cradled for spring's sun

28日 10月, 老中 1119年

≈ Mishi ≈

MISHI DIDN'T HAVE enough breath to curse the plan, Katagi, and Kusuko all at once, so she decided to focus on Kusuko alone. The smell of dust and old parchment tickled her nose, making it even more difficult to keep her breathing steady, and the strain of pressing herself against the ceiling with nothing but two walls for support was starting to wear on her. What had Kusuko been thinking? Fetching the guards? She granted that the girl seemed worried about her, though she would never have believed it if she hadn't heard the quaver in Kusuko's voice when she had led the guard to the staircase that went down to the vault of ancient texts.

"Please... please, I saw her go in, and she looked upset. She's been in there so long, I'm worried... I'm worried what she might have done," Kusuko's voice had said, from the top of the stairwell.

"If you're so worried about her, why don't you go in there yourself?" the guard had asked. Mishi had thought that was an excellent question, and she had eagerly awaited the answer while hurriedly tucking the scroll she had just spent the morning searching for into the elaborate bow of her obi and beginning to look for a place to hide.

"Eee!," Kusuko had said. "She is a visitor and doesn't know it's forbidden to enter the library of ancient texts. I do. I am worried about her, but I am not willing to risk the wrath of the Rōjū! But you are Kisōshi and an Eihei as well, no one will punish you for doing your duty."

By the time Kusuko had finished speaking, Mishi had found a small alcove with a vaulted ceiling and had used feet and hands, along with the small gaps in the stonework, to push herself up to the ceiling, where she now pushed out with all of her strength in order to keep herself suspended at the highest point of the walls.

As Mishi waited for the guard, who had finally succumbed to Kusuko's pleading and entered the vault to find her, she decided that while she wished to curse Kusuko and Katagi, and even 'the plan,' she had no one to blame for this but herself. If she had never allowed Katagi to kiss her, she would never have been so agitated that she missed noticing Kusuko on her journey to the library. Clearly the other girl had seen her, had even watched her enter the vault of ancient texts, and Mishi had thought that she had made it to the library completely undetected. The only thing that could account for such a lapse was the distraction of Katagi's kiss.

And now there was a guard seeking her who was Kisōshi, and 'the plan' was very close to being ruined. She slowed her breathing as the guard moved in her direction. The vault of ancient texts wasn't very large, only twelve tatami or so, and even though there was no light in the dusty stone space, it wouldn't take very long for the guard to find her just by looking. But because he was Kisōshi, he could use his own kisō to scan the room, find another source of kisō somewhere inside of it, and then locate that source. Mishi tamped down hard on her kisō. She needed to maintain her guise as servant girl for as long as possible. She waited. Closer... he was almost there... she was almost tempted to shout at the man to hurry, but she held her peace, and her breath. Finally, the man stepped beneath her.

Mishi dropped, trapping the man's arms with her own before he could reach for his katana. She held him, pinned at the forearm, leaving herself low enough to the ground to get a leg around him and swipe his legs out from under him. The man toppled, and as he fell, Mishi brought her other leg around to strike the side of his head with the heel of her foot. Even through the man's helmet, the force of his fall and the force of her kick were enough to rattle his skull. He slumped, and she knew that he was unconscious.

She thought about taking the man's katana, but decided that it would be unwise. It would be best if she could walk out of the library without anyone knowing she was more than a servant. Kuma-sensei's words still echoed in her mind: *know that once you pick up a sword, your disguise as a servant is completely ruined, so only do it if your very life is threatened.* She had to try to keep her cover for as long as possible.

She sighed as she stepped away from the fallen Kisōshi and the katana he carried. Her fingers itched at the emptiness of her hands, but she let them relax and walked to the staircase that led out of the vault.

She supposed she shouldn't have been surprised, after the way the morning had gone so far, that Kusuko waited at the top of the stairs with yet another Kisōshi guard...

Mishi stalled a few steps below them.

"Woman," the guard sneered, "where is Yoshida-san?"

"Who?" Mishi asked, attempting to sound truly confused.

"The guard who just went down there."

"I didn't see a guard," she said.

"He just went down there," the guard insisted. "You must have seen him!"

Mishi bowed her head and tried to make her body tremble with something akin to fright.

"I'm sorry, O-Kisōshi-sama, I didn't see any guard."

The man looked at her and started in a rush down the stairs.

"You two wait here," he said as he went. "Don't let her go any—"

Mishi pressed herself to the wall and stuck out her right leg as the man went by her, following with her right arm pushing his torso to help him on his journey down the stairs. She didn't pause to see how he would land, but turned and jumped onto his back as he fell, driving him faster down the stairs. As she fell with him, the wind was knocked from her body when he impacted the stairs beneath them, but she gave the man no chance to right himself, no chance to call out or use his kisō to summon a fellow guard. She drove his head into the stone step and heard a sickening crack as it made contact, noticing too late that the man's helmet had come off during his fall. She swallowed hard to keep her stomach from heaving. She might have killed him. She wasn't sure. She hoped not. She hadn't meant to... but there was nothing she could do about it now. He was certainly unconscious, and that was what she needed. She didn't have time to see if he was alive, or to help him if he was in the process of dying. She had to turn and walk back up the stairs.

Kusuko stood trembling at the top of the stairs, her face so washed of color that it stood out like porcelain against the bright red of her kimono. Mishi didn't approach her. She didn't want to have to hurt the girl at all, but she would knock her out if she had to.

"Kusuko-san," she said, "would you still like to leave this place?"

Some of the color returned to Kusuko's face, and she nodded.

"Would today be soon enough?" Mishi asked, the hint of a smile tugging at the corners of her mouth.

Kusuko's face blossomed then, a large smile replacing the blank expanse of white that had stood there moments before. She nodded only once.

"I see it was foolish of me to worry about you," she said, taking Mishi's arm and walking calmly away from the staircase.

Mishi almost laughed, but the thought of that man's skull hitting the stairs filled her mind, and she swallowed back bile instead.

Kusuko looked at her sideways even as they walked forward.

"You didn't mean to kill that man, did you?" she asked.

Mishi shuddered at the implication that she had actually killed the guard. She still harbored some hope that it hadn't been a fatal blow. She shook her head, but didn't trust her voice to speak.

Mishi was taken aback by the venom in Kusuko's voice when next she spoke.

"The man was a pig," she hissed between clenched teeth. "He thought no woman could refuse him because he was Kisōshi. Believe me, Mishi-san, you did the women of Rōjū City a favor by taking his life."

Mishi was surprised to find that the information brought her little comfort. She had still taken a man's life, and worse, she hadn't meant to. She had thought she knew her own strength better than that.

They walked arm in arm, in a strange but companionable silence, until they reached the far side of the lower gardens that separated the libraries from the residential buildings. Mishi pulled them up short, yanking them behind a low tree as the pounding of armored feet came closer. She had to hope that the guards weren't using kisō to search the garden, that they expected to find nothing here.

Her breathing eased as the guards hurried past.

"The first guard must have woken up," she said to Kusuko.

"You should have killed him too," the girl replied, with surprising anger.

Mishi shook her head, reminding herself that the girl had been treated brutally by men her whole life, and maybe particularly by those two guards. She had a right to her anger.

"Too late now," she replied. "With the alarm raised, we'll have to leave as quickly as possible. There's something I have to do first. Meet me at the stables as soon as you can get there. If anyone else arrives before me, hide."

Kusuko grabbed Mishi's arm as she tried to pull away.

"Let me help you. I know the grounds better than you do and—"

Mishi shook her head.

"Kusuko-san, when the guards realize what I've done they will try to kill me. They'll try to kill anyone associated with me as well. I won't risk having you hurt."

Kusuko's eyes widened, and she nodded slowly.

"I'll meet you at the stables," she said.

Mishi wondered briefly at how the girl could go so quickly from cold cynicism and a burning anger to bright eyed fear, but she had no time to consider it. She hadn't been exaggerating when she'd said that the guards would try to kill anyone associated with her. She feared that no amount of denying involvement would save anyone she had been seen with in this city. She had a very brief window in which to save Katagi.

≈ Tsuku ≈

Tsuku sat in the bleachers, watching the Kisōshi on the main floor engaged in sparring and kisō demonstrations with a faint smile on her face. Gaining audience to the Kisōshi tests of rank was one of the few benefits associated with her status as the wife of a Rōjū that she actually enjoyed. Seeing young men demonstrate their skills, so many of their hopes pinned on the outcome of their exams, was refreshing and innocent in a way that many of her duties were not. It was a pleasure to watch Yasuhiko, as he followed the proceedings with such open interest and enthusiasm. This was, perhaps, the one duty of being Rōjū that he truly relished; all else was smoke and mirrors.

She turned to watch him then, his face impassive. He was an expert at masking his true feelings, but she knew him well enough to   recognize the slight spark in his eyes that indicated that he was enjoying himself. It was the only part of being a Rōjū that the man never had to feel guilty about. Just as she was about to turn her attention back to the floor and the testing going on there, a man clad in the uniform of an off duty Eihei, but who Tsuku knew to be the leader of the Rōjū assassins guild, approached Yasuhiko and placed a respectful hand on his shoulder to indicate that he wished to speak with him. Yasuhiko nodded, and even as he did so Tsuku felt the connection of their shared kisō open up. Suddenly, though she could still feel the wooden bench beneath her legs, she heard and saw everything from Yasuhiko's perspective on the dais at the far end of the enormous chamber.

It had taken cycles and cycles for Tsuku and Yasuhiko to develop this connection, and even longer for them to get used to it well enough that it was useful. For cycles, whenever they had tried, it had been so disorienting to them both that if they maintained the connection for more than few moments either they tried to mimic each other's movements and one of them wound up hurting themselves, or else one or both of them began to feel ill. Finally, after more cycles of practice and perfection than Tsuku cared to count, they had taken the basic mingling of kisō that enabled one person to check the health and emotional state of another and been able to extend it to this shared state of hearing and seeing.

Tsuku watched and listened   from Yasuhiko's eyes and ears as he stood,   following the leader of the hishi to the back of the dais.

"Zōkame-sama, I'm afraid that we have an unknown intruder at large in the city. Someone was in the Rōjū Library, the ancient scrolls section. They have evaded apprehension to this point."

Yasuhiko nodded, as Tsuku could tell from the angle of his vision shifting, and then spoke.

"Bring the intruder to me. Attempt to apprehend this thief or spy before the Eihei get ahold of them. I want to question this person. I've recently gotten wind of some kind of conspiracy, and I want more information. Put one of your best people on it."

"Yes, Zōkame-sama," the man bowed, but hesitated before he left.

"What is it?" Yasuhiko asked.

"Zōkame-sama, you should know that the Eihei have been instructed to kill the intruder on sight. Your orders go directly against the ones that they have received."

Yasuhiko nodded again.

"I can understand why my fellow Rōjū might find that to be the most expedient solution to the problem, but I possess information that they do not. We will benefit greatly from having more information about this particular enemy, and the intruder we've detected today is nothing more than a pawn in a much greater scheme. Or so my informants would have me believe."

The hishi leader nodded and walked away. Yasuhiko resumed his seat on the dais, and took up watching the examinations once more. Then he dropped their connection, and Tsuku was left looking through her own eyes once more. She took a deep breath. This was what they had worked so long and hard to be in place for. All the cycles of Yasuhiko pretending to be in line with the Rōjū mandates, all of that time spent supporting a system that they both loathed. All to put Yasuhiko in a place of power when it was most needed. He'd only been in charge of the Rōjū's spy and assassin network for three cycles now, as the previous spymaster had taken his time in dying of old age. But now, here they were, poised to finally enact the plan they'd spent more than half their lives preparing. She only hoped that Kuma-sensei would keep up his end of the bargain.

⇒ Mishi ⇐

Mishi slid cautiously down the large beam she had climbed earlier and took a deep breath to steady her nerves. Her brief inspection of the crawl space above the Rōjū audience chamber had only confirmed her worst suspicions. The chamber was full to bursting with Kisōshi, with more than half of the members of the Rōjū present and the audience full of instructors and test takers from all over the realms, every one of them a Kisōshi of rank, or at least testing for rank. She pressed her back to the beam, trying to find her center and the sense of calm that it brought. So far as she could tell, no one had yet disturbed the testing taking place, but it was only a matter of time before the Eihei would alert the Rōjū to what she had done. It would not take them long to discover that she was the only servant unaccounted for and make the connection between her and Katagi. She needed a plan, and soon.

She heard the rustling of fabric and the soft pad of footsteps, and she shifted to be sure that the wooden pillar she had descended still hid her from the rest of the hallway. The footsteps came closer, and she focused her kisō and prepared to attack. Tension rippled through her as the sounds drew next to her...

And then left her as she recognized Kusuko's kimono. She grabbed Kusuko's arm and threw her other hand around the girl's mouth, pulling her behind the pillar as she did so.

"What are you doing here?" she whispered into the girl's ear. She released her hand enough to let the girl speak, but kept her other arm wrapped tightly around the other young woman's arms and waist.

"Mishi-san, thank the Kami. The guards are everywhere, Mishi-san. I couldn't even get to the stables without being questioned and sent back to my quarters. I don't know what you're doing, but you must leave as soon as you can."

"How did you find me?" Mishi asked, her suspicion rising. She had been very careful not to be followed.

Kusuko shook her head.

"I didn't. I thought you might come here because of Katagi-san. You said they would try to kill anyone who was associated with you, and well.... After how you reacted to killing that guard, it didn't seem likely that you would leave a man here to die."

Mishi nodded and released the other young woman. She supposed that it made sense, though it made her uncomfortable that Kusuko could predict her actions so accurately after knowing her for only a handful of days.

"I can't leave him here," she admitted. "But I don't know how to get him out without getting us all killed."

"Let me help you," Kusuko pleaded.

Mishi looked her up and down. The girl wanted to come with her, and things were going to be dangerous, no matter how they escaped. She might as well be helpful, but... what could the girl do? She looked so small, standing there in her bright kimono. Like her clothes, she appeared made for decoration. Mishi had rarely met a person who she felt was so opposite to herself.

"I can distract the guards," Kusuko said, perhaps recognizing that Mishi was giving in. "Or I can fool them into going somewhere else, or—"

Mishi held up a hand.

"That's it," she said. "I know how you can help."

~~~

Kusuko led the line of eleven fully armored guards to the two giant wooden doors that separated the Rōjū audience chamber from the rest of the building.

"She went in there," she declared, pointing to the two wooden behemoths.

The lead guard turned to look at her.

"No one is allowed into that chamber once testing has begun, least of all a servant."

Kusuko glared up at the man.

"She killed one of your guards, disabled another, and attacked me. What makes you think she cares about what is allowed?"

The guard looked at her and grunted.

"She, huh? A woman couldn't have done those things. Only a fully trained Kisōshi could have overcome my men... killed Saito-san..."

"Fine! He, then! But he's in there, I saw him go in."

The guard shook his head.

"Isn't possible."

"Well, fine. Stay out here. And when the man escapes, in a crowd of Kisōshi, and the Rōjū realize what's been stolen, enjoy telling them that you had an opportunity to catch the man, but you were convinced that two pieces of wood were an impenetrable barrier to someone who had already bested two of your men."

The man grunted again, then nodded to his men.

"You heard the woman, there's a thief in there."

The Eihei pulled open the giant doors and filed through, with Kusuko close on their heels. The moment they entered the chamber, silence greeted them, followed very closely by one of the Rōjū shouting.

"What is the meaning of this?!" came the shout, from a raised dais where the Rōjū sat to judge the testing Kisōshi.

The guard looked around the room, as though willing someone to appear guilty and out of place.

"There is an intruder in the city, sir. This girl said that she saw him or her enter here."

"Him or her?" sneered the Rōjū who had first shouted at them. "How is it that you don't even know the gender of this intruder, yet you are certain that he is within these walls?"

The guard suddenly looked less certain of himself.

"The intruder presented himself as a woman earlier, but he disabled one guard and killed another, so we believe him to be a fully trained Kisōshi."

"And you believe him to be in this room?"

"This girl," the guard said, bringing Kusuko forward, "says that she saw him enter these chambers."

Kusuko nodded and bowed as she came forward. She kept her head bowed as she spoke.

"I saw him enter this room only a few moments ago."

"And yet," said the same Rōjū, "until you all burst in here, no one had entered or left this chamber since the beginning of testing."

Kusuko shook her head.

"I was sure that I saw him…" she looked around the room slowly, then pointed.

"There! That's the man the intruder came with, posing as his servant."

All the blood left Katagi's face as he followed the line from Kusuko's finger to his own chest. All the eyes in the room had turned to him.

"Me? No… I didn't… my servant is a woman, and she's certainly no Kisōshi."

"Seize him!" cried the Rōjū.

"No! I didn't do anything! I don't know what you're talking about!"

The lead Eihei in their little band turned to the guard standing immediately beside him.

"Hold him and bring him with us, we'll need to question him."

The guard crossed the room quickly and took Katagi from the two Kisōshi standing beside him, who had already restrained him. The guard grabbed Katagi's wrists and locked them tightly behind his back, then pushed him forward in a forced march.

"My apologies, O-Rōjū-samatachi," the lead Eihei said, removing his helmet and bowing as the guard leading Katagi shuffled past them. "We will deal with the situation immediately."

The head Eihei followed them out into the hallway.

"Girl, you'll come with us," he said to Kusuko. "You have much to answer for." He turned to the other nine guards standing at attention and waved his helmet at them. "Fan out and search the area—we'll find that bastard yet." Then he turned to the Eihei holding Katagi. "You, follow me."

Katagi began to mumble protestations and objections, but the guard who held him tightened the grip on his wrists enough to make him flinch in pain, and he grew quiet. Once the group of three was halfway down an empty corridor, the guard pushing Katagi stopped. Before the young man had a chance to say anything, the guard whispered into Katagi's ear, "still, not as bad as losing your pants, ne?"

The head Eihei was just turning to see why they had stopped following him when Mishi pushed Katagi to the floor, springing past him to connect her armored hand with the head guard's temple. The man crumpled to the floor, and Mishi turned to see Kusuko smiling and Katagi looking as lost as a rabbit in a fox den.

She lifted the elaborate guard's helmet from her head and smiled at him briefly before replacing it. She stepped forward and grabbed his arm.

"No time for explanations, Katagi-san. We must go."

Together, with Kusuko trailing closely behind, they ran.

~~~

Mishi threw another wall of fire behind her, belatedly wishing that she hadn't flung the katana she'd carried at a following Eihei to give them the time they'd needed to escape the upper garden. Or, better yet, that she had taken the time to grab a sword off of any of the guards she'd felled as they ran through the lower gardens. But she hadn't had time to go back for any of their weapons. She was tempted to take Katagi's sword from him, but she would have felt bad leaving the man without a weapon, even if he still seemed too befuddled to use it.

"Now!" she shouted, as a break in the volley of arrows that came after them gave them the window they would need to make the far wall.

The three of them sprinted to the wall, and Kusuko began climbing instantly. Katagi hesitated.

"Go!" Mishi shouted. She needed him safely over the wall so that she wouldn't have to climb and defend him at the same time. "Go!" Mishi shouted again. How long did he think it would take the Eihei who were charging them to get there? Didn't he realize that the only reason they would have stopped firing arrows was to charge them with swords and kisō attacks?

Katagi nodded, and began to climb. Mishi was about to start her own ascent, when the hair on the back of her neck told her that someone was gathering their kisō for an attack. She dropped to the ground and rolled away from the wall, releasing another sheet of flame above her in the hope that it would create some protection for Kusuko and Katagi as they topped the wall and dropped to the other side.

She didn't have time to see if it worked. She sprang to her feet and rolled backwards, just in time to dodge the sheet of wind that rolled towards her and might have sliced through the armor that she still wore if she had not dodged it.

Mishi's breathing slowed and her mind calmed. She inhaled the scent of the singed ivy on the wall behind her, the ionized taste of air charged with kisō, the sounds of men running, of a katana being pulled from its sheath, of a small blade cutting the air before her. She pulled all the threads of her surroundings towards her, moving without conscious thought. The threads would call her and she would follow. Movement slowed to the beat of her heart, and each breath was a lifetime in which to act.

She dodged the two shuriken that came at her head and tumbled to the left, rising to a run at the end of her roll and throwing two blasts of fire toward the origin of the shuriken. Her mind vaguely registered the cry of the man she had struck, but she would have to mourn him later. She turned around suddenly and planted her feet firmly on the wall that Katagi and Kusuko had scaled, using her momentum to flip her legs over her head and over the man who had an instant earlier been charging her with drawn katana. The man barely managed to stop himself before running into the wall that was now directly before him. She flung her arms out as she descended, grabbing him by the neck and bringing him to the ground with her. She didn't hesitate to snap the man's neck, though she felt a part of herself break along with his spinal column.

This time, she did take the man's katana. She grabbed it even as she rose from the ground and set a wall of flame between herself and the oncoming rush of Kisōshi guards, thankful that there had only been three men at the head of the charge. She turned and climbed the wall, willing the flames she had set behind her to climb higher, hoping that they would be enough to stop the men that followed.

She made it to the top of the wall and down the other side. The look waiting on Katagi's face as she turned to him told her that he hadn't gotten over the wall before seeing at least part of her fight.

"You—"

"Later," she said, before he could get another word out. "To the stables."

She could see that Kusuko, rather than waiting around for her to arrive, had already started in that direction, staying low and following the cover of trees wherever she could.

Ignoring his slight flinch as she reached for him, Mishi grabbed Katagi's arm and pulled him after her.

~~~

Of course, when they reached the stables, all the horses were saddled and waiting for their heavily armored riders to mount them. One patrol was already riding away at a frightening pace, even as Mishi, Katagi, and Kusuko approached in the shadows.

"What now?" Kusuko whispered, the whites of her eyes showing at the sight of so many mounted guards.

Mishi turned to look at her two companions, then back to the guards still getting ready to ride. They hadn't had a chance to organize yet, and both guards and servants were stumbling between stalls looking for available horses and the tack to saddle them.

"Well," she said, with a calm she did not feel, "I am dressed for the part."

Katagi's eyes went wide and he was about to object, but Kusuko beat him to it.

"And what about the two of us? How are we to get horses?" she asked.

Mishi smiled before asking, "How fast can you run?"

~~~

Mishi had thought her plan rather clever, but Kusuko and Katagi hadn't seemed as convinced when she left them to make her way to the stables. She had waited in the shadows until only a handful of guards remained. Then she ran into the stables at full speed.

"Hurry up—we can still catch them!" she shouted, grabbing the reins of a horse from one of the servants. She threw herself up into the saddle without hesitation and turned towards the four armed men behind her.

"Come on!" she bellowed, in the lowest voice she could muster. "They're getting away, you fools!"

She didn't wait to see if they'd follow her; she simply spurred her mount into a gallop and headed towards the small wood by the eastern gate.

A few moments later, she heard the reassuring pounding of horse hooves behind her and she gripped the reins, hunkered lower to her mount, and rode faster.

In the dark of the small wood she saw a brief flash of red and called out, even as she slowed her mount to a trot.

"There they are! Don't kill them! We need them for questioning."

She hoped that the men would heed her, even though it had been made very clear by their earlier pursuit that the Eihei had orders to take them dead or alive.

The men behind her surged forward, even as she slowed, and she only kicked up speed again as the fourth and final guard pulled alongside her. She kept pace with him for a moment, hoping that Kusuko and Katagi could run as quickly as they said they could, and hoping that the man's attention was focused on his quarry. Then she held tight to the saddle of her own mount, leaned her torso out to the left, and kicked high and right, connecting with the guard's head. The force from her booted foot, along with the difference in the speeds of their mounts, rendered the man unconscious even through the protection of his helmet. The man slumped and fell from his saddle, and Mishi felt grateful that she hadn't had to use a sword on him. She slowed her own horse in order to gather the reins of the Eihei's former mount, then pushed both horses to a gallop to catch up with the others.

The other three guards had just cornered Kusuko when she caught up with them, though Mishi noted happily that Katagi was nowhere in sight. They had been smart to divide. The men wouldn't consider Kusuko a threat, which would make them less likely to use lethal force on her than on Katagi. Kusuko cowered on the ground, and Mishi wished that there had been fewer guards present when she had called out for them to follow her. Still, there were only three left, and she thought she might be able to take care of them alone.

Just as she rode up between two of the remaining three guards, a blade of wind struck forth, cutting the third man's armor and leaving a freshly bleeding wound. Mishi smiled, as she kicked the man to her left and let the back of her right hand connect with the nose and mouth of the man to her right. She hadn't known that Katagi knew the bladed wind trick. Perhaps she didn't give him enough credit.

Even as she thought it, Katagi leapt, katana in hand, to slash down the man he had already attacked with his wind blade. Mishi pulled the stunned man to her right down with her, between the two horses, and kicked him in the head, hoping it would be enough to render him unconscious as well. She had already grown tired of killing. The man slumped to the ground and didn't stir.

Just as Mishi turned to deal with the man to her left, she was amazed to see a small dagger fly from the ground to the man's neck. His eyes widened in surprise, even as he fell from the back of his horse. Mishi turned to see Kusuko standing, another dagger already in her grip and a cruel smile spreading across her face.

In the same timespan, Katagi had dispatched the third guard. Mishi simply stared at Kusuko.

"What?" the girl asked. "You didn't think my mama-san would let me be completely defenseless, did you?"

Mishi simply nodded. She wasn't sure what she thought, but she made a mental note to remain in Kusuko's good graces.

"We must ride, before they bar the gates," Mishi said.

"What makes you think they haven't already?" Katagi asked, as he hopped into the saddle of the horse he had just rid of its rider.

"They're still sending out patrols," she replied. "They've no idea where we are, or if we're still inside the city. If you two put on that armor, they may yet let us out." She indicated two of the incapacitated guards.

Kusuko raised an eyebrow.

"They'll never believe that I'm a guard," she said. "Armor or not."

"They might, if we move quickly and don't draw too much attention," Katagi replied.

"And if I use my power to confuse them," Mishi added.

Katagi stared at her, the whites of his eyes growing wider.

"You still have power left, after all of that?" he asked.

Mishi shrugged. She didn't like the way he was looking at her. He seemed frightened.

"We should get going," she said, wanting to get moving and to avoid Katagi's fearful glances. "Quick, get dressed. We'll have time for explanations later."

She didn't say the last part of what she was thinking; *I hope.*

30日 10月、老中 1119年

≈ Taka ≈

TAKA TOOK IN lungfuls of air and delighted in the sudden dips and turns in the trail, the rocks she had to leap over, the boulders she used to stabilize herself, letting herself half run, half fall, over the small cliffs and steep inclines before her. The wind battered her face as tree branches whipped her hair, the cold air of the mountains filled her lungs, and, before she had time to think about it, she was laughing. Nothing was funny, but she was right on Mitsu's heels, and her body was moving so quickly that one wrong move could result in a very painful tangle of limbs and bodies, with no small amount of injury to both of them. She couldn't help but laugh.

Mitsu's ankle had healed well, though they had continued to travel carefully but steadily on it for the first few days after it healed. Today, finally, they were attempting to make up some of the time that they had lost over the past eight days. The wind was in her ears, so she couldn't tell if Mitsu laughed as well while they ran, but when they finally stopped at an incline that would require both hands and feet to climb, a grin split the man's normally stoic features and his eyes sparkled with the same infectious feeling that had gripped Taka.

"Well, you're full of surprises," he said, as he stopped to pull some dried fish from his pack, ripping a hunk off with his teeth.

Taka opened her pack, removing her own piece of dried fish.

"How can anything about me surprise you, when you know absolutely nothing about me?" she asked, biting into her own piece of fish.

Mitsu shrugged, and Taka shook her head as she thought about how little they had spoken since she had healed him. Aside from the exchanges necessary for Taka to tend to his ankle, they'd barely said a hundred words to each other, and Taka wasn't sure if the man had been frightened at her ability to heal him, or merely too stubborn to thank her.

"Well, most spoiled rich girls seem the same to me," he said, in a tone that suggested he was merely stating a fact.

Heat rushed to Taka's neck at the comment, and her fists clenched and unclenched without conscious thought.

"What in all the Kami's names makes you think that I am a spoiled rich girl?" she asked.

Mitsu shrugged again.

"You went to school with Kiko-san, didn't you?"

Taka nodded, but didn't trust herself to speak.

"Well then, there you go," Mitsu said. "How else could you afford whatever special school she went to, to learn how to be a josanpu... or whatever you are?"

Taka didn't know what to say. The anger that flooded her left no room for words, and yet she wasn't even sure why she was angry. How many people knew the true horrors of the Josankō? Certainly, the people in her small village had thought the place worthy of all sorts of dark speculation, but mostly because of one girl who had run away, only to be dragged back and then never heard from again. To be truthful, most of the dark speculation regarding the Josankō that she had heard could have had just as much to do with the girls who attended it as it did with the establishment itself. The orphanage she had been raised in was only a few days' ride away from the Josankō, and her village was bound to hear more, or suspect more, about the things that went on there. In other towns, towns much farther away, places where it would take more than a tenday to reach the school... how much would anyone hear? How much would they know? With a lack of information, it made sense that Mitsu would simply make assumptions. It was what people did, when they didn't have a truth to cling to.

There was no denying that Kiko had come from a wealthy family.... Yet somehow, the mere suggestion that the Josankō was a place that anyone would choose to attend caused her hands to start shaking, and heat to travel from her belly to her neck and shoulders.

Taka shoved what remained of the dried fish back into her pack and turned and walked away from Mitsu. She knew that she was walking in the opposite direction than they were headed, that this would slow them down again, but she didn't care. She couldn't care. She had no words to explain away Mitsu's ignorance, and she didn't know what else to do with the pain that still lanced through her whenever she thought of what had happened to Kiko.

~~~

The sun was riding low in the sky when she finally returned to the spot where they had stopped to eat their snack of dried fish, and Taka didn't say a word to Mitsu as she approached. Mitsu at least had the decency not to say anything, instead turning to climb over the rocky outcropping before them, without question or explanation. Taka fleetingly wondered if the man regretted anything that he'd said, or if he simply thought that she was some simpering rich girl who reacted poorly to being called spoiled. Regardless, the numbness that she had embraced in order to be able to continue with the day's travels pushed the thought aside for her, and she simply focused on placing one foot in front of the other.

They made camp late that night, to make up for the delay that Taka had caused. She felt a brief pang of guilt for having slowed them down once more, but there was nothing she could do about it now. Silence pervaded their small camp site as they readied their bed rolls and small cooking fire.

They were eating a rabbit that Mitsu had killed during Taka's absence when Taka heard a familiar cry above her and looked up. A black speck in the moonlight circled their camp, and Taka felt the numbness that had held her all day slip slightly as she made an answering cry.

Mitsu stared at her, both eyebrows raised to his hairline, as she smiled at the black speck bathed in silver light that was growing rapidly larger.

In a handful of heartbeats, wings spread wide beat near her face, and she lifted her arm up to give Riyōshi a comfortable perch.

Is something wrong? she asked the hawk, worried by the fact that he had been traveling at night when his vision wasn't as effective.

The images and emotions that Riyōshi used to reply conveyed the message that he had been delayed after returning to his nest to inform his mate that he would be going on a journey and was unsure when he would return. He had come back to her cave to find her already gone, and had inquired with other animals to follow her from there.

Taka shook her head. *You shouldn't come with me. It may not be safe, your mate needs you.*

Riyōshi nipped her ear and replied, *my mate is strong, and I can return much faster than you can. I can take messages to Yanagi, and I can see great distances. You need my help.*

I can't let you risk yourself, she countered.

Riyōshi then bombarded her with images of his young chick the cycle before, battered and broken, life slowly slipping away from it, before Taka had stumbled upon them in the woods within a day's walk of her cave. Then he showed her images of her cradling the chick as she healed it, and the chick flying around happily a few tendays later, when it was old enough to leave the nest for good.

And then, apparently unwilling to listen to her argue, Riyōshi leapt from her arm and nestled himself into the crook of a nearby tree.

"Stubborn bird," she murmured.

Taka noted that Mitsu's eyes had not left Riyōshi, from the moment the hawk had perched on her arm, and she almost laughed to see how wide they remained as he took in the raptor on its perch, settling in for sleep.

Taka finished her food without saying a word to either of her companions, then spread out her bedroll in preparation to sleep. Mitsu spread his own roll out on the opposite side of the fire.

"I'll be very tempted to ask you about the hawk tomorrow," he said as he lay down to sleep.

"Surprised you again, have I?" she asked, finding it was somehow easier to keep the bitterness out of her voice now that Riyōshi was here.

Mitsu may have nodded, or he may not have heard her, but he made no audible response. Taka allowed the warmth of the fire, and the warmth of the hawk's friendship, to ease some of the pain from her chest as she drifted off to sleep.

~~~

The following morning, Taka woke in the predawn glow to find Riyōshi perched on Mitsu's arm. She could barely see them from where she lay, the thick morning mist obscuring her vision of where they stood at the edge of the clearing, but she noted the signs that suggested that Mitsu was communicating with the hawk. She packed her bedroll and went to join her two companions.

"I see I'm not the only one who's full of surprises," she said as she approached the man and the hawk.

Mitsu looked somewhat startled by her presence, his face pale and his eyes wide.

"We didn't wake you, did we?" he asked.

She shook her head, but didn't allow for the change of subject.

"Not that many people can communicate with birds of any kind, and fewer still can form a connection with a hawk. Anything you'd like to tell me?" she asked.

Mitsu shrugged and Riyōshi flapped his way to Taka's shoulder, where he affectionately nipped her ear hard enough to draw blood.

Taka eyed the raptor sideways, while wiping the blood from her ear, before returning her attention to Mitsu.

"I..." he opened and closed his mouth a few times. "I don't know anyone else who can do that," he said finally. "Talk to birds that is, or animals at all. I mean, Yanagi can, obviously, and I've heard of others in stories, but you're the first person I've met with the same ability."

His pallor was leaving him, but he looked at her with his head tilted to one side, as though trying to decide something about her.

"What are you?" he asked.

Taka smiled.

"A yukisō," she said with a small shrug. "A healer," she clarified, when all she got from Mitsu was a mystified expression.

"No other healers that I know can communicate with animals," he replied.

"And how many of the healers that you know have ever tried?" she asked. "It doesn't come easily. Well mammals did, but birds took ages. I still can't communicate well with most of them. Riyōshi was the first bird I successfully communicated with, and since then I've only had luck with other raptors. Though, from what Yanagi says, that's more personality than anything else."

Mitsu nodded.

"A healer?" he asked. "I didn't think women could be healers, aside from josanpu that is, but they're not supposed to have enough kisō to..." His voice trailed off, but he looked between Riyōshi and Taka with something like wonder.

"He told you, then?" she asked. "About his youngling who caught a downdraft by accident and smashed into the cliff?"

Mitsu nodded.

Taka shuddered at the memory, and couldn't help reaching up to stroke the feathers on Riyōshi's head and neck for comfort. She received a warning bite for her efforts.

"It was... a delicate procedure," she said, finally shaking off the memory of how close the young hatchling had come to death.

"And my ankle?" Mitsu asked.

"Also a delicate procedure, but not quite as difficult. And your life wasn't at risk... at least, not immediately."

Mitsu smiled then. "So, if you have enough kisō to be a qualified healer, how did you wind up at a school for rich girls with only enough kisō to be josanpu?"

Taka cringed and shouldered her pack.

"We don't have time for me to stand here and talk," she said. "I'll tell you on the way."

And, much to her own surprise, she did tell him. She hadn't really planned to. Yesterday she had been angry enough with Mitsu's ignorance that she had vowed never to correct him of it. Let him blunder along with his misconceptions for as long as he liked. She wouldn't stoop to tell him the truth. He didn't deserve it if he was so eager to make assumptions about her.

But something about seeing him communicate with Riyōshi had changed her mind about that. For one thing, Riyōshi was reluctant to even be in the presence of most humans, and for another, it reminded her that Yanagi-sensei had supposedly raised Mitsu as a boy—they were bound to have a few things in common, much as she might be loath to admit it.

So, as the leagues ticked by, she told Mitsu of how she had come to be at the Josankō, and quickly corrected the notion that it was a place for spoiled rich girls. Mitsu was silent throughout the explanation, but the only time he looked truly stricken was when she told the story of why she had finally left.

By the time they stopped to eat their midday meal, Mitsu looked like he had swallowed a pinecone covered in bird droppings. Taka wondered if she had put him off of his food entirely.

"You..." he began before pausing to swallow air, or perhaps a rising gorge. "I believe I owe you an apology..."

Taka said nothing.

"I... I'm sorry," Mitsu continued after a pause. "Sorry that I made assumptions about you, that I didn't understand... that you had to go through all of that."

He closed his eyes, as if shutting out the horrors, and something occurred to Taka for the first time as she took in just how personally Mitsu seemed to be relating to her pain—a pain that had only truly seemed to affect him when she had reached the part about her final months at the Josankō, with the trials of Kiko's pregnancy and consequent death. Hadn't Tsuku told her that her guide was someone she had known and trusted for cycles? She wondered, then, if maybe that apology had been meant for more than her.

"You knew her, didn't you?" she asked. "Kiko-san... you knew her."

Mitsu rubbed his hands over his face and nodded.

"She... she was a friend," he said, face still hidden behind his hands. "I was young when I started running messages between Kuma-sensei and the Zōkame family. It's... Kuma-sensei is the one who found me and sent me to Yanagi-san after... after my parents were killed. I was five then. By the time I was seven, I knew the forests and mountains so well that Kuma-sensei asked me to deliver a message to an ally of his. It didn't happen often, a handful of times a season cycle, but every time I went, the Zōkame family allowed me to stay the night, and each time I saw Kiko-san. She was always... well, she treated me like any other friend her own age. She never treated me like a peasant, or a serf, or an orphan. No charity, no pity... we played games and... she was like a sister."

He wiped his hands once more over his face, and looked at Taka for the first time since they had begun speaking about Kiko. The look in his eyes made Taka hurt all over again with the pain that losing Kiko had brought her.

"She left without ever saying goodbye. To go to that horrible place... but at the time... I... I thought... I didn't know."

"You thought she had just left to study at a school for rich girls and hadn't bothered to tell you about it?" Taka asked.

Mitsu nodded, pain etching a memoir across his eyes.

"She never wrote," he continued. "She never left so much as a note. She never visited home. From what you've told me, clearly she wasn't allowed to, but I thought she had simply abandoned her former life. It wouldn't be the first time a wealthy girl went to school and forgot about her family."

Taka nodded, though she couldn't say that she knew anything about what wealthy girls did. Kiko was the only one she had ever known.

"And no one ever told you the truth?" she asked.

"Why would they? I was just the messenger boy that Kiko-san had befriended. There was no reason to share family secrets with me, unless I was carrying them to someone else. And besides, it sounds as though Tsuku-san didn't even know the full truth herself, until you told it to her."

Taka sighed and angled her head, as yet another question occurred to her.

"If you knew Kiko-san's family, and you were living with Yanagi-sensei, why didn't he tell me about them at any time in the last five cycles? He knew I was looking for Kiko-san's grandmother!"

Mitsu shook his head.

"Yanagi-sensei never knew about Kiko-san. I didn't tell him about her, at least not by name. He knew that I was relaying messages between Kuma-sensei and others, but he never knew who exactly. You must know how he is—human names and activities mean so little to him, most of the time. I told him what I was doing, but the details never mattered to him. You could have told him every detail you knew about Kiko-san, and it's doubtful that he would have been able to piece together that it was someone I knew."

Taka took a deep breath as the sense of that statement calmed the ire that had started rise. She picked up her pack.

"We should get moving," she said.

~~~

That night, after they had made camp and eaten, and Taka's world narrowed to the sounds of insects and owls in the trees, the smell of wood smoke, and the sensation of a cool wind against her face, she watched the stars pass above her and wondered what Mishi was doing. Was she looking at the same night sky? Did the moonlight bathe her in silver and shadow as it did Taka? Would she ever see her again? She didn't know why it comforted her to think of a friend she was unlikely ever to see again, but somehow it lessened the pain of thinking of a friend she knew she would never see again, at least not in the world of the living.

She sighed, and the sound seemed to draw Mitsu's attention. His voice broke through the crackle of embers between them.

"How did you lose them?" he asked.

Taka turned to look at him, but couldn't make out any of his features on the other side of the fire.

"Lose what?" she asked.

"Your family. How did you come to be raised at the orphanage?"

Taka gave up trying to see his face, and once more let her eyes stray to the stars.

"I don't know." She shifted her arms behind her head as she spoke. "I was just over one cycle old when I was found at the orphanage. I don't remember anything about my life before that. I was too young. Hahasan thinks my parents died somehow, and that a friendly stranger delivered me to the orphanage, but plenty of children are abandoned... there was no real note with me, just a small slip of paper that said, 'Taka.'"

Mitsu said nothing for a while.

"You're lucky, you know," he said, just as she had begun to think he would never reply. "That you don't remember them, I mean. That way you can't miss them. That way... there was nothing for you to love."

Taka considered his words for a moment, as she watched the stars glitter benignly in the sky above.

"You were five when your parents were killed?" she asked.

Mitsu didn't respond for a moment, but eventually, he grunted in the affirmative.

"What happened to them?" she asked, after another long pause.

She wasn't sure if Mitsu would talk to her about it—they had barely spoken since that afternoon. He had seemed caught up in his own thoughts ever since they had talked about Kiko's death. But he had started this line of conversation, so perhaps it was something he wanted to speak of. She waited.

"There was a fire," he said eventually. "I remember that. There was fire everywhere, all through the house. But my mother was completely silent as she brought me to the woods behind our burning home and hid me in the trunk of a fallen tree. No screaming, no crying. She told me to stay there. She made me promise, and then she went back for my father and baby sister. They never came back out."

Taka didn't know what to say, so she remained silent. Eventually, Mitsu spoke again.

"The people from the nearest village insisted it was a tragic accident, that any house could catch fire with a bit of bad luck. I didn't argue with them, since I was only five, but I had seen blackened silhouettes against a sky lit with fire on our rooftop. And I knew that no mere fire could have stopped both of my parents. Kuma-sensei came to find me a few days after that. He had trained my father. For some reason, he's never told me why, as soon as he heard of their deaths, he came to find me. Then he took me to Yanagi-san."

"Why didn't he raise you himself?" she asked.

"He offered. I think he had planned to all along, but he could barely get me out of the village, I was so terrified of people. I had been cowering in that log until Kuma-sensei came to the woods behind the still smoking remains of our home. How he knew to look there after all the villagers had already passed me by so many times... I don't know. I suppose he must have used his own kisō to track mine.... But he found me, and we stayed in the village for one night. I spent the entire night under the futon he had laid out for me, and refused to come out when anyone other than him came near the room. That was all it took for him to realize that I was too terrified of strangers to stay there, or stay with him even. He ran a school, after all, how was he going to keep a child who couldn't be around people without screaming and throwing himself under the nearest hiding place? So, instead of heading to his school, he took me to Yanagi-san. Two cycles later, Yanagi-san took me to visit Kuma-sensei, but by then, even though I could be around people again, I loved the woods and refused to leave them. Kuma-sensei didn't argue with me, he simply offered me work as a messenger between him and some of his contacts. Yanagi-san continued to raise me."

Taka thought about that for a moment, then failed to stifle a laugh.

"What's funny?" Mitsu asked, in a tone that suggested that no answer would be acceptable.

Taka managed to get her voice under control. "I'm picturing Yanagi-sensei as a human father," she said, her voice cracking. "The scoldings must have been terrible! Did he ever sic the birds on you?"

Taka could hear the tension leave Mitsu's voice as he answered.

"More times than I care to count. You're very lucky to have a hawk on your side. I would have done anything to have a hawk on my side when Yanagi-san decided to use the birds as his lash."

It was difficult to see through the firelight, but Taka thought she saw Mitsu rub at his forearm protectively.

"Angry tree spirits are not to be trifled with," he said solemnly, causing Taka to erupt in a fit of laughter.

"You don't have to tell me that," she said. "I had to endure winter training!"

Mitsu started to chuckle then, too.

"What did you do to deserve that?" he asked.

"I got caught in a storm once and came home after dark. Yanagi-sensei was worried about me. He insisted that I rest next to the fire for a full day, kept bringing me soup. He was trying to be kind, but I was... well, it was a period when I was angry all the time. I shouted at him that I could take care of myself."

"Oh, that was a mistake," Mitsu said, chuckling.

"He told me that I could not, but if I insisted that it was so, then he would make sure that I could."

"And of course you insisted."

"Of course I did." Taka chuckled a moment longer, then sighed. "So I spent the next tenday learning to make a snow den that would protect me even in the fiercest winter storm, and how to fashion shoes out of branches that would help me walk across snow as deep as a man..."

She took a breath to continue the list, but Mitsu finished it for her.

"And how to catch a winter hare that's hiding in its den, and make the fire to cook it over, and how to get drinking water from snow, and how to traverse the mountains without causing a snow slide, or disturbing the peace of the forest."

Taka and Mitsu both laughed.

"So you had winter training too," Taka said.

"Yes, but I'm afraid I earned mine more thoroughly than you did."

"Oh?" Taka asked. "What did you—"

A cry from Ryoushi cut the sky and Taka looked up to see a tiny speck of black moving across the deeper blackness of the night sky. She called back. Riyōshi's cries rent the skies once more, and he began his looping descent. Finally, he landed on the ground before Taka and she sat up in her bed roll to look at him. The hawk had flown off on a scouting mission that morning, after Mitsu had asked him to look into a detail that he thought could be important, a piece of information he had garnered from the messages he relayed between Kuma-sensei and Zōkame-san. He hadn't told Taka what it was at the time, and she had worried that he didn't trust her, but perhaps it had simply been something he didn't think she needed to know.

Still, Riyōshi made his report directly to her. So, it was with some confusion that she relayed the message to Mitsu.

"Rōjū City looks like it's going to war."

≈ Mishi ≈

Mishi breathed in the smell of mist and fallen leaves. The trees had turned, even this far south of Rōjū City, and the wind was biting cold even though they were well out of the mountains. The night was quiet except for the sound of wind in the trees and animals shifting stealthily through the darkness. She leaned into the tree that stood behind her, working to dig the bark into her back to help keep her awake.

They hadn't stopped the first night after their escape. They had ridden through the night and all the next day, and even now they only made camp with the blankets from the horses' saddles and not even a fire to warm them.

Mishi tensed as she heard a twig snap behind her, but when she turned to see what had caused the sound, she only saw Katagi walking towards her. She relaxed and turned back to the darkened woods, searching for signs of the Rōjū's Eihei, or worse yet, hishi. Katagi settled his back against the same tree, a hand's span away from her, and looked out at the woods.

"Do you think they've followed us this far?" he asked.

Mishi shook her head.

"I don't think so. I think we outpaced them that first day. Better yet, I don't think they ever knew for certain that we had left the city until we were long gone, and since we've stayed away from the roads... I think they'll have difficulty finding us."

"I still can't believe that we made it through the eastern gate."

Mishi smiled. "When that guard shouted at the man in front of us to stop, I felt as though my heart would jump from my chest and fall to the ground," she admitted.

Katagi shook his head. "I still can't believe you managed to keep them from noticing Kusuko. She was swimming in that armor. You could have put a whole extra woman in there. They should have stopped us."

Mishi shrugged. "I had some kisō left," she said. Then she sighed and leaned harder against the tree, so the discomfort would keep her eyes open. "I'm not sure I could do anything like that now. I'm lucky I didn't fall unconscious from my horse the moment we reached this clearing."

They were both silent for a moment. Mishi kept her eyes on the forest around her, but she wondered if Katagi was thinking about all the things she'd done in the past two days. She wondered if she would see the same fear on his face that she had glimpsed when she'd come over the wall in Rōjū City, if she looked at him now. She was determined to look at the woods instead.

"Mishi-san..." Katagi began, and Mishi tried not to cringe at the uncertainty in his voice. "Mishi-san, I want to know what's going on."

She turned to glance at him then. She supposed that she shouldn't be surprised by this line of questioning, but in the silence that had grown between them, she had been sure that he would ask her about the men that she had killed—sure that he would accuse her of being a monster.

She took a deep breath and let it out. She wasn't sure that these questions would be any easier.

"I'm sorry that I got you involved in this, Katagi-san," she said, turning her eyes back to the darkened trees that surrounded them. "In the original plan, I was to get you to safety before the Eihei could raise the alarm. I'm afraid it didn't work out that way."

Katagi was silent for a moment. When he spoke, his voice was choked with frustration. "While I appreciate that the 'original' plan didn't involve me being chased by the Eihei, could you give me an actual answer instead of that small misdirection? What is going on? Why did the guards have to be involved at all? What did you do, and why? Most importantly, how is it that you are clearly a fully trained Kisōshi, when, to my knowledge, no woman is capable of being such a thing?"

Mishi took another deep breath, and wondered what she could safely tell him. "Have you considered that you might be safer not knowing the answer to those questions?" she asked.

Katagi stared at her. She didn't turn to look at him, but she could feel his gaze on her face.

Blade's Edge

"Can I be in more danger than I am right now? When we return to Kuma-sensei, will the Rōjū and their Eihei stop hunting me? Will they forgive me my association with you, simply because I return to my home? Will they not hunt me till the end of my days as it is?"

Mishi thought about that. She had hoped that would not be the case. She hadn't had much time to think of anything but their escape over the past two days, but she had hoped, briefly, when she had the chance, that they would find a way to expunge Katagi's name and have the Rōjū leave him alone. Of course, that was simply wishful thinking.

"You're right," she said at last. "Of course you're right. It's just... it isn't only me that I'm protecting by not telling you things. There are others' secrets I'm protecting."

Katagi nodded, and hesitated before speaking again.

"Then let us only speak of you and your mission," he said. "You are Kisōshi, ne?" It was barely a question.

Mishi nodded, her eyes still fixed outward, on the woods nearby.

"Kuma-sensei trained you?" he asked.

She nodded once more.

"What was your mission?"

"To steal an ancient Rōjū scroll."

"Why?"

"To use it to protect female Kisōshi... I'm afraid I can't tell you more than that without breaking my word to Kuma-sensei. There is quite a bit more to it than that, and if Kuma-sensei allows me to tell you I will gladly explain more, but for now... I think it's best if I don't."

Katagi nodded and stared thoughtfully towards the woods. Mishi took the opportunity to glance at his face. He didn't seem scared, as she had expected, he merely seemed thoughtful.

"What went wrong?" he asked at length.

She raised an eyebrow at him, unsure what he meant.

"You said the original plan involved getting me to safety before the guard was alerted. What went wrong?"

Mishi shifted her stance and looked around the tree, back to where Kusuko lay sleeping near the horses.

"She did," she said.

"What did she do?" Katagi asked.

"She set the guards on me," Mishi replied.

"And you brought her with us?" Katagi's eyes were wide with incredulity.

"She may have done it with good intentions." Mishi shrugged. "Besides, she was very useful during our escape, and she had reason to leave Rōjū City."

191

"You can't seriously trust her..."

Mishi shrugged again. "I'm not sure that I do, but... she has been helpful, and until she proves herself an enemy, I will treat her as a friend."

"Setting the guards on you doesn't count as proving herself an enemy?"

"She had reason to believe I was in trouble, and I was in a place where she could not go."

"You really believe that?"

"I believe that it's plausible. I also believe that she risked her life to help us escape."

Katagi simply looked at her.

"If she is an enemy," Mishi continued, ignoring his incredulous stare, "it's best to keep her close anyway."

Katagi finally nodded. "Fine, but I don't trust her."

"That's perfectly reasonable," Mishi agreed. She didn't want to believe that Kusuko was an enemy, and part of her was convinced that the girl had truly wanted to help, but she also had to keep in mind that the girl could be trying to gain favor with the Rōjū by working against them.

For a while, Mishi and Katagi simply watched the darkness that surrounded them. Mishi tried to remind herself that falling asleep while standing watch would have Kuma-sensei assigning her five hundred additional high kicks on each leg. Then she wondered if high kicks would help to keep her awake.

"Do you think they'll send hishi after us?" Katagi asked, long after she had suspected him of falling asleep.

Mishi shuddered and told herself it was the chill in the breeze, not the mention of hishi, that caused it.

"I hope not," she said. "I don't think we quite warrant the use of Gensokai's most powerful assassins, do you?" She smiled as she said it, but Katagi didn't return the gesture.

"Maybe *I* don't warrant them, but you might. How many men did you kill during our escape?"

Mishi felt the blood drain away from her face as she thought of that day, and she swallowed to keep her stomach from rebelling.

"I'm not sure," she answered, her voice little more than a whisper.

Katagi reached over and put a hand on her shoulder. "Mishi-san, I'm sorry. I shouldn't have asked, I didn't think..."

She shook her head to try to rid it of the sound that guard's skull had made on the stairs.

"I'm sorry," Katagi said again. This time, instead of just placing a hand on her shoulder, he wrapped her in both of his arms. She stared unseeing into the dark woods that surrounded them.

"I wish I had been more help to you," he whispered. "I wish that I had done more... so that you wouldn't have had to... I wish I could have protected you."

As his words sank through the fog of memory that trapped her in her own mind, Mishi found understanding and stepped back.

"I don't need your protection," she said, pulling his arms from her.

Katagi looked at her with his head tilted to one side for just a moment, then laughed.

"I'm well aware of that, Mishi-san." He laughed again. "It's quite obvious that you don't need anyone to protect you. Least of all me. But... that doesn't... that doesn't stop..." Katagi paused, and Mishi wondered what it was he was so reluctant to say.

"That doesn't stop me from wanting to protect you. Not because you need it, but simply because.... Is it so wrong to want to protect the people you care about?" he asked.

Now the color returned to her face and, suddenly, memories that seemed like a lifetime ago flooded her mind. Katagi telling her he liked her. Katagi saying he thought he loved her. Katagi kissing her, and finally, her throwing Katagi to the floor in a fit of... well, she wasn't sure what it was a fit of, but she thought it must have been a fit. She didn't think most women threw the men who kissed them onto the floor. Heat rushed through her, as embarrassment overwhelmed her senses.

"I still don't understand why you care about me," she said, putting her back to the tree once more, and staring fixedly into the darkness. "You don't even know me.... Until our escape you didn't even know I was a Kisōshi!"

"Mishi-san, how can you be serious?" Katagi asked. "You're a beautiful woman who could kill me with a mere thought, yet you've spent cycles humbly pretending to be a servant at my school. The mystery alone would be enough to draw me in, but on top of that you're brave, calm in an emergency, and a better fighter than I can ever hope to be.... How can any other woman compare?"

Mishi swallowed, and tried to keep the heat from her cheeks. She didn't believe that she was beautiful. A single look at Kusuko, or any of the other women of the World of Winds, made it desperately clear that she wasn't what men looked for in a companion. She was too tall, too muscular, and too lean for any man to want. Her hands were hard from weapons training, climbing the cliff to Tatsu-sama's mountain, and her work as a servant. She had small scars all over her body from training.

No man would consider her beautiful, and that was fine with her. She preferred her strength to any notion of beauty that others held, but it confused her when Katagi said she was beautiful, and it made it difficult for her to trust him.

Katagi must have been paying close attention to her face, or else she was letting her emotions slip out of her control and he was using kisō to read them.

"You don't believe that you're beautiful, do you?" he asked.

Mishi squirmed awkwardly against the tree and remained silent.

"Oh, Mishi-san, I wish I could show you what I see..."

He began to reach gently for her face, but she shifted away at the last moment, just as his skin made contact with hers. She couldn't allow herself to become distracted again. The last time, it had almost cost her the entire mission.

"You were afraid of me," she said, stepping away so that he couldn't touch her, and reminding him of the truth. He couldn't possibly find her beautiful if he also found her terrifying. "I saw it in your face as I reached the other side of the wall when we escaped the lower gardens."

Katagi shook his head. "Fear and awe may look similar on a face," he said. "I won't pretend that you don't awe me, Mishi-san, but the more I learn about you, the more I want to learn. You're dazzling, and I can't stop thinking about you."

He stepped closer then, and Mishi had to step away from the tree to avoid what she feared would be another kiss.

"It's your watch," she said, desperate for something to focus on other than the heat that was pounding through her and the small voice inside of her that was urging her to stand still, or worse yet, move closer to Katagi. "I should get some sleep if we're to travel all day tomorrow. We need to return to Kuma-sensei as quickly as possible."

Katagi lowered his hand to his side and nodded his head.

"Of course," he said, as though he hadn't been moving closer to her only a moment before, as if they'd never stopped talking about their pursuit and how they would return to the school.

"Rest," he insisted as she turned to go. "I'll see you in the morning. We should see about catching a hare or some other small game. We'll need to eat before long."

Mishi nodded, and returned to the horse blanket that she had laid out for herself earlier. She stretched out on the blanket, wrapped one half of it around her, and listened to the quiet sounds of Kusuko's breathing.

She needed rest. She would try to sleep. She wouldn't focus on the strange flips that her stomach seemed to be doing. Wouldn't let her mind stray to thoughts of the light in Katagi's eyes when he told her she was

beautiful. Wouldn't let her body remind her of the feel of Katagi standing so close to her that she could feel his breath on her face.

"There's an army trying to kill us," she reminded herself, in the barest
of whispers. "And maybe assassins, too."

So why was it that she felt her cheeks pink when she thought of the
feeling of Katagi's arms around her shoulders, or his hand against her
cheek? They had a war to fight, one that she had started. This was only
the first move, and there was so much more to be done. Kuma-sensei
would want to move to the next part of the plan as soon as she returned.
There was so much to prepare for, so many details to sort out...

So why did she fall asleep thinking about Katagi's lips against her
own?

1日 11月, 老中 1119年

≈ Taka ≈

THE SMELL OF smoke filled Taka's nostrils and lungs, and she began to cough. She tried to scream, but no sound came forth. The house was completely dark except for the glowing fire, which was slowly getting closer on all sides. She reached for the green jade bird that her mother always placed in her hands to sleep with, but it wasn't there. She tried to cry out again, but choked on smoke instead. Tears streamed down her face, but she couldn't get her body to lift her up from her bed. Then, suddenly, shadows burst into the room and arms reached down to grab her, pulling her from the clutches of the fire that threatened to engulf her.

Taka sat up in her bedroll and barely resisted the urge to scream. As she took in deep lungfuls of air and saw the woods around her, she realized that it had only been a dream. Still, sweat coursed down her back and neck, as though she had been in real danger. She supposed that the dream must have been brought on by Mitsu's story of losing his family, but she couldn't shake how overwhelmingly real everything had seemed.

One look at the sky told her that she would only have one more chance at sleep before the sky began to lighten. She lay back down in her bed roll and tried to rest.

~~~

Taka and Mitsu were moving at full speed. Taka's lungs were burning with the chill air, the scent of coming snow filled the mountains, and she had to put every ounce of her attention into where she placed her feet as they moved over the rocky terrain that lay between them and their destination. Whenever she and Mitsu didn't have to use their hands to help them scramble over rocks, they were running, or as close to running as the terrain would allow.

They had waited until first light to start moving, only because they had agreed that they needed the rest and wouldn't make very good time on this kind of terrain in the dark. They had sent Riyōshi back to monitor what was happening at Rōjū City to the north, as well as on the road south from there to Kuma-sensei's school. The hawk could cover the distance in a handful of hours, when it would have taken them more than five days.

Around midday, they came across a small village nestled in a high valley. They could see it long before they reached it, and Taka wondered why they were headed through it, rather than around.

"Is it worth the risk to travel through the village that lies below us?" she asked, when they stopped to drink water from the skeins they carried.

"Normally I would say no, but the land to either side of this valley is steep and rocky enough to slow down a goat. If we had more time, we could afford to head south of here and then curve back up around the trailing peaks of this mountain range, but with the Eihei on the move towards the south, we can't afford the delay. The small cart path that leads from this high valley into the lower range is the fastest way to cover the ground between us and the school."

Taka nodded. "You seem to know a lot about this area," she said, even as the began their descent into the village once more.

"This is where I was born," Mitsu replied over his shoulder, before turning to the trail and picking up the near-run that the two of them had kept up all day.

Less than a league later, they were in a small clearing that contained nothing more than a grey, sandy circle in its center. A small stone altar had been set up on one side of the clearing, but otherwise the space remained empty. Taka watched Mitsu walk through the circle, and twitched as something in her mind called out for her to stop.

Mitsu stooped before the small altar, removing a stick of incense from his pack, which he then lit and placed in the tiny bowl of sand that rested on the altar for that very purpose. Taka approached the altar slowly, unsure why the sight of it made her skin prickle.

"This was your home?" she asked.

Mitsu nodded, but didn't say anything.

"Why has no one built here?" she asked.

"It's too far away from the village," he said quietly, even as he continued to stare at an object that lay beside the incense holder. "Still another league until you actually reach the village proper. And besides," he said, standing up, "I still own the land."

Taka raised an eyebrow at that and was about to ask him more, when her eye was caught by the small object that Mitsu had been staring at on the altar, previously hidden from her view.

"Taka," she said, reaching for the small green carving.

"What?" Mitsu asked, his eyes suddenly wide as he looked at her.

"Taka," she said again, touching the small jade statue of a hawk that she recognized from her dream. "It… it helped me sleep," she said, before she could think about the words. It had just been a dream. But she hadn't known what the jade bird was called in the dream, the name had just come to her now.

"What did you say?" Mitsu asked. Taka was too mesmerized by the small jade bird to look at Mitsu's face, but his voice sounded rough as he spoke to her.

"Nothing," she said, feeling embarrassed now that she had brought herself back to reality. "I had a dream last night and that bird was in it. Only, in the dream, it was mine."

She stopped then, sure she must sound insane.

"How can that be?" Mitsu asked.

"Where did you find it?" she asked, still taking in the details of the tiny hawk carving. It reminded her of Riyōshi, in a pleasant way. She ran a finger over it and felt another chill run up her arm.

"It was my sister's," Mitsu said, putting his hand on Taka's shoulder and turning her around to face him. "It was mine until my sister was born, and then I gave it to her to help her sleep. We named it Taka. It was one of the only words she could say…"

Mitsu's face was alight with an emotion that Taka didn't understand. His hands reached to her face, and he lowered his eyelids as though trying to see something he couldn't quite focus on.

"How old did you say you were when… when you were taken to that orphanage?" Mitsu asked. His voice was urgent. He couldn't possibly think—

"About one, I think. They were never sure…" she stammered. "Mitsu-san, you can't possibly think… I thought your sister was dead."

"I thought so too," he said, staring carefully at her face. "You look like her, though. Or I think you do. Damn it all, it's been so long since I've seen her! I'm trying to focus on sixteen cycle old memories."

"Look like who, Mitsu-san?"

"My mother," he said, still staring at her face.

"Mitsu-san, the orphanage that I grew up in is a tenday's journey from here. Who would have taken me there? And why? Wasn't the whole point to kill your entire family?"

"How should I know?" Mitsu said. "I was a five cycle old boy forced to hide in a log. How could I possibly know what the point of that kind of destruction was? But... but how else could you know the name of that pendant... or that it was to help her sleep? And your name? Why did you arrive at an orphanage with a note that said 'Taka?'"

Taka shook her head. None of this could be possible.

"What if it was the only word you would say?"

Taka took a deep and shuddering breath... it had just been a dream. Hadn't it?

"It was just a dream, Mitsu-san... my imagination taking all of my worries from the past few tendays, and using your story of a burning house to give it all context."

"I *never* said anything about my sister's pendant. Never. I'm sure of it. I never talk about it to anyone. It's... it's too... personal. But you knew. You knew she slept with it and you knew she called it Taka. How could you know any of that?"

"Maybe... I don't know. Could you have dreamt it, and your kisō pushed it out to me?"

"You said you dreamt you were the girl? Every nightmare I've ever had about my parents' death, and I've had plenty, have all been about me being trapped in that damned log. I have never once dreamt that I was my sister..."

"Mitsu-san, this is too.... How can this be true?"

"I don't know..." Mitsu looked away from her, for the first time since he had turned her around to face him, and his eyes grew distant. "But we're headed to find someone who might."

After a moment, he picked up the small jade bird and handed it to her. "Keep this," he said. "It will bring you luck."

"I can't, Mitsu-san. Your sister... this altar... it would be disrespectful to take it." Taka tried to hand it back, but he folded it into her fingers once more.

"Taka-san, if my sister isn't dead, she doesn't need the altar, and even if she is, I like the idea of you carrying her memory around with you. It feels right to me. Please, take it."

Taka nodded and ran her fingers over the tiny hawk carving while she tried to keep the tears out of her eyes. She looked carefully at the small figurine and smiled at it, a warm feeling spreading through her, even though she thought all of this had to be a crazy dream and nothing more. She kissed the small bird and then tucked it into the pouch at her belt.

When she looked up, Mitsu had his hand extended, and his eyes were alight with something Taka couldn't quite identify.

"Come, on Taka-chan," he said, his mouth curving up in a mischievous grin, "I'll race you to town."

Taka laughed, ignored Mitsu's proffered hand, and took off down the trail that led from the empty clearing into the village. She didn't know what it was like to have a brother, and she still wasn't sure that she had one, but she knew that she wasn't going to start letting Mitsu call her Taka-chan and patronize her. Her grin only widened when she heard a cackle from Mitsu, and the sound of his strides hitting the trail behind her.

4日 11月, 老中 1119年

≈ Taka ≈

THREE DAYS OF some of the hardest traveling Taka had ever done saw them cresting the final mountain between them and Kuma-sensei's school. Pink light tinged the sky and the gathering clouds behind them, as they looked down into the valley. Taka pulled her light fur cape more tightly around her, glad that she was wearing her leathers and not the decorative kimono that Tsuku-san had given her. Not only would she have destroyed the kimono by now if she had been forced to travel in it, but she would also have frozen to death over the past few nights in the mountains.

She heard the soft footsteps of Mitsu behind her and resisted the urge to turn around. Instead, she used kisō to reach out to him and receive his silent reply. She continued to gaze out at the view of the valley stretched before them.

"How much farther from here?" she asked.

"Another day," Mitsu replied, as he stepped up to the same rock on which she was perched.

Taka scanned the sky for signs of Riyōshi. The clouds were low, and the coming darkness made it difficult to make out the shape of a hawk in the distance, so she called out, her voice imitating the high pitched keen of a red-tailed hawk, and waited.

After a few heartbeats of silence, the call was returned from within the cloud cover, and moments later Riyōshi was diving towards them, a small black speck that got larger almost faster than the eyes could track. When he finally spread his wings to slow himself from the prolonged dive, Taka raised her leathered arm and Riyōshi clung to it.

Immediately, the hawk began to convey images to her of the the road from Rōjū City to the town that lay below them now. She saw a troupe of a hundred Eihei riding in ranks along the road, all wearing the symbol of the Rōjū. Riyōshi showed her locations that she didn't recognize, but assumed were markers of distance, and then an image that she couldn't quite decipher. Seven figures riding dark horses, clad all in grey, not in kimono, but uwagi and habaki: clothes that more closely resembled the leggings and shirts that she and Mitsu both wore. The grey clad figures rode through the night, and the village that Riyōshi showed her next was different from any of the ones he had shown her in relation to the mounted guards.

Confused, Taka asked Riyōshi to relay the message to Mitsu. As Mitsu processed the images shown to him by the hawk, the color left his face and the mischievous sparkle that usually lit his eyes slowly faded. By the time Riyōshi flapped his way to the nearest tree, Taka wondered if Mitsu would be able to speak.

"What is it?" she asked.

Mitsu shook himself before replying. "You saw the Eihei?" he asked.

"Yes, but I didn't recognize the towns they passed through. How far away are they?"

"Five days at least. That large a group moves slowly, even when they're traveling at full speed."

"And the last images?" Taka asked, hoping that her guess was far from accurate.

"Hishi," Mitsu confirmed, his voice barely above a whisper. "Less than a day away."

Taka's blood chilled in her veins. She had known that it was unlikely that the figures in the image would be anything other than hishi. Who else covered themselves in grey and rode through the night? But she had hoped that they weren't so close. Would her newest ally be destroyed before she even had a chance to meet him? Would this mean the end of her best chance at undermining the Rōjū?

"We'll never make it in time to warn them," she said, her voice catching.

Mitsu straightened his shoulders and stared into the valley.

"Perhaps they already know what's coming," he suggested. He raised his arm for Riyōshi to come to him, shifting his weight to hold the bird more steadily. "We have to try at least.... Perhaps Riyōshi can deliver a message for us. Kuma-sensei has sent birds to me before. Never a hawk, but.... We can hope."

Taka nodded.

Moments later, Riyōshi took flight, and as soon as the bird was gone Mitsu turned to Taka. "Time to run," he said. So they ran.

⟫ Tsuku ⟪

Tsuku-san carried the tray, heavily laden with her tea supplies, into the large hosting room that she and Yasuhiko kept for entertaining guests when they were in Rōjū City, and set up the items she would need on the low cherry table in front of her. The five voting members of the Rōjū council sat on the other side of the room, their feet tucked beneath them on the comfortable zabuton that the servants had placed there for them only moments before.

Tsuku-san didn't look up from her tea preparations as the men began to talk. Yasuhiko spoke first, as host. Tsuku-san tuned out everything as the formalities were exchanged. She was halfway through her tea ceremony by the time the men reached the meat of the issue.

"Our Eihei and hishi are now closing in on the people responsible for the attack we experienced six days ago," Yasuhiko began, "and I have asked you all here to discuss how the traitors should be dealt with. It is my belief that this heinous act must be met with the utmost deliverance of our authority. I believe we should bring the perpetrators to a very public trial, that we might show all Gensokai what is done to the kind of rabble who would dare insult our authority with this kind of act. It is of paramount importance that we discredit them publicly, with as many witnesses to their execution as we can gather. The seeds of discord that a group like this may have already sown must be weeded out, at all costs."

Tsuku didn't wince at the words that Yasuhiko used to talk about their old friend and his students, but she wanted to. Yet she continued her tea making as though no one else were present, carefully taking herself through every delicate step of the procedure and using each movement to bring calm and focus to her bearing.

"Nnn," said the fourth member of the voting council, a balding man with a large rounded belly that fought to burst forth from his uwagi. "Zōkame-san is quite right. These people should be made an example of. There is no room for this kind of rebellion in Gensokai. I've already heard rumors that one of the Kisōshi in the band that escaped from here was a woman. We can't let that sort of news spread."

"Bah. No one will believe that kind of thing," said the second member of the voting council, who was, in contrast to the fourth member, so thin as to look frail. "The Rōjū has done its job well for the last thousand cycles. No one even believes in the possibility of female Kisōshi anymore. Just because a few crazies are spreading that kind of rumor—"

"For anyone to be saying it," interrupted the third member of the voting council, a short, square jawed man who was almost as wide as he was tall, "someone must believe it. Ergo, it is a problem that must be rectified. If the people begin to believe that female Kisōshi are possible, then they will begin to question why there haven't been any for so long. That is something we must prevent at all costs. But I'm not convinced we have to have a public trial in order to make that happen. Eliminating all of the people involved in this miniature rebellion should be just as effective."

"Simply eliminating them won't suffice," Yasuhiko stated with surety. "My sources tell me that this 'rumor' has spread far enough already that the only way to squash it will be to publicly denounce the entire group, and make it clear that they are frauds."

"How do we prove them to be frauds?" asked the fourth member of the voting council. "The young woman that escaped here was in fact Kisōshi, wasn't she?"

"Of course," said the second member. "She'd have to be one to escape from the middle of Rōjū City, and a damned powerful one, at that."

"How is that even possible?" asked the fourth member. "Isn't the purpose of the whole system of josanpu to keep this very thing from happening?"

"Systems can be avoided," said Yasuhiko sternly, "which is why it's so important that we reinstate the proper amount of fear in the people by bringing this group to a public trial. We must remind the josanpu that their lives are forfeit if they fail to do their jobs, and we must remind the people that female Kisōshi are a myth and that anyone purporting otherwise will be dealt with viciously."

Tsuku managed not to shudder at hearing those words come from her husband's mouth. She used the familiarity of the tea ceremony to ground herself, and made the final preparations on each cup.

"They need to be killed," said the first member of the voting council, his grandfatherly silvering hair and placid brown eyes indicating his rank and stature. The rest of the group was instantly silent. "We cannot suffer them to live, and the sooner they die, the better. Each day that they live is an affront to the Rōjū voting council and all of Gensokai."

Silence followed that proclamation, and Tsuku delivered the individual cups of macha, along with a single sweet bean mochi, to each of the men in the wake of the comment's power.

"We shall vote," declared the first member of the voting council. "Those in favor of bringing the traitors to trial?"

Yasuhiko was the only member who dared to raise his hand. Tsuku's heart plummeted to her feet at the sight, and she worked to keep her face composed as she moved slowly back to her place at the low cherry table at the front of the room.

"Those opposed?" The first member of the voting council asked. Everyone but Yasuhiko raised his hand. "It is decided then. They are to die with the arrival of the hishi. See that it is so."

Three of the five voting members took their leave. Only Yasuhiko and the first member remained to sip their tea. For a long time, the two men simply sat in silence and enjoyed the contrast of the bitter macha with the sweetness of the mochi. When he had finally finished the green foamy brew, the first Rōjū stood up and inclined his head to Tsuku.

"Zōkame Tsuku-san," he said with a gentle smile. "You always prepare the most wonderful macha—it is a true pleasure to watch you perform the ceremony. Thank you for your time and for sharing your talent with us."

Tsuku bowed in return, but said nothing.

"Zōkame-san," the first Rōjū continued, turning his attention to Yasuhiko, "I appreciate your wish to bring these traitors to justice, but I'm afraid that we cannot make it look as though they have a strong enough position to merit our wrath. As long as our hishi are successful at removing them before they gain any more public attention, this whole thing should be put to bed quite easily."

"Of course, Rōjū-sama," Yasuhiko said, bowing his head and keeping it low as the other man exited the room.

Tsuku continued to pick up the small bowls used to serve the macha, while she waited for Yasuhiko to follow the first Rōjū from the room and latch the doors that led to their rooms. When Yasuhiko finally returned, she turned to him and could no longer contain the tears in her eyes.

"Yasuhiko-kun, what will we do?" she asked.

Yasuhiko shook his head. This had been the most important part of their plan, and he had failed. "There's nothing we can do. I can't send contradictory orders without being detected. Nor can I send any kind of warning."

He wrapped Tsuku in his arms, and for a long moment they just stood like that without saying a word. Tsuku didn't know what her husband was thinking at that moment, but she was picturing what would happen to a school full of Kisōshi if they were set upon by hishi in the night, unwarned and unprepared.

"We'll have to trust to hope," Yasuhiko whispered into her hair.

≈ *Mishi* ≈

Mishi lay on her futon, her eyes closed and her breathing slow and constant. After covering a tenday's worth of travel in only five, she was exhausted, but she could not sleep. Her reunion with her sisters, Kuma-sensei, and Tenshi had been joyful, but brief. Katagi and Kusuko had been shown to guest rooms to take their rest shortly after arriving, and Mishi and Kuma-sensei had talked long into the evening after their meal. She had bathed to try to calm herself, but now her mind raced with possibilities and anticipation. She willed her mind calm and her senses open.

For a long time she heard nothing but the quiet sounds of a deep autumn evening. The constant hum of locusts, the wind rattling the shoji that covered her windows. She breathed in the smell of turning leaves and a chilled wind, and her mind stilled further. Her perceptions were open to every tiny detail around her, save sight.

Then she heard a sound that was barely distinguishable from the fall of leaves or rattle of wind. If she hadn't been waiting for it, she would never have noticed. She pulled kisō from the depths of her fuchi, and let the energy surrounding her gather, the threads a web of perception around her, with herself as the focal point.

The shoji that led from the courtyard to her room slid gently open, with barely a sound. Mishi's fingers clenched imperceptibly beneath her sheets, but her eyes remained shut, and her breathing even. A slight whisper through the air above her was her only warning. It was all that she needed.

In an instant, her arm was up and arcing through the air, the katana she held following it in a graceful semicircle that split the night with a flash of moonlight on steel. The sound of swords clashing broke the stillness that had settled so deeply on the school.

Mishi rolled towards the open shoji and angled her legs to sweep at those of her opponent. She connected, and the grey clad figure dropped to the floor. They rose at the same time, Mishi's sword up and ready to parry another attack even as she stood. Her opponent, however, rose with a shuriken in hand and lobbed the small black painted disk directly at Mishi's throat. Mishi's katana met the rotating blade mid air and deflected it into the wall, but her nose caught the slightly acrid smell that accompanied the flying disk and she knew it was poisoned. That knowledge put her on the offensive. Where she would normally be willing to tire her opponent out with defensive maneuvers, she now understood that strategy was a luxury she could not afford. Even a small cut could be lethal, if she was caught by a poisoned blade. She would have to attack without pause in order to keep this hishi from launching another poisoned shuriken at her.

She pressed her opponent, sure now that the hishi meant to kill her rather than capture her. She slashed forward, advancing as she did so, forcing her opponent to lose ground, pressing the hishi towards the wall.

Her opponent tried to press forward, to break out of Mishi's rhythm, but Mishi would not be deterred. The grey clad figure backed, and backed again, until it was pressed to the wall with nowhere left to turn. From there, the hishi grew desperate.

Mishi had hoped that knowing the hishi were coming for them would be all the advantage that she would need. She had hoped that, without the benefit of an ambush, the hishi wouldn't be able to outfight them. The fact that this hishi was still fighting back, that Mishi hadn't already overcome her opponent, made her worry for her sisters and Kuma-sensei.

Finally, she managed a small cut on her opponent's forearm, causing the hishi to drop its katana. The hishi gasped, and Mishi was startled to hear a woman's voice. She had no more time to wonder at the hishi's gender, as the assassin was now scrambling in the folds of her uwagi for another poisoned blade. Mishi made two more shallow cuts in rapid succession—one on the hishi's shoulder and the other near her heart. The woman's eyes, the only feature visible in the grey hood and scarf that covered her face, widened, and Mishi saw understanding dawn in those eyes even as the woman collapsed to the floor.

As the woman went down, Mishi sensed a faint pulse of kisō from her, along with a feeling of panic. The assassin must have tried to warn the rest of her company, whether about the sleeping draught on Mishi's blade, or the mere fact that they were expected, Mishi didn't know, and had no time to wonder. She ran from the room to check on Kuma-sensei and the others.

As she slid from her room into the hallway to see where she was most needed, Mishi went over the plan and her meeting with Kuma-sensei in her head.

Kuma-sensei had expected that the Rōjū would send the Eihei after them, but Mishi had hoped that they would be traveling in larger numbers and consequently be slow to arrive, which Kuma-sensei had agreed was likely. Halfway through their planning, Kuma-sensei had left the room to receive a 'messenger' that Tenshi had announced, and returned insisting that they consider the possibility of hishi arriving right on Mishi's heels.

Mishi had shivered at the mere mention of the Rōjū's most feared assassins. The hishi were likely the people responsible for her parents' deaths, as well as the deaths of Kuma-sensei's wife and daughter. Still, to those who hadn't experienced their violence personally, little was known about the hishi, except that they were thought to use poisons and were as stealthy as they were deadly. The little information that they did have concerning hishi came from Kuma-sensei's personal experience, but even with that experience, he knew very little. The hishi were best known for their secrecy, and most citizens of Gensokai weren't even aware of their existence, or if they were, they generally considered them more fable than fact. One of the most frightening things about dealing with the hishi would be not knowing what to expect.

As a countermeasure to the poisons that the hishi might use, Kuma-sensei had asked Tenshi to concoct a strong and fast-acting sleeping draught. Once ready, Mishi had applied it to her own katana and then to Kuma-sensei's, before taking the oil with her as she made the rounds to 'say goodnight' to her sisters. Along with the oil, Mishi delivered a warning to her sisters that sleep wasn't in their best interests tonight. Mishi silently thanked the Kami for whatever message Kuma-sensei had received that night. If the messenger that Tenshi had announced hadn't warned them, they would already be lying dead in their beds.

Mishi heard sounds of struggling coming from Ami's room across the hall, and she rushed to join the battle. Yet even as she arrived at Ami's door, the hishi that Ami had been battling was pushed through the shoji and collapsed to the ground. Ami followed immediately behind the unconscious figure, looking sweat soaked and disheveled, but ready for action. Mishi caught the girl's eye and nodded, before turning to run towards Kuma-sensei's rooms. Ami headed the opposite direction, towards the rooms of Sachi and their guests.

The shoji to Kuma-sensei's rooms was already open when Mishi arrived, so she slowed her pace and entered cautiously. She could hear the clash of steel on steel and labored breathing in the back room, so she made her way quickly across the tatami floor that separated her from Kuma-sensei's sleeping quarters. The shoji to that room was also open, and as she neared it she could make out the figure of Kuma-sensei and two hishi locked in battle. Kuma-sensei faced the door, and would be able to see her coming. He was either lucky, or had already done some skillful maneuvering, and both of his opponents were in front of him with their backs to the open shoji, though neither of them stood directly in front of it. Mishi assessed quickly and decided that the rightmost hishi would be most surprised by her attack, so she executed a roll that would take her directly behind the man, slashing out with her katana even as she stood from the roll. The hishi had barely registered her arrival in time to turn and parry the slash. The parry was clumsy, and Mishi's next cut tore the cloth and skin of the hishi's upper arm. Another quick cut to the assassin's face and the figure collapsed, the sleeping draught overtaking his consciousness.

Mishi turned in time to see Kuma-sensei's opponent collapse to the ground beside his fellow.

"These ones weren't as much of a challenge as the one in my room," she said, as Kuma-sensei turned to look at her with the beginning of a smile on his lips. "You must have tired them out."

Kuma-sensei was on the verge of responding, when a shriek filled the air. It had come from the direction of the gardens. Mishi didn't wait for Kuma-sensei's reaction, she simply ran as fast as her limbs would allow.

What she saw when she arrived beside the small koi pond that formed the focal point of the garden confused her. Sachi was locked in combat with one of the hishi and seemed to be holding her own, but she was crying and shouting something. Mishi ran directly behind the hishi with whom Sachi was engaged, and the hishi didn't register her arrival until it was entirely too late. Mishi sliced deeply into the assassin's arm, and the grey clad figure collapsed almost instantly.

Sachi was still crying. Mishi didn't understand. The girl appeared uninjured and she had been winning, what could be wrong? Then she saw it. A faint line of red cut across Sachi's right arm. It was barely a scratch. Mishi grabbed Sachi's arm and pulled it towards her. Instantly, she recognized the same acrid smell that had been present on the blades of all the hishi she'd fought with so far.

Sachi shook her head. "It's too late," she said. She sobbed once more, and Mishi could feel her arm start to go limp under her hand.

"No. NO!" This couldn't be happening, not to Sachi. "There must be some way... I'll get Tenshi. She can do something, she can heal you!"

Before the other girl could say anything, before Mishi could register the defeat in Sachi's eyes, she ran. She didn't know where Tenshi might be. The woman was supposed to be hiding until they gave the all clear, but Mishi didn't know where. She was afraid to call out, to draw the attention of yet more hishi to herself. Even worse would be to attract hishi to wherever Tenshi was hiding. The woman was a healer who had never trained in the fighting arts, and she would be hard pressed to defend herself. Mishi turned a corner and came across Ami, who was running in the opposite direction. Mishi stopped her.

"Sachi," she panted, in a whisper that she hoped none of the hishi would hear. "Sachi needs Tenshi. Do you know where she is?"

Ami shook her head, as all of the blood drained from her face.

"Sachi? What happened? Where is she?" she asked.

Mishi couldn't bear to answer the first question, so she only answered the second.

"The garden, by the koi pond."

Then she ran again, desperate to find Tenshi, hoping that the woman would have some miracle to save her friend. No, to save one of the girls who had been her sister for the past eight cycles.

She turned a corner and found yet another grey clad figure stalking the hall before her. The hishi seemed to be looking for an alternate entrance to the kitchens. Suddenly, all the hurt and anger that Sachi's fate had stirred in her overwhelmed her senses. She charged the assassin before he even registered her presence.

The hishi turned at the last moment, Mishi's unrestrained ire making her footsteps louder than usual and alerting the assassin. This time, Mishi's attack lacked all the finesse and grace of her usual motions. She hacked at the figure before her, each strike meant to be a killing blow, her fury pervading every cut. With each attack, she thought of Sachi, the poisoned cut in her arm, the death that awaited her.

Even as the tears came to her eyes, she attacked, dodging and parrying with ease, the movements coming naturally, though fueled by more anger than she had ever felt in her life. A need for vengeance pulsed through her body and she thought the hishi before her must be able to sense his doom, but if so, it wasn't for very long. After pressing the assassin all the way to the end of the hall, she feinted left and let her foot slide back, as though she had lost her balance. The hishi lunged forward at the opening she had created, but the slide was a calculated move, and the opening only a lure to bring him closer. As the man stepped forward, Mishi slid her back foot out in an arc behind her that forced her body to follow it. In seconds her sword, following the arc of her body, had slid neatly across the hishi's chest and opened him from ribs to shoulder. He collapsed, not from the sleeping draught that coated her blade, but because death had taken him.

Tears streamed down Mishi's face. She wanted to continue her search for Tenshi, but she knew there was little point. Finding the healer might only bring hishi directly to her hiding place, and there was nothing that Tenshi could do for Sachi anyway. Mishi had learned that well enough in their basic healing classes. Poisons, particularly the kind that assassins were rumored to use, only needed contact with the bloodstream to take effect. Once that happened, there was no amount of healing that could stop them.

Mishi wiped her face and ran through the hallway. If there were any other hishi left standing on the grounds, they would soon regret ever having set foot here.

5日 11月, 老中 1119年

≈ Mishi ≈

MISHI DRAGGED THE only surviving hishi forward and threw her to the ground, placing her katana against the assassin's neck. The smell of smoke and coming snow tinged the air; some of the last hishi had been trying to set fire to the kitchens, so as to draw Tenshi-san out from her hiding place. The fire had been extinguished, and Tenshi had been found, unharmed. Only the small lanterns that lit the walkway that encircled the garden provided light to see by, but it was enough to catch the koi pond in a dim glow and make out the details of faces within easy reach.

Mishi, Kuma-sensei, and Katagi all gathered by the koi pond and surrounded the grey clad figure. As Mishi regarded the still unconscious assassin, she wondered if the hollow part of her that seemed to grow every time she looked at Sachi's lifeless form, still clutched in Ami's arms, would ever let her know peace.

She tore the mask from the unconscious hishi and stepped back.

She heard Katagi gasp, and as the dim lantern glow finally revealed the face of the woman who she had fought in her sleeping quarters at the very beginning of the attack, she had to fight the urge to slash the assassin's throat on the spot.

She had never been sure of Kusuko's loyalty, but the extent of the young woman's betrayal caused her skin to prickle and her nerves to scream, as she realized the truth of the matter. Sachi lay dead not three arm spans from where she stood, and the traitor behind the attack lay unconscious before her. Mishi's fingers flexed at the hilt of her Katana.

Kuma-sensei put a calming hand on her shoulder.

212

"Questions first, Mishiranu-san," he said quietly.

Mishi nodded. She knew that they needed to find out how much Kusuko knew before they decided what to do with her. Mishi silently hoped that Kuma-sensei would ask her to kill the traitorous woman. Each life that she had taken over the past few days had weighed heavily on her conscience, each one was a scar that her soul would bear for the rest of her days, but now, in this moment, she found that she actually wanted to take someone's life. For the first time since everything had changed for her eight cycles ago and she had discovered what she was, she wanted to use her skill as a Kisōshi to hurt someone else. A small part of her wondered if that made her a monster.

It was only a handful of moments until Tenshi arrived with a small brown jar in her hand. She handed the jar to Kuma-sensei, then crouched beside Ami and began whispering to the still weeping girl.

Kuma-sensei opened the jar and used his index finger to remove a small dab of the paste contained inside. He nodded to Mishi and she replaced her katana at Kusuko's exposed neck. Then he bent down and pulled out Kusuko's lip to wipe the bitter smelling brown paste along the inside of it. He stepped back, and Mishi was shocked to see that the brown paste worked in a matter of a dozen heartbeats.

Kusuko's eyes blinked open, and she struggled against the ropes that bound her hands and legs behind her. Her eyes widened as her tongue shifted through her mouth.

"Looking for this?" Kuma-sensei asked, holding up a small black capsule.

Kusuko's gaze switched from startled confusion to a cold, purposeful glare.

"The few of your companions who did not die fighting us chose to bite down on their capsules when we woke them. As you are consequently the last surviving member of your band, we decided to make the choice for you." Kuma-sensei slid the tiny pill into his obi before continuing. "We have some questions for you."

"I won't answer them," Kusuko replied, in a controlled monotone.

Mishi wondered if Kusuko was actually calm, or if she was merely trained to appear so in all circumstances. Either way, the girl hadn't registered much emotion on her face when informed that all of her fellow hishi were dead.

Mishi adjusted her grip on her katana and pushed it a tiny bit closer to Kusuko's neck. If she was anything like the other hishi they had tried to question, then she wasn't afraid of death, but Mishi wondered if the thought of a painful and slow death might make her talk. It seemed Kuma-sensei was having a similar thought.

"There are fates worse than poison, Kusuko-san. Are you sure you'd like to experience them before you speak to us?"

Kusuko blinked slowly and tried to swallow, the motion drawing a thin red line across her neck from Mishi's blade. Mishi saw the line appear, and wondered what had changed within her in the past few days that she didn't shudder at the thought of causing this girl pain in order to get information from her. As if in answer to her question, Ami's sobs grew louder for a moment before Tenshi murmured words to calm her.

"Besides," Kuma-sensei continued, before Kusuko had a chance to respond. "We don't wish to ask you any questions about the inner workings of the hishi. You can keep your cowards' secrets and take them with you to the grave. The information we seek is hardly valuable to your master, but could be valuable to us."

Kusuko didn't reply, but she flicked her eyes between Mishi and Kuma-sensei once more.

"Why did you befriend Mishi in Rōjū City?" he asked, his voice still mild.

The corner of Kusuko's mouth turned up, and Mishi thought that if the traitorous snake so much as smiled, she would cut her down, unanswered questions or not. Kusuko must have sensed the shift in Mishi's stance that accompanied the thought, as the corner of her mouth dropped before she spoke. Perhaps she had simply been assessing whether or not the leaders of her band of hishi would kill her for answering the question.

"When on duty in Rōjū City, I serve as a spy," Kusuko said, her eyes shifting between Kuma-sensei and Mishi. "My purpose is to look into those that the Eihei would generally overlook. Mishi's guise as a servant was good, but something about her bearing didn't sit well with me. I ran into her while returning from a separate mission, and her interactions with Katagi-san never seemed quite right. She was insufficiently subservient. Then, when Katagi-san was introduced to the Rōjū, I used kisō to scan her and she turned to look at me. If she hadn't had any kisō, she would never have noticed the contact... I took it upon myself to keep an eye on her."

"And why didn't you have the guards seize me the moment you found me suspicious?" Mishi asked, before Kuma-sensei could formulate his next question.

"Because it served me better to know what you were doing than to have you seized for no reason." The tone of Kusuko's voice implied that any idiot should have known the answer to that question, and Mishi clenched her jaw to avoid speaking again out of turn.

"Why set the guards on her in the library and then help her escape?" Kuma-sensei asked, calling on the briefing that Mishi had given him yesterday to formulate his questions.

"Because once I made my report I was asked to follow her, not apprehend her."

"You killed your own men." It was the first time that Katagi had spoken since seeing Sachi's crumpled body by the koi pond. He seemed unable to keep the disgust from his voice. "The guard you killed with your throwing knife in Rōjū City…"

There was a cold sheen to Kusuko's eyes as she replied. "The Eihei are NOT my men." She almost spat the words, and Mishi was reminded of the look of triumph that Kusuko hadn't been able to hide when Mishi had accidentally killed the Kisōshi guard on the library stairs. Suddenly, a detail clicked in Mishi's mind.

"You were telling the truth, weren't you?" she asked quietly, eying the woman with curiosity. "About the start of your life? The orphanage, the man you were sold to?"

Kusuko looked up at her then, and Mishi wondered if the hatred she saw there was directed at her, or at a memory from the young woman's past.

"I was sold, as I told you. But no mama-san ever took pity on me. I was brought in front of my town's council for killing the man who had… kept me… for two cycles."

Kuma-sensei nodded, as though the story made sense to him. "And one of those council members put you in the hands of someone who would make use of your hatred and seeming talent for killing?"

Kusuko only nodded.

Mishi's mind ran through her own childhood, and wondered how close her fate had come to matching Kusuko's. Not for the first time, she wondered if Taka had escaped that fate as well, and shuddered when she considered the possibility that she hadn't.

Kuma-sensei interrupted her thoughts. "Kusuko-san, how many female hishi are there?"

Kusuko shook her head as though she wasn't going to answer, but when Mishi's blade pressed imperceptibly into her neck, she said, "I would imagine there are as many as there are female Kisōshi."

Kuma-sensei nodded. "And how much do you and your… fellows… know about my school here?"

Kusuko tried to shrug, but was hindered by the sword at her throat and the way her arms and legs were tied behind her. "If the rest of my brothers and sisters are truly dead, then my leaders know little more than Mishi's identity and the fact that she and a handful of other girls are

Kisōshi. I didn't have time to make a detailed report before we attacked."

Kuma-sensei seemed to contemplate that for a moment, then he turned to Katagi. "Katagi-san, please escort Tenshi-san to her quarters and help her prepare for a long journey. Prepare a light bag for yourself. Ami-chan, please return to your room and prepare small bags for both you and Mishi. Be sure to bring all of your best weapons."

Mishi waited, her katana still against Kusuko's throat, as the others left the garden. Finally Kuma-sensei turned to her.

"I believe Kusuko-san has told us the truth, or at least part it," he said, as Mishi's eyes met his.

Mishi thought about that for a moment. "She has power as well, and could be deceiving us."

"She could be, yes. But some of what she says is true."

"We can't know which parts, though. She's useless to us as an informant."

Kuma-sensei nodded. "I don't believe we benefit much from her continued presence. Indeed, every moment she remains with us is a moment when we risk her reporting to the enemy."

Mishi nodded, and took a deep breath. She recognized that the other young woman was a threat, that she and the people she loved could gain nothing from the assassin's presence, but could lose much because of it; look what they had already lost. Her eyes flicked to Sachi's cold form once more and her throat tightened, the emptiness within her howling again. She waited for Kuma-sensei to give the command.

"Do you wish to kill her?" he asked, after a lengthy pause.

Mishi searched her own sense of being. She had wanted to kill her. Oh yes, in the moments after unmasking her, she had wanted to kill Kusuko as surely as the sun would light the sky the following day. Did she still want to? She looked at Kusuko, who studied her with a gaze surprisingly devoid of personal interest. Then Mishi raised her eyes to Kuma-sensei.

"I did, but..." she paused for a moment and then shook her head. "If you had not found me, would I have shared the same fate? Did Taka already suffer the same fate herself? What stopped me from becoming just like her? She's only doing what she can to survive in world that has been twisted by the Rōjū for a thousand cycles."

Kuma-sensei looked at her for a long time before replying.

"If we do not kill her, Mishi-san, she will likely find us and kill another of your sisters, or you, or me, for that matter. She is a danger to us all."

216

Mishi nodded. She knew it was true. If she had just struck the girl down at the start, would she have ever regretted it? But now… she no longer knew how many men she had killed since her escape from Rōjū City, although only the most recent ones had been killed in anger, but she also knew that she was tired of adding to that number. Her anger still burned at the sight of Sachi's corpse, and she wasn't sure that the emptiness she felt would ever leave her, but… she couldn't bring herself to kill Kusuko now.

She shook her head again, and Kuma-sensei nodded. Just as she was about to turn to her room and as Kuma-sensei began to pull his katana from its scabbard, a shuffle of feet had Mishi turning back towards the koi pond and reaching for her own sword.

But the sound of footsteps was Tenshi, approaching as quickly as she could.

"Kuma-sensei, Mishi-san, let me guard her," Tenshi said, as soon as she reached them. "I will only slow you in your escape. We all know that the Eihei will be here in a matter of days to finish what the hishi have started, and all of you will need to travel quickly and away from roads. I'm not as fast as I once was. Let me escort our young prisoner somewhere less popular with the Rōjū."

Kuma-sensei looked as though he were about to object, but Tenshi spoke again, before he could say anything.

"Please, Kuma-sensei. Have we not had enough killing for one day?" Her eyes strayed to Sachi's crumpled form as she asked it.

Kuma-sensei only nodded and bent down to pick up Kusuko.

"You'll need to use the horse and cart," he said as he carried the young woman across the garden, with Tenshi close behind.

Mishi watched them go, and wondered what would come of Tenshi's generous spirit.

6日 11月, 老中 1119年

≈ Taka ≈

SMOKE AND THE stench of burnt flesh clogged Taka's throat and
stung her eyes. There wasn't much to see anyway, only ash mixed with
snow and the charred but still glowing remains of what had once been a
school. She wondered if anyone had made an effort to put out the fire,
or if it had simply burned through all of its fuel. Luckily there had been
no houses nearby to succumb to the fire, if it had simply burned its natural course.

Taka watched Mitsu as he picked through the ruins and wondered
how he could appear so calm. Hadn't this place formed some part of his
childhood? Hadn't the man who lived here found him and protected
him? It was possible that that man now numbered amongst the charred
corpses at the center of what had clearly once been a garden, but Mitsu's
face showed not a scrap of emotion.

Taka hadn't known anyone here personally, to her this place was
simply the home of a future ally, but even she felt her insides twist at the
sight of what had happened here. People had died. Someone's home had
been razed. And… she didn't like to let her mind drift to the possible
future of all her plans for revenge, should it prove that Kuma-sensei's
body was among the corpses in the garden.

Taka and Mitsu had known that they had no chance of reaching the
school before the hishi that Riyōshi had spotted. They had sent Riyōshi
ahead, hoping that he would be able to warn Kuma-sensei before it was
too late. If the warning had made it in time, and Kuma-sensei and his
students were the warriors Tsuku-san had led her to believe they were,
then that should have been enough. If the warning hadn't reached them,

or had been ignored, or misunderstood... if they had been caught asleep in their beds, rather than armed for battle.... Well, if that had happened, then it was likely there was no one left.

As she and Mitsu inspected the grounds, it was difficult to tell what had happened. All of the bodies had been brought to the middle of the garden and the whole place had been set on fire, that much was clear. But where the bodies had been before that, and which side the bodies had been fighting for... that was beyond what Taka could discern. So now she waited. Waited while Mitsu did what he did best. While he traced footprints and other small signs, signs that the fire had covered but not destroyed. Signs that would tell him, a master tracker, what had happened here. Or so they hoped.

Taka watched him for as long as she could, but eventually the smoke and stench of death overwhelmed her, and she walked to the edge of the burned area, looking into the road that approached the school compound from town. It wasn't until she was thoroughly coated in a thin layer of snow that Mitsu came to join her.

"It's difficult to sort anything out through the remains of that fire," he said, as he stood beside her.

Taka nodded. "It's far beyond my own skills to discern anything more than that there was a fight, someone died, and then the place was burned down to ash, while somehow the surrounding forest was protected."

"Yes," Mitsu said. "That is a bit of a mystery."

"Which part?"

"How did whoever set the fire protect the forest?"

"Pour water on the trees first?"

"That would take too long. We would have caught them here still, if they'd done that. And besides, none of the trees are wet, or frozen for that matter. I'd say that someone with fire kisō was controlling the burn, but if so, that's an impressive use of power. I've never seen a fire that large contained before."

Taka thought about that for a moment. "Is that the most pressing mystery?" she finally asked.

"No," replied Mitsu. "Just the most puzzling. The most pressing mystery is who all of the corpses are. None of them have enough flesh on them to be recognizable, and I can't even find enough scraps of cloth to identify whether they were hishi or not."

"So you don't know if our allies escaped or were killed?"

Mitsu shook his head.

"But someone escaped," he said.

Taka nodded. "Someone set the fire, so that much is obvious."

Mitsu shook his head. "Not just that," he said. "I found a set of tracks leading into the mountains east of here, on the other side of the valley from where we descended."

Taka perked up at that.

"Can you tell who it is?"

Mitsu frowned. "No. Not without inspecting more carefully. More than one person, traveling on foot."

"And headed for the mountains?" Taka's heart jumped in her chest at the implication.

"Yes. As I said."

"Mitsu, why would the hishi head for the mountains?"

"How should I know? Perhaps they take holidays there."

"Come on, Mitsu. Think. Do they have any reason to come here, kill everyone, burn the place to the ground and then head for the hills? Through the woods? Why not dress like villagers and take the road back to Rōjū City?"

"Are you suggesting that we have any idea what the hishi's motivations might be?"

"No. Obviously, we don't, but come on. It seems far more likely that whoever headed towards the mountains, away from the roads, and in a hurry... was probably Kuma-sensei, or one of his people."

"Maybe." Mitsu stared at the snow falling before him and thought for a moment. "But it could just as easily be the hishi moving on to their next assignment."

"Through the mountains? Into the woods? Is there something between here and the mountains that I don't know about?"

Mitsu shrugged. "Maybe a hermit or two... could be one of them angered the Rōjū somehow—"

"So much that the Rōjū set their elite assassins against them? Against a single hermit? Really?"

Mitsu furrowed his eyebrows and narrowed his eyes at Taka. "It's possible."

"Of course it's possible, Mitsu, but it's not plausible."

"No, you're right. What's more plausible is that the hishi are hot on the trail of the lone survivor from this fight."

"Even if that's the case, it means that one person survived." Taka took a deep breath before continuing. "And that means we have to help him."

"So we're off to traipse through the woods and mountains again, but this time in the middle of a snowstorm?"

Taka nodded. "Good thing we both got in trouble so often with Yanagi-sensei."

"Winter training?" Mitsu asked, a smile teasing the corner of his lips. "I suppose it has its uses."

"Would you be so kind as to lead me to these tracks, Mitsu-san?" she asked, with an exaggerated bow of respect.

Mitsu paused as though considering, though Taka suspected it was simply a tactic to make her keep bowing.

"I suppose my duty requires it of me," he said, with sigh of equally exaggerated responsibility.

Taka suppressed a laugh, and then found any spark of humor wiped from her completely as they turned and made their way across the gruesome remains of the school and its garden.

Just as they reached the far side of the property, being careful to leave as few tracks as possible for the Eihei that they knew were still more than a day's ride away, Taka heard a high pitched cry rend the air. She turned her head skyward to see a small black dot descending rapidly towards her, and she lifted her arm just in time to have Riyōshi spread his wings to slow himself, then settle into a perch atop it.

Relief filled her at the solid weight of the bird on her arm, and the quick scan that she took of him told her he was uninjured. Part of her had worried that if his timing had been all wrong the night before, he could have wound up in the thick of the battle and possibly gotten injured. It seemed that hadn't been the case.

The images that Riyōshi shared with her both relieved and confused her.

"Apparently, these tracks belong to Kuma-sensei and some of his students," she relayed to Mitsu. "They were the survivors, after all."

Mitsu frowned at that. "Then why burn down the school?" he wondered aloud.

"Perhaps to confuse the enemy?" she suggested.

Riyōshi took off, and Taka and Mitsu returned their focus to the trail of bent branches and barely discernible footprints ahead. Mitsu was silent, intent on the trail that Taka would have been unable to find on her own, and Taka was lost in the images that Riyōshi had shared with her.

She had never met Kuma-sensei before, but Riyōshi had connected the man he had delivered his message to the night before with the man who was leading a small group of Kisōshi through the very woods in which she walked right now. But that wasn't what was making her mind freeze and her heart flip. The blame for that reaction could be laid squarely on the brief image she had seen of a young woman in the group of escapees, dressed in the clothes of a Kisōshi, staring into the distance with startling grey eyes.

8日 11月, 老中 1119年

≈ Tsuku ≈

"THEY MUST BE publicly denounced!" Yasuhiko growled, from his seat at the low table in the first Rōjū's chambers.

Tsuku was seated in her own sleeping quarters, the doors shut for privacy, and was once more seeing and hearing through her husband's eyes and ears. Yasuhiko was in the understated but ample reception room that the first Rōjū kept for hosting guests.

"Too many people of Gensokai witnessed our Eihei riding the road to that school, and too many of the village homes were searched before our guards found the trail into the woods. People know that we haven't found who we were looking for, and unless you wish to kill hundreds of innocents, the traitors must be brought to a very public justice to undo all the damage that they have done!"

Tsuku thought that Yasuhiko was putting on an excellent show. Even she was half convinced that he was truly filled with righteous outrage at the thought that Kuma-sensei and his students had escaped, even though she had seen the vivid relief etched on his face when they had privately received word of it earlier in the day.

"Nnn…" the fourth member agreed. "Quite right. It's gone too far now. A quiet death won't do. All the people of Gensokai who have seen our Eihei marching will see them turn around without prisoners or bodies, and think that the traitors escaped. There are more rumors than can be quelled with a quick death."

"But my report said that the school was burned to the ground," the third member protested. "Surely everyone must know that was a Rōjū victory?"

"The school burned down before the Eihei even reached it," the second member said. "Every person in the village will know that. It had been burned to rubble for a full day before the Eihei got there, and then they proceeded to search for the missing traitors and ask the villagers questions. No, you'd have to kill the entire village to silence them now, and that won't do at all. We'd make far too many enemies that way."

Tsuku rejoiced at the fact that the fact that the other men were now making Yasuhiko's points for him. Perhaps there was hope yet.

The third member glanced at the first Rōjū, and Tsuku wondered if everything would fall apart with the older man's next words. There was no rule stating that the first Rōjū's vote counted for more than anyone else's, but one voted against him at one's own risk. Yasuhiko, of course, would look foolish if he didn't vote for his own proposition, but the other three members would likely vote whichever way the first Rōjū voted, no matter what they said in a debate. Tsuku had to remind herself to breathe, as she heard the first Elder begin to speak.

"Indeed, it has gone too far," the first Rōjū said quietly, after taking a small sip of tea. "These traitors must be brought before us, and the Kisōshi from all of Gensokai should be present to see their downfall. The public must be reminded of the power of our reach."

Tsuku's heart leapt in her chest. Could it be true? Would they really vote for such an audience?

"All in favor of bringing the traitors to trial before the entire realm of Gensokai?" asked the first Rōjū.

All five members raised their hands.

"Then it is settled," the first member said. The second, third, and fourth members of the voting Rōjū removed themselves from the room, but Yasuhiko stayed, at the unspoken request of the first Rōjū.

"Zōkame-san," the first Rōjū said, his sharp eyes inspecting Yasuhiko over the rim of his tea cup, "I leave on your shoulders the burden of denouncing these rebels before all Gensokai. Should you fail me in this, the price will be high indeed."

Yasuhiko bowed deeply, his head almost to the floor from his seated position, and said, "This I promise you, Rōjū-sama, the day of the rebels' trial will be a glorious day in the history of all Gensokai. I vow it on my life."

The first Rōjū nodded. "I will hold you to that, Zōkame-san."

Yasuhiko bowed once more, then got up from his place on the floor and exited the room. Tsuku couldn't see the smile on his face, but she knew that it was there, when he whispered, "As will I, Rōjū-sama, as will I."

9日 11月, 老中 1119年

～ Mishi ～

MISHI WATCHED THE moon pass overhead as she listened to the small night sounds and felt the wind tickle her exposed face. She breathed deeply. The air still smelled of snow, both fallen and promised. She wondered at how the rest of their small band could sleep so easily, but then perhaps they were less troubled by their own actions over the past tenday. Or perhaps they were simply exhausted after the crazed pace that they had kept up over the last few days, as they traveled through rough country with no time to rest save a few hours of sleep in the middle of the night. Mishi's mind kept turning to final images of Kuma-sensei's school, her home for the past eight cycles, burning to the ground. The images of Sachi's body and the bodies of all the fallen hishi were charred in her memory, along with the smell of ash from a fire that she had started and fueled with her own power. A fire that had razed the one place that had ever felt like home to her.

Finally, after watching the moon travel from one tree to the next, Mishi admitted to herself that sleep would not come. She rose to find whoever had the current watch.

As she walked to the far end of the camp, careful to make as little noise as possible and let those who were able to fall asleep remain so, she saw that it was Katagi who held the watch.

"Good evening, Katagi-san," she said, in little more than a whisper, as she approached him. He didn't turn around to greet her, but nodded when she stood beside him.

"Good evening, Mishi-san."

"I can't sleep, so I thought I'd relieve you of your watch," she said, even as Katagi kept his eyes glued to the surrounding forest.

One corner of his mouth turned up as he replied, "It's kind of you to offer, but I'm afraid I can't sleep either, so it does me no good to accept."

Mishi nodded. She certainly sympathized with the problem.

"What's keeping you awake tonight?" Katagi asked. "Or is that a stupid question?"

Mishi took a deep breath and let it out. For a long time, she said nothing.

"I'm sorry, Mishi-san," Katagi said, after a while. "It should be obvious what is keeping you awake and… it's none of my business. For—"

"No," Mishi interrupted. "No, it's alright. It might do me good to speak of it… it's just… hard."

Katagi kept his silence this time, and eventually Mishi felt she could speak again.

"Every time I close my eyes… I see them. All the men and women that I've killed over the past tenday. And when I see them, I feel a horrible sense of… wrongness. Like what I've done is… I don't know how to describe it. Like there's a weight in my stomach that I'll never be rid of. And then… then I think of Sachi, of how she was killed by cowards, with poison. And suddenly, the weight is replaced with heat, and I feel as if I didn't kill enough of them. As if I could never kill enough of them to make up for… for losing her."

She leaned against the tree that Katagi had his back to, and closed her eyes for a moment.

"I'm sorry," she said after a while. "I'm sorry I don't make any sense, I just… I don't even know how I feel. It changes so many times a day, a breath, a heartbeat."

"Don't be sorry," Katagi said, still watching the trees and the snow covered ground for any sign of hishi. "I'm honored that you would share your troubles with me. I only wish there were more I could do to comfort you."

"Talking with me is an excellent start," Mishi said, surprising herself. She wondered where the annoyance she had felt at Katagi's company had gone since their journey to Rōjū City. Hadn't his mere presence once made her wish him physical harm? What had changed, that she now found him a comfort? Before she could examine the thought too closely, Katagi chuckled, and the sound brought her back to herself.

"It wasn't long ago that you would have preferred to carry your horse rather than ride next to me," he said, finally glancing at her for just a moment.

"That's not—" Mishi cut herself off, before she could complete the lie. "That might have been true, but... well, I'm confused about everything else these days, why not you as well?"

She had meant it as a joke, but Katagi turned to look at her then, briefly, and the look in his eyes made her desperately wish to change the topic. She turned her own eyes to scanning the woods. One of them should remain on guard, after all, and if she didn't have to see that look in Katagi's eyes, well, so much the better.

"Why can't you sleep?" she asked, wishing to distract him.

"I was thinking about you," he said quietly, and she hoped that she only imagined that he sounded closer than he had a moment before.

"Mishi, I—" Katagi was cut off by the sound of a twig snapping a few arm spans away, and Mishi turned just in time to see a change in the moon shadow that indicated something moving in the darkness. Without thinking, she grabbed Katagi and thew them both flat on the ground. The faint sound of air splitting above them was the only confirmation Mishi had that she had saved their lives.

"HISHI!!!" She and Katagi shouted in unison, doing their best to wake the whole camp, and hoping it wasn't already too late.

The world around Mishi descended into chaos. Between one breath and the next she was dodging and parrying multiple katana, rolling from one opponent to the next with no time to think, barely enough time to breathe, and no way to use her fire kisō without possibly burning her companions.

She couldn't tell where anyone else was. Moments after having dragged Katagi to the ground with her in order to protect him, she had lost all cognizance of where he was. They had been pushed to fight in different directions. She couldn't tell where her sisters were, or Kuma-sensei... she couldn't see or hear well enough, beyond the scope of her own fierce battle with the hishi, to know where her companions were, and she didn't have the time or focus to spare on using her powers to locate them. Each moment was a battle just to stay ahead of her attackers.

After what felt like an age of fighting, with every hishi she defeated replaced with another, and Mishi unsure of where they were even coming from, her arms began to tire. She could no longer hear the sounds of combat outside of her own small circle of death, and she didn't know if that was because her sisters had succumbed to their attackers, or because she'd been driven so far away from the rest of the group that she was no longer be in reach of them. It made little difference; if she didn't cease fighting soon, she would soon fall to her attackers.

She was surrounded by at least three hishi. She wasn't sure how many were actually there, jumping between shadows, but she was beset by three at a time. It was only now, as her arms and legs began to protest her continued movement, that it occurred to her that she was being herded away from the group; that her attackers hadn't truly been trying to kill her, else they would have already succeeded.

She didn't have time to follow that thought. She had little time to do anything at all, save dodge and deflect, occasionally earning the chance to strike down one of her opponents, as if that made any difference with the seemingly inexhaustible supply of hishi she faced. Steel ringing on steel became the soundscape of her world; a world reduced to the rhythm and dance of three grey clad opponents circling a woman in brown and green. Rather than question where they had come from, how they had found her and her companions, or why they weren't trying to kill her, she focused her energy on generating a gap in the circle that surrounded her.

Finally, after a well timed feint on her part, one of her opponents stumbled and she switched to the offensive, pushing the hishi away from her instead of allowing them to keep her on the defensive. Fighting this way took more energy, and she wouldn't be able to keep it up for long, but she didn't need to. With one last, frenzied push, she forced two of her opponents back into a giant pine tree. One stumbled on a root, the other backed against the tree itself, and the third, perhaps thinking that he could compensate for his comrades distraction, lunged forward, as if to shear off Mishi's legs. But the one man's lunge and the other two's stumble was the final opening Mishi needed.

She didn't have the energy to fight much longer, and soon she would make a mistake that would lead to her death or capture. She couldn't afford capture. Not yet, not when she didn't know what had become of her companions, or the final stage of the plan. Finally, finding enough space to call forth fire without burning herself, and knowing that her companions—wherever they might be—were well outside of her range, she called a wall of fire between herself and her would be captors. Then, with no options left, and a deep wrenching in her gut as she thought of Ami and Kuma-sensei, of Katagi, and what leaving them all behind might mean, she ran.

10日 11月, 老中 1119年

⪫ Taka ⪪

TAKA TRIED NOT to look at the blood on the ground. It wasn't that she was squeamish; she was a healer. She was as used to blood as she was to sun on her skin, but every time she looked at this blood, the image of a tall young woman with bright grey eyes flashed through her mind, and her stomach twisted at the possibility that the blood was hers.

Taka crouched on the edge of a very small clearing and watched Mitsu follow the maze of footprints and blood that crossed and wound through each other, like the choreography of some hellish dance.

Despite the obvious signs of a nightmare come to life, the air still smelled of the crispness of new fallen snow, and the sky was heavy with clouds waiting to dispense their burdens. Eventually, Mitsu returned to her at the edge of the clearing.

"They were split into multiple groups," he said, as he crouched beside her.

"Can you tell where they went?" Taka asked.

"Yes, for a little ways, but I can't track them all at the same time."

"Can you tell which way Kuma-sensei went?" Taka hated herself a little bit for asking that question. Part of her cried out wildly to ask if he could tell where the tall girl with grey eyes had gone, but how on earth could he distinguish that from the maze of tracks left behind?

"I'm not sure, not knowing the size of all the hishi involved, but the prints I believe most likely to be his headed that way," he said, nodding to the east.

Taka thought for a moment. Kuma-sensei needed to be their top priority. He was the one who could give them the most information, the one who could best help them plan, no matter what had happened here. Yet her conscience refused to give her any peace until she addressed that blood.

"Mitsu…" she hesitated, unsure how to find the information she needed, wondering if her motives were as clear as she hoped they were. He simply looked at her until she spoke once more. "The blood in the clearing, that larger patch," she said, indicating a large circle of dark red near a tall pine tree. "Can you tell me which direction the person who left that went?"

"Why would you want to know that?" Mitsu asked.

"That person will need a healer," Taka replied.

Mitsu thought for a moment, his eyes never wavering from the patch of blood.

"As it happens, that person went in the same direction."

~~~

The sun was well past its zenith when a faint moan stopped Taka where she stood and made her hold her breath. She heard it once more: someone expressing the soft noises of agonizing pain. She searched around her, wondering how far ahead Mitsu was scouting, and if he could hear the same sounds she could. Finally, a slight movement drew her eyes to a brown and green lump in the snow that they had earlier perceived from a distance as a shrub or a rock, until they happened to catch it moving. She heard another soft moan and ran forward.

Part of her mind screamed at her to be cautious, to approach slowly, that the whole thing could be a trap. But the image of the blood in the clearing that morning mixed with the image of the brown and green clad figure with grey eyes, and nothing could stop her from running as fast as her legs and the snow would allow.

When she was right next to the figure, she collapsed and folded herself onto her legs. This person didn't have grey eyes, and wasn't even a woman. Part of her brain scolded her for having gotten her hopes so high in the first place. Hadn't all of the people in that image Riyōshi had shown her been wearing the same brown uwagi and green hakama? She shook herself. This man, eyes staring unblinking into the trees, needed her help, and badly.

Taka settled herself beside him and put her fingers against his neck. His pulse was mostly sluggish, with occasional surges to a pace that was disturbing. She spread more of her hand against his throat, then breathed deeply in order to focus her ki. Once centered in herself, she sent her kisō outward a little at a time, tracing the pulse that was so irregular, in order to find the cause. When she finally withdrew her hand and her power, she sensed someone standing behind her.

"Mitsu, I am going to need your assistance," she said, as calmly as she could. The man didn't have much time left for her to save him.

Mitsu simply loomed behind her. Finally, he asked, "Do you know who he is?"

"No, but he needs my aid or he will die."

Mitsu said nothing.

"Please build a fire. Collect snow to melt in our water skeins. What I'm about to do will leave this man very thirsty. Also, if you could catch a hare and make a broth from it, that would be excellent. He'll need food, but will find digestion difficult. This will take me some time, and he won't be able to move much when I'm done, so we should make camp here."

Mitsu took a breath that Taka could tell was going to be used to say something contrary.

"Mitsu-kun," she said, hoping the diminutive term of affection would remind him of their possible family connections and make him more willing to do as she asked, "I don't have time to argue. Please help me."

The tracker said nothing, but walked away. Taka had to hope that he would do as he was asked. She didn't have the time to argue, or the excess kisō to reach out to him and see if he planned to assist. She had to reserve everything she had for the task at hand. Poisons were hard work at the best of times, in fact most healers couldn't do anything thing for them, but Yanagi had taught Taka many things that most healers would never learn. However, to make matters more complicated, this man was also bleeding to death.

She focused her ki again, brought herself and her kisō to her center, and then, gently placing a hand on the man's wrist, careful to avoid the long acrid smelling cut that crossed his forearm, she forced her kisō to follow the tainted blood and renew it. The advantage that Taka had over most healers, when it came to poisons, was that she had learned about the properties of plants from a tree kami. As such, she had learned to identify plants in all their forms, even when they had been turned into poison. As a water kisō she could use her connection with the fluid element to cause the blood of a person to reject the plant matter that shouldn't be there. It took time, and it was one of the most difficult and draining things she had ever learned to do.

As her work took effect, the man's breath grew more and more eased. The moans of pain stopped, and eventually his eyes fluttered closed. Little by little, she was able to pull the poison from his body. After that, she began to work on the gashes themselves. After stemming the worst of the bleeding with what was left of her kisō, she looked through her pack and found the silk bandages she had gotten from Tsuku-san. She was in the middle of wrapping the last of the man's flesh wounds when he began to shift, as though in discomfort.

She was just about to pull back from him, worried about how he would react if he woke to find a stranger touching him, when the man lifted a hand and placed it on her face. It was a gentle motion, not a violent one, so she let it stay there.

"Mishi?" the man mumbled.

She looked at him then, looked into his face and his eyes, wondering if she had imagined the word she had just heard. His eyes met hers, clouded with fever and the remnants of pain, and confusion crossed them briefly before he closed them once more. His hand dropped from her face.

"Mishi..." he whispered, before returning to his slumber.

~~~

Mitsu had been a better assistant than Taka could have hoped. He had built a large fire, not far from where she knelt with the man in the snow, and he had found not one hare, but three. He made a broth from one, and the other two he had spitted and roasted over the fire while Taka had worked. He had melted enough snow to hydrate all three of them and go into the broth, and Taka had marveled at the two leather pots the man had assembled with sticks braced above the fire.

"It seems your winter training was more thorough than mine," she said, as she tore greedily into the rabbit haunch that Mitsu had offered her, once her patient was sleeping soundly. The healing had left her exhausted and famished.

Mitsu smirked across the fire, "I can't save the life of a man who has been poisoned and slashed to ribbons." He shrugged. "I need to have some useful skills."

That almost made Taka laugh. Then she thought of what she had to say next, and the laughter died in her throat.

"Mitsu, do you remember the friend I told you of?"

"The one from the orphanage?" he asked.

"Yes. Mishi-san." Taka's stomach flipped as she said the name aloud. It had been so long since she'd permitted herself to say that name.

"Yes. You said she was your closest friend. The only one you knew who shared your abilities."

Taka nodded. "I used to think we shared the same abilities... the more I've learned of what I can do, and the more I think about what she can do, the more I think we didn't actually share all that much. I think... I think she's Kisōshi. I mean a senkisō, not a yukisō like me."

Mitsu raised an eyebrow at that, but said nothing to either argue or agree.

"And..." Taka continued, "and I think that man knows her." She nodded to the sleeping figure on the far side of the fire.

Now both of Mitsu's eyebrows raised to meet his hairline, and Taka had to swallow the strange lump of hope that was forming in her throat.

"Earlier, when I was treating him..." she continued, "he said her name. I think he thought I was her for a moment and... he said her name. I think she was with them. With Kuma-sensei and the rest."

The shadows of flickering firelight playing across Mitsu's face made it difficult to read his expression, his eyebrows neutral, and Taka wondered what the man was thinking. She resisted the urge to reach out to him with her kisō. She shouldn't use it, so soon after such an extensive healing.

"What makes you think—" he began, when the sound of the unknown Kisōshi shifting made them both stop speaking.

"Mishi?" the man's voice muttered in the darkness. They had moved him as close to the fire as they dared, but they had positioned themselves away from him, in case he should wake and think he was still among enemies. Taka and Mitsu both knew how dangerous Kisōshi could be, injured or not.

Taka rose, and moved towards the man cautiously. He didn't react much when she knelt beside him.

"Mishi?" he said again.

"No. Mishi isn't here," Taka said quietly, wondering how present the man's mind was. He made a weak effort to turn his head towards her, and she shifted so that there was more firelight on her face.

"Not Mishi," he said, as though confirming her words.

"My name is Taka," she said, taking his wrist gently in order to check his pulse.

"Taka," he said. He seemed to be becoming more lucid, because he followed with, "That's a nice name."

"Thank you," Taka said, still holding his wrist. "What's your name?" she asked.

The man looked at her as though weighing her trustworthiness, but must have deemed her acceptable, for eventually he said, "Katagi."

She noticed that he did not include a family name. She hadn't either, but in her case that was simply because she didn't have one. She doubted that was true of this man, but it also didn't matter; at least she could call him something other than 'man' or 'Kisōshi.'

"Katagi-san, do you know where you are? Do you know how you got here?"

The purpose of the questions was twofold: she wanted to know what had happened, certainly, but she also wanted to know how well the man's brain was functioning. She considered it a good sign that he chose to look at her with suspicion before answering.

"We're allies of Kuma-sensei," she said. "We were coming to join you all before the attack on the school. We're the ones that sent the hawk to warn you about the hishi. I'm sure it's difficult to trust anyone right now... you're welcome to read my intentions if you like, you'll find that I'm the one that healed you... but, be careful if you do, you're still weak, so using your kisō may drain you."

Katagi nodded, and reached out with his kisō to make very light contact with her own for a single heartbeat. Judging by the way his face paled and his muscles tensed, even that small effort taxed him, but he must have confirmed what she said, because not long after he began to spill forth his entire story.

"I was standing watch and... and I was talking to a friend, to Mishi, when a swarm of hishi descended on us. The battle was chaotic and we were all driven in separate directions. I tried to stay close to Mishi, but..." he trailed off for a moment, and Taka found it difficult to breathe. Did he know what had happened to Mishi? Was she still alive? Had she been killed in that battle?

"They drove us apart," he continued. "All of us. They worked hard to separate us. I never saw what happened to Mishi or Ami, it was all I could do just to keep from getting killed. At one point I was able to make out Kuma-sensei fighting in the distance, so I used my wind kisō and managed to break away from my attackers. I turned to run after him, but they pursued me and kept getting between us. Then one of them managed to cut my arm and I could feel the poison burning... I... it made me think of Sachi... and the distraction... I was overwhelmed. I'm not too certain of what happened after that. I remember still fighting, getting more cuts, stumbling through the woods in the direction I thought Kuma-sensei had gone.... That's all I remember."

Taka nodded, trying to put it all together in her mind. Only one thing stuck out to her, distracted her.

"You don't know what happened to Mishi-san?"

Katagi shook his head. She felt a strange mingling of relief and dread pool in her belly. Mishi could still be alive—or she could just as easily be dead.

"Do you know what happened to Kuma-sensei?" she asked, after a moment.

"No. Nor anyone else." He shook his head for a moment and sighed. "Quite frankly, I'm shocked to find myself alive. The poison the hishi use kills quickly. I don't know how you found me in time."

Taka shook her head.

"Whatever poison was used on you is designed to be slow and painful. It had been half a day since you had received your wounds, and it would have been a few hours more before you succumbed to the poison, had you not also been losing a lot of blood."

"But the hishi, the poison they used on... it was quick... less time than it took the battle to play out..."

"You've seen them use poison before?"

Katagi nodded. "When they attacked the school, one of Mishi's sisters..."

Sisters? Taka bit the inside of her mouth to hold back her questions. Her patient needed to rest. She had already let him tax himself more than she should. He was beginning to sweat and shake in the firelight.

"You should rest," she said. "Your body is far from healed."

Katagi nodded and laid his head back against the tree he was propped on. Taka weighed what he had said quickly, then asked one final question.

"Katagi-san, before you sleep—please, can you tell me, did Mishi-san know everything that Kuma-sensei does? About the plan, I mean?"

Katagi opened one eye, and Taka couldn't make out the emotion that crossed it. She thought for a moment that he wouldn't answer her, but then he spoke.

"It was her mission that started all of this. I don't know what she knew, or what she didn't, but before every major decision our group acted on, Kuma-sensei and Mishi-san met alone and consulted. That's all I can tell you." Katagi's eyes drifted closed.

Taka nodded. She sighed. She had a plan. She didn't like any of it, but she had a plan. Was it worth the risk? Would Mitsu even agree to it?

11日 11月，老中 1119年

≈ Mishi ≈

MISHI PRESSED HER back to the tree and listened again for the faint sound that had shaken her from her reverie.

She had lost track of time while inspecting the site of the battle that had been fought between her companions and the hishi two nights ago. It had taken her a full day to get back to this place. Letting the wind whip the smells of old blood and new fallen snow past her, she had let the setting sun do its best to warm her back, as she had tried to make sense of the maze of footprints and blood before her. She tried to discern which direction any of her companions may have traveled, or been forced to travel, but she could make nothing of it.

She knew a small amount about tracking, but no more than would be useful in pursuing an enemy who had recently fled. Not enough to distinguish anything useful from this tangled web.

Then, the lack of birdsong and the snap of a branch in the distance had brought her back to herself.

Now she stood with her back pressed against the tree she had squatted before mere moments ago. Her breathing was as quiet as she could make it, and her hand rested lightly on the hilt of her katana, as she waited for whoever had made the birds cease their singing.

She hesitated before deciding that it was worth the risk to reach out her kisō to whoever was approaching. Chances were good that the person already knew who and what she was, so alerting them to her kisō would either reassure a friend, or disconcert an enemy. She was fine with either result.

The reading she got from touching the kisō of the man approaching confused her. He was male, but he was neither Kuma-sensei, nor Katagi. He was aware of her presence, and seemed to wish her no harm. He was looking for her. That combination made no sense to her. She prepared for battle, convinced that it was some kind of trick—a clever hishi trap.

She tightened her grip on her katana and began focusing her ki, finding her center and using her kisō to spread her awareness into the woods around her. She would not be caught unawares by a hishi again, no matter how clever his ruse.

She opened her eyes to see a tall figure, taller than she was by a hand's span, all clad in leather, coming forward in the snow with his arms thrown wide, as though to demonstrate that he meant her no harm.

She waited. Just because the man didn't carry a sword didn't mean he wasn't covered in small poisoned weapons, like a true coward. Simply because he wasn't clothed in the more common grey of the hishi didn't mean that he wasn't here to kill her. The fact that she found his blue green eyes startling, and his face handsome, only made her more suspicious of him. Her only hesitation was that she refused to cut a man down without fair warning, as a thrice cursed hishi would.

"You should draw your weapon," she said. "I won't give you a chance to speak, or to throw some poisoned blade at me."

And with no more warning than that, she attacked, not even leaving a beat between her last word and drawing her katana to surge forward. The man fell backwards into the snow, dodging the vicious cut that she had aimed at his midsection, and instantly rolled away from her.

"Stop!" he shouted, as he gained his feet next to a nearby tree. She ignored him, instead turning to slash at his neck. He once more disappeared from her range, this time dropping straight down and rolling forward, leaving her to cut deeply into the bark of the tree that had been behind him. Kami curse him, he was fast. Faster than any of the hishi she'd yet fought.

"Stop, Mishi-san!" he shouted, as he rolled again, this time dodging a downward slash that she'd aimed at his shoulder.

The use of her name didn't slow her. Kusuko could have told any of the hishi her name, or they could have learned it from the Rōjū by now. She shifted, and readied her next blow. How had this hishi gotten to be so fast? He was faster than she was, though she was loath to admit it. Yet he still hadn't drawn a weapon. What ploy was this? She turned to aim her next blow, a feint that would cause the man to move the wrong direction and allow her to run him through at the chest. Just as she completed the feint, though, even as the man began to dodge and place himself perfectly for her next thrust, he spoke again, and this time the words made her falter.

"I'm a friend of Taka-san's!"

Mishi's feet stuttered, and she retracted the sword she had been about to insert into the man's ribs. She placed it gently on his throat instead. He had fallen directly beneath her in his attempt to dodge the blow that had followed her feint. It wouldn't have worked, wouldn't have stopped him from being impaled, had she not recoiled. As it was, the move left him nowhere else to go.

"What did you say?" she asked, listening for the first time.

"I'm a friend of Taka-san's," the man repeated, between heaving breaths. "She sent me to find you. We've found Katagi-san. He was hurt, and we couldn't catch up with you all together. We weren't even sure where to find you."

The man said the last few sentences all in one desperate breath, as though he expected Mishi to slice his throat at any moment if he didn't say everything he'd come to say; perhaps he did. Mishi had certainly expected as much at the beginning of this fight. Now...

Now she let her legs collapse beneath her in the snow. She was careful not to let the katana drop any more of its weight onto the man's neck, though she didn't remove it either.

"I don't understand," was all she could think to say. Taka-san? After all of these cycles? How could... Could the hishi know about her? Could this be a trap to lure her somewhere?

No, stupid. She was alone now. She was an excellent fighter, but she couldn't possibly defend against the full force of the hishi by herself. If they knew where she was, why not send a whole troupe after her? Besides, if they wanted to lure her somewhere, why not say they had Ami, or Kuma-sensei, or just Katagi? She was already fairly certain her friends had been captured. Why bring up Taka at all?

"If you'd be so kind as to remove your katana from my neck, and allow me to sit up, I would be overjoyed to explain."

Mishi looked down at the man in front of her and realized that as she had been contemplating the various explanations for his presence, she had pushed the katana slightly downward into the man's neck. She hadn't shifted forward or back at all, so it hadn't made a cut yet, but even the slightest movement in either direction would leave him bleeding, at the very least.

Fairly certain by now that this man truly meant her no harm, she carefully raised her sword.

Checking his neck with his hands, and coughing repeatedly as though to be extra certain that he remained unscathed, the man sat up.

Mishi didn't sheathe her sword; just because *this* man didn't mean her harm didn't mean that there weren't hishi returning this way to look for her. She shifted back to lean against the tree she had left a gash in, while the man shifted himself into a similar position in front of the tree closest to him.

"Please explain," she said.

"Which part?" he asked. The glint in his eye was mischievous now, as though he wished to put her through some trouble for attacking him.

She couldn't say she blamed him, but she didn't have the energy or patience for that kind of delay.

"Whichever part most expediently enables me to understand why you're here, and where I will find Taka-san," she said, without any of the politeness she most likely owed the man. "She's well? Taka-san?" She was almost afraid to ask, but she had to know.

The man grunted. "She's well enough." He smirked then. "Telling everyone else what to do, so that must tell you something."

The corners of Mishi's mouth quirked up to match the man's. Taka had been bossy even as a child, but it had never bothered Mishi much; the girl was a cycle her senior and always knew what needed to be done. Still, she enjoyed the idea that it bothered this man for some reason. She waited for him to continue.

"The shortest explanation is that Taka-san and I had been sent to meet with Kuma-sensei at his school. We arrived just in time to find it burned to the ground." He paused then, as if considering whether or not to tell her the next part, and her curiosity piqued. "We have a hawk scouting for us, and he was able to tell us that the hishi were closing in on the school the night of the attack. We sent him ahead to warn you, but we weren't sure he made it in time."

Mishi thought for a moment, puzzling out the idea of a hawk that could communicate with humans, then smiled.

"The messenger? Yes, he made it in time. He's probably the only reason we survived the attack that night. The hishi were difficult opponents, even when we were awake and armed, but if we hadn't known they were coming, they would have poisoned us all in our beds."

The man's face blanched, and Mishi wondered if he was as repulsed by the cowardly attacks of the hishi as she was. Then he continued.

"I'm glad he was able to help. The next time we saw him, he was busy showing us your group's escape, and we never asked him about anything else. We've been working to catch up with you since that first attack. Well, I should say, we've been working to catch up with Kuma-sensei. I wasn't aware that you were with the group until Taka-san told me about it yesterday, and I don't think she knew for sure until we found Katagi-san and he said your name."

That caused another quirked eyebrow on the face of the man, and this time, for some reason, that expression, combined with what the man had just said, made all the blood in her body run to her face and neck.

"Is Katagi-san alright?" she asked, hoping to deflect the question that raised eyebrow was implying. "You said he was injured."

The man nodded. "Thanks to Taka-san, he'll live, but if she hadn't found him he would surely be dead by now."

Mishi tried and failed to repress a shudder. The thought of Katagi-san dead at the hands of the hishi was bad, but it was nothing compared to the thought, which his near death conjured in her mind, of Ami and Kuma-sensei lying dead in the woods somewhere.

If the hishi had left Katagi for dead, what were the chances that they hadn't killed Ami or Kuma-sensei? She had managed to convince herself that, since she had been herded away from the group, and it had seemed as though the hishi were deliberately trying to leave her alive, perhaps they would spare her companions as well. The idea of Katagi lying near death in the woods smothered any such hope.

"And the others?" she asked, terrified of what he might say.

"We haven't found anyone. We were following Kuma-sensei's tracks when we found Katagi-san. We haven't seen anyone else… alive or otherwise."

Mishi appreciated that the man tried to say the last part kindly, even if it did no good to keep the words from feeling like a physical blow.

"So, Katagi-san is with Taka-san?" she asked, trying to stick to something she could discuss without feeling like she was being buried beneath the snow that surrounded them.

"He is, and they're both well."

Mishi nodded. She felt lost. So many thoughts careened through her head, with no regard for whether or not she could keep up with them. She latched on to the one clear thing she understood. "We should go to them. We should leave now. The hishi could be headed this way, even as we speak."

The man nodded and stood up. Mishi finally sheathed her sword, as she stood. She leaned against the tree briefly for support, and swiped idly at the snow that now covered her backside.

Was she really about to see Taka after so many cycles apart? Could their reunion be so simple, after so much time? As a counterpoint to the possibility of losing Kuma-sensei and her sisters, it was certainly bittersweet, but a part of her that had been lying quiet and cold, in the deepest corner of her heart, began to warm slightly at the thought.

Taka-san was still bossy, ne? She would know what to do. The thought made her smile. Then she looked at the man before her, with his scruffy but handsome face, entrancing eyes, and leather clothes. He was the only person who had ever been faster than her in battle.

"What's your name?" she asked.

"Mitsu," the man replied, quirking one eyebrow in what she was beginning to recognize as his accustomed look, and bowing slightly.

"Nice to meet you, Mitsu-san," she said, returning the bow and stepping forward to walk next to him—to walk toward Taka.

⟨ Taka ⟩

Taka shifted her back closer to the fire, and shivered as the creaking of the trees in the wind strengthened the pervading sense of unease that she'd felt since sunset.

She'd been reluctant to stay in one place while Mitsu had gone in search of Mishi, but Mitsu had insisted that it would be difficult enough to track down her childhood friend, without then having to track her afterwards. She'd only agreed in the end because Katagi wasn't well enough to move quickly and needed to conserve his energy to finish healing; he would be more useful to them if he was well rested.

Still, the thought of remaining in one place with a band of hishi on the loose, liable to return at any moment to collect the people they had failed to capture or kill in their initial attack, made Taka more nervous than she cared to admit. At the moment, her nerves were serving to keep her awake, which was just as well, since Katagi desperately needed to sleep and she was the only one left to keep watch. Riyōshi was still out on the patrol circuit they'd sent him on not long after they'd found Katagi. She just had to hope that Mitsu and Mishi would return before any hishi did.

She looked out into the darkened woods and wondered what she and Katagi would do if hishi came upon them. What could they do? He was barely healed and still too weak to fight properly. She had a little practice with a knife, nothing that was likely to help her in a fight with a practiced assassin. Would she have a chance to wake Katagi in time for him to protect them? Would she have time to call the woodland creatures to her aid, as Yanagi had once suggested? Would a shifting in the darkness, or a snapping twig, be enough warning for her to do anything at all before they ended up under the sword of some merciless assassin, or worse, a whole band of them?

She decided to pull her knife from the sheath that kept it strapped to her hip, just in case a few seconds would make the difference between being able to defend herself and becoming easy prey. She focused once more on the darkness, hoping her senses would alert her to whatever was coming.

In the end, it made no difference at all. She heard the sound of something hard impacting flesh, and turned to see a dart protruding from Katagi's neck just before she felt the sharp pain of a thin point of metal piercing her own shoulder. In the mere seconds before blackness consumed her, she thought she heard a hawk cry out in the distance.

Mishi

Mishi and Mitsu hadn't agreed to start running through the snowy woods that separated them from Taka and Katagi, it had happened without the exchange of a single word, or even a look.

As they had walked, Mitsu had explained that it had taken him a half a day to reach her from where he, Taka, and Katagi had made camp. Apparently, neither she nor Mitsu were willing to allow the return journey to take that long. Neither of them had to state their fears aloud. They both knew that the hishi were likely still wandering these woods, and that Taka and Katagi were vulnerable.

Mishi exalted in the cold air that burned her lungs, the treacherous snow beneath her feet, and the constant threat of branches, roots, and rocks that made every pounding stride a risk to life and limb.

She and Mitsu were running apace. There was no trail where they ran, they wove parallel sets of tracks between the trees that they constantly dodged and hurdled, and she could see the corners of the man's mouth turned up in a joy that mirrored her own.

Her eyes refocused on the woods before her, but her mind remained fixed on the man by her side. She knew so little about him, but she already found that she enjoyed his company. Had she not already been running, she might have blushed, as her mind questioned what kind of relationship he had with Taka, and she felt a brief pang of jealousy. Why had that thought come to mind? She made herself refocus on the woods before her, and the direction of the man beside her. He was beginning to veer to the east, and she shifted to veer with him. Were they getting close to the camp? How long had   they been running?

She was surprised that she hadn't begun to tire yet. Come to think of it, she had felt more energetic since Mitsu's arrival. Was it simply the knowledge that Taka was alive and she might see her soon, or was there more to it than that?

Her musings were cut short when Mitsu's arm shot out to grab her and pull her to a halt. She had him halfway to her hip and ready to throw over her shoulder before she reminded herself that he was not attacking her. She shifted his weight away from her and stepped back.

"Sorry," she whispered, even as she began looking around them to see why they had stopped so suddenly.

Mitsu grabbed her shoulder and pulled her down and to the right, behind a large boulder a few arm spans away from where they'd stopped. For a moment he said nothing, merely staring into the darkness. Then Mishi saw what he was looking at, and it was only Mitsu's hand clamping down on her mouth that prevented her from saying anything else.

An abandoned fire burned low between two trees, thirty arm spans away from them. Where was Taka? Where was Katagi? Was this where Mitsu had left them? Why weren't they there? She longed to ask, but clearly Mitsu suspected the hishi might still be present.

Tired of waiting to be attacked, Mishi focused her ki, found her center, and sent her consciousness outward with her kisō. Her breathing was less even than it had been that afternoon, when she had sought out Mitsu's consciousness. This time, her mind and body almost vibrated with a need for action. She was tired of sitting still while everything dear to her was snatched away by the hishi and their Rōjū masters. Damn Kuma-sensei's plan, she needed to do something, and if there was single hishi within range of her power, she was going to track him down and...

Nothing. She had reached the end of her range, which extended for half a league or more from where she sat, but... she found nothing, in any direction.

"They're gone," she said aloud, no longer concerned that they might be overheard.

Mitsu nodded, as though he had confirmed the same. She wondered how far his ability to track something ranged.

"More than a league away," he said, answering her unasked question. She was impressed. She couldn't span that far with kisō. She drove away the questions that raised, resolved to ask them later, and focused on the woods that lay before her. They had to move.

"Can you track them from here? Follow the physical trail?" she asked, anxious to close the gap between herself and her enemies.

Mitsu nodded, and the corners of his mouth turned up, though the gesture didn't bring the mischievous glitter to his eyes that it had earlier.

"Even you could likely track the physical trail," he said, standing and walking towards the mere embers that remained of the fire. "They don't seem to be making much effort to hide themselves."

He gestured to the newly trampled snow between the two trees, which looked as though a herd of deer had held a town meeting there. Mishi looked at it closely to see what she could discern from the mess of snow.

"No blood," she commented, attempting to keep relief from flooding her. The simple fact that they hadn't bled enough to leave any behind didn't mean that Taka and Katagi hadn't been cut sufficiently to be poisoned.

Mitsu nodded. "Well, it looks like the herd went this way. Do you suppose they want us to follow them? They might as well have dragged bodies through the snow, for all the effort they made to hide their tracks."

Mishi took a deep breath and let it out slowly.

"If they do want us to follow them, then that's all the better for us," she said after a moment.

"How is a trap better for us, exactly?" he asked.

Mishi thought about her last meeting with Kuma-sensei and all that they'd planned together before the hishi attacks had driven them apart. The smile that pulled at her mouth didn't reach her eyes, but the vibrating need to do something, which had pulled at her earlier, eased off slightly.

"Because it's not their trap," she said, turning to follow the well beaten trail left by her enemies.

21日 11月, 老中 1119年

≈ *Mishi* ≈

"TAKE THIS," MISHI said.

Mitsu looked at the sealed leather case she offered him, but didn't take it.

"What is it?" he asked.

"The thing that started all of this," she said, proffering it to him once more.

"Why should I take it?" He raised an eyebrow as he so often did, this time to accompany an expression of suspicion.

Mishi took a deep breath, and nodded to the high wall of Rōjū City that stood before them. The light snow that fell wasn't enough to obscure the massive warren of buildings, gardens, rivers, and gorges that housed the Rōjū, its bureaucrats, and its guards, so Mishi didn't think it was the cold that sent a shiver down her spine as she contemplated what she was about to do.

"That scroll mustn't fall into the hands of the Rōjū, or the Eihei, or hishi. If it does, the whole plan comes apart. Timing is everything at this stage. I have to go in there, but that can't be on me if the guards capture me."

"So what do I do with it?" he asked, reaching for it, finally.

"I need you to bring it to me."

"And when should I do that?" he asked.

Mishi smiled, though she felt no real mirth. "You'll get an invitation."

~~~

Mishi couldn't help but feel suspicious that her entry to the compound hadn't alerted any guards. Were they expecting her? Most likely. They had left a clear enough trail for her and Mitsu to follow, all the way back to the compound. She knew why she wanted to be here, but she was unsure why the Council would be so keen on having her come. Was it simply because of the scroll? If her friends were still alive, she had to assume that it was because the Rōjū knew that she was the one with the scroll, and therefore everyone she cared for was merely being held as bait.

Well, it was working. She had come for her friends. Time to see how well the trap was set.

She moved through the lower gardens in the cover of darkness, finding the familiar pattern of Eihei, which she had almost grown accustomed to during her last visit, completely altered. There were more guards on patrol at once, and their patrol routes had changed. It didn't make much difference to her, though.

This time, traveling alone and with no need to maintain any illusion of being a servant, she had no reason not to simply take the most direct route to her destination, dodging the Eihei as they came. As she made her way through the narrow streets that wound between buildings and gardens, she maintained a focus that sent her kisō outwards, not to its full extent, but far enough to give her advance warning of where the guards patrolled, leaving her plenty of time to duck behind a decorative shrub or some stone statuary before she was seen.

She made it through the lower and upper gardens without incident. In fact, she had climbed the stairs into the residential hall where she and Katagi had stayed, and was all the way into the guest corridor, before she ran into her first Eihei.

She had been distracted, using her kisō to seek out Taka and the others rather than monitor the guard patrols, and the man had come around a corner just as she had refocused on the nearby area.

It took a moment for the man to recognize her as a threat; perhaps that moment was spent trying to reconcile the clothes of a Kisōshi on the body of woman. Regardless of the cause, Mishi wasn't one to let such an opportunity go to waste. She surged forward, using the momentum of the single stride to propel her fist toward one of the few unarmored places on the guard's body.

The man grabbed at his throat and collapsed to the floor, as his lungs struggled to draw air through a collapsed windpipe. Mishi hoped he would be found and taken to a healer in time to save his life, but she couldn't risk having him raising the alarm before she found Taka and the others. She didn't have time to do anything for him, so she turned and followed the faint trace of familiar kisō that she had recognized on the other side of the city.

She had made it around and through a dozen buildings—sometimes the only way to get across a river was to enter a building and cross using the bridge that connected the second or third floor from one building to the next—before she heard the alarm sound across the city.

She had just entered the Rōjū residence, a building she only vaguely recognized from Kusuko having pointed it out as a place she should never enter, when loud gongs rang from all corners of the compound and she could hear the shouts of guards relaying messages. She cursed the terrible timing—she had only reluctantly entered this building, as it was clearly the shortest way across the next river, and she could sense Kuma-sensei's kisō not far away.

Someone must have found the man she'd attacked. She took a deep breath and centered her kisō on the area around her. There were guards coming from both directions, toward the corridor in which she currently found herself. There was only one room between her and the two patrols that would converge on her soon. Unfortunately, the room was inhabited. Still, there were only two people inside its walls, while there were seven Eihei in each of the patrols that would soon trap her in the corridor. She decided to take her chances with the two people on the other side of the shoji.

She managed to enter quietly enough that the pair within didn't notice her entrance, and she was even able close the door behind her without raising suspicion. As she entered the room, the reason why soon became clear. The couple in the room were having a heated discussion on the opposite side of the chamber. It was a large room, much larger than even Kuma-sensei's chambers at the school. She took a deep breath, trying not to contemplate what kind of fate might await her if she had just entered the room of a member of the Rōjū.

Dressed as Kisōshi and not a maid, with the alarm already sounded, the sensible thing to do was to draw her katana and ready herself for a fight. She drew her weapon quietly, and opened all of her senses to the action on the far side of the room.

"The southern and eastern patrol units will be here soon. They will wish to report whatever it is they have found." The voice came from a man, dressed as a Kisōshi of Ryu-kyū, the highest rank. He stood, facing the window on the far side of the room.

"And if they have already captured her?" This came from a woman dressed in a beautiful kimono of heavy winter silk. Both had greying hair, both faced away from her.

Mishi could not bring herself to attack unannounced, like a dirty assassin. Using another warrior's hesitation was one thing; attacking two unsuspecting elderly people, even if one of them was a Kisōshi who far outranked her, was not something her conscience would allow.

"They haven't caught her yet," she said, by way of warning, even as she charged forward, seizing the elderly woman by the waist and bringing her katana to bear on the woman's neck.

The man's eyes went wide in surprise, and she supposed he must have been tracking the guards very carefully not to have noticed her kisō when she entered the room. Still, he did not reach for his katana. He remained completely silent and still.

"I won't harm her," Mishi continued, before the man could change his mind about attacking. "So long as you allow me passage through this room, and don't send the Eihei after me, I swear no harm will come to her."

The man's gaze traveled up and down her form, in the same fashion that Kuma-sensei's did after a test.

"Mishi-san," the man said, bowing slightly. "I'm glad to finally meet you, though I am sorry of the circumstances."

That had not been the reaction that Mishi had expected.

"I'm afraid that the patrols you are currently attempting to avoid are on their way to report to me."

Even as he said the words, the shoji that she had come through moments before began to slide open. Mishi turned at the sound, keeping the woman, who had remained remarkably still and silent through her capture, up until now, between her and the guards.

"Please," she said, quietly, for only the man to hear, "don't make me harm her."

The fourteen Eihei who she had been so desperate to avoid were pouring into the room, and the only exit available to her was the window behind her, now blocked by the elder Kisōshi.

"Mishi-san, I will not make you do anything. But I do recommend that you surrender," the man said, even as she felt the tip of his katana press against her back.

⟅ Taka ⟆

Taka lay with her back to the cold, stone wall and tried to make out the sounds in the darkness. At the moment, she could hear water dripping down the walls and the occasional sound of a rodent scurrying through the blackness. Her eyes told her nothing; there was no light that she could sense. Her nose told her slightly more; the air smelled of stale urine and the kind of mold that generally inhabited caves and other lightless places.

She had woken up in this room, arms and legs bound behind her, and a few calls into the darkness had proven both that she was alone in the stone chamber and that she was out of earshot of anyone willing to respond. She didn't know where Katagi was, or even if he still lived.

She hoped that Mitsu had found Mishi, and that the two of them had avoided capture. Perhaps they would even be able to find Kuma-sensei and help him finish his mission.

Then, in the distance, she heard the sound of metal on stone, and the creak of hinges. After that she heard the sound of footsteps getting closer and a murmur of voices.

"Here," said a gruff male voice she didn't recognize. "The Rōjū said to put her in this one."

She didn't know if any other words or looks were exchanged. She remained in total darkness, but soon the sound of metal scraping on stone was much closer, and the light that filtered in nearly blinded her as the sound of hinges creaking echoed through the tiny chamber. A moment later she heard the thud of cloth and flesh hitting stone, and a groaning breath escape from someone near by. The hinges screamed, the light slipped away, and metal scraped stone, then clanged with finality.

"Thank you!" shouted a voice that made Taka's insides jump and dance. "I hadn't seen this part of the grounds yet!"

Taka's heart sped up and she wished she could see. Wished that the door opening hadn't blinded her, that the room weren't pitch black anyway, because she was sure that the face that accompanied that voice contained a gloriously familiar pair of grey eyes.

~~~

"Mishi-san?" she asked, almost afraid to breathe the word aloud. Silence was all that met her. Had she imagined it all? Was she still alone in the cell, the past few moments simply some sick hallucination brought on by the sleeping draught that had poisoned her?

"Mishi-san?" She tried once more. "Is that… can that really be you?"

"Taka-san?" the other voice sounded hoarse suddenly, as though it had been constricted while escaping Mishi's throat.

"Mishi-san!" She tried to roll away from the wall, to move towards the friend she had half expected never to see again, the friend lost to her for the past eight cycles. But her arms and legs were tied behind her, so the effort only caused her to flop face-down a mere arm span from where she had been a moment before.

"Taka-san!" She felt Mishi's arms awkwardly pull her over so she was on her back, face to the still invisible ceiling, and she felt a cheek press down on her own. "It's truly you," Mishi whispered.

Taka could feel the warm wet of tears flow over her cheek, and she was unsure if they were hers or Mishi's.

"Why have they tied your arms and legs behind you?" Mishi asked, after a moment.

Taka almost laughed. Eight cycles of separation, and that's the first question Mishi asks? Then again, no one could have asked for stranger circumstances under which to be reunited.

"I don't know. Are your arms free?" she finally replied.

"No. They're tied in front of me, and my ankles are tied together, but they haven't taken the trouble to truss me up like a pig as they have you." Then Mishi chuckled. "You must have really pissed them off."

Taka laughed then too. Oh, how she had missed this girl!

"I may, or may not, have woken on the trip here and tried to claw my way to freedom with whatever was handy."

"Which was?"

"Nails and teeth."

That had Mishi laughing all the harder, and soon Taka joined in. There was nothing funny about their current situation, but she wasn't sure she cared anymore. She finally had her friend back.

"And you came quietly, I suppose?" Taka asked, once the laughter had quieted some.

"Well, you know... I may, or may not, have taken a high ranking Rōjū's wife hostage."

"Mishi-san!"

"I didn't hurt her."

"And they didn't truss you up like a pig?"

She could hear Mishi sigh, though the girl had pushed herself back some and was no longer touching her.

"Not as fully as they have done you." She paused for a moment, and Taka wondered if she was trying to decide how to break bad news to her.

"And Mitsu-san?" Taka asked, before Mishi could speak.

"He's fine," Mishi said, her voice sincere. "Or, he was, when I left him. I don't know how well he'll stay out of trouble, but he had better stick to the plan, or..."

"He does have a tendency to incite one to violence, doesn't he?" Mishi chuckled.

"I can see why you like him," Mishi said, her voice sounding less open than it had a moment before.

Taka laughed. "I have come to be able to tolerate his presence over the past tendays. 'Like' might be an exaggeration." She paused then, worrying that she was making Mitsu sound worse than he was. "I do trust him though," she said at length. "I trusted him to find you."

Now that she took time to think about that fact, Taka felt a flicker of anger in the pit of her stomach.

"Mishi-san, you aren't supposed to be here. Mitsu-san was supposed to find you, and you were supposed to find Kuma-sensei together, and finish what you started!"

Mishi was silent for a moment.

"You didn't honestly expect me to abandon you, when I knew you had been captured," Mishi replied, at last.

"You weren't supposed to come after me! You're supposed to finish the mission!"

Again, Mishi's silence dragged out, and Taka was beginning to wonder if the other girl had fallen asleep before she finally replied.

"Taka-san, Mitsu told me that you were trained at the Josankō. That you know all of their secrets. Is that true?"

"Mishi-chan, what does that have to do with anything? Why are you changing the subject?"

"I'm not changing the subject. I'm asking you a question." Mishi's voice had gotten quiet. She sounded much more serious than she had a few moments before. Did she sound sad, too, or was that just Taka's imagination?

"It's true. I was there for a few cycles and... and I saw things... learned things. They're horrible, Mishi-chan. They're as bad as the monsters that buy young girls for... they're worse."

Taka's voice had broken at the end of her admission, and Mishi said nothing for a time. Taka cursed the darkness for keeping her friend's face hidden.

Tentatively, unsure of how Mishi might react to the contact after so many cycles apart, Taka sent her own kisō outward to make contact with Mishi's.

Taka's breath drew in sharply, as she picked up on the confusion of emotions that rolled off of Mishi's kisō. Pain, fear, remorse... Mishi must have been projecting on purpose, because Taka had never been sensitive enough to pick up so much without Mishi's help.

"What happened, Mishi-chan?"

Mishi was silent for a while longer, apparently unable to speak of certain horrors, but she let her memories flood outward for Taka to pick up. Had Taka thought of her friend as a girl? Mishi was a girl no longer.... Images of men dying, dying at Mishi's hands, overwhelmed her until her breath started hitching on a remorse that was not her own. Only then did Mishi pull her emotions and memories back into herself.

"I'm sorry, Taka-chan. I didn't mean... I haven't shared that way with anyone in so many cycles and... it's a relief, but... I.... You shouldn't have to experience all that I..." Mishi's voice trailed away as she drew farther into herself.

Taka shook her head, and wished again that the her friend could see her. Instead, she forcefully sent out her own emotions, not as vivid as Mishi's had been just now, but hopefully enough to make her feelings clear. The words wouldn't come to her, but acceptance and love, even some of her own need for vengeance... she could project those things and hope that Mishi understood.

A long while passed before either of them spoke again. When Taka next heard Mishi's voice, it sounded clearer, more forceful.

"I didn't ask about your history at that 'school' in order for either of us to relive memories that we would rather leave behind, but I'm afraid that you'll need those memories soon. I understand now why Zōkame-san sent you to us. You'll play an integral role in our plan."

"Mishi-san, you know Zōkame-san? Tsuku-san, or her husband?" Taka asked, trying to contain her surprise. Could she have been the only one who didn't know that she had been headed to Mishi-san all along?

"No," Mishi said in the darkness. "I've never met them. I hadn't even heard of them, until Mitsu explained why you had come to us. Kuma-sensei had told me that we had important allies with the Rōjū, but he never told me who they were. Perhaps out of regard for their safety, perhaps out of regard for mine. If I had been captured before now, and had known who they were, that could have gone poorly for all of us."

Taka thought for a time, before responding.

"You refer to your plan as if you can still make it happen. How are you going to accomplish whatever it is you intend to do when you are trapped in here with me?" Taka couldn't fathom what it was that Mishi planned to accomplish, now that they were locked up in their dingy little cell, but she had never been told the details of Kuma-sensei's grand scheme. She had only known that Kuma-sensei was working against the Rōjū, and that she would somehow be able to help. Mishi's confidence startled and confused her.

"My darling Taka-chan, this *is* the plan. We are right where we need to be, about to be handed exactly what we need most, in order for our plan to work."

"And what is that, Mishi-san? What is it you need for the plan to work?"

"An audience with all of Gensokai."

23日 11月，老中 1119年

≈ Tsuku ≈

"COME IN," TSUKU called, as she made her way to the sliding door that separated their personal rooms from the hallway of the Rōjū residence. The door slid slowly back before she reached it, and a young woman wearing a beautiful crimson and black kimono entered, bowing low immediately.

"Zōkame-sama asked to see me," she said.

"Of course," Tsuku replied. "Please, follow me." She turned then, and led the young woman into their smaller, less formal reception room, where Yasuhiko waited before a low table set with a fresh pot of tea and two cups.

"Yasuhiko-san, your guest has arrived," she said, indicating the empty zabuton on the other side of the low table with her hand. The young woman folded herself into place on the small cushion and bowed her head.

"Thank you, Tsuku-san," Yasuhiko said, nodding slightly to his wife. Tsuku nodded back, and walked to the far corner of the room where she folded herself to the floor in front of the door. From here she could watch, listen, and protect as necessary.

"Thank you for taking the trouble to join me, Kusuko-san," Yasuhiko said, as he poured them both some tea. "I hear you've had a trying few tendays."

Kusuko's face blanched at that comment, and Tsuku wondered if the girl didn't know that the man she now conversed with was the man in charge of the entire hishi and spy network at the Rōjū's disposal.

"Yes, Zōkame Rōjū-sama," the young woman said, when she could get her voice to work. "It has been a most vexing time for me. Please forgive my ineptitude. I will work harder not to fail you in the future."

Tsuku kept her face clear of all emotion, but she smiled inwardly at the obvious sign that the girl did indeed know with whom she was speaking.

"Ah... you are young, ne?" Yasuhiko said, as he sipped his tea. "And the young often make mistakes. Poor judgment, too much confidence... such are the follies of youth."

"Yes, Zōkame Rōjū-sama," Kusuko said, as she bowed her head once more.

Tsuku-san had to restrain a laugh, then. Did the girl think that they believed her sincerity? Did she not know that they could read her scroll? Ah well, she supposed the girl had to remain polite, even if she knew that they knew it was insincere.

"Yet, of course," Yasuhiko continued, "it can be difficult to recognize our own faults when we are young. In fact, I would say that the greatest benefit of age is a clearer understanding of our shortcomings."

Tsuku wanted to prod her husband to get him to hurry up. He was trying to make the girl uncomfortable, a tactic she understood, but she hoped he would get to the point soon.

"Now then," he said, setting his tea cup on the table once more, and placing his hands on his knees. "I'm told you were captured by these rebels, ne? A... what was his name... Gunma-sensei?"

"Kuma-sensei, O-Rōjū-sama," Kusuko corrected, with her head still bowed.

Yasuhiko smiled then, and Tsuku knew it was because he admired the girl's spirit. Correcting a high ranking Rōjū was not something most grown men would dare to do.

"Ah yes, Kuma-sensei," he said, wiping the smirk from his face as the young woman's head came back up. "You were captured by him, yes?"

Kusuko nodded.

"And yet, he let you live?"

Kusuko nodded again.

"Why is that, do you think?"

Kusuko sat there in silence, and Tsuku wondered if the girl thought that it had been a rhetorical question. Eventually, she looked up at Yasuhiko and met his gaze, which was sincere and penetrating.

"What do you mean, Zōkame Rōjū-sama?" she asked.

"I mean what I said. Why do you think he let you live?"

"It was all in my report, Zōkame-sama. He and Mishi-san were talking about whether or not to let me live when the woman, the healer, Tenshi-san, came back and said she would guard me—"

"I know what the report said, Kusuko-san. I'm not asking you how it was arranged. I'm asking you *why?* Why would a man who has every reason to hate hishi, and everything that they represent, spare the life of a young woman who had just aided in the attack on his home and the death of one of his students? Keep in mind that Kuma-sensei's students are like daughters to him. He rescued the girls at birth, from a world that would otherwise see them dead, or, as was the case with Mishi-san, saved her from an orphanage and who knows what kind of fate. You do know what happens to so many girls who are left to grow up in orphanages, don't you? He saved those girls, as he could never save his own daughter, and then... then he raised them to be Kisōshi. Raised them to be strong young women that even a young assassin, and all her fellow elite assassins, couldn't defeat in a fair fight. Instead, one of her fellows killed one of those students with poison. And still, Kuma-sensei let the one remaining young hishi live. Knowing that she would likely escape her captor, knowing that she would likely return to her masters and inform them of everything that she had learned about his plans, knowing that she would once more join the ranks of his enemy and possibly return to fight, and maybe even kill, the people he holds dearest in this world, he let her live. Why do you think that is?"

Kusuko's face had drained of all color, and her eyes were wide with something between awe and fear. Tsuku wondered what the girl thought was happening here. Did she fear for her life? Did she consider this a strangely veiled threat? Tsuku hoped the girl had enough sense to discern the true meaning behind Yasuhiko's questions.

"I—I don't know, Zōkame-sama," Kusuko finally stammered, after watching Yasuhiko placidly return to drinking his tea.

"Oh?" Yasuhiko asked, as he put his cup on the table once more. "Well," he said, as he locked gazes with the young woman again, "perhaps that's something you ought to think about."

Kusuko's eyes went wider still, and Tsuku wondered if the poor girl would be able to stand up, now that it was time for her to leave. Tsuku rose from her own place before the door and came to stand beside the girl, to usher her back out of their apartments.

Long after the young woman had left, Tsuku returned to her husband's side.

"Do you think it will work?" she asked.

"There's no way to know," Yasuhiko said, as he poured his wife a cup of tea. "But I am hopeful."

"Oh? And why is that?" she asked.

"Because when she escaped from Tenshi's captivity, she left the healer alive."

Kisaki

1 1 1 9 年

Winter's bright talons
exposing the snow white bone
pain and truth released

1日 12月、老中 1119年

≈ Mishi ≈

"THE PRISONERS ARE to be brought forward! Let all of Gensokai know what is done to traitors!"

The crier stood atop a raised dais on the far side of the enormous square. Mishi could barely see the man, raised though he was, over the dense crowd before her. She had never seen so many people gathered in a single place.

She was being escorted down the middle of what was normally Rōjū City market square. The space was long enough to hold a hundred or more market stalls in a single file, and wide enough to hold at least five such rows, with plenty of space for people and even horses to pass in between. There was no sign of the market here now, though; no stalls, no merchants, only an open gravel surface writhing with humans.

The wind was cold against her face, and carried a hint of snow with it, but there were so many people present that she could feel the warmth emanating from them, and the smell of tightly packed bodies overwhelmed her nostrils. She supposed that the size of the crowd explained why she and her companions had been forgotten in their cells for a tenday. It would have taken that long to assemble so many highly esteemed individuals from all over Gensokai.

The faces that crowded together in the snowy sunlight were attached to bodies adorned in the finest silks; at least that was true of the ones closest to the center of the square. Mishi couldn't see far enough to know what the masses gathered farther back looked like.

She didn't have long to inspect the gathered crowd before she and her companions were dragged forward, each held by the shoulders and arms between two Eihei, save herself and Kuma-sensei, who had been granted the dubious honor of a third Eihei each.

As the audience parted and brought her towards the dais, she saw that it was lined with Kisōshi, all dressed in ceremonial uwagi and hakama rather than armor, but armed with katana and wakizashi. Mishi shivered as she took in the Rōjū in its full ranks, as well as the armored Eihei that now lined the opening the audience had left between her and the dais. This was the moment that she and Kuma-sensei had been waiting for, and her heart jumped and stuttered in her chest, as she lifted her chin and gazed at the assembly before her.

She hadn't had a chance to speak with anyone, aside from Taka, during their days of captivity. She and Taka had been locked in darkness the entire time, given water and rice only sparingly, for the duration of their stay in the cells beneath Rōjū City. She hadn't known if anyone else was even alive, until they had been brought, stumbling and blinded, into the sunlight this morning.

She had been overjoyed to see Kuma-sensei, Ami, and Katagi all standing between the two guards that held them, looking battered and worn, but alive. Kuma-sensei looked the worst off of any of them, with his right arm tightly bandaged and wrapped close to his body, and his face pale and haggard as though he had lost a large amount of blood. It didn't look as though the time in captivity had given him much of a chance to heal.

Mishi had swallowed, as she considered how old her mentor appeared at that moment. Kuma-sensei had always seemed so vibrant and full of life, but as her eyes adjusted to the sun, and she gazed at him, she had wondered for the first time how old the man actually was. The grey that peppered his hair had suddenly looked more pronounced, the laugh lines that creased his face had looked deeper, and seemed to have multiplied since she last saw him.

He kept his head raised, and his eyes were piercing, his grim nod somehow encompassing their long awaited reunion and all that was still left for them to do, in a single swift motion. The man might be battered, but he was far from broken. That simple knowledge had bolstered her, even as they were practically dragged by the Eihei through the massive throng of citizens.

Now that they stood only a few arm spans before the Rōjū's raised dais, fully armored Eihei restraining her and lining the path that led to where they stood, even the reassurance of Kuma-sensei and Ami's presence couldn't keep the slight tremble that coursed through her body at bay. So much depended on what happened in these next few moments.

She glanced at the form of Taka beside her, held between two Eihei, and shuddered as she considered the possible fates that lay before them. Had she been reunited with Taka so recently only to get them both killed at the hand of the Rōjū? She took a deep breath to center herself. She wouldn't allow her thoughts to travel down that path. She remembered all the details that she and Kuma-sensei had discussed, all the new information Taka had added to their plans. Even if it got them killed, today would change everything. She had to believe that.

Mishi's eyes focused on the five Rōjū at the center of the stage. The other eight members stood behind them, in a protective semi-circle. The rightmost of the five Rōjū at center-stage was a man Mishi recognized. He was the man whose wife she had briefly held as a hostage, the man whose silver hair and jagged scar made him easy to recognize. The man, Zōkame-san, who Mishi now understood, after conversing with Taka over their days of imprisonment, was the one on whom all of her precious plans relied.

She tried not to draw attention to him by staring. Instead, she scanned the other men assembled around him. They looked like normal men. Some were short and slightly rounded with an abundance of food. Some were tall and gaunt. They all looked at her with varying expressions, ranging from curiosity, to a barely contained disgust, to… did she detect fear in the man seated directly ahead of her? Yes, some of these men were looking at her with the kind of loathing that most people reserved for the kind of vermin that destroyed food stores and brought famine, but none of them looked evil to her. The one who sat four men to the left of Zōkame-san looked like someone's kindly grandfather. She was a bit shaken by that. She had expected any, perhaps all, of the men responsible for the atrocities of the Rōjū council to seem more… vile.

She was startled from her consideration of the Rōjū by the crier who had called earlier from the dais, causing the crowd to part so that she and her companions could be brought forward.

"The prisoners who stand before you have been charged with treason!" the man called out, and the crowd suddenly grew silent enough that she could hear the breath of the individual Rōjū before her. "They are accused of conspiring to steal and destroy an ancient scroll, to have women impersonate Kisōshi, and to kill thirty Eihei, all of them ranking Kisōshi."

The crowd murmured at that bit of information, and Mishi wondered if they were more startled by the overall accusation, or the idea that three women and two men had caused so much trouble. She herself was startled at the number of Eihei they were accused of killing. She wondered if the hishi she had killed were rolled into that number. She supposed the Rōjū council was unlikely to announce that it had sent hishi against them, let alone that any of them had been defeated.

The crier stepped down from the dais, and one of the Rōjū in the center of the stage spoke next.

"Normally, we would not bother to hold a public trial for a clear case of treason," the man said. He sat to the left of Zōkame-san, so Mishi assumed that he was a higher ranking Rōjū. "But," he continued, "these accusations are so heinous that we feel these treasonous criminals must be made an example of." Then the man turned to Zōkame-san. "Zōkame-san, I believe you have been charged with interviewing the criminals." He bowed slightly then, as though leaving things in Zōkame-san's charge.

The man with the silvered hair and jagged scar across his face turned to look at them now. Zōkame-san took in each member of their group, and stopped finally with his eyes directed at Mishi.

"Mishiranu-san," he said, his face unreadable, "you in particular are accused of stealing the ancient scroll, impersonating a Kisōshi on more than one occasion, and assisting in the murder of a number of Eihei. What do you have to say for yourself?"

The other members of the Rōjū grumbled. One man hissed, "Do not let the traitor speak."

Zōkame-san's face was unperturbed. He didn't turn to face the man, but spoke to the audience that surrounded them.

"This young woman is accused of crimes that she will die for, if they are true. I am curious as to her motives. What could cause someone to so thoroughly betray her own land and people?"

The grumbling amongst the Rōjū lessened, but Mishi knew she had to be very careful how she proceeded. The wrong words could get her cut down before she'd accomplished anything. She took a deep breath, as all the eyes in the crowd turned to her expectantly

"I am guilty, Rōjū-sama, of stealing the ancient scroll to which you refer," she admitted. A murmur went through the crowd as her admission rippled through them. "However," she continued, raising her voice slightly to be heard above the murmur of so many voices, "I am innocent of the other two charges."

At this, Zōkame-san raised an eyebrow, as did a number of the Rōjū beside him.

"You deny both of the other charges?" he asked, unable to contain his surprise.

Mishi nodded, and gathered her courage before she spoke again.

"Yes. I did not assist in murdering anyone." She had to wait for the collective intake of breath that this statement stirred in the crowd to die down. "I killed those men myself, and it was not murder, but self defense."

"Lies!" shouted one of the Rōjū next to Zōkame-san, the one who had been looking at her as though she were a rotting rat corpse.

Zōkame-san held his hand up for silence, and Mishi was amazed that he dared do so to a Rōjū who outranked him. Yet his voice remained calm, when next he spoke.

"Possibly, but let us hear what else she has to say. That is only one charge, Mishiranu-san. What do you say to the final charge, of impersonating a Kisōshi? You stand before us wearing the hakama and uwagi of a Kisōshi, and you were found wearing a katana and wakizashi. Can you honestly deny impersonating one of the most honored protectors of Gensokai?"

Mishi took a deep breath and nodded once more.

"I am not impersonating a Kisōshi," she said, attempting to keep the calm in her voice. "I am one."

Now the crowd roared behind her, and some of the Rōjū on the dais before her looked as though they were prepared to kill her where she stood. Her heart skipped, as she wondered if they would try it.

"Impossible!"

"There are no female Kisōshi, everyone knows that."

"She's insane!"

"Deluded!"

All those voices came from the Rōjū platform. The roar that came from the audience around her was too great for her to hear what was said exactly, but she imagined it was more of the same. This time it was the man farthest to the left of the central five Rōjū who raised a hand for silence.

"Mishiranu-san, I'm afraid lies such as that will only incriminate you further," the man said, once the crowd had quieted around them.

"It isn't a lie," she said, keeping her voice firm, despite the fear that now coursed through her. She didn't have long, she thought, before the Rōjū would simply order her executed, and she had to make sure that the people around her—the people who didn't know the secrets of the Rōjū—heard the truth, whether they believed it or not, before that happened.

"It's true," came Kuma-sensei's voice to her side. "She is a Kisōshi—so is Ami-san—I trained them myself."

Mishi knew that Kuma-sensei's word would mean nothing to the Rōjū, but it wasn't the Rōjū that they were trying to convince. The men on the dais already knew the truth, they just didn't want anyone else learning it."It's true," Katagi-san echoed. Mishi inhaled sharply. She hadn't expected him to speak. She had hoped that she would find some way to exonerate him of his association with the school before they were all sentenced to die, but now that he had spoken there was little chance of that. "She is a Kisōshi, one of the finest I've ever seen."

Mishi took a deep breath to contain her emotions. The thought of Katagi-san wrapped up in whatever was about to be done to them was painful, and she tried to push it aside.

One of the Elders behind Zōkame-san spoke up then, bringing all eyes to him. "Do we really have to listen to this? Simply because they are all delusional, do we have to sit here and hear them babble?"

Zōkame-san turned from the Rōjū who had spoken back to the audience. Just before he spoke, Mishi saw a glint in his eye that sent a chill down her spine.

"Isn't it interesting though," he said almost casually, "that they all share the same delusion?" The Rōjū that surrounded him began to shift uncomfortably, but he continued before anyone could object. "I wonder, Mishiranu-san, if you could explain how on earth there could be such a thing as a female Kisōshi? Wouldn't we all know if such thing were possible?"

Mishi took a breath to speak, then shut her mouth when Taka's voice spoke out beside her.

"Female Kisōshi, the few that are conceived anymore, are killed at birth," she said, stepping forward, only to be pulled back harshly by the guards that held her. This caused a grumbling from the crowd, but Taka continued before she could be silenced, shouting to be heard above the rumbling populace. "I was trained as a josanpu by the Josankō, and learned the horrors that all josanpu are expected to participate in. Your babies," she shouted, above the growing roar of the crowd and the dais in front of her, "your babies are taken and killed if they are Kisōshi born of the wrong gender!"

Taka had turned to face the crowd as she shouted this, but she was being roughly maneuvered to face the dais again. One of the Eihei holding her struck her across the face, when she opened her mouth to speak again.

"SILENCE!" shouted the leftmost Rōjū of the voting five. "I have had enough of these lie—"

As he spoke, the crowd shuffled apart as a scuffle to the right of the dais tumbled forward through the guards. At first Mishi was shocked that the guards weren't restraining whoever was tumbling through the audience towards the dais. Then she recognized the two figures grappling on the ground before her. One was clad all in leather, and moved with a speed she instantly recognized. The other was clad all in grey.

Mishi cried out as Kusuko finally restrained Mitsu's arms, pinning them to his back, and pulled him up with her wakizashi to his throat. She supposed the Eihei knew better than to attack a hishi at work, even if that hishi was a woman who didn't have her face covered.

Mishi's stomach dropped at the sight of the two, and her legs began to buckle. If the Eihei restraining her hadn't been there, she might have collapsed. Kusuko was supposed to be Tenshi's captive. Had Tenshi let her go? Had the young woman killed Tenshi and escaped? She didn't give herself time to consider it. She was too busy considering how wrong everything was now that Mitsu was captured. Mitsu had the scroll, which meant Kusuko now had it, or would in a matter of moments.

~~~

"What is the meaning of this?!?" shouted the Rōjū who had been interrupted by the tousle.

Kusuko bowed as deeply as she could without releasing Mitsu.

"Rōjū-sama," she said, "I found this man trying to make his way to the center of the crowd, and suspected that he was part of some plot."

Mishi raised an eyebrow at this confession. Didn't Kusuko-san realize that admitting to this crowd that she was a hishi would defeat everything the Rōjū were trying to do?

"That may be," said the Rōjū, looking flustered. "But why YOU, woman, would have anything to—"

"And I found this on him," Kusuko said, interrupting the Rōjū. Was she trying to get herself killed? She held up a small cylinder with the hand that had been holding Mitsu's wrists, while her other hand still held the wakizahsi to his throat. "I believe this is the scroll that Mishiranu-san stole."

Kusuko looked at Mishi when she spoke, and Mishi wondered what was going on in the young woman's mind. She couldn't reach her kisō out from where she stood without the guards picking up on her power and thinking that she was preparing to attack. There was no telling what they would do, if they thought she was using her kisō on the offensive. So she simply held Kusuko's gaze and waited to see what the woman planned to do.

Without breaking eye contact with Mishi, Kusuko flicked the scroll open with one hand, and said, "Shall we read it, to see why this group of traitors thought it worth stealing?"

Mishi couldn't believe her ears. Did Kusuko understand what she was doing? This was the very goal that Mishi and Kuma-sensei had been working towards all along: to read the scroll in front of the largest crowd of citizens possible. It was the reason for the theft of the scroll, and the chase that followed, the reason that Mishi and her companions had wanted to draw out the search for them long enough that it would infuriate the Rōjū, enabling Zōkame-san to suggest that their trial be public. Did Kusuko think she was helping her precious Rōjū somehow? Did she even know what was contained in the scroll? Mishi braced herself, sure that at any moment the Rōjū would strike her dead for what she threatened.

Then, a small, elderly woman, who Mishi hadn't even seen approach, stood before Kusuko and held out her hand. Kusuko bowed her head slightly, finally breaking eye contact with Mishi, and handed the scroll to the silver haired woman. Mishi's breath caught, as she recognized the wife of Zōkame-san; the woman she had held hostage a tenday ago.

"Zōkame Tsuku-san," the Rōjū who had been speaking before Kusuko produced the scroll said, sounding surprised and slightly relieved. "You honor us with your presence. Please be so kind as to deliver that scroll to us."

Tsuku-san didn't reply, but rather turned away from the dais, facing the gathered crowd that now stood silent in shock.

"Nezumi Rōjū-sama, I rather think I'd like to read this," she said. Mishi wondered at the elder woman's bravery. Did she think that the Rōjū would refrain from killing her because she was Zōkame-san's wife? Was she right?

"Zōkame Tsuku-san!" shouted Nezumi, "Anyone who reads that scroll will be guilty of the highest trea—"

But Tsuku-san didn't even wait for the man to finish before she began to read aloud, and the crowd hushed around her. Her words rang like cold steel above the crowd, and Mishi's eyes went wide at the scope of the small woman's voice.

"This pact, accorded by the newly formed Rōjū council, in this the first cycle of the Rōjū's reign, agrees that after the destruction of the Yūwaku, and all the harm that said organization has wrought upon people of the realm, henceforth any female determined to have the power of a Kisōshi, regardless of her elemental ties, will be eliminated before she may bring any harm to Gensokai or its people. All existing female Kisōshi have already been eliminated. To address the point of future Kisōshi, the order of josanpu has been created. Its members shall be trained at the newly founded Josankō and assigned two at a time to every birth of a child, to detect and eliminate any threat that may arise at birth. Any woman, or girl, with detectable power in her later cycles shall be taken for the realm and trained as a josanpu. Further, the Rōjū shall hereafter protect the knowledge of the existence of female Kisōshi, preventing that knowledge from spreading by whatever means necessary. They shall be obligated to use force, as needed, to prevent the same scourge that arose in the Yūwaku from ever arising again."

As Tsuku-san paused, perhaps for emphasis, or perhaps to draw breath, an armored hand clamped down on her mouth and she was seized by an Eihei.

No order had been given audibly. Mishi supposed that the Rōjū would pretend later that the guard had acted of his own accord. But before the Eihei could snatch the scroll from Tsuku-san's hands, the elderly woman stepped down on the man's instep, using the back of her head to crush his nose. That was the last thing that Mishi saw clearly, before the world around her dissolved into chaos.

⟞ Taka ⟝

Taka was never sure what happened first. To her, it seemed that the attack on Tsuku-san and the descent into chaos on the dais of the Rōjū council happened at precisely the same moment. All eyes in the crowd had been focused on Tsuku-san, as she read the damning words contained on that ancient scroll, and Taka had still been reeling at how perfect Tsuku-san's timing had been, when she had glanced up at the stage and seen the Rōjū seated behind Zōkame-san slowly begin to pull his wakizashi from its sheath. Not knowing how else to warn him, while the man's own eyes focused on his wife, Taka used her kisō to convey imagery and emotions to him the same way she would Riyōshi: an image of the man behind him, the feeling of surprise, alarm, and fear.

It had worked. Zōkame-san had turned and caught the other Rōjū's wrist, just before the man's wakizashi had cleared its sheath. In her peripheral vision, Taka saw an armed guard struggling with Tsuku-san, and then everything around her had dissolved into chaos.

As if all acting on a hidden cue, Mishi was fighting with her three captors, as was Kuma-sensei, as was Mishi's 'sister' Ami. Even Katagi-san, health still not fully recovered after so many days in captivity, had begun struggling against his captors.

She had a brief moment to wonder where all of her companions had managed to find katana, when they had been unarmed mere moments before, *had they all just taken them from their captors?* then she felt the guard behind her shift.

Realizing that the man might have assumed that she was just as capable of cutting him down as her companions seemed to be, and worried that he would decide to attack first in order to give himself the best chance at survival, she began to move away from him.

For a moment, she was deeply jealous of the fighting ability of all the Kisōshi that surrounded her, and then she was collapsing to the ground in order to avoid being run through by the guard behind her. Startled by her sudden absence, the guard hesitated a moment, before realizing that she had simply dropped to the ground. Luckily, that small hesitation was all that Mishi needed to sever the man's hand at the wrist, causing hand and katana to fall lifelessly to the ground beside Taka.

Taka gasped, revulsion for what had just been done and admiration for the skill it had taken warring, as she watched Mishi work her way through the guards that surrounded them. From her vantage point on the ground, she could see the beauty in the deadly dance her childhood friend was engaged in, and its usefulness could not be denied at a time like this, but part of her rebelled at the thought that, since the two of them had been separated, Mishi had been trained to kill.

She shook herself and attempted to stand up, only to find herself tackled to the ground once more. Her heart tried to leap its way out of her chest as she fought the weight on top of her, sure that she was about to die. Her hands grabbed for any purchase they could find, scrabbling against smooth leather as she writhed and screamed, only to hear a voice whisper in her ear.

"It's me, Taka-chan, and believe me, it's safer down here for the moment."

She wasn't sure if it was relief or anger that made all the blood in her body warm for a moment, but she allowed the sound of Mitsu's voice to calm her, regardless. After a moment, the pressure of Mitsu's body relinquished, and she felt herself being pulled to a standing position.

"Here," Mitsu said, thrusting a knife into her hands. "Take this and use it on anyone you don't like." He winked briefly, then was gone, rolling towards a fully armored guard and launching a series of small knives through the air into the few small patches that the guard's armor didn't cover, even before he was fully standing again.

Taka felt the comforting weight of the knife, which was about the same size as her own hunting knife, and suddenly felt more secure than she had since the moment that she and Katagi-san had been captured. Even as she adjusted her stance to prepare for the possibility of being attacked, she saw the motion of a guard moving towards her. Suddenly, the bottom dropped out of her stomach. The knife might have reassured her briefly, but her opponents were fully trained, fully armored Kisōshi—armed with katana and wakizashi—and all she had was a hunting knife and an excellent understanding of anatomy.

She took a deep breath, and turned to meet her opponent. She reminded herself that she didn't have to be a better fighter than her enemy, she simply had to find a way to get close enough to touch him.

If the Eihei hadn't underestimated her, she would probably have died in the first few seconds of combat. The guard, presumably thinking she would do little to resist, raised his katana high, in order to slash straight into her. Luckily, the man assumed that her first feint, in which she pretended to stumble while slashing at the man from left to right with the blade in her right hand, was true ineptitude. Instead of using the opportunity to run her through while she appeared off balance, the man simply stepped to the side and back from where he had been, then followed up as though to catch her. Perhaps he thought that she would be unable to defend herself if they grappled, but as he moved to catch her, she brought her left hand up to his neck and grabbed the base of his throat lightly. The man had just enough time to widen his eyes in shock, before her kisō flowed through him and rendered him unconscious.

Taka shook herself, even as the man collapsed to the ground, recognizing dimly that she wouldn't be able to do that to many more opponents without using up all of her kisō. She looked around the battle that seemed to have spread out, with the dais as its epicenter, and tried to determine friend from foe.

She and her companions should have been grossly outnumbered; she had grimly counted the number of Eihei that had surrounded them, even as the Rōjū had been accusing Mishi. It had been a depressing exercise, thoroughly swallowing any hope she might have held of escape. She had stopped after she reached fifty and realized that was well less than half of the total number of Eihei present for their trial. Yet, now, the majority of those guards seemed engaged with the people that surrounded them.

How many Kisōshi had heard what was said and decided that the Rōjū was a force that needed to be stopped? How many had simply decided that any attack on a small and elderly woman, such as Tsuku-san, could not be countenanced? She couldn't begin to guess their reasoning, but the mere fact that they were distracting so many Eihei, and even some of the Rōjū who had tried to escape the dais as soon as the fighting broke out, gave Taka hope that they might yet find a chance to escape alive. She even caught a brief flash of a bright gold uwagi in her peripheral vision—it seemed to be attached to a Kisōshi who was attacking at least two Eihei at once—that brought to mind memories of the night she had learned the location of the Zōkame residence. And for a moment, a smile began to tug at the corners of her mouth.

Then she saw the first Rōjū draw his katana and charge Mishi.

≫ *Mishi* ≪

Mishi saw the motion out of her peripheral vision just in time to roll backwards, away from the guard she was fighting and the newcomer at the same time. Doing so put her back to back with Ami, and she took comfort in having her back protected by one of her companions. Yet all that move had accomplished was to prevent the charging figure that she had seen in her peripheral vision from running her through from the side. As she had rolled away, he had turned to follow her. Now the guard that she was already fighting stood slightly ahead of the man who had charged her. That gave her a very brief window in which to take out the guard, before the other man arrived.

Not for the first time this battle, Mishi cursed how close and inter-mixed with the enemy her companions were; she couldn't use her fire kisō at all, without risking her friends.

Instead, she kept herself centered and let her kisō reach all around her, the rhythm of her heart and lungs becoming the drumbeat to which she danced. The Eihei directly before her, the man she had first been fighting, came in with a direct overhand slash, perhaps expecting that it would have taken her longer to recover from her roll. As it was, she simply extended her stance, dropping under the man's guard and aiming to impale him beneath the ribs. His armor would protect him partially from that assault, but not if he continued with his forward momentum. In order to dodge being impaled, and also use his katana to deflect Mishi's, he was forced to step sideways and rotate his torso; in doing so he began to lose his balance, his guard leaving a small opening that led to his throat. Mishi didn't hesitate. She slid her katana into that gap, slit-ting the throat that was exposed beneath the man's helmet.

She had no time for remorse, or any other thought, as she turned her attention to the Rōjū, who had closed the distance between them in the time it had taken her to dispatch the guard. Mishi barely had time to recognize the man as the first member of the Rōjū voting council, then their katanas met and she was forced to put all of her skill to use.

Mishi had wondered, when a number of the Rōjū had made moves to escape the dais as the fighting had broken out, if the Rōjū were Kisōshi in name only, or if they were truly trained in combat as she had been.

As she engaged with the first Rōjū, her doubt left her. Within seconds of crossing blades, Mishi understood that this opponent would put all of her skills to the test.

For every feint and thrust she made, every combination she tried, the man had a counter. The man's hair was all silver, and his face resembled the ancient parchment of the scroll that Mishi had stolen, yet, despite his evident age, the Rōjū's precision and reflexes were at least as good as Mishi's own.

What was more, the man had only joined the fight when he decided to charge Mishi a few moments ago, while Mishi had been fighting for minutes already and was beginning to feel the fatigue of extended combat. It would be a long time yet before she would truly tire, but any slip in her reflexes could be a fatal mistake, with an opponent like this.

She redoubled her efforts to break through the Rōjū's defenses. Shifting forward, away from the benefit of having Ami directly behind her, she pushed the man into a retreat, in the hope that she might gain an advantage in footing. But the Rōjū kept pace with her forward surge, continuing an even and balanced defense. Mishi continued her press, but the Rōjū seemed unperturbed. As Mishi began a third surge, this one angled to press the man back towards the dais, a blur of grey launched into her peripheral vision, and Mishi sidestepped in order to avoid her newest attacker.

But the attacker didn't engage with her—instead, the grey clad hishi was attacking the Rōjū, helping her to drive the man towards the dais.

Mishi was unsure what to make of Kusuko's arrival. Was this an elaborate ploy to get her to let down her guard and open herself to attack? Had the woman truly switched over to their side, after handing the scroll over to Tsuku-san? She had little time to consider it. She kept her distance from Kusuko, both in order to flank the Rōjū they were now both driving backwards, and to leave a buffer between herself and the woman she still didn't trust.

The Rōjū, eyes widening in shock at the apparent betrayal of one of his loyal hishi, seemed to realize the inevitability of being cornered against the dais. Mishi expected the man to lash out, in a desperate attempt to prevent that from happening, but she never expected him to do so with an attack that would risk killing his own people.

When the Rōjū was only an arm span from the dais behind him, and a final surge from Mishi and Kusuko would have him cornered, he launched a final attack. Seeing him recoil for an instant, as though gathering the air that surrounded him closer, Mishi had prepared to dodge a wind blade, like the one that Katagi had used when they had escaped from Rōjū City tendays before. But then the Rōjū threw his arms wide, and Mishi realized that no amount of dodging would save her, or the people around her. The Rōjū released an impact force of wind, which flung everyone in his vicinity over thirty arm spans into the air.

Mishi barely had time to register her surprise at an attack that was guaranteed to kill as many of the Rōjū's own people as his enemies, before gravity caught up with her and she was forced to recognize the terror of falling from such a height. She, Kusuko, Ami, and a handful of Eihei had all been caught in the blast of wind, thrown at a ninety degree angle from wherever they had stood fighting a moment before.

The force of the wind that had thrown her was almost sufficient to render her unconscious, but she was still aware enough as she reached the apex of her arc to note that Ami and Kusuko were falling with her. *No. Not Ami,* Mishi thought, in the instant she had to think of such things. Not another of her sisters. She couldn't lose them all. She had failed to protect Sachi. She couldn't fail to protect Ami too.

Terror filled Mishi, as she started her very rapid descent. She had risen high enough, and been launched far enough, that there weren't many people below her. Just the snow covered gravel rushed to meet her. As she hurtled towards the ground, Mishi recalled falling another time, cycles ago, with Tatsu's thunderous voice roaring in her ears and a vision of fire spilling all around her. Memory mixed with reality, and the strange sight of fire, enveloping not only her, but also Ami, Kusuko, and all of the guards who happened to be falling with them, filled her mind, even as blackness claimed her.

≈ Taka ≈

Taka's throat locked around a scream, as she saw Mishi launched from where she had been locked in combat with the Rōjū who had attacked her and flung to the far reaches of the battle that continued below her. The scream finally broke free, as Mishi began her plummet towards the earth and Taka's brain told her that there was no chance of surviving a fall from that height.

Taka had just finished rendering another guard unconscious, when she had looked up to check on Mishi and had seen the Rōjū launch not only

Mishi, but Ami, a handful of Eihei, and even the female hishi, violently into the air.

Now she didn't wait to see if any more opponents were making their way towards her, she simply ran towards where she saw Mishi falling. She pushed her way between combatants locked in battle, with little regard for whether or not she would mistakenly take a blade intended for someone else. She dodged and rolled as best she could, running straight forward whenever space allowed. A thick wall of people still stood between her and where she expected Mishi to land, when she saw a giant plume of flame explode on the other side of the crowd.

She stopped, as did a number of the people fighting around her, to look at the phenomenon before her: a handful of bodies, suspended on a bed of fire, mere handspans from the ground. Taka shook herself and pushed forward, even as the bed of fire collapsed before her eyes and the figures contained within it hit the ground heavily.

The rest of the crowd, between herself and Mishi, disappeared in a blur. She thought they might have ceased fighting momentarily, but she wasn't really sure. Her world had narrowed to the breadth of Mishi's face.

As Taka crouched beside Mishi, she had to shift the grey clad woman beside her slightly out of the way, and she was heartened to find that, though somewhat singed, the other woman was clearly breathing. Then she focused more closely on Mishi, and panic started to overtake her. Mishi wasn't breathing. Taka shoved the terror filling her aside, blocked the panic that was trying to overwhelm her, and carefully raised her hand to her friend's neck.

She found no pulse.

No. No. She couldn't be dead, she couldn't be. How could Mishi have died, when the girl next to her, who had fallen the same distance, still breathed and moaned beside her? She brought her head up briefly, and saw Ami moaning a few arm spans away. The other girls had only suffered some burns from that bed of fire. Why they hadn't all been completely incinerated by it, Taka wasn't sure, but Mishi appeared untouched by the flame.

So why wasn't she breathing? Where was her pulse?

Taka clamped down on the panic that tried to overwhelm her, and spread her hand across Mishi's neck. There was a chance she wasn't truly dead, that even though her heart and lungs had stopped, her brain and organs would still respond to Taka's kisō.

Taka took deep breaths, until her kisō centered in her chest, and then she sent it out, pulsating as quickly as her ability would allow, through the body of her friend. Blood vessels, muscles, organs, everywhere that there was water to be drawn to, she spread her awareness through them all.

No physical damage. Taka could find nothing that would explain why Mishi wasn't breathing, why her heart seemed to have stopped. She pushed farther, deeper, into the pieces that made up Mishi's life. There was nothing physical for her to fix.

Taka took a shaky breath, then traced the small bundles of wiring that attached the body to the mind. She traced them all the way to their source and found... nothing. Where she should have found Mishi's fuchi, she found nothing. Taka controlled a sob. She wouldn't give up yet, if she could just find.... There.

In the vision she saw, within her head, that represented Mishi's life, she saw it: a faint glow that represented Mishi's own kisō. It was almost completely depleted—there wasn't enough to even go beyond the small central place where her core resided—but there was a tiny spark left. Would it be enough?

Taka inhaled deeply, and on the exhale she pushed her kisō along the pathways where Mishi's kisō would normally travel, forcing her kisō into Mishi's almost empty fuchi. She felt a strange tingling, as her kisō met with the tiny spark that was all that remained of Mishi's. She pushed her own kisō further, forced it to mingle with Mishi's and entwine. Mishi's kisō accepted Taka's, wrapped with it, and then Taka did something she'd never tried before, or even heard of in all of her studies. She transferred her own kisō to Mishi's, and pushed until the little spark grew, to a round ball the size of her fist. The ball sat there and glowed in an otherwise dark world, and then Taka transferred more of her kisō, before gently beginning to pull back. Slowly, as she retracted her kisō, the kisō at the core of Mishi's fuchi expanded and followed her, and a faint trickle of light began to fill in all that had been dark and empty.

Taka opened her eyes and tried to maintain focus on her hand. For a long moment, she could barely distinguish her hand from the skin beneath it. Then, she finally was able to tell where her hand ended and Mishi's skin began. A moment later, she thought she felt a faint and unsteady twitch beneath her fingers.

She felt a hand grab her shoulder, just as she thought she felt a stronger beat beneath her finger tips.

"Taka-san, is she..." Katagi's voice trailed off, and Taka could hear that the man's voice sounded hoarse, either from shouting or crying.

For a long moment she didn't answer. She kept her hand incredibly still, careful not to apply too much pressure to the spot where it lay against Mishi's artery. Finally, after a longer delay than she would have liked, she felt the pulse again.

"She's not dead," she said finally, after she felt a few more fluttery beats beneath her finger tips, and the truth of that brought tears to her eyes. "But she's very weak, and I don't know…"

Taka fought to form the words. Her field of vision was beginning to darken. She was having difficulty making her mouth do her bidding.

"We… need to get her out of…" Taka's shoulders began to droop. She tried to make herself sit up, to keep her hand on Mishi's pulse, but suddenly the effort was like pushing her way through a hundred giant sacks of rice.

"We've got almost everyone," Katagi replied, but his voice sounded more distant than it had earlier, even though she could still feel his hand on her shoulder. Also, his response didn't make any sense, in the context of what she had just said.

"Can you carry her?"

That was Mitsu, Taka thought vaguely, as she started to slide slowly to the ground. *Carry her? Was he crazy? Couldn't he see that she could barely hold herself up?*

"I've got her. Can you carry Taka?"

"Yes. Did you see Riyōshi?"

"Yes, he was the one who led me here. I think he's already headed out of the city."

"What about Ami?"

"Let's get these two out of here, while…"

Taka could barely feel the arms around her, and the voices now sounded as though she were listening to them from underwater. *Was she dying? Had she used so much of her kisō that she wouldn't be able to recover? Was this what dying felt like? Like a blackness that called to you, promising peace?*

She tried to take a deep breath, and on the exhale, she let the darkness claim her.

21日 12月、老中 1119年

≫ Mishi ≪

MISHI FELT THE thunder more than she heard it. *Was she outside in the middle of a storm? That was strange. And why was it dark? She couldn't see anything at all. Why was that? What had she been doing? The last thing that she remembered... she wasn't sure. Had she dreamt it all? Taka, the cell underground, Tsuku-san reading the scroll to the Rōjū.... The Rōjū who had used a blast of wind to launch her and everyone around her... falling. She had fallen. She had been falling... and then, a sudden burst of flame, but that had been her imagination, hadn't it? Tatsu had said that if she were ever to use that trick again...*

Mishi's eyes popped open, and for a moment everything was still dark, or at least, so out of focus that it might as well have been dark. Slowly her vision began to clear, more light seeped through her eyes, and she saw... teeth.

A snort that shook every bone in her body sounded above her.

"You certainly took your time coming back to us," said a voice that explained why she had felt thunder earlier.

"Tatsu-san?"

"Oh, child, you must be unwell. You didn't call me sensei, or even sama."

Mishi would have laughed, but she didn't feel like she had the strength. Her eyes focused further, and Tatsu moved his head farther away from her, so that she was able to see more than just teeth.

"Tatsu-sensei... I was... I had a dream... or.... What happened? Why am I with you?"

"Ah, Mishiranu-chan…. So much to experience in such a short life," Tatsu's deep voice rumbled above her. The vague response made Mishi assume the worst. Tatsu was a Kami after all.

"Tatsu-sensei… I'm not… dead, am I?"

"What! For Kami's sake child, no, you're very much alive. Can't you tell?"

"I don't know." Mishi thought for a moment. She supposed that, if she were dead, she wouldn't feel so weak, but how should she know? "I've never been dead before, I have no basis for comparison."

Tatsu's laugh rolled out over the nearby mountain peaks, and Mishi realized that she was at Tatsu's shrine.

"Tatsu-san…." She was tired, and the extra syllable that 'sensei' and 'sama' required was more than she could deal with. "If I'm not dead, how did I get here?"

"Hmm…. An excellent question… one that I am not best qualified to answer. Just a moment." Just then, Tatsu stopped speaking, and made a high pitched bugling sound that Mishi had never heard from him before.

She expected him to start speaking again immediately, but when he didn't, her mind began to wander, and she decided to save her energy and not ask her questions just yet. *How had she gotten so tired, so weak? Had the dream been real? Had she truly been fighting in Rōjū City? If so, how had she gotten here, and how was she still alive?*

Her thoughts were brought back to focus when Tatsu's voice grumbled out, "Here they are," and she opened her eyes, which took their time refocusing.

When her vision finally cleared, Mishi could hardly believe what she saw. Taka, Katagi, and Mitsu all stood before her. What were they doing here on Tatsu's mountain? All three of them were smiling, but… Mishi could sense that something wasn't quite right. The light that usually sparkled in Mitsu's eyes was dim. Katagi looked more gaunt than usual, as though he wasn't quite well. And Taka… Mishi knew that face so well, even after all these cycles. Taka was hiding something from her. Before Mishi could ask what it was, Taka rushed past Tatsu's protective claws and knelt beside her. Mitsu and Katagi lingered just on the other side of Tatsu's claws, looking on eagerly.

"Mishi-chan! It's so good to see you awake! How do you feel?" Taka wrapped her in a careful, but breath reducing, hug and then instantly placed a hand on her neck. Mishi had to stifle a laugh as Taka went instantly into healer mode, checking all of Mishi's vital information.

"I feel fine, Taka-chan," Mishi replied. "Quite tired, and weaker than I've ever felt before, but as long as no one asks me to move, I should be fine."

Taka smiled at her. Apparently her yukisō confirmed Mishi's statements, because she nodded and removed her hand from Mishi's neck. Taka's vision clouded momentarily, and Mishi took a deep breath.

"Are you going to tell me what has all of you acting like frightened foxes?" She tried to smile as she asked it, but something about the looks on her three friends faces made the action impossible. Three friends.... She swallowed.

"Where is Ami-san?" she asked, trying to keep her voice from breaking.

"Oh, Mishi-chan..." Taka began, but her voice trailed off and she looked to Mitsu and Katagi, as though hoping that they would speak for her. Mishi felt her stomach drop and go cold.

"Did she..." she couldn't finish the question.

"Ami-san is fine," Taka said quickly. "But... she couldn't come because... because she and Tenshi had to continue the vigil at the shrine for... for Kuma-sensei." The way that Taka's face fell at those last words left no doubt in Mishi's mind as to the truth.

"How... how did it happen?" she asked.

It was Katagi-san who answered, his voice sounding slightly choked.

"His arm was broken, from when he was captured by the hishi. It hadn't had time to heal, and no healer had been sent to us in the cell."

"You were with him?" Mishi interrupted. "In the cells, before the trial?"

Katagi nodded, and continued. "He wasn't well; it wasn't just the broken arm, something was infected—he had been fighting a fever for days, and it was his sword arm that had been broken."

Katagi stopped, as if he couldn't bring himself to say what came next. Mitsu must have taken pity on him, for he continued from there.

"He was fighting one handed, and with his off hand. You saw him at the start. He managed to take on the three guards who held him, but... later on, he was outnumbered and one of the Rōjū turned on him... there wasn't anything we could do..."

Mishi nodded, even as Mitsu's voice trailed off. She knew how chaotic the battle had been. There hadn't been time to make your way to the aid of a friend, not fast enough, if that friend had been completely overwhelmed. She was still amazed that any of them had gotten out with their lives.

"We didn't... did we lose anyone else?" she asked quietly. It was taking more and more of her energy to speak. An emptiness had taken over part of her body at the knowledge that Kuma-sensei was gone. Where there had once been warmth and light, there was now a hole that she didn't think could ever be filled. How did one go on living with such a hole? She didn't have the energy to deal with that kind of truth at the moment. She tried to focus on her friends, here and now. She hoped that she didn't fall asleep before she'd finished talking to these three.

Taka shook her head, unshed tears in her eyes.

"You saved Ami-san and Kusuko-san with your bed of fire. They were both singed a bit, Ami-san more so than Kusuko-san, since apparently Kusuko-san's element is also fire, which gave her some protection, but it saved both their lives. We're not sure what happened to Kusuko-san—she was carried away by a Kisōshi that I've only met once before, but I imagine she's in good hands. Even Zōkame-san and Tsuku-san made it safely away from the trial," Taka said, wiping at the corners of her eyes. "They've been working to build a new council. The Rōjū have been forced into hiding, those that weren't captured the day of the trial, that is. Word spread quickly after Tsuku-san read from the scroll, and anyone assosciated with the old council has had half the Kisōshi in Gensokai chasing them down. Now, the highest ranked Kisōshi who weren't associated with the Rōjū have banded together to start the process of forming a council with women on it."

Mishi tried to process this new information, but wound up scowling as the facts failed to add up. "They work quickly. And spread word quickly! How many days have I been asleep?"

Taka seemed to hold her breath for a moment, and Mishi wondered what could possibly have caused her face to pale so much, in so little time.

"Two tendays," she said softly.

"What?!?" Mishi grimaced at the volume of her own reply. Shouting was definitely out of the question. Her head was still vibrating with her own words.

"Two tendays?" she asked, more quietly. "How is that possible?"

Tatsu finally joined the conversation. His giant bulk had been there the entire time, circled around her protectively, but he hadn't chosen to speak until now.

"Mishiranu-chan, you know full well why you've taken two weeks to recover." He sounded impatient, perhaps a little upset, not at all as sympathetic as she expected him to be. "I warned you, did I not?"

"The fire bed," she murmured.

"Indeed," humphed Tatsu. "Had the greatest healer of the age not been present to attend to you immediately, we would have lost you as well."

"The greatest healer of the age?" Mishi asked, before her brain could catch up.

Mitsu took that opportunity to punch Taka in the shoulder.

"He means this one," he said, as Taka rubbed her arm and glared at him.

Mishi smiled at that, yet even as she did so her heart began to heat up in the center of her chest, torn with a sensation she hadn't experienced before, even with the loss of Sachi. She tried to turn her mind away from the loss of Kuma-sensei and focus on all that they had gained instead.

"This new council, you said that there would be women on it?"

Taka nodded, and light filled her eyes once more, but it was Katagi who answered this time.

"Tsuku-san's reading was perfect. Your plan worked beautifully. The wives and daughters of all the highest ranking Kisōshi and local leaders had been invited, just so the Kami forsaken Rōjū could show them what happens to 'women who make trouble.' How many of those women and their husbands are now questioning every 'still birth' they've ever had in the family? How many of them have daughters who have been sent to the Josankō? We couldn't have requested a better audience if we'd written out the invitations ourselves."

The thought brought some comfort to Mishi, even as the pain in her chest flared at the thought that Kuma-sensei wasn't here for her to share the triumph with.

"I want to…" her vision was blurring once more, and it was a struggle to form words. "I… want to see…"

But she couldn't get words out past her lips anymore. Grief mingled with exhaustion, and her weaknesses overtook her.

"You'll be fine, Mishi-chan," she heard the deep thunder of Tatsu's voice mutter to her. "Rest now. I will watch over you."

Sleep overtook her, and her mind filled with images of her mentor, eyes bright with a smile that never reached his mouth, as his face crinkled with lines that marked a life lived in joy, despite all the sadness that he had been forced to endure. In one image, he yelled at Mishi to keep kicking until she finally got it right, in the next he gave her a birthday gift, the first she had ever received from anyone but Taka. Love and loss filled Mishi's throat, even as her dreams carried her away to a place where bears played in the woods, hawks flew free through forests full of talking trees, and dragons circled a full moon wrapped in a thin ring of startling grey.

Saya

1 年

Phoenix flight spreads ash
all that fire cannot consume
still returns to earth

30日 1月, 新議 1年

30 Ichigatsu, Year of the New Council 1

TAKA STARED INTO the cold grey distance and let the smell of dry wood and fresh snow fill her lungs. She held the branch loosely in her hand, and let her mind relive all the memories that haunted her, all the memories she was about put behind her.

It hadn't taken Tsuku-san long to convince the New Council that the Josankō should cease to exist. The New Council's hold wasn't as solid yet as the Rōjū's hold had been, but they had the benefit of allowing all of the Kisōshi of Gensokai, along with all of the merchants, village leaders, and anyone else who wanted to speak, to have a say in their meetings. While things took longer to agree upon than they had under their predecessors, people were listening to their decisions because they felt that they had some input in them.

Once they had established themselves, one of the first items of business had been to end the program that had necessitated the Josankō. New programs were being created to replace it, programs that, rather than requiring that young women with the power to become Kisōshi be killed or brainwashed, were being established to train them. Real schools were being opened all over Gensokai. Ami and Tenshi were rebuilding on top of the ashes of Kuma-sensei's old school, establishing a school to train female Kisōshi openly, the first of its kind for over a thousand cycles.

Taka herself had already been invited to teach at a school for female healers. She had told them she would, but there were some things she had to do first. There were a few such places opening across Gensokai. They were formed with two goals: the first, to train young women with the kisō to be healers of any kind in their work, and the second, to retrain the women who had been trained by the Josankō. Undoing the work that the Rōjū had spent hundreds upon hundreds of cycles cementing would take a long time, but Taka thought she might enjoy teaching at a real school. She wondered what that would be like. She knew what it *wouldn't* be like.

She took a deep breath, and pushed the branch she grasped into the pot of flaming oil until it caught. She turned to her side and caught Tsuku-san's eyes. The silver haired woman nodded. As Taka exhaled, she threw the branch onto the building before her. It hit the wood and paper wall that sat beneath the snow covered tile roof, and slid onto the large pile of oiled wood waiting at the base.

Flames spread across the oiled wood in a flash that left a white imprint behind, even when Taka closed her eyes. She only blinked briefly from the initial flash, and then she focused on the the flames that consumed what had been one of her longest and worst nightmares.

***

MISHI stood back from Taka and Tsuku-san, as she watched the building before her curl and writhe in the flames that consumed it. She had lit the pot of oil, but it was Taka's place to light the fire that would bring this building down.

Mishi shuddered, as she thought of all that Taka had experienced there, and took a deep breath as the thought brought on memories of her own nightmares. She closed her eyes briefly, to try to forget the effects her own flames had had on men whose names she had never even known.

Ami hadn't understood her, when she refused her invitation to be an instructor at their new school for female Kisōshi, but Ami hadn't understood why she woke up screaming in the night, reliving the deaths of people whose names she didn't know, either.

It had been Tatsu's suggestion that she take on the work that Tenshi had largely done for Kuma-sensei, in the days of the Rōjū. Tenshi had insisted that she should stay with Ami to run the business side of the school, an intricacy that she understood far better than Ami, and so Mishi was the perfect person to take up Tenshi's former role.

Mishi knew that she wasn't yet ready to make fighting part of her life again, and sometimes she wondered if she ever would be able to, but she thought the idea of wandering Gensokai, looking for babies or young girls with the budding powers of a Kisōshi, would be something she could enjoy.

Katagi had offered to accompany her, but she had declined the offer, for now. He would be aiding Ami with her new school, as an instructor in Mishi's stead, and she thought that was an excellent place for him to be.

She didn't know how to tell him that he was tied to the nightmares in ways that she couldn't yet separate from reality, that she needed to be away from him for a time. Instead, she had simply explained that she thought he would be most useful to Ami at the school grounds, helping them to rebuild and plan for the new students' arrival.

Mishi had invited Taka instead, who had accepted and asked if they could bring Mitsu along as well. Taka had told her recently that she and Mitsu had a mystery that the two of them needed to solve together. She hadn't shared what that mystery was, but she had suggested that traveling back to the orphanage where she and Mishi had been raised might be useful, and that answers might even be found in Rōjū City.

Since Mitsu's face didn't appear in her nightmares, and Taka's presence was always soothing to her, no matter her mental state, she had welcomed them both as traveling companions.

She sighed as she watched Taka and Tsuku-san stand before the flames, even as the heat reached a level that would have been unbearable for most people. To Mishi, whose element was fire, the heat felt like an embrace.

Mitsu leaned against a nearby tree, to her right.

"We should go," he grumbled. "We've a lot of ground to cover before dark."

Mishi smiled. Mitsu hated to admit how uncomfortable fire made him. Sometimes she wondered if her mere presence intimidated him. She hoped not.

"Give them some time," Mishi replied, with a flicker of longing. She didn't envy the memories that accompanied this place, but she longed for a pain that could be even partially cleansed by fire.

***

TAKA stared into the fire until it was nothing but cinders, just as she once had so many cycles ago. Then, as now, Tsuku-san had stood beside her, and they had both tried to let the fire take the pain away.

Then, as now, it was only the beginning.

When all that remained was smoke and cinder, Taka turned around. Mitsu, unmoving, leaned with his back against a tree and his eyes closed. Mishi stood in a relaxed fighting stance, her eyes glued to the ruins that remained.

Taka breathed deeply, the air fresh with the wind that carried the smoke and ash away from them. Taking in her friends' postures, she wished that their pasts were as easily erased as her own. She sighed. Weren't they both proof that fire didn't always cleanse?

She stepped towards them, wrapping Mishi in a brief embrace, and then turned to put her arm around Mitsu as well.

"Thank you for waiting," she said. Then she turned, and, followed by her closest friends, walked away from the Josankō for the last time.

Acknowledgements

THERE ARE SO many people to thank for helping me with this process that it's difficult to know where to start. The next section after this is for the Kickstarter backers, so I won't mention them here except to say that what you are holding in your hands would look very different if not for them (as in, you might not even have picked it up due to how shabby it looked).

I suppose I'll start with my husband (I think that's a thing people do). I'll keep all the sappy bits between us (after all, I do see him almost every day), but I want to publicly state that without him I would most likely be a puddle of overwhelmed, exhausted, dribbling, incoherently muttering, mess on the floor. He props me up, feeds me, makes me tea and coffee, and reminds me of all of my positive attributes and faults as needed on any given day.

Next up comes my family and friends. I'm not going to start naming you all because... well sheesh people, I'm trying to get this book to print soonish. But if you've met with me and asked me how it's going (and then listened to an answer much longer than you were hoping for/expecting) or given me a hug, or bought me a coffee, or a meal, or just been kind enough to meet me somewhere and distract me from my own thoughts for a bit: THANK YOU! I love you all.

Next is my Copy Editor Extraordinaire, Aurora Wilson McClain. Is it cheating that I'm both related to and friends with my copy editor? If so, oops. I like to think it's just truly fortunate that my brother decided to marry an English major turned architect who also happens to be a free lance copy editor. Thank you Aurora, for bolstering me when I needed it, making my writing better, and just generally being fabulous (all while taking care of a newborn!).

Let us not forget my wonderful beta-readers! Thank you Jessica Henderson, Shannon Ralph-Pierce, Shayla Elizabeth, and Corey Ticknor (ok he's technically an Alpha Reader but why be picky).

I'd also like to thank the talented Juan Carlos Barquet (www.jcbarquet.com) for producing cover art that is so good it made me worry that my book wasn't good enough for it, and Andrew Brown at

Design for Writers (www.designforwriters.com) for taking that cover art and highlighting it with a sleek and beautiful cover design.

Special thanks must go to Gavin Greene for his help with Japanese both real and imaginary. ありがとうございました！ In addition, many thanks go to Ray Caldito for help with contracts!

Finally, I'd like to thank my mom and dad. They are no longer a unit in the traditional sense, but they and their amazing partners in crime have become a giant four person parenting paragon. (And no, just because I'm not a kid and haven't been one for a long time, it does not mean that my parents aren't still parenting.) The book is dedicated to my parents because no matter what else has been going on in their lives, they have always supported me, encouraged me to pursue my dreams no matter how crazy, and looked the other way when I do things they consider dangerous (like rock climbing). It's been a long time since we've been a traditional family, but traditional is boring. Thank you for always being there!

Kickstarter Supporters

BLADE'S EDGE WAS produced with the support of 92 amazing human beings, also known as Kickstarter Backers. They are listed below in no particular order. Please note that some backers opted not to have their names included.

Jeremy, Bridget, and Tesla Broomfield
Khali Wenaus
Darrin Moore
Aurora Wilson McClain
Alex Liobis
Shannon Pierce-Ralph
Sam Knowlton
Natalie Miller
Caroline Diehl
Jonathan Coustick
Jared Collie
Jesica Tsuzuki
Dave Nicar in honor of Linda Jennings
Ryan Ashford Pricington, III
Sean Louvel
Joey D
Scott Ticknor
Peter L. Trinh
Jason P. Crawford
Michael Downey
John Taylor
Kimberley Whipp
Charlotte Nortman
T.J. McClain
Andrea McGovern
Pat and Steve Pickering
Melissa McChesney
Jason Q

Luis R. Suazo
Judy Prins
Nick Bryan
Steph Wyeth
Jessica Schulze
Kendall Chun
Linda Jennings
Janine Lawton
Gavin Greene
Andrew Hatchell
Robin and Steve Dettman, Faith and Hope
Tasha Turner
James
Jim & Anne Ticknor
Michelle, Scott, and Daniel Kerenyi
Mark White
Nicole Hall
Patrick Hershey
Jerry Fan
Garth & Gail Smith
Brenda Bearden
Jane Hilton
Dawn Del Sontro
Hans Lassooij
Jennifer Dixon
R.C. Matthews
Wendy Treash
Benjamin Parry
David Russell
Bran Mydwynter
Dylan Madeley
Jill Fineis
Ryan Young
The McNortmans
S. Sullman
Other Wench
Kat and Jay Liegl
Karla Ferguson & Sean McManus
Clarinda Harriss & Tom McClain
Claire Brislin
Corey Ticknor
Mide Burns

Lauren B. Andrus
Lei Anne Sharratt
Warren K. Fincher
Seffa Bee Klein
Jeanne Péloquin
Nic Plum

I cannot thank my Kickstarter backers enough. Without the people listed here (and some who chose to go unnamed) I would never have been able to produce this book at the level of quality which you hold in your hands. If you read this book and found it indistinguishable from a traditionally published book it is because of their contributions and support. Independent publishing is a long and lonely road, but the friends, family, and total strangers who supported this process kept me company, cheered me on, and generally made the entire journey not only possible, but downright pleasant. Thank you!

About the Author

VIRGINIA THINKS dangling from the tops of hundred foot cliffs is a good time. She also enjoys hauling a fifty pound backpack all over the Grand Canyon and sleeping under the stars. Sometimes she likes running for miles through the desert, mountains, or wooded flatlands, and she *always* loves getting lost in new places where she may or may not speak the language.

From surviving earthquakes in Japan, to putting out a small forest fire in Montana, Virginia has been collecting stories from a very young age. She works hard to make her fiction as adventurous as her life, and her life as adventurous as her fiction. Both take a lot of imagination.

She recently moved to Winnipeg with her husband (a Manitoba native) and their dog.

Find out more about Virginia McClain and her writing at
www.virginiamcclain.com.

Made in the USA
Middletown, DE
05 July 2016